MW01204218

Beyond the
ROADHOUSE

PATRICIA BARLOW-IRICK

Beyond the ROADHOUSE

PATRICIA BARLOW-IRICK

Little Wind Talks
Friends and Family Publishing
Largo Canyon, New Mexico

Little Wind Talks
POB 620
Blanco, New Mexico 87412

Patricia Barlow-Irick decided to write a novel about the people who most annoyed her. It took several years to figure out how to get them to work together as a cast of characters. She holed up in her office in NW New Mexico for several months and finally emerged with this manuscript. She claims it is fifty-seven percent true and forty-three percent total fabrication.

Copyright © 2016 Patricia Barlow-Irick
All rights reserved. No part of this work may be reproduced or transmitted without written permission from the author.

ISBN: 978-15398465836

Printed by Createspace

For all the victims of covert-aggression.

I hope you are inspired to listen to your

intuition and trust your instincts.

"Any person I have been influenced by, I've been obliged to betray in a sense. It's only through freeing ourselves from the obligation of being beholden to others that we are really free... You have to deny yourself too, your own past, because it's your own past that's going to then constrain you."

Isamu Noguchi, sculptor

PROLOGUE

A preface for my dear readers,

I started writing this story when I was in prison awaiting trial. I've picked it back up and added some of my blogs and filled in some of the story I didn't know at the time. I hope it gives you the sense of what it means to live on the fringe.

From the urban environment in which I currently find myself, it's clear to me that I needed to spend those years where the wild things are. I needed that creative, expressive space, where the noise and confusion of "civilization" was muted. It was there, in my self-imposed social exile that I learned to think my own thoughts, honor my unique perspective, and develop my personal form of expression and living. I learned to see the rules for the mere suggestions that they really are.

The mental health community designates areas with population densities of less than six persons per square mile as "frontier." as if those six or fewer persons were pioneers with teams of oxen and covered wagons. That's not who lives there. Most conventional people would never make the choice to live in a lonely landscape with only themselves for company. That choice is typically made under the duress of powerful contingencies. Some of these folks are simply hiding out from real or imagined social trauma and their own propensity for deviant behavior, but other humans are there on a sacred quest. It is well known that experience of isolation often results in self-induced altered states of consciousness characterized by depersonalization, hallucinations, altered sense of time. It may also give rise to an intense feeling state—oceanic, yet simultaneously detailed perception of environmental wholeness, intuitive intellectual insight, and a resultant prophetic understanding of reality. For those on this quest, living on the frontier is a legal hallucinogen, a short cut to the numinosity of the sacred.

And this quest is *absolutely* archetypal. Moses and Jesus both found their connection to God clarified in the wilderness. Beyond the protection of civilization, you are *Homo sacer*, a person on their own. In early Roman religion *sacer*, much like the Hebrew *qadoš*, denotes anything "set apart" from common society and encompasses both the sense of "hallowed" and that of "cursed". The Hebrew rabbis specifically taught that opening to the truth of the Torah may require danger, solitude, and an untamed spirit, while teaching about the Torah requires safety, community, and structure. We learn from the rabbis' vision of wilderness that acquiring holy spirit requires risk and a willingness to stand alone, beyond the conventional boundaries of society.

Civilization has come to mean control, organization, and homogenization. The frontier offers relief from these dehumanizing tendencies; it encourages individuality. It's a place where every person you cross paths with can be important to your world. It's a place where you don't have to look the other way as a psychological defense against strangers. The frontier is an arena where man can experiment, deviate, discover, and improve. The frontier represents freedom, a geography of hope, inextricably linked to the preservation of free people. It's the only place big enough for those other archetypal symbols of freedom, the wild horses of America.

I apologize to my readers, especially the *Dine' Hataali*i Association members, if I have taken liberty with the facts in order to generate a more beautiful interpretation (this has become a common criticism of my work).

May you always know how to access your own personal geography of freedom!

Dr. A. Ramsden, Ph.D.

January, 2018

Navajo City Roadhouse Blog:

The Menu

Monday, October 20, 2011

I might as well tell you about the menu here. I *did* mention that we serve burgers, didn't I? We do. We serve a lot of burgers—cheese burgers, green chile cheeseburgers, mushroom Swiss burgers, Aussie burgers, patty melts. If it is a ground up cow between buns, we serve it. I don't eat red meat so I just don't get it. They must be good, but, sorry, I have never tried one

In a place like this, you only have to ask a rare customer what kind of dressing they want on their salad. Only asking once a day makes it easy to forget.

Most of our customers drink iced tea whether it's summer or winter. Not too many drink coffee. The coffee gets old and has to be thrown out, but the ice tea keeps flowing. We also serve lemonade and fountain sodas. The drinking water comes out of the reverse osmosis system; it even smells nice. We have an espresso machine but it's mostly used to make hot tea and hot chocolate.

Our appetizer menu used to be a lot bigger when this was the City Bar at Navajo City. They used to serve jalapeno poppers and Rocky Mountain oysters (bull testicles), but the new owners got rid of all that bar food. You can still order nachos or onion rings.

The New Mexican food menu is being developed. The owner has this idea of real New Mexican food, but the oil patch isn't exactly a culture open to ethnic foods. To make it in this crowd, it's got to be beef between buns to be in the food category. Ketchup is their idea of a vegetable. Tonight we had chicken enchiladas on special. The cook fixed me a plate for my employee meal. Buster is the only customer that ordered the special. I know he thought it was good, because it *was* good. The owner is a taco man himself. He has made a lifetime study of the taco, trying them in every town and every cafe he can. He says if we can hold a candle to the Cuban Cafe, in Cuba, NM, we will be doing good.

Part of the problem with developing the New Mexican menu is that the cooks are not from New Mexico. One was born in New York and the other in Alabama. You could serve them clam chowder and tell them it's authentic NM cuisine, and they wouldn't know the difference. The owner encouraged the cooks to study New Mexican food by going to various restaurants, but they're kind of addicted to the China Buffet. I don't know if they serve hamburgers at the China Buffet, but it wouldn't surprise me. The redemption is that one of the cooks considers himself a master of sauces. That covers up a lot of other culinary sins.

In the unlikely event a customer turns out to be a vegetarian, the cook will make something specially for them. Last Saturday someone came in and said they wanted an exotic sandwich but didn't know anything more specific than that. I went back and said "Invent an exotic sandwich" and when it came out the customer was pleased.

The cook just came out and told me to start mopping up. Guess I better sign off. I work again on Thursday and Friday. You can write some comments for me in the meanwhile ... just click on the comments link below.
Yours truly,
Aletta

{Chapter 2}

The Riddle

Aletta, the waitress, stood backed up to the kitchen stove, which was definitely the warmest spot in the restaurant, thinking she really should have brought a sweater to work. It was going to look a little extreme if she wore her down jacket to serve customers. "Guido, I think it's finally starting to feel like fall," she said to the cook, who responded by lifting the spoon from the pot of sauce he was preparing, waving it in the air, and bending the lyrics to suit him as he sang.

Take my job and shove it!
I ain't cookin' here no more
One of these days, I'll take all my money
And you won't see me no more ...

She was grateful he was in a good mood. She knew he loved to cook the big batches of the green chile sauces that gave the Roadhouse food its distinctive flavor. He loved sauces as much as he absolutely hated cooking breakfast items. Woe be to the waitress who accepted an order off the breakfast menu on Guido's shift!

"It's been busy today," she went on, knowing that he probably wasn't listening. "I ran the cash register report and it said we had done seven hundred dollars by the end of lunch, I bet we've done another four hundred since then. It's not a hunting season right now ... I think it's just that the oil field is super busy getting ready for winter."

Guido pulled out the large chopping knife and held it—pointed end up—next to his face. He grimaced, pulling back his lips to expose all of his teeth, raised his eyebrows, and said, "Here's Johnny!"

"Wow, Guido, that's a great Jack Nicholson impression. Got any plans for Halloween?"

Guido responded by stabbing an onion. She realized that she might be more comfortable out of the kitchen and so walked back down the hallway to the front

13

of the restaurant. She stood by the cash register looking for some little something that might be cleaned without too much work. The front door caught her attention. Grimy fingerprints at eye level prompted her to get a sponge and some cleanser. The door was dirtier than she expected. She washed the window glass, and wiped off the squarish copper cowbell that hung from it by a metal spring. The door could not be opened without the cowbell announcing the event.

Satisfied, she rinsed the sponge and set to wiping the barstool seats. Five bright orange rotating bar stools were tucked along the bar counter that separated the customer area from the staff area. She was scrubbing the sixth barstool, the one for the waitress behind the bar, when the cowbell clanked.

She looked up to see a tall, blond man with a fuzzy handlebar mustache and a dark-eyed brunette coming through the door. They were both smiling, but the man grinned more broadly when his eyes met with Aletta's.

"A Dutchman and a Gypsy walked into a bar in the middle of nowhere .... then what happened?" he boomed.

The waitress replied to the apparently boisterous stranger with, "I don't know."

"They ordered a beer!" he chortled.

Aletta's face dropped. "We aren't really a bar. We don't have a liquor license. It used to be a bar ... but," she looked up and smiled, "we have *very* good food."

"Good enough, we'll settle for *very* good food since we have not found a beer in the last fifty miles." They moved to sit in the newly clean barstools at the counter. "May I introduce myself ... I am Luuk Koningh and this is my lovely wife, Lala, which means Tulip in Bulgarian."

"Well, I'm Aletta, and I don't know what that means in Bulgarian." she said as she set menus and silverware rolled in paper napkins in front of the pair. "What would you like to drink?"

"Beer ... but I will happily accept iced tea as a substitute," Luuk said.

"Coffee for me, I was getting sleepy," said Lala.

As Aletta was getting their drinks, Luuk looked up from his menu to ask what she would recommend. She set the beverages down in front of them and replied, "We have good hamburgers, that's one of our main things, but we are also famous for our New Mexico green chile sauce which comes on our Mexican food items."

"What is the most typical New Mexican food?" asked Luuk.

"Probably enchiladas, probably green chile chicken enchiladas," the waitress replied.

"Inchy-ladas ... yes! Pinchy-ladas! That's what I want. With chill-A." chortled the happy man.

"I was thinking of a mushroom swiss burger," started Lala, "but I think I will instead have the pinchy-ladas. Same-same as Luuk."

Aletta took the order back to Guido who was pleased at the opportunity to use some sauce. As she walked back into the front, she asked the smiling couple, "So are you from Bulgaria?"

The couple howled with laughter. Aletta giggled, but she didn't know why.

When they were done laughing, Luuk took a sip of tea, set his glass down, tried to look serious, and folded his hands in front of him on the bar. "No, we are from the Netherlands, which you probably know as Holland ... Well, actually Lala was born in Bulgaria ...she is a Gypsy ... but my family adopted her as a baby. So when we grew up, we knew we could never fall in love with anyone else, so we just got married. Yes, I married my own sister who was no relative at all!"

Aletta looked doubtful, "How did your parents feel about that?"

Luuk and Lala looked at each other affectionately, then turned back to the waitress, "They were happy!" said Lala.

"My mother-in-law loves me like a son," said Luuk. "But enough about us, tell us about this bar-that-is-not-a-bar in the middle of nowhere. Wasn't this place the hangout for the Del Fuego biker gang in the movies?"

"No, I have heard that we were a biker bar in the 1960's but no movies were made here as far as I know. We are more of an oil field kind of place these days."

"Why are there so many white trucks and why are they all flying orange flags?

That is our national color! Are they soccer fans?" asked the Dutchman.

"No, I doubt any of them are soccer fans," the waitress laughed. "The white trucks are guys working in the oil-field, and those are safety flags so they can see each other coming on the narrow back roads. There are about 17,000 wells in the local area."

"That's a lot of oil!" responded Luuk.

"Actually, they get natural gas and not so much liquid oil. It gets shipped to California in pipelines from here. I think we are the third largest gas field in North America. All these guys need to eat, so ... we're right here in the middle of it."

Guido rang the waitress call-bell signalling their orders were ready and Aletta quickly went to get them. The cheese covered stacks of tortillas and chicken were smothered in a rich green chile sauce on a heavy oval plate. One end of each oval was covered with steaming hot beans, while the other was piled with a salad of lettuce, onion, and tomato. Luuk and Lala looked pleased.

"No cowboys and Indians in this area?" asked Lala.

"Yeah, we have cowboys and Indians," Aletta launched into her well practiced tour-guide monologue that she used on curious tourists. "The last town you drove through, Dulce, that's the headquarters for the Apaches. West of here, maybe 40 miles, is the Navajo Nation. North, across the Colorado border are the Ute Indians. Truckloads ... yes, literally truckloads of cowboys come in for lunch whenever it's time to move the cattle around. But these days the cowboy and the Indian might be the same person since a lot of the Indians raise cattle. Either way, no one is going home for lunch when they're out this far from town. Everyone tries to eat at the Roadhouse."

Her audience had their mouths full so she went on, "We also get a lot of hunters. The various hunting seasons continue from September to January every year. A lot of hunters come in for three meals a day, so things get really busy then. Of course, just five miles north of here is Navajo Lake, which is huge. We get a lot of recreational traffic in the summer.

"This week we have another set of people, government people, coming in for a wild horse roundup. They've been getting ready for that. I'm kind of excited about getting to see some wild mustangs up close. Of course, people drive up to the forest to photograph the mustangs all year around. It's just one of our many recreational activities."

"Are you and the cook the only ones who work here? Can you feed all of these people lunch everyday?" asked Lala.

"No, I only work in the afternoon four days a week. There is a girl from down the road that takes the other three days. In the morning there is a different set of people who work here. Penny, the morning waitress, is the senior staff member so she gets her choice of shifts.

"Penny and I share the lunch hour since it would be too much for one person and it's where all the tips of the day come in. Then we split the lunchtime tips."

"I like these pinchy-ladas," Luuk said between bites.

"We sell a lot of breakfast burritos; it's our main product, even more than hamburgers. We get them all ready and keep them hot in that case over there," she said pointing to the far end of the bar. "Guys grab them on the way out to the oil patch and eat them on the road. We sell maybe fifty of those every morning but Sunday. We are pretty proud that instead of buying burritos in town, our customers wait 30 miles until they get here. We have really loyal customers.

"One thing that is *really* cool about working here," continued Aletta, "is that people like to buy each other lunch as a surprise. The oil guys are generous not only with us, but with each other, so someone will come up and secretly pay for someone else. We are not supposed to tell who did it. It makes it a lot of fun."

She paused to listen to Glen Campbell sing the last two stanzas of *By the Time I get to Phoenix.* "Do you know this song?" she asked, when they responded with blank looks she said, "It's about a guy that leaves a woman. I am always trying to figure out why. I was hoping you might have an idea

"Anyway, where are you two headed?" she asked

"We are going to Las Vegas. I am going to a Furry convention, and Lala is going to see the Elvis Festival," replied the Dutchman.

"Elvis impersonators? A convention of Elvis impersonators?" the waitress asked. "We have an Elvis Impersonator working in the oil field. He actually got up on this very bar one time to sing."

"I love Elvis," said the gypsy, pushing her clean plate to the side.

"Now, Aletta, if you would like, I will read your palms and tell you your future," offered Lala.

Aletta looked at Luuk, who was smiling and finishing his iced tea, then she held out her hands to the dark-eyed woman.

"Ahh ... a long life and much creativity ... You need lots of freedom ... I see some trouble coming in the next few months, but, do not worry, it will work out for the best because you will find a way to turn it into an opportunity. You are an amazing person, Aletta. I can see all of this in your hands."

Aletta was skeptical that Lala was even looking at her hands because she delivered her prognostication with closed eyes, but, still, it was nice to see reason for hope against any trouble that might befall her. "Thank you, Lala. I will write it down, so I will remember it should dark times befall me."

Luuk finished rubbing his mustache with a napkin and rose from his barstool. "We'd best be on our way, but now we know how the joke turns out ... A Dutchman and a Gypsy walk into the bar and ... they order pinchy-ladas." Everyone broke out laughing.

Aletta was sad to see them leave, but they gave her a generous tip. She gave them each a hug before they walked out the door. Then she sighed and prepared to scrub down the tables and refill the ketchup bottles. She heard the noise of the back door and realized that Guido had been out back taking a break. He came through the kitchen, through the hallway where the dishwasher sat, and got himself a cup of coffee at the waitress station. He sat down at the bar.

"The thing about this job, Guido, is being prepared. That is all you and I ever do, get ready for the next order," said the waitress. "Once in awhile, though, some magic comes through that door."

{Chapter 3}

If you were there ...

If you had been sitting on the corner barstool that morning, you would have seen Aletta at her laptop, watching a YouTube video, typing through the tears running down her face. You wouldn't have thought her pretty, dressed in jeans, boots, a crimson-colored apron, shoulder length brown hair and wire-rimmed glasses, but you would have guessed—from those fingers flying on the keyboard— that she was smart. You would not have noticed the other waitress and the cook smoking cigarettes outside the back door. If you looked over your shoulder and out the window, you might have noticed the man in the parking lot, standing by his truck, talking on his cell phone and eating a hamburger and fries. You then would have noticed the white government plates and his khaki shirt that marked him as a government employee. Of course if you (or he) were on the barstool, the waitress would have waited on you instead of paying attention to the screen, served you a meal, refilled your drink, made a little polite chat to test if you wanted to talk to her, and if you did, she would have gotten you to tell her your whole life story. You would have been lulled into verbosity by the rare pleasure of engaging with an active listener, eager to learn what makes you tick and makes you special. You might have surprised yourself at how much you were willing to reveal to a stranger. She had a lot of practice getting strangers to open up as if they were library books and then, after they paid the bill and drove away, she would make notes in her journal because she wanted to become a writer someday and she would need characters. This café was a gold-mine of characters. But you weren't there to be waited on, the fellow was on the phone with his girlfriend, the highway in front of the cafe was momentarily quiet, the big take-out order for the BLM had been picked up, and everything was prepped for the coming lunch rush, so she wrote about elephants and cried:

{Chapter 4}

The Elephant Story

Sand and clay, the gray beach with a surface packed like brown sugar. Dense and hard when dry, grainy gray slurry when wet.

Mother elephant the size of a Mack truck, baby the size of a cow.

Their smooth gray color only a shade less brown than the beach. Both screaming; hysterical with fear. Mother pacing frantically along a hole in the ground.

A natural sinkhole formed where the high water table liquefied and washed out the underlying sand, allowing the top clay layers to simply cave in. A death trap waiting for a victim. The youngster had wandered too near the edge and slipped in on the greasy clay.

The baby elephant leaped and scrambled up the crumbling walls valiantly but despite the effort, time after time, only managed to slide back to the bottom. Its tiny trunk grabbed desperately but only grasped loose sand as it slid back down. The bottom of the pit was liquefying with the pounding steps of the youngster. Soon it would dissolve into quicksand and provide the young frightened animal with a slow death in a watery grave.

The mother's agitation attracted the attention of three men in a Land Rover. Leaving the road, they ventured out onto the beach but stayed inside the vehicle. "The little guy's in trouble. The muck will swallow him alive."

The anxious mother would be extremely dangerous. It would be foolhardy to get out of the truck with an angry frightened female elephant who might misunderstand their intentions toward her calf. She would have to go and the Land Rover was their only tool they had to get that done.

A determined Safari-guide behind the wheel matched his will to save the little one against the mother's desperate attempts to return to her baby. The honking horn and sharp prods with the bumper of the Land Rover convinced her to flee down the beach to the rest of the herd.

They didn't have much time as the mother was sure to return with herd-mates.

Returning to the pit, they found the panicking baby circling and screaming. It was now slogging through slop halfway to its knees.

Pulling the Land Rover as close to the pit as possible, the guides drug out the tow ropes from where they were kept for emergencies. Two thin men worked quickly to throw a loop around the baby, who had no idea the project required her cooperation. Time and time again, the loop slipped off, but they discovered that by pulling more up with their arms, the rope would catch and could be held. It was an awkward angle, but the two men pulled with all of their might, as their partner inside the vehicle backed up, stretching the rope between bumper and elephant.

Suddenly, without warning, the tiny elephant was pulled upward and off its feet. It slipped so quickly through the greasy mud that, for that one moment, the animal seemed almost weightless. The black man in the yellow shirt, who was pulling the hardest, fell backwards onto his right hip, but quickly caught himself and bounded up for a new hold of the rope as the elephant slid onto the sandy beach surface. He wasn't sure if he should be afraid of the baby elephant, but he stretched forward to undo the knot that formed the loop.

The loop slipped off and the baby bolted for freedom. The men stood, with arms and hands dangling in exhaustion, watching her go. She screamed with every step of the way across the beach and her calls were answered by mother as the beach rolled under the mother's giant strides. The trumpeting suddenly went silent as the elephants touched. The little ones head dropped low as the mother reached across her baby's back with her trunk and pulled it close. The mother turned to let the baby into nursing position as the rest of the herd surrounded them.

{Chapter 5}

Tears vs. Saliva

Dear reader, you may be wondering why a waitress in a small roadside cafe would be interested in tears. We have prepared a brief lesson on this timely subject. Today, we will compare and contrast crying and salivation. They have more in common than you may expect.

Both of these aqueous products are produced from spongy-looking glands that sit near your temples. It is true that a few bits of salivary gland can also be found under the jaw and under the tongue, but the largest of them, the glorious Parotid gland, is lurking somewhere between your ear and your eyebrow.

The ductworks for these products are not fully formed in the newborn human, so the human infant can neither salivate nor cry real tears. At 12 weeks, with termination of newborn status, the ductwork is finished and tears begin to fall. Infants only drink milk and haven't needed saliva. Suddenly they must learn to swallow their saliva to keep from drowning in it. This is why babies have a bit of a drooling problem.

All vertebrate animals salivate as adults. Some insects also produce saliva. Crying tears of sadness is uniquely human. Animals simply cannot provide a research model for the topic of emotional lacrimation.

These behaviors are under the control of the parasympathetic nervous system rather than conscious control. We don't decide to salivate or to cry; our body decides for us. Yet, both can be activated by learned associations. Ivan Petrovich Pavlov, a Russian physiologist, most famously associated with salivation noticed that his dogs would salivate when anticipating food arrival, and that if he always presented some kind of stimulus, such as a bell, before the food, soon the stimulus alone would cause the animals to salivate. He called it a "conditional reflex".

It would be thoroughly unethical to intentionally induce fear activated lacrimation in the service of science in today's ethical climate. Lucky for inquiring minds, in the 1920s people weren't so socially responsible and scaring a little boy seemed a worthwhile endeavor. With a loud noise and a rat, two scientists frightened a child they affectionately called Little Albert. At first he was willing to play with the rat, but after the scientists paired reaching for the rat with a thunderous noise, he was soon fearful of the rat and all other fuzzy creatures. Some of his response involved simple lacrimation, but at other times the response was the less interesting response of mere dry-eyed avoidance. Little Albert's lacrimation, despite his lasting traumatic memories, has limited value for Chapter Five's pedagogical endeavor. We can, how-ever, try to sever lacrimation from fear in a brief thought experiment. If Pavlov's theory of conditioned association is applicable to non-emotional lacrimation, we should be able to reliably create tears by merely viewing onions. Pavlov predicts that, after multiple onion-induced lacrimation events, the cook should then start tearing-up whenever he or she happens to see an onion. This experiment will require that we start with cooks who have never seen an onion prior to the test. Perhaps the thirteen week old babies will volunteer?

The ductworks for these aqueous products can be rerouted to supply tears to the mouth or saliva to the eyes. The slightly salty flavor of tears could conceivably create a gourmet market for this medical procedure; however the commercial vi-ability of such surgery has not yet been tested. Expect prime-time advertising and side-effect warnings soon. In contrast, the rerouting of saliva to the eyes has been done to relieve chronic painfully dry eyes. However, the surgeons found that the patients are then doomed to a life of crying through their mealtimes. How much better if they had tongue lengthening surgery so they could lick their eyes moist at their own convenience? The surgeons, dismayed as they were by the weeping diners, did not give up.

Happily, these surgeons soon determined that salivary gland tissues could be transplanted into the lacrimal glands and would generate substitute tears in appro-priate context. This gives a whole new and more literal meaning to "spit in your eye". The recipients don't seem to mind.

The aqueous products of these glands both contain lysosomes, an enzyme whose function is to break down the cell walls of pathogenic bacteria. Any of the microbial evil-doers that resist lysosomal disintegration are trapped in mucus and swallowed where they are, hopefully, destroyed by stomach acid. Take that, you bacterial interloper! Gulp!

Salivation has been thoroughly studied since 1899 by men such as Pavlov. Still science has not defined, with any accuracy, what kind of stimuli, other than pain, reliably elicit crying in adult humans.

Emotionally controlled secretion offers an interesting challenge for a waitress/novelist: She could make you cry or salivate and you couldn't stop her. You wouldn't even know it was merely psychological manipulation.

{Chapter 6}

Alright Guy

Aaron Shauner, Wild Horse Range Specialist for the Farmington Area Bureau of Land Management, came speeding past milepost 87 much faster than government employees were supposed to drive. He was pulling a large white stock trailer behind his government truck. Today was the long awaited wild horse round up. Yee-haw!!!

As he crested the hill, the Roadhouse Cafe came into view, and— just his bad luck—his boss was in the parking lot with a cardboard box. *Better slow down, Hotrod!* Aaron's foot went heavy on the brake pedal just in time to make the turn into the parking lot. The truck and trailer shuddered to a stop. Aaron jumped out of his truck grinning.

Randall Tapia dropped the heavy box of catered food into the front seat of his truck with a thud. Twenty-five cheeseburgers for the roundup crew, French fries, a whole bottle of ketchup, and a to-go cup filled with chopped green chile were stuffed around the edges. The crew would be satisfied today!

"Hey, boss!" Shauner offered, eyeing the burger box.

"Hey, Aaron." Tapia replied less enthusiastically.

"Mind if I do?" Shauner pointed to the box.

"Go ahead, Aaron. I'll see you out there."

Shauner retrieved a burger and fries from the box as Tapia started his engine. Shauner shut the truck door and lifted his burger as if in salute as Tapia drove off.

Taking a bite from the burger, he walked through the front door of the cafe. The cowbell hanging from the door clanked, and the waitress looked up.

"Got a take-out menu?" he asked. Seeing he was already eating, she simply handed him the traveling menu and said, "Just call ahead, Aaron."

"I will. Tonight after the round-up. On my way home. Talk to you then."

He returned to his truck and set his french-fries on the hood. A perfect opportunity to call his girlfriend, Angela. If anyone had been in the parking lot this is what they would have heard:

"Hey, girlfriend!"

"Don't hang up, please! ... Just give me a chance to explain. It's not like it seems ... No, no, don't hang up, Angela. You are everything to me. Give me a chance to straighten things out ... Angela, calm down; that wasn't mine. Tim forgot it on the couch. It wasn't mine ... Yes, there were naked pictures of Madonna. Yes! But I wasn't looking at them, I was merely moving the book. It is not a crime to move a book, is it?

"Angela, what do I have to do to make you understand that I am *not* a scumbag? I swear I wasn't looking at it. Madonna is not my type. I don't like blondes. Next time it needs to be moved, I will ask you to do it. Will that work for you? ... Okay, I'll get Tim to take it back to his house right away. I will call him about it the next time I have a free minute ... No, I won't forget. I promise ...

"Honey, listen I am at work and I have to go now. I just need you to calm down and remember how much I love you. You're sexier than Madonna any day of the week. You're my girlfriend, not Madonna. Okay?

"Bye, Babe"

{chapter 7}

Trust Your Instincts

As the BLM truck and horse trailer pulled back onto the highway, Rex Roundy pulled off the highway. Aletta didn't notice the chubby man's approach until the cowbell on the front door clanked and the man stood before her. She quickly closed her laptop and brushed the tears from her eyes.

"What's this? Is the cupcake girl crying? Did I come at a bad time? Just broke up with your boyfriend? I seen him leaving. He's not your kind anyway."

Aletta didn't reply. Engaging with Rex was never any fun. His game was to find the weak spot and torture his victim.

"Just as well, Cupcake, you don't need a government man. You need me in your life."

Still ignoring the banter, Aletta looked him in the eye and asked, "A pack of cigarettes?"

"How did you guess, Darlin'? See, you do love me!"

"Smoking is going to kill you, Rex," handing him a pack from the shelf behind her.

"I knew it! You do care!" he said handing her his credit card.

Without looking at him, she swiped the card in the reader and waited for the ticket. He opened the end of the pack, took out a cigarette and hung it in his mouth. She handed him a pen for his signature and as he signed the ticket, he went on, "Now that lover boy is gone, what do you say you and me plan our honeymoon?"

She knew better than to try a comeback. They never worked with Rex.

"Have a nice day, Rex," she said as she turned on her heels and retreated to the kitchen. "Guido, will you cover the front for me for a couple of minutes?"

Guido rinsed his hands and dried them on a white bar-towel as he walked into the dining room. The cow-bell clanked and Rex was gone. Rex did not know how to tease Guido.

Aletta walked out the back door into the alley between the restaurant and the modular building that served as Guido's residence. The heavy smells of the containers of old fryer oil and gravel which had been splashed thousands of times with the night's mop water were strong, but not unpleasant. She felt, for a moment, totally protected as she walked down the alley to where her Jeep was parked. She thought about the emotion of security as she got in and started the jeep. She knew what she needed to do was not think, but just listen to her own inner strength.

She knew it never worked to just try a little harder, possibly become a little more compassionate, understanding, and loving; hoping everything will work out. Instead, her best hope was to learn to control her sensitive nature, grow her intuition, and become more self-aware. Her quest was to see people as they really are and learn to trust her awareness. As she pulled her jeep around to the gas pumps, she admitted to herself that her intuition told her that Rex Roundy was bad news and the less she said to him, the better off she would be. She wished the owners would quit selling cigarettes because then Rex wouldn't have a reason to stop in outside of mealtimes.

She had read that a person can develop their self-awareness and intuition by spending a few moments alone each day, closing their eyes and asking themselves, "What am I feeling?" The point was not to think, just to listen. "Trust your instincts," Aletta told herself out loud as she swiped her credit card in the pump's card-lock. She closed her eyes as she pushed the trigger to start the gas pump flowing.

Narcissists seem to beat a path to her doorway. Why didn't Penny have a problem with Rex or anyone else for that matter? Penny would have just said something to make the fat man blush and run.

"Why am I so sensitive? Everyone thinks I am too shy, too reserved, too quiet, too anxious, too depressed, too insecure. Heavens, does it ever stop? I don't really want to be the perennial victim."

She stood, eyes closed, telling herself she had to quit playing the role of the victim, when a truck and horse trailer pulled off the highway and into the fuel lanes across the pump from her.

Her eyes opened to see a palomino horse tail hanging out of a fairly new two-horse trailer. It was hitched to a nice clean truck with a New Mexico license plate, not like all the muddy dusty ranch trucks with broken shocks and squeaking brakes. This person must be someone from town going somewhere interesting.

A tall man stepped down from the cab. He wasn't wearing a cowboy hat, but instead sported a hairstyle that was all at once sexy, shaggy, and stylish. His outfit was color coordinated to look good on a palomino horse, and he wore a turquoise bandana around his neck. It seemed, to Aletta, that a Wild West show had come to town.

As he swiped his card in the gas pump, she reckoned him to be in his mid-forties and the words "mid-life crisis" popped into her mind. After he had the gas running, he turned to her and smiled, "Howdy, ma'am." Then he twisted his nose and sniffed.

She smiled back, "Looks like you might be going somewhere interesting ... what kind of horse is that?"

"Oh, he's Arabian. We're just going camping for a few days."

Interesting outing that's going to be, she thought tightening the gas cap on her jeep, imagining him with a guitar next to a campfire. She pulled the receipt from the gas dispenser, wadded it up, and tossed it into the trash can.

He raised his eyebrows and said slowly, "Tickle your ass with a feather?"

"What!?" she gasped.

"I asked if you're expecting nasty weather. Think it's going to snow?" He stroked the fuel line in a rather sensual way. Then he grinned at her and sniffed again.

Without another word, she scooted into the jeep driver seat and drove back around the building to her parking spot. He pulled her receipt from the can, looked it over. "Aletta Ramsden is a cute name," he said to himself, then stuffed the receipt into his front right pants pocket.

{Chapter 8}

Tapia is Ready

Tapia heard his stomach growling down somewhere near his silver belt buckle. "Not now honey, you have to wait" he said thinking how much his wife and his stomach had in common. Insatiable appetites, one polishing one side of the belt buckle, and the other doing her best to keep the other side shined with her dancing dresses. Did the stomach look forward to Saturday night on the dance floor as much as Danielle did? Hmmm, he'd have to think about that. He gripped the steering wheel tighter to stop his hand from diving into the box of burgers and stepped a little harder on the gas pedal. Eighteen miles on the highway, 12 miles on a secondary road, and 10 on the dirt road that ended at the roundup site ... okay, an hour of driving. He opened the window, took off his glasses, and let the cool air wash his face.

Randall Tapia could have told you everything you might need to know about this wild-horse roundup—including the fact it's called a *gather*—because he was the official in charge of this event. He and his assistant, Aaron Shauner, had everything arranged. The helicopter-gather contract, the catch-site environmental clearance, a media and advocate interface plan, parking with a designated "Free-Speech" area, the portable toilets, and group seating provided by hefty cottonwood logs circled up for lunch time, it was all under control. The Safety Briefing would take place at lunch with this captive audience. He and Shauner had even planned their simultaneous morning absence from the site to discourage the wild-horse advocates in hopes that some would pack-up and leave before the helicopter arrived. Not that they totally wanted to discourage all the advocates. Actually, Tapia had even arranged for the participation of an officially sanctioned wild-horse advocate. The Society of Humane Treatment of Animals had sent him the perfect representative, Sephra Brooks, 20 years old and city-raised, still wet behind the ears. Not that he or Shauner really minded the advocates, (someone needed to speak up for the horses) but creating obstacles for them was just part of the BLM's game. It would be unconscionable to not mess with them a little. As he recounted the many details of the plan, he couldn't help but feel he had done his best. This round-up, he hoped, just might turn out perfect. He was riding high on self-confidence as he pulled into the round-up site with the burger box intact except for the one Shauner had taken. He had even remembered to bring extra napkins.

Several trucks and trailers were being parked as the helicopters popped over the ridge and landed in a clearing.

Shauner pulled in right beside him and started unloading the few pieces of gear tucked into the bed of the truck. He had a pile of seven or eight four-foot long stock whips with white flags tied to the end. He had a camera and a few clipboards. He pulled out a folding table and carried everything to the circle of logs. The contractor that was doing the gather had brought all the major pieces of equipment: the fence panels, the burlap for the long trap chute, the loading ramp, the Judas horse, and the helicopter.

Tapia put on his grey cowboy hat and then unloaded the burgers and the napkins. It crossed his mind that he didn't bring toilet paper for the outhouse, but then he remembered that the portable toilet company provided it. The office ladies who had managed to wrangle a field day out of the office were not going to have much to complain about. He broke into a whistling tune as he strode across the parking lot.

Jessica, his secretary, was already sitting on a log bench chatting with Sephra, the young woman from the Humane Treatment Society. They were giggling about something like old friends, although Jessica was old enough to be the young woman's mother. Jessica jumped up to help Tapia with his load of food. Tapia and Shauner opened the folding table, and suddenly it was a picnic. Jessica set a case of bottled water on the table and opened the napkins. Tapia opened the box, pulled out a burger, and offered it to Sephra. The rest of the gather personnel swarmed in and soon the box was empty. Everyone had a cozy seat on the fat logs while Tapia stood with one foot up on a log. His hat bobbed around as he talked.

"It's really important that we are all on the same page, so I am going to briefly review what we went over at the Safety Meeting yesterday. The way this works is the helicopter has already spotted and moved some of the horses closer. They'll go out for the final push which won't take long. The contractor's people will set the gates and bring out the Judas horse. They will let the Judas horse go just as the wild horses are about to overtake it and it will lead the horses in. You BLM people will remain on the truck side of the corral system away from the incoming horses until I signal. Keep quiet as the horses approach. Once the horses have run in and the contractors have closed the gates, the horses have to get sorted as quickly as possible. They will be highly stressed and the stallions will start fighting. Yearlings and small horses get put in the west pen, stallions in the north pen, mares in the east pen, and mares with foals in the south pen. Sephra, I want you to stay with Jessica. Jessica will be photographing mare and foal pairs. Any horses with obvious physical problems should go in that little pen in the southwest corner. We have a vet on call in case we need one.

"We shouldn't have any problems with the advocates or media, but just in case, Officers Sanders and Bennett will be stationed in the public viewing area. The public will not be allowed to approach the trap area, but I expect law enforcement will try to maintain a professional but congenial atmosphere over there.

"Aaron will be the Point-of-Contact for the gather contractor. All official communication goes through the POC. Jack Lily, from Catorr Chopper Company, is the contractor's representative. The Forest Service sent us two experienced wild-horse specialists, Karen Sorensen and Erin Tate. They will be ready to assist anywhere. The rest of you BLMers should be documenting the gather with video and photos. We want a real 'show and tell' after it's over, so photograph everything.

"The important thing is that no one gets hurt and that we don't kill any horses. Working with these horses is a case of cowboy wisdom: the slower you go, the faster you get there. If you feel yourself getting anxious, step back out of the action and calm down. Adrenaline is not your friend today. No mistakes allowed."

"Aaron, do you have anything to add?"

The response was a barely discernible quick shake of the head.

"Jack Lily, do you want to add anything?"

"Just keep your people back from the pens and things should be fine. It's not our first time to this dance."

Tapia looked around for any sign of residual confusion, then said, "Okay, let's go!"

Everyone rose from their seats and set about their business. Jessica picked up a few stray napkins from the ground and tossed them in the trash.

Tapia excused himself to check the toilet paper supply in the port-a-potty, as Jessica and Sephra cleaned up after lunch. Nary a French-fry had been left behind. Jessica put the empty water bottles back into the food box to deliver to recycling. Then the women sat down with their clipboards and cameras to wait.

Tapia returned, wiping his hands on a towelette, looking quizzically at Sephra. "Why in the world does an animal advocate have a gun rack and a shotgun in her truck? I thought you were all pacifists or something ... or should that be vegetarians? No, you just ate a cheeseburger, so what gives, Miss Sephra?"

"Oh! I've had that thing since last spring when I first moved here. I was driving home alone one night when this naked man ran across the road. It was the middle of nowhere, and it was pretty chilly to be naked. It really scared me. I was coming home from church, so the next week, I mentioned it to my pastor, and he insisted that I take the gun. He said to keep it, so I just have had it there ever since."

Tapia smiled mischievously. "Wait, Sephra .... are you telling us that you keep that gun to shoot naked men? Oh, my!!! Are you serious?"

Sephra nodded sheepishly.

Jessica broke out into a giggle. "Are you going to apply for a hunting license or just take these naked men illegally?"

"Well, I didn't actually plan on shooting anyone. I just wanted the gun to look like I could defend myself if needed."

Tapia chortled and turned to see Shauner bee-lining straight to him.

"Hey, Boss. They're calling on the radio for you to come to the Advocate Viewing Area."

"Gotta go now, ladies. See you later," he said, tipping his hat as he walked away.

{Chapter 9}

Roundup Time

The advocates were standing in a semicircle with the law enforcement officers. The officers stood with their backs to the roundup area. Officer Sanders stood tensely in a parade rest posture. His eyes were hidden under his hat and dark sunglasses, his arms close to his sides with elbows bent to keep his gloved fists clenched next to the pistol grips. Officer Bennett stood relaxed, smiling, with his foot up resting on a small boulder. They shifted sidewards to make room for Tapia and Shauner to join the circle.

"These ladies want to make an official for-the-record statement, Sir," announced Bennett.

Everyone looked at Beth Hudson, the de facto leader of the wild horse advocates.

"I have a statement to make. You know, I think we want to go on record as making a statement that we don't think this roundup should start today. Most of the horses have been put in canyons that are relatively far from here and to get this done today will require that the horses be moved too far in a short period of time. Too far, certainly, for Dr. Grandin's welfare standards for young horses.

"Several of the foals are only three months old and this will be quite difficult for them. We were told that it was contractor availability that was the reason for doing it in this season, however, given that we only have 6 hours, the pressure on these young animals will be too much.

"We represent tens of thousands of people that would not want this to proceed. Here is a copy of my statement for the record." she said, handing a folded paper to Tapia.

He self-consciously adjusted his big gray hat before he spoke. " Beth, ladies ...

35

thank you for coming today and thank you for caring about the Bureau of Land Management's Wild Horse and Burro program. We've put several months of preparation into this gather event and delayed it until the last possible moment given the timing of hunting season and predicted weather. We've timed how long the horses should take by riding these ranges ourselves, and we've put the bands with the youngest foals in the closest canyons. For the record, I think we have addressed your concerns. Now, if you will excuse me, I have a few things left to do. Oh, by the way ... do you all like the port-a-potty that we set up for you?"

Lynne Wagner, standing behind her camera and tripod, gave him a thumbs-up gesture, but the rest of the advocates looked somewhat shocked by the question. Tapia grinned before he and Shauner retreated back to the pens. The officers retreated to the edge of the parking lot.

The sound of a helicopter in the distance immediately brought the group to its feet. Get those cameras ready! As tripods were extended and long lenses attached, a beat-up black pickup pulled into the parking lot. An older man got out, pulled a cane from behind the seat and hobbled over towards the viewing area.

Bennett greeted him kindly, "Hello, Sam! Good to see you here. You'll have to stay here with the advocates until the first batch is in. Randall told me to minimize any confusion and not open the inner gate during helicopter approaches, but I'll radio over and let Shauner know you made it."

He barked into his radio, "Shauner, Sam's here." Although the officials had already reached the pens, the advocates saw Tapia and Shauner both turn their heads to look back for just a moment. Tapia touched his hat in greeting and then went on his way.

Lynne Wagner approached, "Are you Sam Elkins, the horse trapper?" to which Sam nodded and broke out into a wide grin.

"And who are you?"

36

"Lynne Wagner"

"Lynne!! My girlfriend has your book on her coffee table! Lucky meeting you here, gal. Can I sit with you? We need to talk about the Salt Creek Basin herd. I heard they're in trouble."

"Sam, sit with me, yes! I don't know if we have time to talk now with these horses almost here, but meeting you is like meeting a living legend. You have been the voice of sanity when it comes to gathering mustangs. We need to talk about how to make some changes in the system. We need your help with the Basin mustangs."

Beth picked up her camera and moved 20 feet away as she spitefully muttered "That ol' horse-killer is not going to help you!"

"Oh, Beth," Sam replied, "you're always going to blame me for that aren't you? Do you think I called those mountain lions down to eat that foal? "

"It was killed in *your* trap! All that I can say about it is that you're an asshole," and with that she turned her face to her camera viewfinder. Everyone else turned to their own cameras as well, because the helicopter had just come into view. It was a long way off, but from their high vantage point, they had a great view.

From around the edge of the mesa, a line of horses came trotting and cantering down a dirt road that ran through the sagebrush covered valley. The horses looked remarkably relaxed as they traveled. A few ran behind the main herd, and the last was a small foal, who struggled to keep up.

"Look at the conflict in that stallion at the back. He wants to be in front and direct the band to safety, but he can't leave the mare and foal behind. He's getting frantic. *Hold on, boy, you're almost there,*" whispered Sam.

Dust swirled up from the open ground as the helicopter passed. Its shadow trailed close behind the horses. From the perspective of the viewing area, the helicopter appeared to be almost on top of the foal.

Suddenly, a second helicopter, this one gray, popped over the ridge. It hovered over the mouth of the side canyon, blocking it until the leading horses had passed by. Out of the dust of the gray chopper, a buckskin horse came running down the sandy arroyo and joined the herd. This horse was not the least bit relaxed and galloped hard to overtake the lead.

"Is that the herd stallion?" Lynne asked, as she stared into her viewfinder.

"No, they've managed to get four bands together, there are four stallions already. That horse"—Sam hesitated—"That horse is one I call The Phantom. I'm counting thirty-two horses in the first pass. Hot, damn! At $700 per horse, they pretty much already earned their day's wages.

"Now look what ol' Phantom's doin'! He's trying to lead those horses off the path. He seems to sense it's a trap. If he gets them to run into those trees, they'll be able to hide from the choppers. They might get some on horseback, but most of them will be gone.

"It's bad news for Phantom! Look where the fella's are standing with the Judas horse just before the trap. They're lettin' it go."

The Judas horse faithfully ran, as it had been trained to do, straight into the trap system. The lead mares swerved from following Phantom into the brush to follow the Judas horse down the more open pathway. The herd thundered into a long funnel shaped runway bounded by burlap material fence spread between metal posts. Men hid crouched behind the burlap.

As the little foal passed into the funnel, a man waving a white flag tied to a whip sprinted out of the bushes. He struck the rump of the lagging foal with the flag several times. Confused, the foal turned his head to try to look at the man, but then doggedly cantered on to follow his mother.

The Phantom ran into the trap, thundering past the mare and foal to overtake all of the horses. As he passed the lead mare inside the funnel, he turned to head straight to the burlap wall. He didn't even try to jump it, but just plowed into it, hooves first, creating a gap where he knocked it down. The leading mares close behind Phantom swerved away from the burlap and slowed to a standstill. Men scrambled to block the breach in the fabric. The horses were half way down the chute and looked confused as more horses crowded in behind them. The man ran up, still pushing the foal, flapping his white flag high and low. The horses snorted and jumped into what seemed to them the only escape route ... an S-curve in the panel system. The lagging foal received another strike from the whip as he stumbled forward. The man slammed the gate closed. Men popped out from their hiding places, throwing chains around the gates. The horses were trapped!

With stage one complete, the cowboys took a moment to stop, lean on the gate, and look at the harvest. Mostly bays, a few buckskins, some blacks, and a cremello— and that tiny sorrel foal.

Several of the men jumped over the burlap wall to get to the place where the saddle horses were tied. They swung quietly onto their mounts and loped off. As if the company had a dress code, the men all were wearing knee-high boots, tight jeans, and wide-brimmed cowboy hats. Those who are not wearing their leather gloves had them sticking out of their hip pockets. Some wore fleecy vests, some denim jackets. They looked like they were born for the saddle; they could give the Phantom a run for his money.

The wild horses stood steaming in the cold breeze. Some of them, like the foal, had coats wet with sweat. Suddenly, all hell broke loose as the stallions realized other stallions were sharing the pen. Long standing conflicts suddenly burst a-fire as the stallions showed their arched necks and savagely screamed. The lunging and kicking stallions crowded their bands between them and the fences. The sorrel foal fell in the press and was trampled. Men ran to break up the fights with their white flapping flags and the wild horses scrambled away, rearing up to try to leap the high fences. The mares started looking for places to escape along the bottoms of the fences and in the corners. Someone tapped the foal with a flag to get him up. A few men started climbing over the fence, flag/whips in hand. The horses wheeled to watch the humans.

Gates opened. A few horses were hazed deeper into the labyrinth of pens. The small pens made of tall gray panels were covered with visibility reducing plastic mesh. The cowboys perched along the top of the pens with no regard for the terror of the captives. They moved the horses around by threatening them with their long flag/whips. Tapia kept a tally of the horses as they passed by his checkpoint at the second gate. He would be the one who approved the invoice for this operation.

From the tiny pen in the center of this maze the horses were sorted into genders for shipping. The stallions were removed immediately to reduce the danger to the men. The mare and foal pairs were turned in circles with flapping flags until the gate could be opened in front of the mare to let her escape, leaving the baby trapped for exit into the foal pen. Jessica tried to photo document the mare and foal pairs, but otherwise no one kept track of which band any one horse came in with. The familial relationships of the bands were destroyed forever. In the stallion pen, the overwhelming fear stifled their aggression toward each other temporarily and they frantically screamed to their mares.

The tiny sorting pens filled quickly. Most of the horses were mares and as the mare pen became crowded, Karen Sorensen backed a long covered stock-trailer to the exit gate. Very little was visible from the distance of the Public Viewing Area because the tall walls there were covered with canvas tarps.

Every mare struggled to avoid being the first horse onto the trailer. They curled their necks around each other and tried to push away from the trailer. The cowboys waved the white flags from behind fence panels to push them in and after a moment a horse stepped up and onto the trailer. The other horses followed until the trailer was crowded. The last few horses were still standing on the ground. The cowboys climbed the fence and started kicking the horses' backs and rumps to encourage them in. Finally, by banging the gate on the legs of the last horse still on the ground, the cowboys forced this unlucky animal to find a way to squeeze in. The group was surprising quiet in the trailer as it was too crowded for the horses to kick each other.

Sorting happened quite quickly, as the contractor's men needed to be ready for another incoming band. The truck and trailer pulled away from the exit gate and were already heading for the short-term holding facility seventy-three miles away in Bloomfield. The sorrel foal's mother called to him from the truck as it disappeared down the road. He screamed in his isolation and crashed into a fence panel, but he was firmly in captivity.

Horses were not the only animals terrorized by the helicopters. A large herd of deer ran by. The photographers in the Public Viewing Area rotated their tripods in perfect unison.

"Okay, Sam. You're clear to go on down." Bennett broke the silence.

Sam touched Lynne on the shoulder, picked up his cane, and hobbled back to his truck.

{Chapter 10}

Red X Campsite

David reached over for the map sitting in the passenger seat and pulled it onto his lap. He wanted to check directions, but he didn't want to stop to do it. He twisted his nose and sniffed. The excitement of being on his journey was exhilarating, but he was worried. He knew that Forest Road 310 shouldn't be too hard to find because if you pass it you see the welcome signs for the Apache Reservation, but what if he missed it? He concentrated on being aware of the surroundings. The sky was filled with white, fluffy clouds, the pine trees so tall and stately on the ridges, sandstone boulders jumbled at the base of the sheer rock cliffs, the sea-green patches of gramma grasses scattered among the fading reds and golds of the oak brush, the cool air in his face; it all made him feel so alive. At last, he spotted the little brown sign saying "Forest Road 310, Carracas Mesa". The turn had plenty of room to pull his truck and horse trailer over and still be out of the way. He parked, and then quickly unfolded the map as he sniffed.

Oil field roads are notoriously hard to navigate, and these, running along the valleys and mesas of this canyon country, were some of the worst, but David was prepared. He had spent many exhilarating hours planning this trip. His map had a blood-red line connected the turnoff, where he now sat, to a red x. The distance between every turnoff was written in pencil beside the winding red path. The x was on a mesa near a gas well. North of the red x, the canyon bottom was circled and marked "roundup". She, herself, had provided him with the location. He pushed the button to reset the mileage indicator to zero as he pulled back onto Forest Road 310.

An hour later, David coasted his truck past the gas well and followed a two-track behind the trees to his Red X campsite. His neck felt tense from the drive and he stretched it in several directions and sniffed before he jumped down from the cab. He grabbed a rope from the back of the truck and tied a highline between the trailer and a tree. Once the palomino, Apostle, was out of the trailer, David gave him some water in a bucket and tethered him on the highline. Apostle stretched his neck and legs.

Camp consisted of a two-man tent, a shotgun, and some high-powered binoculars. No guitar, no campfire. "The clouds are darker," David thought as he saddled the horse and put the shotgun in the scabbard. Could, indeed, be nasty weather, and he realized with surprise that precipitation hadn't been considered in any of his plans to watch the young lady. Sniffing, he pulled a camouflage jacket from the cab of the truck and put it on.

It only took a few minutes to saddle the quiet gelding. The scabbard for the gun was tied on the left side. The shotgun shells, except for one, went in the saddle bag. "Just for emergencies," he told himself, stuffing the shell into his left front pocket next to the gas receipt.

He swung up onto Apostle, and set off northwards through the trees. He savored the moment, wondering if it was possible to be something more than merely alive. "Vibrant" is the closest word to it. He wondered if Jesus had felt vibrant during his life on earth and decided that was probably what made Jesus so special, besides being the son of God. Jesus just radiated this vibrancy and with it lighted the world. He felt a special blessing to have this moment of vibrancy. He loved his connection with God and having his own ministry. Life was good. Manhood was good. How could it be wrong to appreciate young women? God made them beautiful for a reason. *Sniff.*

It wasn't long before David reached his destination overlooking the roundup. Apostle stood quietly after being tied to a tree. David felt his face broaden into a smile as he pulled the binoculars out of his saddle bags. The rock David chose to sit on was covered with gray and orange lichens, matching the camo jacket. He had a clear view of the roundup below.

The vehicles were mostly parked together near a fork in the road on the west end. He spotted her truck right away. He could see quite a few people, mostly women, it seemed, in a group on a rocky ridge above the pens. A few men in uniform stood leaning on a government truck. "Watchmen," David said in a whisper. The women sat along the edge of the cliff behind cameras and seemed rather occupied. None of them looked like her.

He lowered his binoculars to look at the pens. Horses were stirring up the dust and it looked like only men were in the pens near the horses. Cowboys and watchmen. A little knot of women with cameras stood well outside the pens, but she wasn't in that group either. He was watching the men open a gate and move a horse, when a movement caught his eye. The plastic mesh was blocking part his view, but she was there. It only took a few minutes to ride to a better view.

From his new rock, he first checked what she was wearing. Jeans and a checkered western blouse. The word "cute" came to mind, then the word "cunt". Vibrant and alive. He felt his temperature rise as he thought about her having no clue she was being watched so carefully. He took off his coat as the sun peeked out from behind a cloud. He spread his legs apart to let the sun warm his pants. Vibrant. Look at the way that woman moves. Look at how her breasts push at that checkered cloth. She's wearing makeup. She wants to be pretty for me. She feels so secure; she doesn't have a bloody clue.

He lay back on the rock and closed his eyes. His hand reached for the sun-warmed zipper. He felt oh, so vibrant.

"Hallelujah, Jesus!" *Sniff.*

When he looked again, she was sitting on a log near the trucks. He got up and adjusted Apostle's saddle. He pulled out the shotgun. "Let's go target practice, Mr. Apostle," but before he dropped the binoculars into the saddle bag, he turned them to look again at her truck. She still had the gun rack and shotgun he had given her. He chuckled to think how disappointed she was going to be if she ever tried to use it. *Sniff.*

{Chapter 11}

Mop-Up Operation

Sam was a little bit hot under the collar when he found Tapia.

"Dammit, Randall. These helicopter boys are doing everything they can to provide the advocates with the kind of publicity you don't need. The ladies are sitting up there filming your horses getting whacked, run into fences, foals getting whacked, and the contractor has you where you can't do a thing about it because you don't see it happening. Get Shauner to take over the inventory and get this show under control!"

"What's happening, Sam?" Tapia winced.

"You'll see it on the nightly news ... BLM Abuses Horses. I sat in the peanut gallery with the advocates and they've got everything you didn't want to happen on film. I spent twenty years out here bait-trapping horses and in all that time I never committed half of the abuses that these boys pulled off in forty-five minutes."

"Sam, if you can give me a list of these things, I can do something about it."

"Let me borrow that clipboard. Can I write on this? Gimme a pen. The thing is, Randall, this is where horses start figuring out what humans are all about. Bob Browning used to tell me 'You never get a second chance to make a first impression.' That's what we're doing here, Randall; we are making our first impressions. What the horses learn here today will stay with them for the rest of their lives. We owe them a better start of their lives in captivity. Horses aren't like cows, Randall. They have to trust us to be able to perform their jobs. We ruin that right out of the box and what the hell for? It's really not necessary."

Sam concentrated on his list—pen flashing in the sunlight— for a moment then handed the clipboard to Randall Tapia.

1. Unnecessary touching
2. Hitting animals with whips
3. Use of flags and prods to move animals
4. Shouting

5. Climbing on fences
6. Moving fast
7. Appearing suddenly
8. Chasing animals like a predator
9. Banging gates,
10. Banging legs with trailer door to make them move.
11. Rough handling of foals.

"Crap," muttered Tapia. "Let's go find Jessica."

Jessica and Sephra were sitting in the shade of the loading pen tarps with their backs against the fence looking through the photos. Tapia dispensed with any pleasantries, "Jessica, did you bring any work order forms? I've got to write these guys up before we get the next horses in. Are they in your truck? Can you run get one?"

As Jessica ran off towards the parking lot, Tapia introduced Sam Elkins (venerated horse trapper) to Sephra Brooks (neophyte Welfare advocate). Even for Tapia it was an honor to be in the presence of the legendary horse trapper who had spent his life demonstrating that bait-trapping was a humane alternative to helicopters. He knew every one of the horses on this range by sight, even the almost indistinguishable bays, from having studied the herd for twenty years. His photo documentation was phenomenal. He would help to pick out the horses to be returned to the range today. The plan was to maximize genetic diversity while maintaining color and conformation. Sam was uniquely qualified to make those decisions.

Tapia asked Sephra if she had noticed any welfare issues going on.

"They were a little hard on the foals, but Jessica and I took that job over so now we move them." she replied. "The poor babies are so terrified. I haven't had time to look at anything else."

Jessica returned with the form. Tapia slid it into the clipboard clip and started writing. "I'm not going to let this go south on me. Jessica, call John Lily and ask him to come to the loading chute immediately. Also call Shauner and get him over here too."

Sam looked down at Sephra who was still sitting on the ground. "Miss Brooks, did they tell me you have photos of all the horses caught today?" Sephra nodded. "May I see them?" he asked. Sephra stood up and handed him the camera, but the glare of the sunlight obscured the screen.

"Let's go over by that tree," she suggested when she saw him squinting. As they were leaving, Shauner trotted up, sending the nearby horses crashing into the far side of their tiny pens. He instinctively veered, ducked his head, and crouched at the sudden noises.

"Shauner, you just violated Item six of this work order. Here, read this and don't let me catch you doing *any* of it. Then when the next batch comes in, you are to be taking the inventory I was doing. What *were* you doing anyway?"

"Watchin' 'em try to catch that rogue stallion. He's a lot smarter than those cowboys! I don't think the contractor is going to be too happy about these rules, Boss." Shauner said as he handed back the clipboard.

It turned out that Shauner was only partially right. It wasn't the first time the contractor had been forced to 'play nice' and his cowboys knew how, but not without a certain amount of grumbling about the *damn advocates*. When the next wave of horses came in, the action had a whole new feeling of professionalism, efficiency, and lowered energy. The mania went away and the rest of the afternoon was relaxed.

Even the horses themselves seemed to relax. Panting and sweating from their travels, they stood quietly in the s-shaped pen. The adults surrounded the foals as they recovered from the chase. The stallion would always be the first to raise his neck in vigilance. His sharp ears would twist to catch every sound. When the horses had calmed, the gates would open and a single quiet cowboy would prove sufficient to make them move past Shauner's checkpoint into the sorting labyrinth. The horse advocates in the viewing area grew bored of filming improved horsemanship.

{Chapter 12)

Mop-Up II

Picking out the best mares to be returned to the range was harder than Sam had expected. It was easy to let the ones with crooked legs, big heads, or big withers get put into captivity, but the delicate ones, the ones with brilliant colors, and the ones with handsome foals were all ones he wanted to keep in the herd. Tapia had been adamant that only 30 horses were to remain on the range. It was starting to give Sam a headache.

The little corner pen for horses with physical defects was starting to fill up. A bay stallion was half blind, his left eye missing. A bay mare had a clubfoot, its hoof sitting at an unnatural angle. Two—one bay and the other black—were thin, old horses who probably didn't have much left for teeth. One was a dun yearling colt with a severe eye infection. A sway-back pinto mare was added in one of the final drives. No humans wanted to linger by their little pen, but instead hurried around that corner of the setup.

The light breezes of midday gave way to gusty winds rolling tumble weeds and whipping up sand, causing the horses to turn their tails to the west. Many of the horses in the pens stood with their eyes closed to the sand. Tapia held on to his cowboy hat as he moved another set of mares towards the loading pen. There wasn't much blue sky left.

From the catch-pens, it was not possible to watch the incoming herds. The people stationed there could only hear the helicopters and thundering hooves as they approached, so only the advocates in the viewing area saw how Phantom was finally rounded up. The wild horse had not given up trying to intercept and redirect bands away from the catch-pens. Finally, every man with a saddle horse rode out between drives and stationed himself in the sage and rabbitbrush. One helicopter drove the band forward as normal. The band was additionally followed by the men on saddle horses forming a phalanx of riders across the canyon bottom. When Phantom made his run for the front of the small herd, the second helicopter appeared over the ridge and flew along the western edge of the valley, discouraging any horse from running for those trees and freedom. The riders moved at a gallop to surround Phantom and the band, pushing them into the burlap-lined runway. The helicopters hovered along each side of the runway. By the time Phantom turned to run, any possible escape route was totally blocked. He was soon inside the s-shaped pen.

With most of the contractor's staff out on horseback, Erin Tate, the USFS Wild Horse specialist, was manning the gate at the s-shaped pen. He managed to get it latched and turned to face the horses. He held a flag pointing toward the ground and put out his hand toward the horses to shoo them into the labyrinth, where Shauner had opened the gate. Phantom cantered in a circle around the edge of the odd-shaped pen, brushing by Tate and stepping on the flag. The horse turned, nostrils flaring, and hammered the earth with his left front hoof, pawing and pounding. Phantom stared at Tate, and then started another cantering circle. Tate raised the whip and tried to turn the horse away with a strike to the chest, but the horse just cantered by and kicked Tate in the thigh as he passed him. Tate fell to his knees on the ground and held his leg until the shock of the impact subsided into a dull throb. It was going to hurt like hell tomorrow, but it wasn't broken.

Shauner shouted "Man down!" Cowboy and government agents approached quickly but cautiously lest they panic the horses into running over the fallen man. "That horse attacked Tate!"

"I'm alright," Tate countered. He stood up and dusted off his jeans. "But that horse is loco."

All eyes turned to the horse. Phantom was perhaps 9 or 10 years old, a golden buckskin with a large white star and a white forelock. The rest of his mane and his tail was inky black, matching his legs and hooves. As stunning as he might be, he was obviously equally cunning and extremely dangerous. Tapia called out to Shauner, "Put that one in the corner pen. He's too dangerous to keep."

Erin Tate harbored a grudge so he lingered at the corner pen after his nemesis had been hazed in. "Now, you'll get what you deserve. A bullet between the eyes. You and these other misfits." Phantom puffed himself up and ran straight to the fence. He shoved his head and neck through the bars moving the fence panel three feet closer to his intended victim. Tate jumped backwards as he saw the flash of teeth, looked around sheepishly, and left looking for something else to do.

Sephra and Sam remained to look at the magnificent animal. "What do you know about this horse, Sam?"

"I call this horse Phantom because I've only seen him three times out on the range. I've never seen a band with him. I never saw him as a foal. I don't know if he was domestic and someone dumped him. His lack of fear of humans makes me think he might have been dumped. I just don't know much about him. Maybe I could find him in the photo archives. He looks like he'd be a son of Rocket. Rocket led a band in Cabresto Canyon back in the 90's. Maybe I forgot a foal, though it's hard to imagine forgetting one like him."

"What will happen to him, Sam?" the advocate asked.

"I don't know," Sam lied and then changed the subject. "Looks like a storm is moving in. Might be a little tough to get this setup out of here tomorrow. A heavy rain could really lock this place down."

***

Bennett sat in the passenger seat of the BLM Law Enforcement truck doing a crossword puzzle. Sanders stood unobtrusively near the bumper doing isometric exercises by pushing one hand against the other. They tried to hide their utter boredom from the advocates cameras because they knew if they weren't careful they could end up as the example of slovenly BLM cops on some website or, worse, the nightly news. It was a relief when they spied a heavy duty Ford truck heading toward their post. Sanders, seeing a hard-shell cover over the bed of the truck, quickly considered the possibility that it could be covering a load of ammonium nitrite with a suicide bomber at the wheel. Bennett, on the other hand, knew it was the veterinarian; he'd seen her before. Before she pulled up to their checkpoint, he had already radioed Tapia.

As she stopped, Sanders motioned for her to roll down her window. Bennett did not want to correct him, so he waited for Sanders to ask to see her license. Emily Nelson, DVM. As Sanders handed back her license, Bennett said, "Go ahead, Dr. Nelson, they are expecting you." Neither the police nor the vet noticed Beth taking their photos.

They didn't have time to return to boredom before an equally heavy duty, but much muddier truck approached. This one held three men in cowboy hats. They could have passed as members of the contractor's crew if they had been wearing the correct identification badges.

Sanders requested identification from each of them. Beth turned her camera again to take the picture. Don Cabot, age 24 sat on the passenger side. He had a clean, pudgy face, or at least his buzz-cut made it look pudgy. Behind his dark sunglasses he seemed to be staring at the glove-box. In the center, Michael Cabot, at 26, wasn't so clean with a few days stubble covering his cheeks and a drooping mustache over his upper lip. He eyes glowed darkly under straight and narrow eyebrows, seemingly staring straight at Beth's camera. Shep Cabot wore sunglasses under a dove-gray cowboy hat. He talked with the officers. The newish cowboy hat had a narrow dark leather and silver hatband. Shep was more than twice as old as his boys and his manicured gray goatee and long gray sideburns suggested he was more than just a lonely rancher. The law enforcement officers sent them down the hill to the roundup area after returning their identification cards.

The advocates watched from their perch as the vet entered the roundup area. Tapia met her at the loading gate and ushered her to the small corner pen where Phantom and his six companions stood. Carrying a clipboard, she began writing and pointing to the horses. Tapia held up a camera to document the horses as she indicated them. She bent over to look at the club-foot on the horse. She waved her arm in a downward arc as he photographed the swayback. She tilted her head from side to side before she pointed to the yearling.

Phantom seemed to have very little interest in the veterinarian. He stood dozing as if he had simply gone off the clock from his vigilant demeanor. The veterinarian looked at him, looked at Tapia, and shook her head. Tapia seemed to be emphatic. He motioned for Jessica to come. Jessica brought her camera, which she showed to the veterinarian. The veterinarian nodded affirmatively and wrote on her clipboard. Tapia looked relieved and held out his hand to accept the paper the vet handed him. The vet returned to her truck and left the area as Tapia turned his attention to the loading of the foals.

The foals were confused about jumping up into the dark trailer. The contractor's cowboys had forgotten protocol. The advocates filmed them doing more than physically pushing the youngsters. The cowboys were documented twisting the foals necks, pulling their manes, hitting them on their butts, and lifting them by the tail before Tapia arrived and civility was restored. As soon as the foals were loaded into the trailer, Erin Tate departed with them for the Bloomfield holding facility.

Tapia ushered the three cowboys to the small corner pen. Phantom lunged at them. They instinctively put their hands on their hats and turned to look at each other. Tapia and the older Cabot shook hands before the trio returned to their ranch truck and left.

By this time, Beth was beside herself with anger. "This really sucks!" she announced to the group. "The vet's already signed the order condemning Phantom, the hangmen have arrived, and the assholes can't stop themselves from torturing the foals. I hate these people with every fiber of my being!" She threw her gear into her carrying bag and stormed to her car, pausing only long enough to screech insults at the bemused law enforcement officers.

The other advocates stayed put, knowing the best footage was yet to come. They didn't have to wait long. The BLM staff and Sephra assembled outside the burlap fence, all cameras at the ready. John Lily himself walked through the complex, leaving gates wide open behind him. Sam stood by the gate where the horses to be released waited uneasily. John and Sam shook hands and Sam opened the gate. Cowboys emerged to push the selected horses out, back through the labyrinth, and the s-shaped pen to freedom. Everyone cheered, even Sanders. They were broken bands, but the five stallions and twenty mares would be the start of a new herd. In four years there would be 50 horses, in eight 100. It would be more than a decade before they would have to schedule the next gather.

The advocates started packing and departing as the last stallions were loaded on the trailer. The contractors started disassembling the pen system from the burlap fence end. The BLM office ladies drove away in a Chevy Suburban. Tapia and Shauner supervised the loading of the horses condemned by vet as having 'poor prognosis for suitability as a riding horse.' They made sure no one was foolhardy enough to enter any pen or alley with Phantom. Several cowboys and their flags were needed to force the beast onto the trailer. After watching Phantom be loaded, Sephra and Sam left as a convoy, heading to his camper to look at horse photos.

***

Tapia pulled away from the pens, thinking things had gone reasonably well. No accidents. No horses injured. The contractor had made a poor showing, but the BLM had behaved impeccably. Fifty-five horses caught, of which twenty-eight were fairly young and would be easier to adopt. In the meadow that was filled with purple daisies there was a fork in the road. He followed the well-traveled fork to the left, under the watchful eye of a black Angus cow.

***

Aaron Shauner started his vehicle and listened to the engine. This was normally Tapia's truck. It had all of Tapia's stuff in it; it even smelled like Tapia. He thought about how it would feel to be the boss. Too much paperwork, he decided, as he turned right onto the less-traveled little two-track, still under the watchful eye of the black cow.

He was headed into a zone of few cell towers, so he had some business to take care of while he could.

"Hello ... I'd like to place an order to go .... I'd like one of those Roadhouse Roadkill's ... Curley fries ... I'll be there about 8, is that too late? ... Okay, see you then."

{Chapter 13}

The Murder

Shauner was fiddling with the radio tuner when he drove into the meadow. He failed to notice the man by the clump of aspen trees; a man mounted on a palomino horse loading a shell into his shotgun, a slip of paper fluttering to the ground. He would not have failed to see the dead deer next to the road, if he had gotten that far. Instead, Shauner stopped to check his left rear tire and stepped out of the vehicle.

"Bad timing, Watchman. You should have kept going.

"I am not going to let you ruin my life. I didn't kill that deer, but if I am caught here with a weapon, they will take away my church. I don't get another chance, they've already told me that. Who would I even be without my ministry?

"God is testing me. I must be strong!"

He cocked his weapon.

The horses in the trailer, smelling the near-hysteria of the hidden man, became agitated. Their frantic movements rocked the trailer wildly. The noise of them kicking the walls of the trailer put the potential victim on edge and distracted him. Aaron felt sorry for the fearful horses as he bent down to feel the too warm tire. He didn't notice the perpetrator before the shotgun blast slammed his body against the trailer.

"Hearken Watchman, Jesus has called you home. Deliver your soul to its maker!"

The saddle horse bolted at the sound of the blast, but the rider jerked the reins, cruelly pinching the horse's tongue. The horse broke into a sudden canter but the rider responded by forcing the steed to lope in circle in order to settle him down before heading back to the fence, where a jump over the locked gate let them disappear into a leafy oak forest. Blowing leaves quickly covered their tracks.

A human seems to be locked in the trailer with the horses, as a hand reaches out through the trailer gate and jerks the latch. With the urgency of true panic, the gate is thrown open and a naked man leaps into the sand, running hard to stay in front of the frantic bolting wild horses. The horse-hooves pound the road like thunder for a moment then fade as the horses disappear over the rise.

The naked man stops running after 30 yards and looks back at the vehicles. In the blink of an eye, the man has disappeared and in his place stands a coyote.

The animal walks back to the victim and sniffs the pooling blood. He knows the spirit is gone; he can't change that. He trots away down the trail left by the fleeing horses.

No one ever saw a coyote like that one before. He had a white forehead.

{Chapter 14}

Last customer of the day

He walked across the porch looking anxious and jumped when he opened the door with its clanking cowbell. He stood in the doorway looking wide-eyed until he saw that there was only an aproned waitress looking back at him from across the counter. She was putting away red plastic glasses as she dried them with a white bar-towel. His posture relaxed and he stepped inside.

"Can I get something to eat this late?"

In Aletta's experience, ordering food was an unusual behavior for a Native American male traveling solo. They usually only stopped if they had a backseat full of hungry kids. Also, this fellow was not wearing the mandatory oil-field uniform of fire-retardant clothing, so he must not be from around here. Aletta smiled at the prospect of meeting a stranger, then grabbed a menu and some silverware wrapped in a napkin and said "Sure", placing the items on the counter in front of a barstool. He didn't take her bait to sit and chat but picked up the items and carried them to a table, sitting on the far side where he would be facing the door but not facing her. "What would you like to drink?"

"Black coffee."

She carried the steaming cup to his table, "The cook is already gone for the night, but I can fix you anything except Mexican food."

He grunted and studied the menu. His broad and handsome face seemed to be Navajo. His hair was jet black except for a streak of silver-gray shining above his left eyebrow. She noticed he wore a traditional ornate necklace of silver, turquoise, and orange coral. His feet were clad in buckskin moccasins. She also noticed he wore her favorite perfume, the warm scent of horses.

"Green-chile cheeseburger with fries."-

56

"Coming right up." She retreated to the kitchen and soon the sounds and smells of sizzling food brought the café atmosphere to life. The radio played a song about a truck stop at the end of the world. She delivered the man's food, re-cleaned the kitchen, refilled his coffee and then perched on a barstool near the cash register to listen to the radio.

"*Me and Billy the kid, never got along, ...*" As she listened to the music, her eyelids grew heavy. She struggled to pull them up several times, but then they quietly overpowered her and the world faded away.

He stood at the register. "Excuse me, young lady. I'd like to pay my bill now."

"Oh, sorry. I just kind of drifted off for a moment. I know why I am so tired! It was one of the busiest days ever with that horse round-up going on. We catered it, and I've been here since four this morning when we started making the breakfast burritos."

His eyebrows dropped to an interested slant. "I heard about that horse round-up. Where did they take those horses?" he said handing her a twenty dollar bill.

"Oh, they're down in Bloomfield. They have a place where they get them ready for adoption. They have to brand them and geld them before people can get them." The cash register printed the receipt, and the cash drawer popped open. She put the twenty in the correct compartment and took out a ten and three ones.

"What do they do with the old ones that no one wants to adopt?" he asked as she handed him his change.

"I dunno. I heard they got 52 this time, so probably 10 of them are going to be old ones. You could call the BLM and ask, I have their number here. They surely will need homes for those old ones."

"That's okay. But I think they got seven less than that. I just have a feeling about it." He said with a little grin as he dropped the ones into the tip jar and walked out the door.

Feeling unsatisfied with the brevity of the conversation, she consoled herself by pulling the tip out of the jar and stuffing it into her pocket. It was time to sweep and mop.

As she was dumping out the end of the coffee and rinsing the pot, she realized the call-in-order customer is probably not going to show up before she closes. She moved the brown paper bag out of the warming box and put it next to her purse so she could take it home to be used as training treats. She regretted that her dogs were getting slightly chubby on Roadhouse leftovers, but they had, at least, learned many tricks they could perform to earn the treats.

Midway through the locking and powering-down ritual, she realized she had forgotten to turn on the open sign when it got dark. "Would it have made any difference?" she asked herself, trying to imagine who might have stopped in. Too bad that quirky Navajo hadn't been more chatty.

{Chapter 15}

Phantom Photos

Sam pulled up to his camper trailer, retrieved his flashlight from the glove box, and watched Sephra park her truck. It would be hours before the moon rose, so he clicked the light on and illuminated a path for her. He was a little self-conscious about having a young lady visit him in the evening hours, but, she had insisted that it would be difficult for her to get to his camp any other time. The two hours between him and town had benefits for his desire to live like a hermit, but sometimes company was nice.

They walked to the camper, chatting about the herd of deer that had crossed their path on the way from the roundup. Hunting season started in three days—deer beware! Sam wanted to have his trailer moved to his girlfriend's place in Santa Fe by then.

Sam's camper was fitted with energy-saving LED lights, which he flipped on as he walked through the unlocked door. Sephra was impressed by how tidy the camper was. She had a stereotype projection of a hermit as messy. The wall by the kitchen booth/table was covered with tacked on photos. Impressed again, she realized that Sam was quite a photographer! Not only horses, but stunning landscapes inhabited by bear, elk, mountain lions, and antelope. It was obvious that the hermit put his solitude in nature to good use.

While she studied the wall photo collection, he pulled two trout from the refrigerator and put a black iron frying pan on the tiny gas stove. "Do you eat fish?" he asked. Many advocates didn't, but she responded affirmatively. Breaded in cornmeal, the fish were soon sizzling in their frying pan. He boiled water to make instant mashed potatoes and heated a can of corn. He was *never* accused of being an inhospitable hermit. He set out glasses of water next to plates and silverware. A vase with wildflowers completed a rather elegant camp cookout.

Sephra ate quietly, racking her brain for something to say. She was having dinner with Sam Elkins, a living legend in the horse advocacy world. She felt like a little girl at the table with grownups. She refused to let herself play the "cute little girl", because she wanted more than anything for him to take her role as a horse advocate seriously. She pulled the bones from the trout and moved the corn around on her plate self-consciously.

Sam stripped the bones from the fish with a practiced hand, put them on the side of the plate, and proceeded to chow down. When his plate was clear he looked up, pushed his plate away, and said, "Corky caught those trout from the San Juan River and brought them to me last night. Do you know Corky? He's about your age. Fly fishing guide. Nice guy. I think he was up here scouting for this hunt, but it was sure thoughtful of him to remember how much I like trout."

Sephra relaxed and started eating what she now realized was a pescatarian treasure. "Do you know what species of trout it is?" she asked, pleased with herself for having thought of something to say.

"I believe that's a rainbow," as he cleared the table of the items he'd used. The teapot of water started to sputter and he pulled it off the camp-stove and poured it into a plastic dishpan. He washed his dishes quickly, then took up her now empty plate and washed it too. The dishrag was squeezed almost dry before he wiped the table off, then he tossed her a dry cloth and said, "Dry it while I get the photos down."

The photo collection was in file boxes that looked like shoeboxes for children. Each box was labeled with a year and inside there were dividers labeled with the months. He took the cloth from her and hung it on the towel rack. "You start in 2010, I'll start in 2000. We are bound to find something of Mr. Phantom; he can't be more than 10 years old."

"I didn't make it up to the advocate viewing area today. Who all was there?" she ventured as she flipped through the photos.

"Let's see," he said, as he raced through his stack. "Hmm. Beth Hudson was there; she doesn't like me. Hmm ... I met Lynne Wagner today for the first time. She sure seems positive. Do you know her?" to which Sephra nodded her head *yes*. "Then, there was, uh, Sally, uh ... Sally Horne and Kathy Kipper. There was a couple of others I didn't recognize. I did know the law enforcement officers though!" he laughed. "I don't think that impressed Ms. Beth."

"Sam, do you think the advocates have any chance of working together?" to which he chuckled and snorted in response. She continued, "I've been trying to find some sense of community between my job and the other advocates. Maybe I have been spoiled by being brought up in the church and just expect community to exist, but so far I feel like I've just gotten a cold shoulder from everyone. Don't they need each other or is it somehow competitive?"

She reached for the 2009 box as he replied, "Girlie, it is a dog-eat-dog world among the advocates. They are fighting for public recognition that their organizations are doing the most because whoever is doing the most will attract the most and biggest donations. You and I are lucky. You have the Society for Humane Treatment of Animals to do the fundraising you need. I have my contract to dart horses to fund me. This birth control darting is very well funded. You and I have it made, but the advocates have to fight and scratch each other for every dollar. Of course, in your case, your organization can just steamroll them and out fund-raise them at every corner. No, they couldn't actually be friends with you."

"Bingo!" he blurted out. "2002, Mr. Phantom was already full-grown." He flipped out the photo and studied the writing on the back. "Carracas Mesa, near Eul Point, so—right in the heart of the designated Wild Horse Territory.

"He's standing with a young mare. I know her ... did I already trap her? Was she in the group I released? Did we send her down to Bloomfield? Oh, why can't I remember her? I know I gave her a name, but it's not on the back of the photo."

"Here they are in 2008, Sam!" She pulled out a photo. The mare was a bay with a big white blaze on her face and high white stockings on her hind legs, next to her stood a black foal who duplicated his mother's stockings. Phantom was touching noses with the foal and the foal had his neck stretched and his mouth open. "Cute family," she said turning the photo over. "'Middle Mesa' ... Sam, is that near Eul Point?"

"Directly across the canyon! Do the notes have her name?"

"It says 'Phantom and Daisy's new son Clipper'. Do you remember Clipper and what happened to him?"

"We gathered him today. He was one of the studs I turned out," breaking out into an infectious grin.

She grinned back, "Oh, Sam, at least Phantom's line will live on!" Then suddenly, tears filled her eyes. "Are they going to euthanize Phantom? No one would tell me."

"Yeah," he replied with sudden despondency. Tears rolled down his cheeks.

"Damn it, Girlie, we are going to get my photos wet. Here, take a paper towel." He wiped his eyes and blew his nose.

"Can we do anything to save him, Sam?" she asked as she dabbed her eyes.

"Oh, Sephra, everyone falls in love with some horse that their heart tells them doesn't deserve the fate the person imagines is awaiting them, whether that fate is getting caught, starving to death in a bad winter, getting euthanized, or even just getting adopted by an animal abuser. That is one thing we advocates have to remind ourselves: it's not about the individual horse. It's the herd and their genetics. That is the part we have to preserve. Horses get old and die. That can't be stopped. The herd has to stay young. Phantom has lived a long good life. He's more than ten years old even if he looks like a young stud. He's had his day. His genes live on."

"I know you're right, Sam, but it's hard. He's my first ... but," she said resolutely, "he won't be my last. I'll fall in love with every one of them, if it makes me a better advocate. I am not the kind of person that gives up."

"Oh, look how late it is. I won't get home until midnight if I leave right this moment," she exclaimed, getting up.

"Can you find your way at night? I could follow you until you get to Forest Road 310."

"Is Rosa Road harder to find?" she asked. "I know my way that way." They headed out the door with the flashlight. The moon was on the eastern horizon.

"No, I just usually go the other way from habit. At the first fork, turn west, that is left, it will take you into a canyon. Just stay on that road and it goes to Rosa Road. It's a little bumpy, but your truck will be fine."

She jumped in her truck but before she could start the engine he said, "Sephra, you don't know how much it means to me to see young people take up the mission to help save the mustangs. I am really happy you asked to see my photos."

"Sam, you have no idea how much this has meant to me. I don't feel so alone now. There is a chance to make a change. Next time I see you, I'll give you the hug I have for you, but right now, I better skedaddle. Bye now."

She was still glowing brighter than the moon when she got to the city lights of Bloomfield.

{Chapter 16}

Cowboys to the Rescue

By half past ten, the Cabots had grown tired of waiting for the BLM truck, so they piled back into the cab of their ranch truck and headed up the single-lane ridge road Shauner should be on. They crossed the cattleguard that separated their private lands from the public lands and crawled up the switchbacks in first gear. The road had been built to accommodate oil field traffic so the turns were comfortably wide although the road was steep. This was the most dangerous section of road, but there was no sign that the government truck had fallen off the mountain along this stretch.

Shep had bought the ranch back in the 1960's back when it wasn't a crime to gather wild horses and sell them for slaughter. They didn't really belong to anyone back then. He liked to tell his boys about the old days, but since they had become adults they never seemed to listen. Yessiree, he had gathered a lot of wild horses in his day. It was enough to cover the mortgage. Those boys were born to run this ranch, how could they even consider moving to town?

The rabbit brush was growing up in the center of the roadway between the two dirt tracks. This road rarely had any traffic. Not too many people knew about it, and if anyone bothered coming over the top, after passing the *No Trespassing* sign at the cattleguard, they landed in the ranch yard, and if they managed to get through that, the road out of the ranch was closed by a locked gate. Shep had told Shauner about this shortcut before he left the roundup.

As they crossed the cattleguard that separated the bull pasture from the mesa pasture, they caught a glimpse of a vehicle ahead in the dark, but before they got there, they could see a brown shaggy hump lying partially in the road. It had bled out and laid in a dried pool of blood and as they came closer, they saw it was a deer with antlers.

"What the hell is going on here, boys?" Shep asked.

"Don't know, Pa," replied Don anxiously. Michael's scowl grew deeper.

They rolled past the deer slowly to the truck just across the meadow. It occupied the entire roadway, but the government truck wasn't moving so they crept toward it until the two trucks were almost bumper to bumper. The government cab didn't have a driver sitting in it, but they could see the back door of the trailer swinging open in the wind.

"There is something back there on the ground on the driver's side," said Don.

"Well, get out and look, damn it, Don! I'll keep the headlights on. You too, Michael. Get out and see what's going on." The old man scowled at them.

Don stepped out, took one step, froze then shouted, "Oh my god! He's dead! Oh my god! They blew his brains out! Shep, he's dead!"

Michael finished climbing down from the truck and walked toward the body. "No point in calling the ambulance, this one is a goner."

"Get back in this truck, boys, and don't touch nothin'. Don't leave any more tracks than you have and don't leave any fingerprints. We want nothin' to do with this. We don't know if the killer is still here."

Don got in the truck, but Michael stayed in position near the headlight.

"What are we going to do, Dad?" asked Don. "What if the killer is still here? Can he get all three of us?"

Michael answered for him, "The killer is not going to be sitting around waiting to get caught, Don. If I was him, I'd be seven counties away by now. Killing a government guy is against all kinds of federal laws. This is FBI kind of stuff. Killing the deer was stupid, but killing the BLM guy was a lot worse. Damn it anyway, we are going to lose the money for gettin' rid of those nags. I was countin' on that to make my car payment."

Michael continued, "I think we should take anything worth havin', put the deer on the hood, load the body on the truck, drive it down to the hill, light it on fire, and push it off the hill. He'll be just as dead and we will have gotten something out of the deal. Too bad we can't keep the trailer." He was proud of his plan.

Shep stepped out of the truck and bounded around the front of the truck, grabbing Michael by the collar and pulling him up to his own body. "You idiot! The horses are gone. How are you going to explain the missing horses!! Get back in the truck. I'm calling the cops."

Shep turned and walked back around the truck. He faced away and dialed 911. Michael tiptoed towards the government truck, reached through the window and stole the sunglasses off the dashboard without touching anything else. He was back in the ranch truck before Shep even started talking.

{Chapter 17}

Midnight at the Oasis.

When Guido realized he could rent "The Diary of Sacco and Vanzetti" from Netflix, he had a dilemma. He had not spent a penny of his earnings since he had been working at the Roadhouse; would he succumb to being a video rental consumer? But he wanted to see the old anarchy classic! Finally, Penny—trying to get on his good side—offered to rent it for him. She had no issue with being a consumer. The movie had arrived in today's mail.

He was watching it a second time through, taking notes on restaurant guest check pad, when he noticed a bright light moving around the field next door highlighting the sprinkles of rain. Crap! He threw on his jacket and took the order pad in case he needed to write down a license number. Coming around the west side of the building he saw it was the BLM Law Enforcement guys apparently looking at things with their spotlight. He instantly wondered if a crime was in process. Was he in danger?

The spotlight turned on him. He put one hand up to shield his eyes and with the other he waved the order pad but he kept walking towards the truck. They turned the spotlight off and he could see three men were sitting in the truck. Sanders rolled the driver's window down as Guido stopped beside the truck and raised the order pad and his pen.

"Will this order be to go?" he joked. Then he looked serious. "What's up, guys?"

"We're waiting for the medical investigator," replied Tapia from the far side of the truck.

"Is he walking cross country?" asked Guido, turning to put his right hand over his eyes, as if shielding it from the absent moonlight, and peering into the dark.

"No, he's coming in on a helicopter; we're meeting him here. We were just looking for the best landing spot."

"Is the chopper going to be parked there for a while?" Guido asked, shifting from his typical comical self to his helpful self.

"No, they're picking me up." Tapia replied.

"Across the road there are no power lines but there are trees and behind the building there are no trees but power lines and fences. Will it fit on the parking lot?" Guido queried.

"That's what we were thinking. Might get a bit breezy on the porch for a minute, but I don't see anything that will be bothered."

"Do you need to park the truck? It could go over by the fuel pumps or back by my apartment."

Sanders spoke up, "No, Bennett and I are going on in the truck."

"Can you tell me where you public servants are headed to, this late, with the medical investigator? Halloween party?"

"Someone got killed in the backcountry. We got a call about an hour ago and we're the first responders."

"Is it something to do with the horse roundup?"

"Don't know yet."

"Can I make you something to eat to take with you? Thermos of coffee? Hamburger? On the house. I have a big thermos you can take."

"If he comes while the coffee is brewing, we'll have to just go, but if you don't mind trying, I have an idea that coffee is going to be needed."

"Anything else? Restroom? ... last one for 100 miles!"

Bennett nodded his head, and Tapia got out to let him slide out and follow Guido into the cafe. Bennett was gone a little while, but when he came back out he was carrying the thermos and a box of individually wrapped sweet rolls. The helicopter was on approach. Tapia waved his flashlight, beckoning the helicopter down. With his down jacket stuffed under his arm, he climbed aboard and the helicopter departed quickly to the east. Sanders and Bennett pulled onto the highway and followed.

Guido stood on the porch and watched them go. There wasn't anything left to clean up, so he just locked the door from the inside, picked up the order pad and walked back through the cafe and across the driveway to his apartment. Watching the rest of Sacco and Vanzetti had lost its appeal. He looked through his notes on the pad absently, then lay down on his bed.

Anarchy was a good thing, he assured himself. It was important to have strong values, but, damn it, he was glad four guys were heading off into the night as public servants. He was glad someone was gonna find out why someone else was dead. Providing cops with coffee and donuts in the middle of the night made him feel pretty good, even if cops were politically unacceptable.

{Chapter 18}

Medical Investigator at Work

Anne Parsons, MD, scooted into the backseat and fastened her seat belt as Tapia climbed aboard. He would be the guide to get them to the scene. This was his territory, but she hoped that giving him her seat wasn't a sign to him that he could dominate her. It might have sent the wrong signal, she thought, so she took the initiative of introducing herself.

"I assume you are Randall Tapia of the BLM. I'm Anne Parsons, Chief Medical Investigator for the State of New Mexico, and the pilot is Mitchell Loomis with the New Mexico State Police. It's going to be a little noisy, so we'll have a formal introduction once we arrive at the scene."

Tapia barely got his seatbelt fastened before they were flying east over Highway 64. "I've got the GPS coordinates and there should be some cowboys waiting for us there. I told them to back away from the site and stay in the truck until we get there. Does this chopper have a GPS navigation system?"

Mitch pointed to a colorful display screen. "It's a Garmin dual-screen system. Put your coordinates in here," he pointed to a keypad. "It consolidates all primary situational information regarding our position, speed, vertical rate, altitude, and flight progress. This screen shows GPS waypoints in addition to the desired and actual track."

"Can it tell if we are going to crash into a mountain?" Tapia asked.

Mitch chuckled, "I sure hope so."

Tapia relaxed and watched the earth and sky around him. The clouds were still high, but rather solid. The moon was behind the clouds. He could barely make out some of the landforms below.

Dr. Parsons did not look out the window and she did not relax. Apparent murder of a federal employee was an extremely serious matter. She could expect the U.S.

Marshall to show up on this one. The Federal Bureau of Investigation would certainly be there as well. Normally a lower ranked medical investigator would be dispatched from the local office, but given the rank of everyone else that would respond, it was best that she do it herself.

She felt herself start to grind her teeth together but managed to stop before she got going. Teeth clenching she allowed, but grinding teeth was unprofessional. She consciously checked the hair band around her braid and then folded her hands on her lap. She tried to take a mental inventory of the forms in her briefcase. There was a lot of information to collect between now and the inquest. That was the easy part. Dealing with the dead people wasn't the hard part either; it was dealing with the live ones, who were almost always men.

On her last trip the local responders had been total jerks. She knew in her rational mind that the men's anxiety about being in the presence of grisly death was the set-up for their juvenile behavior, but sexist remarks to the Chief Medical Investigator! That was over the top for inappropriate. If only she could just totally ignore the idiots, but no, she always had to get emotional. Sometimes mad and sometimes hurt, but either way, it led into a cycle of self-recriminations. She started feeling inept when it happened; it made her feel like a big sissy girl.

This big sissy girl, she thought, is a medical doctor and has scraped up more dead bodies than any law enforcement officer ever would in an entire lifetime. The idiots would never realize how meticulous her work was. That is what got her through the ranks to the status of Chief: attention to detail. *That is my life*, she thought. *I pay attention to details*.

The helicopter swung around to the left and started to descend. Mitch switched on some lights to see the ground conditions. Tapia could see his truck and the trailer in a meadow, and then he saw the Cabot's ranch truck on the other side of the cattle-guard. Two young men were laying in the back, but started climbing out of the bed as the helicopter got closer.

"We'll land in this meadow behind the rancher's truck. We don't want to contaminate our scene with rotorwash," Mitch said.

"Are these men witnesses?" Dr. Parson's asked.

"No, they just found the scene. The victim was delivering some horses to them and they got worried when he didn't show. They called 911 when they found him," Tapia explained.

"Okay, we don't really want to hold them up, but there are some preliminary things we have to do, and we will need to ask them some questions. We'll include them in the introductory briefing, and then you detain them while I check the victim. Then, Mitch, can you do the interview with them to get all their personal data? I'll follow up with any questions that come up in the preliminary check."

With that, they climbed out of the helicopter under its slowing blades. The area was lit by a bright tail light assembly that Mitch had positioned toward the road. Tapia started wondering what it was that he should be doing and regretted not asking, but things started happening quickly.

Dr. Parsons introduced herself, and then introduced Mitchell Loomis. Randall Tapia introduced himself as the BLM representative, and then started to introduce Shep Cabot and his two boys, Michael and Don, but Shep interrupted to ask if they could go home now.

"Sorry, Shep, but there are some things we need to ask you," Tapia offered.

"I know it's late," Dr. Parsons said, "and you are probably cold and hungry, but state law says we have to do a few things. It won't be long; then we can let you go. I will be the lead investigator until we remove the body. Mr. Loomis will be assisting me to collect evidence. Mr. Tapia will be responsible for protecting the scene. Now, Mr. Cabot, are you aware of any hazards on this site that may be a problem for the investigators? Have you seen any sign of any animals or other humans in the area? It looked like the ground is flat around the scene, are you aware of any hazards like cliffs or holes? "

Shep shook his head no and said, "It's normally real safe around here. Just don't get stuck in the cattleguard."

She shined her flashlight toward it and asked, "Randall, what can we do to make it safe to cross?"

"We'll just open the barbed wire gate next to it and then we don't have to walk across it. I'll pull the barbed wire back against the fence so it's out of the way."

Dr. Parsons turned back to Shep, "Mr. Cabot, you entered the site with your truck. Can you tell me what you did?"

"We drove in. There is a dead deer halfway between the cattleguard and the BLM rig. We drove past it and almost up to the rig. Don and Michael got out and started walking toward the rig, but then they saw the body and stopped. The body is on the driver's side back by the rear tire. I came around the truck once too, then I stood beside our truck to call 911. We didn't walk around and we didn't touch nothin'. After I called the cops, I backed out and parked here. We haven't been back across the cattleguard."

Dr. Parson looked visibly happier, "Good work, fellows. So we can expect their truck tracks in and out, then just a very small area of their footprints at the end of the tracks. I think we should make the cattleguard and fence the boundary of the crime scene and limit ourselves to making tracks down the right side of the road if there are no footprints on it. We can use this side of the cattleguard as the staging area. We don't have a lot of light, but, Randall, are your men bringing a portable light tower? We'll pull that on top of the existing tracks.

"Okay, Mr. Cabot, I have to go check the body, but I need you to wait here a little longer. Mr. Loomis will be collecting your names and contact information. Randall, could you fix that gate while I get my gear?"

Tapia set his flashlight on the top of a fence post so the light would shine on the gate. It was made simply of a post with four strands of barbed wire and held closed by a loop of smooth wire that slipped over the top of the post. The gate was tight and he struggled to pull the smooth wire loop off the top of the post. Once it was opened, he lifted the gate post and pulled it back along the fence. He didn't notice the horse tracks where the horse and rider had jumped the gate.

"Randall, come with me. You can make a positive identification of the victim. Here, carry this flashlight for me, please. Remember to stay on the right side."

She entered the area through the left side of the gate opening and stepped into the track and tire print they would use as their path. Their narrow beams of light cut a small slice out of the inky blackness surrounding them.

It occurred to Tapia that there was no way his wife would lead the way into a murder scene. Even he had the heebie-jeebies. Dr. Parsons was clearly no ordinary woman.

The deer carcass lay to the left of the road. The lights on it highlighted the white hairs of its coat, making it look more gray than brown. The blood that it lay in looked black under the lights. "We'll need to know if our victims were killed by the same weapon." Then she mused, "Two victims, one homicide. Sounds like a coroner's riddle."

They continued toward the truck. Anne noticed the ground where the Cabot boys had got out of their truck. She pointed to the tracks, but Tapia was too distracted by the eerie specter of his truck to give it much attention.

She stopped at the headlight. "Okay, there will be tracks along the truck that we don't want to disturb." She tied the end of a roll of flagging to the grill of the truck, taking care not to touch anything, and then lifted the camera from where it hung around her neck. "I'll get a photo of these tracks before we contaminate them with our trail. Stay here until I get this marked."

Resting the camera again, she pulled a fiberglass stake from her backpack. She crossed the boy's trail and then searched for more tracks. She pushed the stake into the ground about three feet away from the corner of the truck and fastened the yellow tape to it. "We'll make a protected corridor along the truck with the tape."

Then she shined her flashlight back along the side of the truck, until the light was on the body. Not much chance of this one still being alive; no need to rush. She studied the ground in front of her to continue designating the trail. At the body, she determined there were no tracks between it and the tailgate, so when she finally reached the body it was from the far side. She slid her hands into baby blue surgical gloves and touched the victim. The body was cold in the armpits and the blood was dry. Rigor mortis had set in down to the arms. Parsons reached into Shauner's light jacket with a thermometer and left it for a moment. When she pulled it out she announced "94 even, he's been dead about 10 hours." Pulling a tiny tape recorder from her pocket, she noted: "The victim was found dead at 2:24 AM October 30, 2011.

Based on a body temperature of 94 and upper body rigor mortis, the time of death was more than 10 hours earlier."

"Okay, Randall, go around the stakes and come down here to identify the victim. Just stay on my path ... you're okay."

Tapia didn't want to have to look, but he reminded himself he was a grownup as he approached the body. He quickly shined his light on the body. It was Shauner all right. "Hey, Boss!" echoed in his head. Tapia shuddered and confirmed the identity to Dr. Parsons. With the death pronounced and the victim identified, the first stage was done.

Tapia sucked in a deep breath and willed himself not to bawl, but on the way back to the staging area, tears blurred his vision and ran down his cheeks. He dried his eyes on his sleeve before the Cabots could see him.

As they approached Loomis and the Cabots, Dr. Parsons asked Tapia, "So, you said he was hauling some horses. What happened to the horses?"

Shep spoke up, "They was gone when we got here. The trailer door was wide open and flappin' in the wind."

"Who is the owner of these horses and how many of them were there?" Loomis asked.

"There were seven. They belong to the US government. They are wild horses. We were sending them to the Cabots to be euthanized."

"Euthanized?" Dr. Parsons asked.

"Yes. Horses with poor prognosis to become domesticated can be euthanized. A vet certifies it. The paperwork will be in the truck that Shauner was driving."

Dr. Parsons turned to Shep, "Mr. Cabot, I don't think we have any more questions for you at this time. You are free to go. We will contact you if we need more information. Thank you for the care you took to protect the evidence."

As they left, she pulled a clipboard from her pack and the tiny tape recorder from her pocket. Loomis adjusted his clipboard to have the yellow pad on top. As she went down the checklist on her clipboard, she spoke rapidly into recorder. Loomis wrote out the details in shorthand on his pad. There would be many forms to fill out, Tapia suspected, but these people would have something ready for every box.

{Chapter 19}

Investigation 2

Tapia suddenly noticed that the sprinkles were looking more snow-like. A man, whose life work revolved around leasing government grass to ranchers, had an automatic pro-precipitation attitude. It always made him smile. Parsons and Loomis, he noticed, were looking annoyed as they finished their note taking. Snow on the crime scene was not going to help. He comforted himself with the thought, "Well, it's too warm to stick anyway."

"We need to do the walk-through, Tapia, but is your crew is bringing a construction light pole? Which direction will they be coming from?"

"Wow, I forgot about them. They will be coming up from the roundup side—the same way Shauner came. We probably need them to check that road for tracks before they drive it. It's about two miles long and not used often. There is a gate on the other side, but the Cabots unlocked and opened it for Shauner and the horse trailer."

"Can you contact your men?" asked Loomis. "Do they have any experience tracking?"

"BLM law enforcement actually does a lot of tracking. Animals and trucks, not so much human. I'll get them on the radio."

"You and I can search the roadway starting at the trailer and establish a staging area for their truck on that side. Tell them to stop every 10th of a mile and look for changes. Document everything with photographs. If they find anything they should call before they drive over it."

While Tapia returned to the helicopter to get his radio and contact his men, Loomis drew a site plan map. Parsons lit up the meadow with her camera's flash attachment as she created a panorama of the view that would have been visible to Shauner in his last moments.

Tapia returned with news. "My officers are at the gate at the other end of our road. Some of the horses that escaped from the trailer here are in a field in the canyon. They said they counted six of them. They said that it looks like the only vehicles on this road since the last real rain were Shauner and the trailer he was pulling. The horses were moving at a trot when they came through the open gate. We better get that staging area designated because they will be here in about 30 minutes."

"I want some better light to start really searching around. I think I will help you with the road until they get here. Let's designate a corridor to travel on the right side of the truck since we know the blast came from the meadow on the left." She pulled out more fiberglass rods and started methodically searching and designating a pathway. "Don't touch the truck, Tapia, until Loomis gets the fingerprints off it."

"Good of you to remind me, Dr. Parsons, because that is normally the truck I drive. Seems a little strange to not just get in and go. Kind of like it's a sacred object now."

Once they had passed the rear door of the horse-trailer, they could see an aggregation of horse tracks where the animals had hit the dirt running. With a photo and a promise to take a closer look on their way back, they moved on, confining their footprints to the west side of the road. The search yielded nothing but the tracks of galloping unshod horses. The lights of the approaching BLM truck started casting a glow in the trees far down the road. The three stopped and waited.

"Either the trailer door came open by itself, or someone let these horses out," Parsons offered. "What is the chance the horses got out unassisted?"

Tapia remembered helping secure the latches before the truck pulled away from the loading chute. "Something might have broken, but otherwise, the door has to be opened by hand. I helped close the horses in, and I remember securing the latches."

"Then we should have tracks and finger prints on the trailer. Loomis, let's check that as soon as we get your light tower in place."

The BLM truck coasted to a stop as Loomis motioned them forward to where the group stood. Bennett leaned out and asked if it was okay to get out of the truck; Loomis and Parsons both motioned them to join the group. Bennett was stiff as he descended from the truck, putting his hands on his rear pockets until he could stand upright. Sanders jumped out with a clipboard and a flashlight. Tapia briefly introduced everyone.

"Is that a construction light trailer behind your truck?" Parsons asked.

"Yes, a portable light tower," responded Sanders.

"Let's get it to the edge of the meadow. Sanders, you follow us in the truck. We'll double check the roadway again. Then we'll pull it by hand around your truck. The five of us will have no trouble moving it."

The trailer was soon in place, Bennett flipped the light on and Parsons, Loomis, and Tapia instantly turned to get a good look at the trailer. Each person stared hard, expecting their best evidence was about to be found. Bennett and Sanders looked confused, but watched without comment.

"I don't see any problem with the door hinges or latch from here," Tapia said.

"Look how the horses tore up so much dirt as they hit the ground," said Loomis, "I'll go get the finger print kit for the door handle."

Dr. Parsons started taking photographs from various angles. Sanders asked, "Do we know who let the horses out? Hey ... that looks like a footprint right there on the right side below the latch. "

Everyone turned to look, but no one replied before Sanders continued, "It's a barefoot print heading away from the trailer."

"I see it," said Dr. Parsons, "Good call, I was looking for something like a vibram sole print. Do you see more?"

The men shined flashlights at low angles and turned up two tracks in horse poop inside the trailer by the corner with the latch, and a fading set of tracks where the bare feet had run away from the trailer. Dr. Parsons laid a ruler next to the tracks and set her camera to work.

"This case is getting weird. Let's do a walk-through with what we've got right now," said Dr. Parsons

"We have a dead deer and we would like to know if it was killed at the same time as the victim. Our victim was killed with a shotgun at a distance of less than 50 feet but more than 25 feet. We have a time estimate of late afternoon, but he wasn't found until 10:30 pm. It appears that he was not standing up when he was shot, given the location of the blood splatter on the truck fender. The direction of the shooter had to be in the north-west quadrant of the meadow. Now it appears that the person who let the horses out was barefooted.

"We have located corridors along the roadway and on both sides of the truck. We need to search the meadows and look for fingerprints on the truck. I will examine the deer next. Loomis, can you call up and order some Search & Rescue dogs to follow the human tracks?"

"Hey, the Roadhouse sent up some coffee and sweet rolls. I almost forgot. Do we have any cups?" Bennett interrupted.

Tapia remembered the food service items in his truck. "I think I have paper cups in the jump seat of my truck, if we can get it searched and cleared. If that truck was not off-limits at the moment, I'd be curled up in the jump seat snoring loud enough to wake the dead."

Loomis offered, "Why don't you just go rest in the back seat of the chopper? It would be very useful to have Mr. Shauner awake to answer some questions." He winked. "Sanders, I'd like to have you search for blood or tracks on the west side of the road starting at the deer. Bennett, go ahead and fetch that thermos. The door handles of that truck are my first priority."

"Won't the fingerprints be ruined in the rain?" asked Sanders.

"Actually it doesn't hurt them at all. They are oil based and so won't mix with rain. I have a spray can of Wet Print. It actually works better than the dry methods. I get photos of the stained print, then I lift the print with tape and store it on a print card. Tapia, before you go lie down, let me photograph your fingertips. This is your truck, right?"

Parsons crouched on the balls of her feet, camera flash illuminating the whole meadow as she photographed the deer. She tried lifting the deer's head to see the wound but didn't find it. "I want to see the bullet that killed this animal. Sanders, will you help me flip it over?" The deer was not very stiff. She shined her flashlight into the deer's nostrils. "Flies are just starting to hatch. This deer has been dead at least 24 hours if not longer. It was dead long before Shauner was killed." She stuck the thermometer into its rectum and set about cutting the bullet out of the body. When she finished, she dropped the slug into an envelope. "The deer is at ambient temperature, same as the soil under it."

"I have a pretty good trail of blood and deer tracks across this meadow. It goes on into the forest, should I follow it?" Sanders asked.

"I think the deer was there at least twelve hours before Shauner was shot. I doubt that it's trail will tell us much. Can you and Bennett get the lights moved to illuminate the body? Hey what happened with the coffee?" Loomis responded by opening the truck door and pulling out a plastic bag with paper cups. Tapia poured a cup for each of them and then asked if they would mind if he went and slept in the helicopter.

Parsons sensed Bennett was also exhausted, so she sent him to sleep in the law enforcement truck before asking the others to help her move the light tower. Once it was in place, she examined the body more carefully. Livor mortis had turned his face and hands a splotchy blue. She found no fly eggs in the wound or in his ears. It would have been too cold for bot flies by late afternoon. Her camera seemed to flash constantly.

Sanders stood watching her with a vacant expression on his face. She suddenly realized he might not have any experience with a death scene. "Have you helped on other homicides?" she asked. He shook his head in reply.

"I just finished up my associates degree in Criminal Justice. I'm trying to get into the Department of Homeland Security program. Homicide, suicide—I don't really want to make that a career. Why in the hell would a woman as good looking as you get involved with this crap? Are you a Femi-Nazi or something?"

She blew out a breath and looked straight ahead for a moment, then she replied, "People ask me *why*. Why not be a housewife? Why trade a position many women are perfectly happy with, for a continuous stream of work and corpses?' I've got this natural curiosity." She shrugged, her hands twisting her camera from side to side. "I do want to help people—seriously. At the point where I enter their lives, they have no control and very little predictability. I want to get to the bottom of things for them; I want them to feel like the judicial process is serving them.

"I get the sense that you are the same. You want justice. Am I right, Sanders?"

He pushed his lips together in an unhappy grimace, an unconscious expression of his conflicted emotions. It was fun to play investigator but it was horrifying to deal with death.

"I think Loomis could use a hand with that east meadow. That's where the action will be."

Looking back, she noticed that the tops of the trees on the other side of the helicopter were illuminated, just before the noise of an approaching vehicle made her realize it was headlights. She walked back down the designated corridor and around the cattle-guard and stood waiting as a law enforcement vehicle pulled into the staging area. 'Rio Arriba County Sheriff's Department' was announced by the sign on the door. A Hispanic man with a long handle-bar mustache rolled down the window of the truck.

"I'm Attencio Candelaria with the Sheriff's Department. We heard there was a 911 call from the Cabot ranch, so I came to check it out. What's happening?"

"Homicide investigation. I'm Anne Parsons with the OMI and Mitchell Loomis of the New Mexico State Police is the other investigator. And you? I'll need to see your badge to go in the site record."

"Mr. Cabot told me a BLM guy got killed. *Mira*," he said as he handed her the badge. "I thought I would just drive around over here and see if anything looks suspicious. Anything in particular I should be looking for?"

She finished writing down his name and badge number as she thought of how to answer. Then she looked at him and said, "Crazy as it sounds, a barefoot person. Barefeet tracks. Someone maybe five foot eight, with wide feet." She shook her head and shrugged her shoulders. "Hey, we're expecting the NMSAR dog team and the morgue van, if you see them, can you help them find us?"

"*No problemo, Senora*. You have a nice night now. *Hasta la vista*," he said just before he rolled up his window and turned around to leave. She noted the time for the record: 4:08 a.m. 10/29/2011

{Chapter 20}

Investigation 3

She returned to the body to look for shotgun pellets. Size and number could possibly yield the manufacturer, but with internet sales of ammo perfectly legal, there was little hope of using the brand to track down the criminal. The pellets had not lodged in the flesh, but rather traveled all the way through Shauner's skull. She counted nine divots where the pellets had hit the truck fender panel. Shells with nine pellet were the most common type, diminishing the likelihood they would provide useful evidence. She searched in the coagulated blood under and around the body. She picked up each bloody pellet with forceps and put them into a small envelope.

"Loomis, did you find the shotgun shell wadding?" she asked.

"I think it's stuck to that purple daisy plant directly between us. I haven't gotten that far because I am stuck in a mess of horse tracks. Looks like one horse didn't just run with the rest but circled the meadow a few times. Or maybe the perp was on horseback ..."

Sanders spoke up from where he was searching. "There was a crazy stallion with those horses. He didn't act like a normal horse—kinda fearless. Loco. We saw the others down in the canyon, but he wasn't with them. I sure wish we knew his hoof prints because he might do anything. They were going to euthanize him because he was dangerous. He tried to attack someone at the roundup."

"It doesn't look like any horses came near the body," said Parsons. "I'll measure the distance from the body to the wadding before I collect it. Loomis, I am getting a pretty meager collection of evidence to turn over to you—just bugs and bullets."

Suddenly the sound of a helicopter broke the stillness of the night. It circled around, and then landed in the meadow of the staging area. Two men in black tactical gear jumped down and waited as Dr. Parsons walked around the cattle guard to meet them. "Ted and Greg! Thanks for coming. Ted, do you have dogs coming?"

"About an hour behind us. The morgue van is coming up the hill right now. Let's get the scene reviewed so we are up to speed." said the taller of the two men.

Dr. Parsons called to Loomis and Sanders to break off for a meeting if possible. As the investigators picked a careful path back to the designated corridor, Tapia stepped down from the helicopter, yawning. "I wish I hadn't seen you do that, Randall. It's highly contagious," said Dr. Parsons just before she broke out into her own yawn. "At five A.M., no one is immune." Ted and Greg looked at each other, and neither one was yawning, until they looked away from each other, then almost simultaneously their jaws dropped in big yawns. Everyone was laughing as Sanders and Loomis walked up.

Dr. Parsons quickly introduced everyone. The tall one was Ted McDade from the US Marshal's Office; the redheaded one was Greg Stribling from the FBI. When she introduced Sanders to the men, she described him as an up-and-coming rookie eager to acquire some experience, which seemed to please him. She then reviewed what they had found, the site layout, and what still needed to be done. Loomis reported that most of the prints found on the truck seemed to be either Tapia's or Shauner's, but he had gotten a different print off the trailer handle.

Tapia looked pained, but spoke up, "There is a good chance other people touched that handle at the roundup. Anyone of the twenty-five roundup folks might have had their hands on it."

Dr. Parsons put the end of her pencil across her lips, then opened her mouth and bit the pencil in an unconscious gesture of frustration. As soon as she did it, she realized she was putting an unclean object in her mouth at a crime scene. Once the pencil was back on paper, she looked around to see if anyone had noticed. "*I must be getting tired*," she thought.

Lights on the treetops announced the impending arrival of the refrigerated morgue van. There wasn't anything left to do with the body that the pathologist wouldn't do better, so they zipped the body into a bag and carried it around the truck. It was loaded as soon as the driver had the back of the truck ready for it. "*Bye, Aaron Shauner*," thought Tapia, "*You were a good man and I'll never see you again.*" He found a handkerchief in his pocket and stood on the dark side of the helicopter until the van was gone.

There wasn't a lot left to do except look for tracks, but with the dogs coming that seemed counterproductive. Tapia found the thermos and got a cup of coffee. He stood quietly, watching snowflakes fall into his steaming coffee.

The snowflakes had grown bigger and with the drop in temperature of the approaching dawn, the snow started to stick. Tapia wondered if the El Nino pattern would continue bringing extra moisture into the range. "That would make a good winter," he told himself and tried to picture grass growing next spring. If there was anything good about this night, it was precipitation. He glanced at Sanders and Bennett to see how they were reacting to the change in weather and their relaxed postures seem to confirm his appraisal. He was unsure if his own relaxation was anything more than resignation.

Parsons assigned Sanders the job of collecting Shauner's medical and personal, history. She gave him a copy of a form to fill out. "If you have any trouble with this, give me or Loomis a call. As soon as you get it done, say ... Monday afternoon ... fax it to me. I'll write the fax number here on top of the first page. Then get the original over to Loomis. You know where his office is in Farmington, right?

"Greg, will you do an interview with Tapia? He was the victim's supervisor and they were in the process of finishing a big project. Let's get any possible leads and you can coordinate with Loomis to follow them up."

Greg and Tapia looked at each other. "Let's sit in the State Police helicopter." Greg suggested. "I have a thermos of coffee. I'll get my clipboard and be right there."

Tapia appreciated the opportunity to talk about what had happened. Greg asked probing questions. It gave Tapia an opportunity to think through parts of the puzzle he had pushed to the back of his mind. Someone at the roundup did have a shotgun. There was a whole gallery of people there that might not like what Shauner was doing. He'd have Bennett prepare a report on the horse welfare advocates present.

It was getting light as the Search & Rescue dog, Tippy, arrived with his handler in a black Toyota Land Cruiser. Tippy was a red hound with reddish brown eyes. Everyone watched expectantly as the handler showed Tippy the track in the trailer, then the track on the ground. Tippy bayed once and started pulling his handler along the path of the barefoot tracks. He ran about 30 yards out, stopped and ran straight back to where Shauner's body had been, then he turned and ran along the road in the direction the fleeing horses had traveled. Ted stopped the handler so they could look for physical tracks, but the only thing they found was a coyote track. They started Tippy over, but again he was soon on the coyote track. The handler was embarrassed and the snow was now covering the ground. Ted called off the dog search.

Parsons led the final scene debriefing, covering all the physical evidence they had managed to find. A few responsibilities remained. Loomis would be responsible for keeping the evidence. Once she had the pathologist's report and the victim history, she would prepare the final report. "Tapia, you can have your truck back now. It was good to work with your team. Thanks for being here and sticking with it."

Everyone shook each other's hands. Everyone handed Tapia a business card. Then, as the BLM men watched, the four crime professionals were in their helicopters and gone.

Tapia turned to Sanders, "What do you say we wake up Bennett and get out of here?"

"I like that idea a lot," returned Sanders. "I'll fold up the light tower if you want to go get him."

"There's a backpack pump with water in the back of my truck. See if you can wash the blood off the truck before I get back," Tapia suggested. "That wouldn't look so good coming into town."

It looked pretty good, though, by the time Tapia pulled into Navajo City where Milton was sweeping the snow off the walkway. He recognized the old man who cleaned the parking lot every morning. "Ya'll open yet? Is Aletta here?"

"Who?" asked the old man.

"Aletta, the waitress."

"Oh her ... Aletta won't be here until afternoon."

"Can you do me a favor and give Aletta my card and have her call me, please?"

"Yeah, I'll put it on the register for her and tell her," the old man mumbled before Tapia headed on towards home.

{Chapter 21}

The Quietness of Snow

Milton stuck the business card in the left front pocket of his jacket and slipped his leather gloves back on to continue sweeping the snow away. The broom handle was old and a little bit splintery. In his opinion, this wasn't really much of a snowstorm—by December there would be real snowfall and he'd get out the snow shovel. Maybe he would get some sandpaper and fix the broom, or maybe he would just wear gloves. It was all the same to him.

Every day Milton got up early to feed his dog, then walked across the highway and cleaned the Roadhouse parking lot in exchange for breakfast. He had retired from a long career as an electrician then tried to become an artist. The waitresses still had some of his paintings hanging on the wall of the dining room, though, to be honest, no one had ever tried to buy one. Now his hands weren't steady enough for oil painting, and he didn't feel like dragging his painting gear up into the mountains like he used to. He liked being part of the team at the Roadhouse, and he liked betting on race horses, and that was enough.

This morning, with a black garbage bag in one hand, he found some papers and cups stuck in the fence slats as if it had been very windy in the night. A few of the plastic letters from the marquee sign had blown off and were lying by the road.

He assumed that it must have been windy, but he couldn't remember feeling the wind shake his little house trailer. "Must have slept right through it." He thought about the sound of wind, and he wondered if he would ever hear it again. He recalled hearing wind on the prairies of Kansas as a kid, but now he couldn't hear worth a darn. The thought that he could probably still hear a tornado sent a momentary flash of a smile across his somber visage.

Thoughts of his prairie upbringing brought forth more thoughts about trout fishing with his twin brother who was still alive in Kansas. He wondered if his brother was also losing his hearing, but Milton would never imagine trying to call. It would be embarrassing to have to shout at each other. He thought about his brother having a FaceBook page that Aletta showed him one time. Maybe she could send a message for him ... but what would he say?

Once order was restored to the parking lot, Milton went inside, washed his hands, and sat down at the corner of the bar. Penny automatically set a coffee, a teaspoon, and a tiny pitcher of cream in front of the old man. She shouted, "How are you doing today, Milton? What do you want for breakfast?"

"Eggs over easy, one link sausage, and toast with *no* butter," he replied.

"No butter, the same as every day," Penny said in a normal voice.

"Did I tell you no butter?" He asked with concern. "I can't eat butter; it disagrees with me."

She patted his hand and took the order back to the kitchen.

Milton thought about his son in Colorado. He was proud of the boy for having made a name for himself as a chef. Now the boy would be getting married. She was a nice woman and would make a good mother to his grandchildren, but Milton doubted that they would ever come visit him. They were city people. Having a grandson and not being able to hear his voice was a very depressing thought.

His ex-wife lived in Aztec. She had always been decent to him, even after the divorce. He could visit her sometimes, but he knew it was hard for her to try to have a conversation with him, so he stayed away except for holidays when there would be big groups of people.

His dog didn't really care if he could hear or not.

As he finished eating and pushed his plate away, he drained the last drops of coffee from the cup, and turned to Penny with a rare smile. She was rolling silverware in napkins and smiled back. He pulled the card Tapia had given him out of his pocket and waved it in the air. "This is for Aletta. He wants her to call him."

Penny leaned over to take it from him, and then studied it. "I'll call her right now" she said, pulling the cell phone toward her.

"Aletta, good morning ... Randall Tapia ... yeah, that BLM guy ... anyway he dropped by a business card and asked that you call him ... sure ... you got a pencil?" Penny read the number carefully then continued, "No, we didn't get very much, it's pretty much melted ... see you later."

Penny placed a fork and a table knife on the napkin, and then folded the napkin around it, creating a roll of silverware. She needed at least 60 for lunch.

Milton looked back and forth between his plate and Penny's hands several times, then blurted out, "Yesterday I went to dinner at the Senior Citizen's Center."

"Oh," she responded, "was that good? What did you have?"

"What'd you say?" he asked.

She raised her voice to repeat it.

He looked happy to tell her that they had lasagna and salad. "Then I went down to the racetrack, but I didn't have any money, so I didn't stay long. Just watched a couple of telecasted races."

She rolled her eyes and spoke loudly, "Milton, you know I don't want to hear about your horse racing conspiracy theories. You get too excited and I can't understand what you are talking about. Tell me about something else."

"Well, I saw something *real funny* on the way home. Yep, it was real funny. It was after dark. There was a convertible headed to town and a big ol' English sheepdog was driving. You couldn't tell it was a costume, but the dog had to have been headed to a Halloween party."

Penny seemed to be lost in her napkin folding and didn't respond to the old man.

He was excruciatingly aware that it was hard for people to respond to him. He stared at his hands thinking how disgusted people got when he tried to talk to them. Deaf, defective, deficient, and stupid. He didn't know what to do.

Frustrated, he took a pen out of his shirt pocket and started doodling on a clean napkin. He drew the dog driving the car. Wind whipping its gray fur, its white forehead shining in the moonlight as the car raced on.

"How cute!", Penny picked it up and laughed. "Can I show it to Mary?" Then they were laughing in the kitchen, *he could hear it*. Returning, Penny asked if she could keep it. He nodded emphatically as she pinned the sketch to the wall.

Milton then clicked his pen and returned it to his pocket. He trudged into the kitchen to pull a sack of garbage from the trash can and took it out to the dumpster. Mary gave him a paper bag filled with scraps for his dog. His life was in order. His social security check would be coming on Monday. Milton wondered if there might be any horses worth betting on this month.

{Chapter 22}

Chile Verde Accent

A phone conversation with Randall Tapia! The prospect of it was extremely exciting! Aletta had been studying the northern New Mexico accent for months now. She never had time to listen that carefully when she was at work. A phone call meant she could record it. She wouldn't even have to tell him.

She had been to the library looking in the language section, but had found nothing useful. She had spent hours in the western fiction section and had only found Texas drawls and Mexico Spanish. Her internet research had turned up very little. She stumbled onto some videos narrated by a horse trainer named Joe Fernandez that sounded right, but she wasn't sure where he was from. She searched for videos from Espanola, but only found things narrated by Anglos, mostly news reports of people getting shot.

One book had actual percentages of how many people pronounce certain words certain ways by state. She learned that in New Mexico 'Aunt' is pronounced like the insect 'ant', but she knew that in northern New Mexico, the right word is '*Tia*'. It's not really about the pronunciation, she suspected, it's more about the rhythm under the words, a sprinkling of Spanish, and the sound of the vowels.

Randall certainly has to be from Northern New Mexico. She could ask him. If she just asked him a few questions, she could get him to pronounce some of the words that she most wondered about.

There were many Roadhouse customers spoke with what she had come to call the Chile Verde accent: Freddy, Arturo, John Salazar, Fidel, Emilio. For example, they would say "chile" as "CHEE-leh", not as "chilly" the way most Americans would. They would also pronounce "enchilada" as "en-chee-LAH-thah" rather than as "en-chuh-LAH-duh".

Unfortunately for her research, really focusing on their speech meant ignoring what they were trying to say, so it could only be done as an eavesdropper. If there was more than one customer, she didn't have the time to really listen. If she did too much they might misunderstand and think she was flirting.

If she could manage to describe the Chile Verde accent, despite all of these obstacles, she could start a literary revolution among the writers of Northern New Mexico. That is what she wanted at least.

It made her feel a little uncomfortable to actually set up the recording equipment. 'Sneaky' wasn't a word she wanted to apply to herself, though 'resourceful' was something she could be proud of. She wished that she had a chance to test the equipment first, but she dialed his number and held her breath until he answered.

"Hello."

He sounded sleepy. Was he taking a nap?

"Hi, this is Aletta, from the Roadhouse. You wanted me to call you?"

"Oh, yeah, Aletta, thanks for calling me. I need to ask you a favor."

"I need to ask you a favor too, Randall."

"What is it?" he said sounding surprised.

"I need you to tell me a few things, like where you were born and what your favorite foods are."

"Well, I was born in Espanola, and I like steak and potatoes."

"Last question, how do you pronounce your full name?"

"Randall James Tapia. Top-ee-uh," he said sounding out his last name. "Why do you want to know this stuff?" he asked.

She realized the anxiety in his voice was strongly affecting his speech pattern, probably destroying the whole effect.

"It's your turn, Randall, what favor did you want to ask me?"

"This is a personal favor, Aletta. I'm asking you this not as my job, but personal to me, okay?

"I need you to not write in your blog about the murder investigation until things sort themselves out. Everyone in western Rio Arriba County reads your blog since there is no newspaper out there and the Roadhouse is the hub of all the action. Hell,

I even read it. But right now is a time to hold back and not get into speculating. If you would treat this as if you were a professional news reporter and just stick to verified facts, I think it would help the investigation."

He is sounding so official. She thought it was destroying the accent totally. Maybe the sing-song accent was only strong when the speaker was not anxious? What is bothering him?

"Did you say 'murder'?"

"Yes, Aaron Shauner was killed last night. I was up all night at the investigation."

"Oh my God! Aaron was murdered?"

"Yes. We don't know by who, but just do me a personal favor and don't blog about it for a few days. Personal favor ..."

"I can do that for you, Randall. Gosh, I am so sorry to hear this. I saw him yesterday about midday."

"Aletta, I can't really give out any information, but let's pretend this conversation never happened, and I'll make sure you have the facts and get copies of any press releases ... Thanks, Aletta," and he hung up.

She sat there stunned for a moment, then erased the tape without even listening to it.

{Chapter 23}

Gossip Explosion

Penny was carrying two plates of *huevos rancheros* when the phone rang. She sat one of them down in front of Tim Tucker and the other in front of John Aragon. They were having a late morning breakfast on their weekend rounds tending gas wells. The call would go to voicemail so she remained focused on the tipping potentials of her current customers.

So far, for a Saturday, tips had been good. The highway was busy. The rifle season for deer would be opening tomorrow, so she anticipated a steady flow of customers. Lots of fuel sales, lots of sit-down dinners. The prospects for tips were good.

Those few extra dollars were going to be especially appreciated because tomorrow was the start of her annual vacation. This year she was going back to Las Vegas, Nevada to do a little gambling. Rita Mae Castleberry would be filling in for her next week. If Penny managed to hit the jackpot, Rita Mae could keep the job.

Traipsing back to the counter, she picked up the phone and played back the voicemail. It was Aletta asking her to call. She sounded worried and Penny instantly felt her stomach tighten with fear—what if Aletta called in sick? Penny's plans had no room for working an extra shift, especially the afternoon shift, so it was with some trepidation that she returned the call.

"Penny, what is going on? Did Aaron Shauner really get murdered?"

"I haven't heard anything like that. Where did you hear that?"

"I think he got murdered after the wild horse roundup. I just wanted to know if you had any more on it. I'll be in a little early. See you then."

Penny wasn't sure what to do with such news, so she started washing some cups. With the water splashing in the sink, she shouted back to Mary in the kitchen, "I heard Aaron Shauner, that cute BLM guy, got killed last night."

Mary shouted over the sound of frying bacon, "Car accident or what?"

"No, murder," Penny shouted. With the cups soaking in a sink full of hot soapy water, she returned to the counter and picked up the phone, not noticing that the overheard conversation was disturbing to her diners.

Her best friend Sandy would know if anyone would. Sandy partied with everyone.

"Sandy, did you hear that Aaron Shauner got murdered?" she asked, noticing that customers were looking at her. She picked up the coffee pot and walked over to refill their cups as she talked. "You sound like you have a hangover, girl. Okay, let me know if you hear anything. I hope you feel better. "

Sandy called Pamela Anderson, who worked for the Forest Service, and had a cousin that worked for the BLM. Pamela didn't know anything so Pam called her cousin, Jessica, but Jessica didn't know anything. Jessica called Shauner's phone number, but he didn't answer. She didn't want to call her boss, Randall Tapia, because he and his wife had probably stayed out late last night dancing.

Meanwhile at the Roadhouse, Penny's customers hastened to finish their meals and pay their checks. There was a line at the cash register. Between the moment that the change hit the tip jar and the cowbell on the door clanked, they had dialed and had their cell phones to their ears. The news radiated through the community at an exponentially increasing rate. Within minutes the cell tower servicing that part of the oilfield was going into overload.

Oilfield drivers started flagging over their peers and coworkers. Trucks everywhere in the oilfield were stopped in the middle of the roads, driver's window to driver's window. No one knew any details.

Tim Tucker, Shauner's best friend, sat at the table with a half-eaten plate of *huevos rancheros*, drumming his fingers on the table and staring into space. When he finally moved, he picked up his cellphone and called Shauner's mother. She confirmed it saying his boss and a State Policeman came at about 7 A.M. to tell her.

With tears running down his cheeks, Tim pulled out a ten dollar bill and put it on the counter in front of Penny. "It's true. His mother says he's dead." Without another word, he walked out the door, got in his truck and drove away.

As the morning wore on, the gossip began to take a life of its own. Oilmen came in saying they heard it. Some heard a hunter got him. Some heard a horse activist got him (damn that PETA!). Some heard the Apaches got him. Some heard that he had gotten mixed up with a bad drug deal. Some suspected that it was the aliens. No one really knew anything.

Guido came in from his back lot apartment to get a late breakfast. He was humming and carefree. "Penny, I just want to thank you for renting the movie for me. Here it is ready to be sent back. 'Long live anarchy!' that's what Sacco said before they fried him. Another black moment in American history!"

Penny never knew how to respond to Guido so she just said, "Aaron Shauner, one of the BLM guys was murdered last night."

He responded with, "I know. The cops came by about midnight with a helicopter, but they didn't want any hamburgers to go." She tried to get him to tell her more, but he refused to be serious about it. "Long live anarchy!" he said as he walked out the door. Now Penny was mad.

As she looked for consolation, she noticed her tip jar was not as full as she expected. This murder was impacting the generosity of her customers in a negative way. A group of camouflage-clad hunters walked in. If there was any hope of salvaging the economic potential of the day, Penny knew that she had to take control of the atmosphere and get out of the gossip funk. She started by changing the radio to classic country and putting on her best smile. She carried the menus out to the waiting customers.

While Penny was getting coffee for the group, Aletta walked in and answered the ringing phone. When she realized it was not a call-in order, she took the phone and retreated to the kitchen for some privacy. It was Sephra. The cops had taken her shotgun for testing. Aletta consoled her, "They would have arrested you if they thought that you did it. They are just being thorough and doing their job. Don't worry. Let's take the dogs to the lake tomorrow afternoon ... okay ... see you then."

When she stepped back out of the kitchen, Penny was standing by the register. "I think I'll start on my way to Vegas right after work. There is a killer on the loose. I don't think I would sleep that good around here.

"Something else, Aletta—I figured out that it's better if we just don't talk about Aaron around here. It really hurt my tips this morning."

High noon and the trucks started filling up the parking lot. Every table was taken and customers were even eating outside on the deck. It felt strange for Aletta to tell people she didn't want to talk about it, but the truth was she really didn't have time anyway. By the time the lunch rush slacked off, Penny had her Vegas nest-egg and then some.

Business never really slowed down that Saturday. By closing time, Guido was quite irritated that he had not been able to prep for Sunday morning. That meant that he'd have to stay late and make sure the bacon and potatoes were cooked. If it was going to be Mary cooking, he might slack off and not do it, but not on Sunday. Sunday was a short day where the owner did all the cooking.

Aletta drove home with all of her tips in her pocket, and plans to spend them dancing in her head. Maybe she'd take that James Patterson Novel Writing class she had seen on the internet.

{Chapter 24}

Sunday Morning Comin' Down

When John Irick arrived, Milton actually had the snow shovel out. Milton grinned and waved as John drove past to the employee parking spaces at the back of the building. He raised the fingers of his left hand off the steering wheel in a return salute, but with this much snow, John's instinct for safety kept both hands on the wheel. Highway 537 had gotten his adrenaline flowing. He might live only 8 miles away, but it was the curliest and steepest eight miles of pavement imaginable. He sighed with relief as he turned the key off and got out of the truck. John's keys were left dangling from the ignition.

John pulled a box of groceries from the bed of the truck and walked across the gravel of the alley behind the building noticing that the snow blocked the smell of old mop water. The back door was unlocked as expected. He considered locking and keys to be a nuisance. His house, back at Navajo Dam, was unlocked as well, the keys having been lost long ago.

He turned on the lights and lit the big gas range to start the cooking flat-deck heating up. Guido had left it polished. Then he carried the box into the walk-in cooler to put away the food. Cilantro, jalapeno chiles, cheese, and tortillas. He was planning a Mexican food special. Sundays brought in less oilfield traffic and more local ranchers. He also had picked up a newspaper on the way. He set it on the plastic chair he kept by the door.

He snapped on the satellite radio and adjusted the volume so he could listen to his favorite station, Outlaw Country, a blend of alternative country music and Americana. He was in the mood to hear Waylon Jennings. Then he started the coffee brewing. He didn't expect the waitress to come in until closer to eight o'clock, this gave him time to get prepped. He appreciated the fact that Guido had left the precooked bacon and the boiled potatoes ready and waiting.

The back door opened and Milton stepped inside, snowflakes on his shoulders.

The two gray-bearded men looked at each other, John towering over diminutive Milton as Milton struggled to get his words out.

"There's some people out front that want to know if we're open," Milton finally blurted out.

"Okay, thanks for telling me," John said before he turned, walked through the dining room and unlocked both the cow-belled front door and the wrought iron exterior door that was kept propped open during business hours. He looked at the customers—a traveling family with one child. "We're not really open, but you are welcome to come in, have some coffee, and use the restrooms."

While John let the folks in, Milton started a fire in the little cast-iron stove. It smoked for a minute and then the generated heat started pulling the smoke up the chimney. Milton stood backed up to it waiting for some heat.

The man emerged from the restroom first and stood by the fire with Milton until his wife came out, looking refreshed. They asked for two large coffees to go and picked out a bag of peanuts for the child. John poured their coffee into large styrofoam containers and then more coffee into ceramic mugs for himself and Milton.

"Two bucks. Thanks, have a great trip," and the cowbell clanked them goodbye. John motioned to Milton to come get his coffee, knowing that Milton would want to have cream. The old man would have to help himself; John had to get back to work.

It was an ominous start for the day. Yes, customers were good, but really John just wanted to enjoy a day of mindless cooking, listening to the radio, and then do some napping in the plastic chair.

He had bought the Roadhouse on a whim and never really had plans to operate a cafe in the middle of nowhere. His wife, Miriam, had been well-insured when she died from being bitten by a Komodo Dragon while leading a field trip to Indonesia. She was unlucky enough to be allergic to the proteins in the normally innocuous venom of the dragon. The University she worked for as a botany professor had been generous with him and when he noticed the old run-down restaurant was up for sale at a ridiculously low price, he just paid cash for it. He tried to make it the kind of place where she would have wanted to have lunch.

He thought that Miriam would have liked Aletta, but been less approving of the other afternoon waitress, Naomi. However, as a retired accountant, he had examined the records and determined that the number of fuel sales and sit-down customers increased by ten percent when the beautiful and scantily clad Naomi was on shift, though the actual difference in gross sales was insignificant. John saw the economic potential of an attraction like Naomi, however he had not figured out how to exploit it. He liked Aletta because her cash drawer always counted out correctly, because she left notes about supplies that were running short, and because she was witty. She was a keeper.

He was thinking about her when she stepped through the back door, taking off her coat as she walked. "Good morning, Mr. Irick! How are you doing on this snowy Sunday?"

"I'm doing good. How did your Jeep do coming up Manzanares Pass?"

"There wasn't any snow until I got about halfway up the pass. It wasn't too bad at all. The snow is only in the shady parts of the road on the other side of milepost 85.

"Hey, what time did you close last Friday? Rex Roundy called me and said you were closed when he came by for dinner."

"I closed at 8, but Guido had left at 7 to get a ride to his AA meeting.... oh, yeah, I had forgotten to turn on the 'open' sign; it's kind'a wonky for him to complain that it's closed anyway. Rex never eats dinner here. That guy is a pain in the rear."

"Yeah, he is the type to want to cause trouble. You have my permission to eighty-six anyone that is causing trouble."

"Eighty-six?"

"Oh, that's bar lingo for someone getting kicked out and banned from coming back."

"I can eighty-six Rex?"

"If you need to. Here take this hopper of pork-chop burritos and put it out in the warmer."

Feeling pleased, John put away the tubs of cheese and the burrito wrappers, then brushed off the crumbs of grated potato, green chile, and meat crumbs. He refilled his cup and sat down in the plastic chair.

The headlines read: HOMICIDE AT THE WILD HORSE ROUNDUP

He had heard about it on Saturday afternoon, so he read the article with interest.

FARMINGTON, N.M. (AP) – U.S. Marshals Service say a BLM employee working on a wild horse roundup earlier this week has been found dead along a dirt road near the round-up site.

The Marshals Service spokeswoman Georgette Jacquez says a citizen called police after spotting the body of Aaron Shauner of Farmington on Friday evening.

Shauner's body is being examined in Albuquerque at the Office of the Medical Investigator. The case is considered a homicide.

Saturday, New Mexico State Police Chief Mitchell Loomis said police—at this point—are not chasing any one person, but continue to cross off potential suspects from their list.

"A lot of what we are doing now is eliminating people from suspicion as much as we are trying to track down those who might be of interest in this investigation. There are a lot of leads to follow," Loomis said. "We've had a variety of major cases that have taken two to three weeks, sometimes a couple of months, sometimes years. And I'm not projecting any particular timeline will be the case with this investigation; it just depends on a variety of factors."

Loomis went on to say that no clues point to this homicide being a random act, meaning the public should not worry about their safety. Emphasizing that further tips are vital to the case, Loomis asked the public to share any information they may have.

John had always been proud to say that Navajo City Roadhouse built its customer base one customer at a time. He thought ironically, now we are looking at them one customer at a time. The cowbell signaled incoming customers, so he rose from his chair and shifted back into cooking mode.

"Looks like trouble," he thought, "the men in camo are invading. Hunting season, humph ..."

***

Aletta was plumb tired by 1:30 when the lunch rush slowed down. Even though there were a lot of non-residents, everyone wanted to talk about the murder. It seemed to her that a lot of folks were just hoping for something they could get alarmed about. Like unidentified killers on the loose. Didn't the paper say that the police had reason to think it was not a random act? Nevertheless, several of her regular customers had expressed concern that she was not armed and did not own a weapon.

She finished refilling the salt shakers when John walked out of the kitchen to dispense a coke for himself. "You doing okay?" he asked.

"Yeah, hey, what do you think? Should I get a gun? Do I need protection? Is there something to actually be worried about?" she asked the man she most trusted.

He snorted. "Aletta, you have been talking to gun nuts all morning. Do you think you talked to anyone who doesn't have at least one gun in their truck? Maybe one of the oilfield guys .... but this is a community that had lines in front of the gun stores for months after Obama's election. This is a community of gun nuts even before you add on three hundred rabid hunters."

"Do you own a gun, Mr. Irick?"

"I do," he admitted. "I have a 302 and a 22 but I don't know what closet they might be in. I never use them. The 302 was my dad's, and I bought the 22 when I was a kid with money I made mowing lawns. I don't like to hunt. I'd have to go buy bullets if I wanted to use either one. I just don't think you really *need* a gun, Aletta."

"Do you think I should not worry?" she asked.

"You are in a lot more danger of being shot every time you go to a big city. Or even Espanola. People get killed in Albuquerque everyday, but out here, not much chance of anything happening. I wouldn't worry too much, if I were you."

The cowbell signaled an incoming customer, so Aletta stepped back into the front area behind the counter. It was only Eleanor Vicente stopping to use the lady's room.

John had settled into his plastic chair for a timely nap as Aletta stuck her head back around the corner.

"Do we have a company safety policy? Should I allow people to carry weapons into the restaurant?"

"Let me think about it. Don't you need to fill up the ketchups or something? Find something to dust?"

"Oh, you're going to take a nap ..." she replied.

"Something like that." He closed his eyes thinking about how to keep his employees safe.

***

Later that day, Aletta noticed John had posted a hand-lettered sign on the refrigerator with a magnet.

SAFETY POLICY
IN CASE OF HOLDUP:

• *Give them the money.*

• *Don't leave the building with them.*

• *Ask them what kind of burger they want*
because they must be pretty hungry
to hold this place up.

{Chapter 25}

Dogs at the Lake

On her way to meet Sephra at the lake, Aletta stopped by her house to get her dogs. She pulled into the driveway and got out to open the gate. No use in checking the mailbox since it was Sunday.

The dogs were at the gate before she could pull the Jeep in, but they had no intention of escaping. Their human was home!!! They joyously followed the Jeep down her sandy driveway and around the low hill that hid her trailer from the road. The trailer had a little fenced yard where last summer's flowers and a tomato plant had frozen but not yet been discarded. Along the north side, it had three elm trees, which shaded it nicely during the summer. She was making payments on the land. She had found the trailer in the Thrifty Nickel. It had required a lot of work, but now it was home.

She dropped her purse on the kitchen table and grabbed the dogs' leashes. They knew instantly that adventure was in the wind.

Superficially her two dogs looked similar. Both were mutts with Airedale in their ancestry. Bones, a young male, was mixed with Afghan Hound. Koby, an older female, had the markings of a German Shepherd. Somehow, Aletta found owning Airedale mutts more satisfying than owning the purebreds themselves.

The dogs vibrated with excitement as they waited for her to open the back door of the Jeep. She asked them to sit before she opened the door, then she invited them in one at a time. "Bones, hup! ... Koby, hup!"

Sephra, who had a purebred Australian Shepherd, was training him toward the AKC Companion Dog title. Sephra's family had shown dogs. It was a world that Aletta found strange, but since they had been working their dogs together, Aletta's dogs had been happier and easier to manage. Bones had even quit biting at the tires of the Jeep when she left for work.

Sephra was already waiting at the little dirt turnout with Duke. His glowing chest looked like a snow patch, while his gray and black mottled body was perfectly proportioned. *The only thing wrong with that dog*, Aletta thought, *is he's not part Airedale.*

Sephra was at the Jeep door even before Aletta got the key out of the ignition. The young woman's dark eyes were red and her cheeks were wet. She wrapped her arms around Aletta before Aletta could shut the door. The older woman put her arms around Sephra and let her sob.

"What is it, Sephra?" Aletta asked. "Is there something I don't know?"

"The whole thing is so awful. How could they think I had anything to do with it? What would happen to Duke if they arrested me? I feel so overwhelmed," she sobbed.

"It's just that you had a shotgun in your truck and you were there. They had to examine your shotgun so they could cross you off of their list. You read the paper, didn't you? Sounds to me like they have no leads at all," offered Aletta.

"Everytime I think about it, my heart starts pounding and I can hardly breathe. I can't even think, my mind is just totally blank. Poor Aaron!!!" the young woman bawled.

She collected herself enough to be able to talk, "I was hoping I could talk to Pastor Donisthorpe after church this morning, but he was out of town and the Deacon led the service. I have no one that I trust to talk to about it but you, Aletta. I feel like I am losing my mind. Things are going from bad to worse. What if they decide that I did it?"

"If you get arrested, I'll take care of your dog. If I get arrested, will you take care of mine? Yes ... well, we have a deal. Now, when was the last time you used that gun? Did you ever get it working?"

"No, I never actually used it."

"Well, what they are looking for is how long ago it was fired. They are looking for a weapon that was fired on Friday afternoon. Your gun isn't the one they are looking for. Have a little confidence in the system, Sephra. You know where you were and what you were doing. Do you have an alibi?"

"I was having dinner at Sam Elkins' place. We were looking at his photos of the horses that were captured. Aaron was hauling some horses to be euthanized. Naturally, they will suspect either me or Sam. There was one horse on that trailer that we were both interested in and everyone knew it. Now those horses are dead and Aaron's dead. And I am a suspect. This is so unfair," she started sobbing again.

"Wait a minute," Aletta said tenderly. "I heard that the horses got away. I heard that seven horses escaped—could that be right? I don't remember who told me, but it was someone that I believed. I think your horses might be alive.

"Hey," she continued, "Remember the time we brought your shotgun out here and tried to target practice? Somebody should have made a video of that because it was definitely funny. It was like a Bugs Bunny cartoon where the gun doesn't work and they look down the barrel, but neither you nor I were going to chance looking into the barrel even if there were no bullets. That gun wasn't functional in my opinion. I took the tin-can targets home and put bulk food in them, so much for blasting them to pieces!"

Sephra managed a vague smile at the memory. Then she asked, "Doesn't the idea of someone you know getting murdered freak you out?"

"Honey, I live in the gossip capitol of the universe. I've heard every version of every theory that could possibly exist. Did you know the aliens killed Aaron Shauner for getting too close to the secret underground airbase? I heard that one too. It's sad and it's unfortunate, but things happen. Your preacher might have told you that it is just God's plan and a test of our faith. Have a little faith, Sephra. Things will be okay. Maybe God's plan was to let those horses go."

"Does someone *really* believe it might be aliens?" Sephra asked.

Aletta ignored the question and said, "Hey, let's get some dog training done. How about a game of 'Sit, stay, fetch'?"

Bones and Koby sat, their tails fanning the air. Duke seemed in no mood to focus on the game. Instead he whined and pressed his body against Sephra's legs, unwilling to leave her.

"Your dog is worried about you. You have no choice; you simply have to pull yourself together, Amiga."

Sephra wiped the tears from her eyes and said "Let's just run. Duke and I need to burn off these stress hormones. It's my only hope."

"Let's go!" Aletta said bounding down the dirt track.

{Chapter 26}

Monday, Monday, Can't Trust that Day.

Rita Mae was polishing the tops of the pepper shakers. She had already scrubbed them with a scour pad until the glass was crystal clean. The tables were glistening. The floor had been mopped twice. Rita Mae didn't believe in standing around chit-chatting when there was work to be done.

She noticed the dead flies and dust in the window sills. Something for the afternoon waitress to take care of. There simply wouldn't be time to get it done before lunch.

When John called her about coming for the week, she had jumped at the chance to get out of Nova Scotia and head to the land of green chile. She flew into Albuquerque and rode the shuttle up to Farmington. John picked her up and brought her home to stay for a week. She'd been here before, several times when Miriam was alive, and once after John bought the Roadhouse. She had helped him get it organized. She threw out the bull testicles and jalapeno poppers. She showed him how to keep the place spotless. Clean is something she specialized in. She had spent forty years in the service of cleaning and being prepared. Waitresses have a lot to learn from surgical nurses!

Retiring from her nursing career had been easy, and now she was free to explore the hopes and dreams that had sat on the backburner all those years. On the top of her bucket list was being a truckstop waitress. John was giving her the chance to live out that fantasy without having to get a real job.

The cowbell clanked as she put away her polishing rag. She looked up to see a small Hispanic man in a navy blue work uniform. He headed straight to the restroom. Since he was occupied, she walked to the window and looked out at his truck. It was a flat bed with three portable toilets lashed on. The sign on the door said Cerandos Incorporated. Behind her, she could hear the bathroom sink running for quite a while.

He ultimately stepped out of the restroom looking refreshed. His hair was newly combed. He took off his jacket, with its 'Cerandos, Inc.' logo and folded it neatly before he put it over the back of a barstool at the counter. "It's time for lunch," he said grinning.

She looked carefully at his navy blue shirt. Its logo said 'Ernesto'. It was clean and freshly pressed. But the idea of a man who hauls human feces around for a living unsettled her.

She was, after all, a Canadian: polite and clean.

She handed him a menu and set a glass of water and a roll of silverware down on the counter in front of him.

She looked at his narrow Hispanic nose and an image popped into her mind of tiny molecules of outhouse chemicals being trapped in his snot. She did not realize he was trying to order his food. She was preoccupied with the thought that fecal molecules from one patient at a time was something she could deal with; however the thought of the biotic output of dozens of guts being hauled around on a truck was simply too much. Too much information!! It must be stuck to every surface he comes in contact with. How many bottles of bleach would it take to erase all trace of him?

He has that look on his face like he just told me his order, she thought, coming back to the present moment. Aloud, she said, "Sir, could you repeat that order for me?"

On her way back from handing Guido the order, she realized that he is probably starting to suspect this new waitress is a racist bitch. She did not want to be a racist. No one was going to accuse Rita Mae of being racist if she could help it.

"So, do you work in the oil-patch?" she asked.

"Sometimes ... I deliver porta-potties wherever nature calls. I was just out picking up at the wild horse roundup site. I barely got in; there was so much snow.

"Hey, did you hear about that BLM guy that got killed? *Ay! Dios mio!* That was a helluva deal."

"I did hear a bit about that," she replied, "I'm from Nova Scotia and just got in yesterday, but the tragedy seems to be what everyone is talking about," Rita Mae said. "What do you think happened?"

He started explaining his theory, but Naomi came in, the parking lot filled with trucks, and the cowbell started going crazy. Rita Mae and Ernesto looked at each other. He raised his hands, palms up to about the level of his shoulder and shouted over the din, "I'll come in earlier tomorrow and we'll talk. I'd like to hear about Nova Scotia."

The prospect of a new friend did not displease her.

{Chapter 27}

The Adult Crying Model of Vingerhoets

We have accumulated enough examples of adult crying, that we are now in position to evaluate the Adult Crying Model of Vingerhoets, 2013. This model has five variable states with many sources of moderating factors.

1. Objective situation
2. Appraisal
3. Internal association
4. Emotional state
5. Crying with or without Lacrimation

As we have seen, the objective situation itself is not the predictor of tears. For example, the death of a government employee has led to Tim Tucker's lacrimation, but few other males in the community emitted this behavior in response to the news. It is apparent that the objective situation is merely a catalyst.

Appraisal appears to be a key factor. Appraisal is the answer to "what is the personal significance of the objective situation?" In this case, the demise of Aaron Shauner means that members of the community will never see him again. In Tim Tucker's appraisal, this is significant as Tim shared a certain amount of his free time with the departed. He lost his drinking buddy. To many workers in the oil-patch, the personal significance is that they no longer have to worry about the BLM guy that drives like a crazy hillbilly. We can safely predict they will not cry.

The internal association is the internalized interpretation of the objective situation; it combines all the personal belief structures already in play with the appraisal of the event. Tim Tucker experiences the event as a loss. Other internal situations that frequently lead to adult crying are personal inadequacy, criticism/rebuke, and rejection. Sephra's lacrimation may reflect personal inadequacy or feelings of rebuke, but probably not loss itself. It should be also noted at this point that extremely positive internal situations, such as your daughter getting married, can also lead to adult

111

crying.

The internal association produces an emotional state. Modern science has come to see emotional states as neurochemical states. Here we find sadness, which researchers have correlated with separation distress circuitry in the brain. Sadness is treatable.

Finally, when the stimulus of the objective situation has successfully cascaded through these stages, it reaches the psychobiological machinery of crying, not limited to the eyes, but also associated with breathing patterns and vocalizations. Individual variations in the functional status of this machinery lead to characteristic individual responses. Some people weep copiously or sob loudly, others barely moisten an eye, or perhaps merely whimper.

Armed with this knowledge, we are now ready to venture into an experiment in process. Our next chapter gives us the opportunity to evaluate simultaneous presentation of a single objective situation to a wide assortment of subjects. Can we predict where the tears will fall?

{Chapter 28}

The Funeral of Aaron Shauner

"*Yea, though I walk through the valley of the shadow of death, I will fear no evil; for Thou art with me; Thy rod and Thy staff, they comfort me. Psalm 23.*

"If you will allow Him, God provides comfort, even in your darkest hour of grief and pain.

"Let us read together from Psalm 46:1-11.

"*God is our refuge and strength, a very present help in trouble. Even though the earth be removed, and though the mountains be carried into the midst of the sea; though its waters roar and be troubled, though the mountains shake with its swelling there is a river whose streams shall make glad the city of God.*

"*God is in the midst of her, she shall not be moved; God shall help her, just at the break of dawn. The nations raged, the kingdoms were moved; He uttered His voice, the earth melted. The Lord of hosts is with us; the God of Jacob is our refuge.*

"*Come, behold the works of the Lord, Who has made desolation in the earth. He makes wars cease to the end of the earth; He breaks the bow and cuts the spear in two; He burns the chariot in the fire.*

"*Be still, and know that I am God, I will be exalted among the nations, I will be exalted in the earth! The Lord of Hosts is with us; The God of Jacob is our refuge.*

"God's message to you now is that although we feel helplessness in these times, God's grace offers us strength and hope that will carry us through these dark hours. How hopeless we feel when the lives of our young sons and brothers are unexpectedly lost in tragedy. Most of us would do anything to change the course of events, and yet, there appears to be little, if anything, any of us could have done to change the events that led to Aaron Shauner's death. The Sovereign of the Sudden, God Almighty, had called Aaron home.

"Inevitably, without knowing of the grace and love of God Almighty, the tragic loss of a loved one leads us survivors into the sea of hopelessness. There may not be mountains that are visibly being carried into the sea, but in a very strange way, the earth *is* trembling, and you seem to find yourselves under the influence of a very powerful force— the force of death, the emotion of grief. Grief shakes us at our deepest level. Grief creates fear. Our world may appear to be crumbling and turned upside down, but God is there to help us.

"We know very little about the force of death, a force that very quickly puts us in touch with our limited capacities as human beings. However, the insecurity that God provides in these times is the impetus for the renewal of faith. We become open to his healing message in a crisis of consciousness. The Psalmist exhorts us to listen to the still quiet voice of God, by being still and knowing that God is Almighty and He has everything under control.

"'Be still and know that God is God.' He is with us. Jesus has said, *'I will never leave you nor forsake you.'*

"It is in the midst of this kind of trouble and grief that God comes to us and offers us the kind of refuge and strength we need. Jesus said, *'I will not leave you as orphans, I will come to you.'* Recall that Joseph and Jeremiah each went to prison. Job lost everything but his life. Paul had an affliction that plagued him all his life. All of the original disciples were martyred for their faith in Jesus, except one. And he was an exiled prisoner. Jesus never promised them a 'rose garden'. However, he did promise, *'I am with you'* (Matthew. 28:20). It may be tough to be in a storm with Jesus, but imagine being in one without him.

"Death does not have to be the destructive and totally mysterious force that we fear it to be. If our hearts are properly prepared death can be an event we all look forward to. God's plan and purpose for our loved ones and for our lives are not subject to whims, accidents, circumstances, illnesses, or evil. God works through these to bring about his will. We stand on the assurance, *'Fear not, for I have redeemed you; I have summoned you by name; you are mine. When you pass through the waters, I will be with you; and when you pass through the rivers, they will not sweep over you. When you walk through the fire, you will not be burned; the flames will not set you ablaze. For I am the Lord, your God, the Holy One of Israel, your Savior'* (Isaiah. 43:1–3).

"Depression must give way to celebration. The Sovereign of the Sudden was, is, and always will be in charge. In our pain and sorrow, we stand on the everlasting truth, '*Our Lord reigns!*'

"Let us pray".

***

Who knew Shauner would have so many friends gather to say goodbye? Almost everyone from the BLM and Forest Service offices showed up. His mother and sister sat in the front row and looked numb. All the permittees who ran cattle on the BLM rangelands and their immediate families had their hats off as they stood in the back of the church. Sephra and a few other horse advocates sat in the pews with Sam and his significant other, Karen. The rest of the pews were filled with Shauner's high school friends and friends of friends. The church was crowded.

Pastor Donisthorpe stopped the sermon several times to sniff, dry-eyed, into his handkerchief. Everyone cried, even Erin Tate.

Lunch was served in the church recreation room. It was mostly a potluck, but the Roadhouse Cafe sent fifty bean and cheese burritos wrapped in silvered paper. Aletta brought them with her, putting out bowls of both green chile and of onion, with big plastic spoons to serve them.

Aletta had never been to this church, but somehow Pastor Donisthorpe looked vaguely familiar. He avoided even looking at her.

{Chapter 29}

Freedom's Just Another Word ...

The cowbell clanked at four P.M. on Friday afternoon. Aletta looked up from her laptop and smiled. "Hey, did you find any feathers?"

"Just a few red-shafted flicker feathers under a piñyon tree," replied the medium-sized woman wearing a US Forest Service uniform and hiking boots. She walked to the bar counter and pulled up a stool.

"I saved a piece of cake for you, Pam. Decaf?" inquired Aletta.

Pam nodded and put her hands on the counter. She fingered a napkin absent-mindedly. Aletta set down two plates bearing carrot cake squares, then brought two cups of coffee and two forks before she seated herself across the counter from Pam and pulled one cake and coffee in front of herself. She enjoyed her Friday afternoon visits with Pam.

"What a week!" the uniformed woman sighed. "You can't imagine the hell going on in the Wild Horse and Burro program. Everyone's gone bonkers. Jessica says it's the same over at the BLM office. She said if anyone popped a balloon in that office, three people would die of a heart attack."

"Except for the funeral—and by the way, I loved the blouse you wore—I've just stayed in my office and avoided the ruckus. I had a stack of archaeological site reports to write and this week was just what I needed to keep my nose on the grindstone and get 'er done. My desk is clean for the first time in years! What about you; what's been happening up here?"

Aletta took a sip of decaf to wash the cake from her teeth. "I have only been here yesterday and today, and yesterday I was at the funeral for three hours of my shift, so I really couldn't tell you. Penny's on vacation, so Rita Mae is here. Do you remember her? ... the nurse from Nova Scotia? ... Well, she's the owner's personal friend and tried to get Naomi to do some housekeeping. That didn't turn out so well, so next week, I get five shifts, which is going to really help my bank account."

116

"Yes," Pam said, "I noticed this place looks pretty spiffy. Clean windows and all."

"You know, Rita Mae really inspires people to greatness. Even Guido likes her. About Aaron, though, do they have any suspects yet?"

Pam sighed, "Aletta, the District Ranger and the Forest Supervisor brought us all into a meeting and explained why we should not discuss the case with anyone. They basically asked us to not talk about it."

"Randall Tapia asked me not to blog about it."

"Did he?" the older woman interjected, widening her left eye. "For how long?"

"He didn't say. But then it came out in the newspaper, which kind of hurt my feelings. I think Randall just forgot about me."

"This community depends on that blog to know what is happening in this part of Rio Arriba County. He shouldn't do that, but ... He probably has a lot of other things on his mind right now," Pam said.

"I do have some news though," Aletta began. "Sephra got her shotgun back and they said that not only had she not used it, it wasn't actually functional. She's going to give it back to that guy who loaned it to her."

"Aletta, I am going to tell you something because we are friends, but please do not repeat it or put it in your blog. The only important evidence they found was some barefoot tracks in the horse trailer. Well, it could not have happened at a worse time for sure, because now there is eight inches of snow on the ground and no chance for further scene investigation."

"Someone was barefooted at the murder scene?" Aletta asked.

"Yep."

"Well, that should make it easy. Not too many barefooted people around."

Pam looked down her nose at Aletta. "Silly goose, when was the last time you were barefooted? This morning, I dare say. Every human on the planet has a set of those—well most everyone."

"Oh, yeah. I see what you mean, " Aletta said thoughtfully. "Actually, I like to go barefoot. I keep all the goat-head stickers cleared from my land just so I can go barefoot. Sometimes I even go barefoot in the snow. Things like that make me feel alive!"

Aletta took another bite of cake and another sip of decaf, then asked "Do you think that this 'Cone of Silence' we are in is an infringement of our rights. Is it a curtailment of freedom?"

Pam tilted her head and fidgeted with her napkin before replying, "Well, I think that is why they didn't tell us we *couldn't* talk about it, they just made it our moral responsibility to keep tight lips."

"Same with Randall. He said it was just a personal favor."

"I read a magazine article where they had surveyed people about freedom." Pam took a sip of decaf and continued, "They had asked young people in the United States if they had to choose one, would they rather be free or happy. More than half of them, chose happiness. The majority felt that freedom doesn't count for much if they couldn't be happy. Young people are typically so idealistic, this result surprised me."

"Does the archaeological record have anything to say about the correlation between happiness and freedom across time?" Aletta asked.

"That is an interesting question, girlfriend. I'll check it out and get back to you. As I recall, the French Enlightenment linked the two. In this culture we seem to think that democracy is necessary for happiness and assume people living under any other form of government are unhappy."

"I love having a smart friend!" Aletta sighed. "What about the freedom of the wild horses? What do they gain or lose by being brought into captivity?"

"That is an interesting question too, but I am sure the archaeologists have not researched it. First you would have to define freedom and happiness for a horse, then you would have to figure out how to quantify it. They are doing a lot of amazing research with neurochemistry and measuring stress, but it's not exactly the same as the opposite of happiness," Pam said thoughtfully. "And how would you measure it in a wild horse without making it unhappy? That's hard."

The cowbell clanked. In stepped a tall grizzly-looking man with long grey hair and a beard. Through the open front of his jacket, the women could see his t-shirt brightly proclaiming 'Liberty or Death' around the skeleton of a hand illustrated in red, white, and blue flag motif. The fingers held a gold star.

His truck was parked at the gas pump. "Hey, JL. Let's see your t-shirt. We were just talking about liberty," Aletta said as she took the ten dollar bill he held out to her. She tapped out the transaction on the cash register as he held his coat open and turned to flash it to Pam. "What'cha been up to? Go to town?"

"I had to pick up some ammo," he replied. "That nigger is gonna take away our guns. This ain't gonna be a free country much longer. We are not even going to be able to defend ourselves. We'll all end up deader than Aaron Shauner!" The man turned abruptly, grunted, and stomped out the door.

"Who was that?" asked a wide-eyed Pam.

"Oh, that's JL Hartman. He lives in a little fortified house at about milepost 97. He's a character. He is such a stereotype that he amazes me."

"He creeps me out," said the archaeologist.

"He never stays long. Weird can be interesting in small doses," the waitress said. "Hey, you didn't tell me about your adventures today."

"Don't have too much to tell. I managed to get to two more little caves, but there wasn't anything there except packrats. No bones, no feathers, no skulls ... darn! Hey, it's getting late, I better head for the barn," she said, stepping down from her bar stool.

"Pam, thanks for coming by. I really enjoy your company," Aletta said with a smile.

"See you next week, same time, same place ... Bye, now." and the cowbell clanked again.

Navajo City Roadhouse Blog:

Sweeping and Mopping

Saturday, November 5, 2011

Did I tell you that you have to be a mudwrestler to work here? Argh!!!

Yours truly,
Aletta

ps. Will write about the murder of Aaron Shauner when I get any new facts, meanwhile, don't believe everything you hear—especially about the aliens.

{Chapter 31}

Honky-Tonk Heroes

When Aletta started pulling chairs out from under tables on Thursday afternoon, Guido thought she was going to mop again. But when she started dragging tables around, it was clear bigger plans were afoot.

"Aletta, why are you moving the tables?"

"John is letting the Wild Horse Advocate Coalition meet here this afternoon."

"Hmmm, wild ... horse ... advocate ... coalition. The W.H.A.C. *Whack*! For wacking BLM employees? Wacking government agents is a dangerous business! I am not sure I want to be in the same building with this meeting. Someone finds out an anarchist made the french fries and, *boom*, we all go to jail."

"Well, I doubt if that is their mission. Sephra Brooks organized it," Aletta countered.

"Oh, the girl with the shotgun? You know, I think I'll just go back in the kitchen and sing along with the radio if you don't mind." He picked up his glass and disappeared through the kitchen door.

Aletta was pushing the last chair into place, when the cowbell clanked and Sephra walked in carrying a whiteboard easel and some markers.

"Oh, this looks nice. A circle of tables! That's great!" said the dark-eyed girl.

The sound of a truck pulling up made the two women look out the window. Attencio Candelaria was climbing down from the cab.

"Rio Arriba County Sheriff?" Aletta said. "They never come this far west. What the hell?" Guido's warning replayed in her head.

"I invited them, Aletta. Don't worry. I also invited the BLM and the FBI."

"The FBI?"

"Let's put napkins on the tables. I think people will be ordering pie," Sephra said, ignoring the question.

The cowbell clanked and Attencio walked in. He looked around the room, then

121

took off his broad-brimmed hat.

Sephra waved a napkin at Attencio and said, "Come sit down. Would you like some coffee?"

The cowbell clanked as Lynne Wagoner came in carrying a large package wrapped in brown paper. It clanked again and Sam Elkins walked in. He started by shaking hands with Attencio and greeting him in Spanish. The cowbell was working overtime when Beth Hudson and Sally Horne pushed open the door. Three men arrived in quick succession; one Aletta recognized as Officer Sanders, but the other two were strangers. Sam shook hands with everyone.

Aletta announced the location of the bathroom and that everyone could help themselves to coffee. Sephra took the package from Lynne as she waited for everyone to finish their visits to the restroom. When almost everyone was seated, she held up the package. "The first order of business is to present John Irick and the Roadhouse this token of our gratitude." She ripped off the brown paper and there was a framed photograph of the horse roundup. Cowboys were shaking hands or looking at horses, Phantom was rearing up most elegantly, Sephra was looking at a foal. Aaron Shauner was standing in the middle of it all, looking serene and smiling. "This is how we want the community to remember Aaron Shauner."

Sephra held out the picture to Aletta who took it and hung it on a nail in the wall.

Sephra continued, "I organized this meeting to have a way to exchange information without the jeopardy of a conspiracy, therefore we are holding our organizational meeting in a public place with members of law enforcement present. I think most of you know Officer Sanders as he was at the round-up. This," she said, indicating the red-headed man, "is Greg Stribling from the FBI."

"Let's go around the room and I will introduce you all. I'm Sephra Brooks. I work with the Society for Humane Treatment of Animals. To my left is Lynne Wagoner from Wind Knots Photography, Beth Hudson from Wild Forever, Attencio Candelaria with the Rio Arriba County Sheriff's office, Sally Horne from Four Corners Animal Alliance, David Quinn from Wild Horse and Burro Association of Colorado, Andy Milligan from New Mexico Equine Protection Services, Dan

Sanders from the BLM, Sam Elkins, everyone knows Sam, private contractor, and, finally, Aletta Ramsden from the Roadhouse.

"The best way we can start is to make a list of questions we have about the issues. I will write them on the whiteboard."

Beth spoke up, "Do we want to make a public statement for the record?" Sephra wrote *public statement*.

Sally asked, "Are we still suspects?" Sephra wrote *still suspects*?

David raised his hand. "Will they use this to further restrict access to wild horse roundups? Sephra wrote *impact to roundup accessibility*.

Lynne looked around, "Who all has been questioned in respect to this murder? Don't write it on the board, Sephra; everyone who has been questioned, raise your hands." All the advocates raised their hands and looked at each other.

Lynne continued, "Well, the question is then, are there suspects other than horse advocates?" Sephra wrote down *other suspects*?

"I guess it's my turn," said Andy Milligan. "I want to know how we can keep ourselves from being caught up in a hunt for Animal Liberation activists and eco-terrorists."

"I don't know what to write down for that," said Sephra.

Beth answered, "Write 'Not ALF'; underline not." Sephra did so.

"I have a question, okay," Attencio smiled. "I heard we are going to have pie. What kind of pie?"

Everyone laughed and the tension in the room lowered. Sephra asked, "Shall we break for pie?"

Stribling stood up. "I think in the interest of time, I can address a lot of your questions. Why don't I talk and you eat pie."

Aletta and Sephra dished out slices of apple pie, put forks on the plates, and passed them around. Several people helped themselves to coffee refills.

"Terrorism is terrorism, no matter what the motive," Stribling began. "There's a clear difference between constitutionally protected advocacy—which is the right of all Americans—and violent criminal activity. My office investigates terrorism, domestic and international. We have a special unit for Animal Liberation activity. A man was killed and animals were liberated, so I am on this case.

"In 2006, the Animal Enterprise Terrorism Act toughened penalties, created additional protections for people—the original law only covered property damage—and included secondary targets. We have a lot of legal precedent to go after the perpetrator of this crime.

"Now, you people have a constitutionally protected right to have an interest in the welfare of the mustangs. Your free speech is protected. You, however, have no right to murder people or let government-owned horses go. If you do that, you'll go to jail. If you have a conspiracy to engage in any kind of violent criminal activity, including letting horses free, it won't matter if you actually commit the crime. We find out and we prosecute. The laws have changed. We can pick up terrorists without a warrant. We can hold them indefinitely. The cause that you have aligned yourself with is problematic. If your mission is freeing animals, you are on the slippery slope into Animal Liberation terrorist activity.

"I've met with each of you individually and we've discussed reasons to take you off my list of suspects. Most of you seem pretty clean to me. Other than that, I can't tell you who is or isn't a suspect in this case. We recently had an arson at the Bureau of Land Management Wild Horse Corrals in Litchfield, California. These incidents may be connected."

"I've heard you can't even have a website that is critical of animal welfare in agriculture," said David.

"If it were damaging or interfering with the operations of an animal enterprise, it would, yes, be criminal," responded Stribling.

Beth got up and strode to where the photo was hanging. "So, standing between this horse and the rancher with his gun who was being paid to euthanize it would make me a terrorist in the same class as Timothy McVeigh or Ted Kaczynski?"

"You don't want to do that, young lady." Stribling cautioned. "It's against the law."

Sam spoke up, "Well, I guess the best way to get out of the searchlight, is to get the searchlight turned off. What can we do to help the investigation so it goes away?"

"Keep your eyes and ears open. Call me if you notice or remember anything that might be significant," said the federal lawman.

"In contrast to our federal partners, Rio Arriba County," said the sheriff, "still requires warrants for arrest and still respects habeas corpus. We are old fashioned ... *que no?*"

Andy Milligan stood up to speak, "It is my firm belief that we have to be realistic about the political landscape we are in. Speciesism is still strong in this culture. Animal welfare issues are a fringe concept. We can delude ourselves that this is not, or should not be, the case, but this is an era in which the possibilities for change for non-humans is extremely limited. We must focus on reform and accept the fact that there are great obstacles before us."

"I move," said Lynne, "that we issue a public statement that as a coalition, we support expediting the investigation of Aaron Shauner's murder and that our members offer their services and support to the law enforcement community."

"I second that," said Sam.

"Any more discussion ...?" Sephra paused and looked around the room. "If not, all those in favor of issuing a public statement that we support the expedited investigation of the murder, please raise your hand." All of the advocates raised hands.

"The motion carries," Sephra said.

"I move to adjourn," said Andy. "It's a long way back to Santa Fe."

The shadows were getting long as the cowbell fell quiet and the various vehicles pulled onto the highway.

{Chapter 32}

Send Me Anywhere but Bulgaria

When Pamela Anderson didn't show up on Friday at exactly 4 P.M., Aletta was instantly worried about her friend. What if the murderer got a second government employee? Who would do a thing like that? She finished cleaning the countertop and then reached for the phone. Instead of dialing, Aletta set it down on the counter and looked at it. She would make herself wait until 4:15 P.M. before she called. It would be embarrassing to call too early.

She poured herself a cup of decaf and sat listening to the radio. *If she is not going to show up, I should scrub the drink dispenser,* she told herself, but she just continued to sit. Ray Wylie Hubbard was singing about the Snake Farm. *Where did he get an idea for a song like that?* she wondered.

The government truck coasted off of the highway and pulled into one of the closest parking places. Pam got out of the truck limping slightly. Aletta watched her friend walk up the boardwalk. The cowbell clanked.

"Hey, I was about ready to call the search and rescue department! It's not like you to be late."

"Yeah, I sure know it. I got stuck in the snow up off of Rosa Road. I just slid off into a little soft spot and then my truck wouldn't go into four-wheel drive. I had to wait for someone to come along that could pull me out. Shep Cabot was nice enough to get his chain and give me a little tug. My truck popped right out," said the archaeologist.

Aletta set the cake slices and a cup for Pam on the counter. The two women pulled their plates in front of them. This time it was lemon cake with a thick vanilla frosting. Before she took her first bite, Pam asked, "So what's been happening in Navajo City?"

Aletta swallowed her bite and turned her fork, so that the tines were sticking straight up into the air. "Well, we had a meeting here of the Wild Horse Advocate

Coalition. It was eye-opening. I didn't realize that there were such tough laws protecting animal operations. You can be a terrorist without even trying. Sephra had a man from the FBI come and talk to them. No one but me seemed surprised, but everyone was worried."

"Was it about the murder?" the archaeologist asked.

"Yes, the members voted to do whatever they could to expedite the investigation to get the cops off their backs."

"What can they do to expedite it?"

"No one talked about that. I don't know." replied the waitress. "What about your world, Pam? What's happening with the Forest Service?"

"Thank goodness it has quieted down in our office. It's finally between hunting seasons so things seem pretty normal. However, Jessica says things are still crazy at the BLM. Randall Tapia brought his own personal shotgun in and asked Jessica to take it to the police to be tested. He said it was just to clear his own name, but we think it might be because it was his truck at the crime scene and maybe someone was gunning for him. Who would have access to the gun besides Mrs. Tapia? But, it's all speculation. The gun came back clean having last been fired three years ago.

"Then better news, the day after the gather, people started coming by to adopt some horses. I guess this man adopted two of them, kind of older mares, and he comes to see them every day. They will be branding them next week and then they can go. Isn't that sweet? I think Jessica said the man was Navajo. She said that he can already pet them."

The women ate a few bites of cake as the radio finished playing "Folsom Prison Blues."

"Hey, that reminds me, I had time to do a little research on the freedom question," said the archaeologist. "The problem is that both freedom and happiness are constructs. Each person has their own experience of what they mean."

"What's a construct?" asked the waitress.

"A construct is a phenomenon or category created by cultural consensus. It has no objective reality other than individual perception."

Pam continued, "It's very difficult to elicit such abstract concepts from the archeological record. We might find evidence of oppression in human remains—blunt trauma injuries from being struck, stress fractures from carrying heavy loads—which would be occupation markers—foot binding of females as in traditional China, economic inequality where one class gets the best and the others almost starve. Oppression leaves traces, but freedom does not.

"We can ask anthropological questions of modern peoples. For example, we could ask if the Navajos who had no central authority were more or less happy than tribes with a strong chief. How we are going to measure happiness is another question."

"I've noticed that some tribes are a lot more serious and less likely to tease me. The Apaches are pretty serious, but I don't know if they are unhappy," said Aletta.

Pam said, "And the Zunis always have a joke, but are they happy? I hope so. Well, I found this anthropological research paper from the Netherlands that compared relative freedom and happiness scores in more than forty countries. It was very tough for them to define the two constructs. They defined freedom as the opportunity and capacity to choose—to both have things to choose from and to actually make choices, which is an individual action.

"Wow," said the waitress, "so freedom depends on having alternatives to choose from. Someone who liked hamburgers would get a sense of freedom from our menu, whereas a vegetarian would not experience freedom at all. But ... wait, I thought freedom was not having someone telling you what to do."

The archaeologist replied, "You can have freedom in that sense as well. Freedom from impediments, such as restrictive laws or oppression by the powerful. That is where freedom starts requiring responsibility. Making choices involves uncertainty *and* responsibility. Often people shy away from this.

"The research was done using various measures that other institutes and study groups had done. Extensive surveys for the most part. They had three categories of freedom: economic, political, and personal. What countries would you think are the least free?"

"The middle east, maybe Iraq," the waitress guessed.

"In the 1990's when they did this research, the bottom three, by far, were Nigeria, China, and India. India's caste system overcame its good education system. People wouldn't choose to violate the caste system. The top three were Switzerland—by every measure—Canada, and either New Zealand or the Netherlands."

"Not the United States?" asked Aletta.

"The U.S. was close to the top but never in the top three. For the measures of happiness, the researchers used Quality of Life surveys done in these same countries. They basically asked people about their satisfaction with life. Bulgaria is the least happy country, and is closely followed by several other Eastern European countries. The Netherlands is the happiest country, with Iceland, Sweden, and Ireland close behind. The USA came in 10th and it is probably much worse now. The 1990's were an economic bubble.

"But we are always taught that we are the best country in the world, how can we be neither the most free nor the most happy?" asked Aletta.

Pam was sarcastic. "We do have the most weapons stockpiled, the highest murder rate, and the biggest defense budget, if it makes you feel better!" Both women laughed.

The archaeologist continued, "What they found when they looked at the correlation between the measures was that in general freedom and happiness tend to rise and fall together, but the relationship also seemed to relate to economic prosperity. When the researchers controlled for that by comparing rich countries with rich countries, and poor countries with poor countries, the correlation between happiness and the measures of freedom were not nearly as strong. Economic freedom was tied to happiness in the undeveloped countries, while political freedom was tied to happiness in the developed countries."

"So would poor countries actually have a different construct they call freedom?" asked Aletta.

"Exactly! Now you see the problem with investigating *freedom*, whatever that means."

"The research paper didn't talk about it, but I was looking at their correlation tables and noticed that public acceptance of homosexuality was by far the biggest predictor of happiness for a nation. Isn't that interesting?"

"Pam, if that is what it takes for the United States to be happy, I guess we better just get used to being the tenth. Homosexuality is a hot button out in this corner of the world, but ... hmm, come to think about it, if you can't make choices about who you find attractive, you have already lost in the freedom category anyway. This is going to be enough to keep me busy thinking for at least a week."

Pam sighed and looked at her napkin. "That's another thing I need to talk to you about. With this much snow, I am going to have to suspend my archeological investigations until spring. You'll have to come have lunch with me in town instead."

"Friday afternoon is going to be so boring without you," sighed the waitress. "At least you could call me if you read any more cool stuff."

"Will do. Ciao, *amiga*!" and with that the archaeologist was out the door. The cowbell clanked.

{Chapter 33}

Kleenex Alert

Aletta simply couldn't think of anything else that needed cleaning. She imagined Rita Mae pasting on a Seal of Approval on the wall. John had even run the floor buffer, but now he was asleep in his plastic chair. The radio was playing "Too Long in the Wasteland." She listened to the words, then she scribbled some of the phrases onto an order form.

- *hear the trucks on the highway*

- *ghost of a moon in the afternoon*

- *bullet holes in the mailbox*

- *mothers tell their children just leave that man alone*

"*Great images,*" she thought. She pulled her little black notebook from her purse and slipped the order inside. *"Maybe working at the Roadhouse is like being in the Wasteland?"* she mused. The image of frightening town children with her mere presence did not displease her. Next time she was outside, she would have to check the mailbox for bullet holes; then she would know for certain.

Thinking about bullet holes made her think about hunters. It was pretty darn quiet without a hunt going on. She considered pulling out the hunt schedule, but instead pulled out her laptop. It was time to make another stab at her animal sob story project. She had the video saved on the hard drive.

A moose has fallen through the ice into freezing water. Its shaggy brown head is visible in the ice, but it seems resigned to death. A man is chopping the ice away from it with a pulaski. He works earnestly and will not let this animal die if he can save it.

A helicopter lands on the snowy field behind him and two men in blue jumpsuits disembark with hand tools to help. Soon the hole is large enough to pull the shaggy sodden body from its watery grave. They manage to get straps around the animal and begin to pull. The odds of 600 pounds of men pulling 1200 pounds of moose are weighted by the men's sheer determination. Heaving with every bit of energy they can muster, the moose is pulled to the surface where the air and midday warmth can begin to dry it.

The moose is nearly lifeless, but in the Arctic it is common knowledge that something is not dead until it is warm and dead, so the men continue their work. They repetitively flex the legs. Bend, straighten, bend, straighten, forward and back. Time is suspended as the men work, willing the animal to live.

The man who found the moose will not give up. He turns the moose's muzzle upward and begins to blow his warm breath into the sodden beast. The rhythm of artificial respiration becomes hypnotic. Breathe in, blow out, breathe in, blow out. The man simply refuses to give up. The beast groans. He manages to give it a few more breaths before it moves its head, then struggles up to rest on its sternum. The man joyfully hugs the wild moose, who can do no more than stare vacantly across the snowy landscape. Its fate is not secure in this Arctic environment, but the men have given it a chance for survival.

"That story is not going to make anyone cry," she said to herself. "I cried when I watched it, but why can't I capture that emotion? Maybe I'll work on it later."

She emptied and rinsed the coffee pot, turned off the 'Open' sign, locked the front door, told John goodbye, and went home. Her half-Airedales would cheer her up.

{Chapter 34}

Breakdown

Danielle Tapia pulled up to the emergency entrance of San Juan Regional Hospital. There was plenty of room to park in front of the doors, but there was no one to help her. She glanced at her husband and decided he would be safe until she ran inside and got help.

The security guard was standing inside by the window, so she shouted "I need some help out here!", and motioned for him to follow. He barked something into his radio and two orderlies burst from the inner office, racing through the front door to follow her to the car.

Randall was slumped over in the front seat. Danielle opened the car door. Randall's arms were wrapped around his knees and he was sobbing. "He's having some kind of emotional breakdown."

The orderlies glanced at each other. "Wheelchair," one said and the other went to get it.

"What is his name?" the orderly asked Danielle.

"Randall ... Randall Tapia," the woman replied.

"Mr. Tapia, can you sit up for me?" the orderly asked as he touched Randall on the shoulder. The response was a momentary loosening of the knee hug, but then he started sobbing again and pulled himself tighter.

"We need to get you inside so we can find out what is wrong, Mr. Tapia. See if you can sit up."

The wheelchair arrived just as Tapia struggled to an upright position. He grasped the dashboard in front of him to steady himself, his elbow buckling several times into a partial collapse as he sobbed harder.

The orderlies moved into position to assist him out of the car and without any effort Randall was suddenly sitting in the wheelchair.

"Are you Mrs. Tapia?" one of them asked. She nodded.

"Mrs. Tapia, if you could move your car to the parking lot, we'll take Mr. Tapia into the hospital. Just come right to the desk and we will bring you to him."

The orderly turned the wheelchair and headed to the entrance; the other walked by Randall's knee, keeping one hand near Randall, should Randall need support.

Danielle watched the three men moving toward the entrance for a moment. The orderlies were twenty-some year olds, college types. "Kind of cute," she thought before she got in the car to move it.

As they rolled up to the intake desk, Randall put his forehead in his hand and rested his elbow on his knee. The orderly said, "Let's just stay here until your wife comes in. Are you comfortable?"

Randall did not reply. Mrs. Tapia came striding through the automatically opening entrance doors, her long, black hair swaying with each step. She was wearing tight black slacks and a turquoise blue shirt. Her nails were long and polished a deep red. She had applied fresh matching lipstick before she left the car.

A younger woman approached her and said, "Hi, I'm Lynette Spurgeon. I'll be your client advocate. My job is to help you through the hospital experience with as little trauma as possible. Is this the patient?" she said indicating Randall. "Do you have an insurance card?"

Danielle fished it from her wallet and dropped the wallet back into her purse. She watched the young girl swipe it against the card reader and start some forms printing. The girl's blouse had a frilly neckline, which Danielle thought was too low. She turned Randall's wheelchair so he couldn't see it.

"Are you ... Danielle?" Lynette asked looking at the paper. "Okay, I think all of your intake information is already in the system. We can go on back to see a doctor."

Carrying the paperwork, Lynette motioned for Danielle to follow her with Randall who rode with his head still in his hands.

"You are going to need to sit on the bed, Mr. Tapia. Do you think you can get up there yourself, or should we help you?"

Randall lifted his head from his hand, then he raised his hand and made a grasping gesture.

"You need some help. Great. We can do that. I'm going to let you take my hands and pull yourself up ... there we go. Good job. Now just sit back onto the bed and relax until the doctor comes in."

Danielle felt herself wish the young woman wouldn't touch him. "I'd like to be the one to help him if he needs to move again," Danielle said.

Lynette acknowledged the request and went to find the doctor. Within minutes, she came back through the door in front of Dr. Sands. "This is Dr. Carla Sands. She is our mental health specialist."

Danielle blanched at the sight of the vivacious, full-lipped, big-bosomed blonde doctor wearing a white lab coat. "Isn't there a male doctor?"

"Yes, Dr. Daly is here, but he is working on an accident victim. He can probably see Mr. Tapia in about an hour. His specialty is orthopaedics. Do you want to wait to see him?"

Danielle bit her lip considering the alternatives. "Okay, Dr. Sands, but ... well, I just love my husband very much."

"Mrs. Tapia, I really like working with patients who have strong marriages. It makes their recovery so much faster."

Dr. Sands turned to Randall, "Mr. Tapia, are you feeling sad? Just lift your hand to say yes if you can't talk ... okay, you feel sad, now I need to know if your body hurts too. Does it hurt anywhere, just raise your hand a little to say yes."

Randall pointed to his head and struggled to sit more erect.

"Your head hurts?"

Randall nodded, but then grimaced in reply, so she went on. "Is it like a headache?" He lifted his hand. "Does it hurt to nod your head?" His hand came up again. "Does it hurt to talk? Can you try that and check to see if it hurts?"

Randall managed some throat sounds and a weak "Okay."

"Great! That's good news!" she said quietly. "Now, I need to check your heart and your temperature. I have to look in your ears, your eyes, and your throat. Then we can get you some pain relief." She turned to Danielle. "Mrs. Tapia, can you unbutton the top two buttons on his shirt for me to put the stethoscope on his chest?"

As she worked recording his vital signs, Dr. Sands thought about the problems that morbid jealousy presented. Insecurity was always at the base of the problem. Whatever Randall Tapia's presenting problem might be, it wasn't going to help him to have to deal with the accusations and interrogations his morbidly jealous wife would invariably fling at him. She was acutely aware that Danielle had already decided that a blonde female doctor was a threat. She hoped the patient didn't already see the handwriting on the wall and fear his wife's wrath.

"Okay, Mr. Tapia. I'm going to give you an injection to help your headache. It will be pokey for just a second. I want you to just lie there and relax as much as you can. We'll be back in five minutes. I am going to talk to your wife while you relax. Everything is under control now."

"Mrs. Tapia, let's go out to my desk so we don't disturb our patient." She exited the curtained-off room and turned to wait for Danielle. She pointed to a little cubicle tucked in against a wall. "Go ahead and sit down." The doctor picked up a phone, dialed three digits, and waited for someone to answer.

"This is Dr. Sands in the ER. Can you squeeze another scan in your schedule? ... okay, great. He'll be there in about twenty. Bye."

She turned back to Danielle. "I've ordered an MRI to see if there is anything changing in his brain. How long has he been this way?"

"He got this bad maybe two days ago. Before that, he wasn't sleeping hardly at all."

"When you say he wasn't sleeping, what exactly do you mean?"

"He would just be lying there awake almost all night. I tried to comfort him, but he was too stressed out."

"Why is he stressed?"

"He works for the BLM and someone murdered one of his boys ... one of the men that worked for him."

"When did that happen?"

"A couple of days before the end of October. It was right before Halloween. Since then, well, he's just been going downhill. I found him like this after I came out from getting dressed this morning. I put the blow-drier down and asked him 'What the hell is wrong with you?' That's when he started bawling his eyes out. Maybe that was a mean thing to say? But, really, he hasn't been any fun lately.

"I thought there might be another woman, but I haven't found any evidence of that, so I think it is just his job. Will you be able to get him back on his feet, Doc?"

"If we can rule out physical problems with his brain, he'll probably be back to normal before you know it. I'll just make some notes in his file, if you just want to wait with your husband for the orderlies. He'll probably be asleep. He doesn't need to wake up to go—he can have his MRI and nap at the same time, but I'd like you to be there in case he does wake up. He will be less confused if you are there."

Danielle left and Carla picked up the paperwork and started writing. When she was through describing Randall's condition, at the bottom of the page she wrote: 'Wife: helpful DSM-5 BPD? Would like husband to be cared for by male staff.' "If she has a BPD, she'll be nosing around this file for sure," thought Carla. She added bronchopulmonary dysplasia in parenthesis under BPD, hoping it would satisfy the poor woman. It wouldn't help for her to know Carla suspected a full blown case of Borderline Personality Dysfunction, but it would help the other staff to know how to treat her.

She returned to the room with the orderlies. One of them pulled back the curtains and pushed in an empty bed, as the other pulled the bed containing the sleeping Randall into the hall. Carla dropped the patient file into the file holder at the end of the bed. "Mrs. Tapia, he'll have the MRI, and then they will take him to his room. I will meet you up there in about an hour."

Danielle looked horrified. "He's going to have to stay here?"

"At least a few nights, until he is on the mend. We'll talk about it after the MRI."

{Chapter 35}

The Devil Made Me Do It The First Time.

Danielle wasn't allowed to accompany her husband into the MRI facility. The orderlies instructed her to wait in the MRI waiting area, which was crowded with all kinds of people. She sat down next to a couple waiting to use the miracle of modern technology to see the man's kidney stones. They were preoccupied with their conversation, comparing the probability of the stones just passing against the possibility that the doctors would want to zap the stones with ultrasound. Either way, it wasn't something Danielle wanted to imagine. She looked around for another seat, but all of the empty ones were near children. A magazine rack on the wall caught her eye. It was the perfect opportunity to catch up on Cosmopolitan. "Hmmm, '*The secret of luscious lips*'... that looks interesting."

She had tried the sugar and water exfoliation method, it made them softer, yes, but it didn't plump them up. She had considered the surgical injections, but she didn't trust the technology. Lip liner was what she was doing now. It worked, but it was a pain in the ass, really. Reading about essential oils, cinnamon or peppermint was sensually very appealing... she remembered she had missed breakfast. A little oil of cinnamon sounded like a sweet roll without the carbs.

Hydration: yes, there is a water fountain. She got a drink and sat back down. Exercise: smiling and puckering up for a pouty kiss, she could do that. It seemed that twenty reps of each should be a good, so she started alternating between smiling and puckering as she turned the pages looking for other beauty ideas. She was on her 15th pouty pucker, when she self-consciously lifted her eyes from the magazine and realized she was being stared at by a man at the door, a man in a black shirt with a while clerical collar.

"Pastor Donisthorpe, how nice to see you!" Danielle said, setting the Cosmo aside. "What are you doing in this rat-trap?" She crossed the room to stand directly in front of him.

"Well, Danielle, I am making the rounds. Visiting the sick. Ministering to the needy. What are you doing here? Are you ailing?" he said solicitously. *Sniff.*

"I have never felt better, but Randall is having some kind of stress headache problem. I brought him into the ER this morning. I think he is going to be stuck here for a few days. I'll probably be hanging out by his room, if you want to.. uh.. come minister to me. I'm going to be freaking out on my own for a few days."

He momentarily puckered his lips into the masculine version of the pout, then said, "Yes. It's a small hospital. I'll find you. *Sniff.* Jesus loves you, don't ever forget that." And with that he was gone.

Navajo City Roadhouse Blog:

Community News

Sunday, November 20, 2011

Book mobile in Western Rio Arriba County?

The New Mexico State Library has informed me that if five card-holding patrons commit to using their services, they will create a bookmobile stop at Navajo City. Please contact me if you are interested. John says the Roadhouse will provide free coffee during bookmobile stops.

Journey of Trust

The Benedictine nuns of the Monastery of the Virgin of the Canyons have asked me to share a link to their newsletter. They are preparing to construct a guesthouse. They would like to share the adventure with community residents. They are inviting anyone to come and get some hands on experience of the Benedictine tradition. They have overnight accommodations for women, and the guest house will allow them to also have male guests. They have submitted grant requests to several foundations and expect that their project, which they call Journey of Compassion, will be funded for spring construction. More information is available at www.virginofthecanyons.org.

During the visit, they told me about Advent, the Christian holiday leading up to Christmas. This year it started on the 27th of October. It is the celebration of the pregnancy of the Virgin Mary. Advent has a color theme: purple—proving it's not just the color for crazy cat ladies. In the last week of Advent, the color changes to pink or particularly rose-pink.

The hanging of a wreath during Advent has a lot more symbolism than most people are aware of. It is made of evergreens to symbolize eternal life. It is a circle to remind us that God's mercy has no beginning or end. Its four candles (which should be white and purple or pink) symbolize the light of God coming into the world through his son, as well as symbolizing the time period between the prophet Malachi and the birth of Christ. Who knew it wasn't just a holiday decoration?

Valentino, the Lucky elk

Friends of the Monastery will also be glad to know that their resident elk, Valentino, survived the fall hunting season. The Monastery grounds have been posted with NO HUNTING signs and they are hoping no one kills their beautiful mascot.

Randall Tapia

The BLM district manager, Randall, collapsed from exhaustion earlier this week. His doctors have ordered him to stay away from his cell phone. Cards and friendly letters can be sent to him in care of San Juan Regional Medical Hospital. For business matters, contact the BLM.

Navajo City Roadhouse Blog:

Guido Bails

Saturday, December 10, 2011

I've got some bad news about Guido, so here it is. He cooked for a good part of the summer and fall. Kind of a crotchety cook, the kind that gets pissy if you take an order for eggs after 11 A.M. so he usually had the afternoon shift. But yesterday, he was supposed to do Mary's morning shift because the weekends have been so slow.

At 11:15 A.M. Jonah the water-hauler from Crownpoint came in and placed an order. Jonah is one of our super-loyal customers. It is the same identical order he places every single day that he is out here on the job: three eggs over easy, pancakes, and ham. Penny turned the order in to Guido who had no other meals in preparation. There were no other customers at the time. After a while Penny went back to check how the order was coming. Guido wasn't in the kitchen and the order hadn't been started, so she just cooked it up. After Jonah was chowin' down on it, she went looking for Guido. He was nowhere to be found. She went and looked in his room since he was staying in the guest room out back. All of his stuff was gone. He had packed up his backpack full of gear and hitchhiked out of here without so much as a see-you-later.

The boss says it was because he and Guido had been discussing philosophy and the boss said that people basically are motivated by money whether or not they admit it. Guido was adamantly and categorically against the profit-motive. However, we all noticed that he didn't give back any of his paychecks when he left. We figure, based on how many weeks he worked and the fact that he never spent a dime, he was carrying about $3,000.

Anyway, poor Penny! There she was just before the lunch rush with no cook. I would have collapsed in a dead faint at that, but nope. She just put on an apron and did both jobs. What a waitress!!!!
Yours,
Aletta Ramsden

Navajo City Roadhouse Blog:

Quandary

Monday, December 12, 2011

Well, I have been in a real quandary since yesterday. Something happened and I don't know whether or not to tell the boss. It's really a big dilemma for me.

The boss decided the computer in the employee apartment was better than the one we had running the credit card machine, which has been acting up lately, so he asked me to exchange them. My qualification to fix the problem is simply that since I have a blog, I must be a computer whiz. Which means you must be a real nerd to be reading this blog!

We normally have the main computer display the photos on the hard drive as the screensaver. We like to keep photos of good customers, tasty meals, beautiful sunsets, or happy waitresses popping up all day.

Anyway, part of the assignment was to get any photos the cook left behind off the desktop. So I ran a search over the hard drive for any image files, hoping to just find and delete them. There were 476 images in the temporary storage and I made the mistake of clicking on one.

Geez! I think it was some kind of transvestite porno stuff, but I didn't stick around to analyze it too carefully. No amount of analysis was needed to determine it was anatomically a male despite how it was dressed. Yikes! I clicked on a couple of other files in the temp folder and they all came up equally trashy so it wasn't just an accidental foray into a porno site. Yikes! Suddenly even touching the keyboard was too creepy. I deleted the contents of the folder and emptied the trash. Let's just say that there are some things you really don't want to have to see.

So, now the dilemma—do I tell the boss about this? Give me some advice.

Yours,
Aletta Ramsden

{Chapter 39}

Lakota Legends

"Grandpa, Tina said you were a medicine man."

"No, little one, if I was a medicine man, I would be like Doctor Bob. Medicine is a cure for sick or wounded people, in our language we call this *pejuta*. So a Lakota doctor is called a *pejuta wacasa*."

"Is Dr. Bob a *pejuta wacasa?*"

"No, he is a white man, so we call him a *wasica wakan*, a white doctor. I am a *wicasa wakan*; do you hear the difference in the words? *Wacasa ... wicasa.* Do you hear the difference?"

The little girl nodded and asked, "What is *wakan*?

"Oh child, you ask difficult questions! *Wakan* is what is inside of things that makes them what they are. Every object in the world has a spirit and the power of that spirit is *wakan*. You have some *wakan* in you; the spirit beings put it there with your families help."

"I might have told you about the spirit beings before ... do you remember?"

The little girl nodded again and said, "Yes, they were never born and can never die. The sun is one and the sky is another. They are magic and they can help us. All of them together make *Wakan Tanka*."

"You remember well! Now, what I do is help the spirit beings move the *wakan* to where it is needed."

"Grandpa, will you tell me a story?"

I could tell you about the beginning of time, when the only thing that existed was rock. No sky, no sun, no water ... just a very big rock named Inyan. All the *Wakan Tanka* was inside of Inyan. But Inyan got lonely, so he tried to create our lovely planet, Maka, the Mother Earth, out of himself. He squeezed out his blood to make the water. Now he was dried and hard, he had given most of his *wakan* away to the water. Maka wasn't strong enough to control all of the *wakan,* so she created the sky. The sky didn't want all the wakan so it created the sun and the wind. The sun was

146

strong and was able to hold much of the wakan, and that is how it became the leader of the spirit beings. That is how the world came into being, all the spirit beings created other spirit beings until the world was full."

"Grandpa, tell me the story about the rabbits."

"Okay, little one, but you have to get in your bed to listen. Get in your bed and close your eyes to help you imagine. I am going to turn off the light.

"In the olden days, people could talk to animals and animals could talk to people. People could turn into animals and animals could turn into people. The earth was not quite finished. The spirit beings were still creating things.

"In these far-gone days, lived a rabbit. He was a good-natured rabbit, always happy, always helpful.

"One day he was walking down a trail when he found a little lump of blood. It was like jelly inside of a clear plastic ball, only tiny, the size of a pea. No one ever found out where it came from, but the rabbit was interested. The rabbit started rolling his tiny ball of blood with his nose, then he kicked it with his foot, then he rolled it down a hill. He pushed it with his paws.

"The little lump of blood began to change as the spirit of motion, Takuskan-skan, made it come alive. It formed the stomach first, then the arms and legs, the heart began to beat, and soon it was a tiny little boy. The rabbit was surprised at what had happened, but he decided to take the little boy home with him.

"He named him '*We-ota-wichasha*', which means Much-Blood Boy, but later the boy was called Rabbit Boy. The rabbit took the boy to his wife and together they became a family, for they loved Rabbit Boy as if he were their own son. They dressed him in a beautiful buckskin shirt all decorated with beads and porcupine quills.

"One day, when Rabbit Boy was almost fully grown, the old father rabbit took him aside and said, "Son, I must tell you that you are not what you think you are - a rabbit like me. You are a human. We love you and we hate to let you go, but you must leave and find your own people."

Carl Klinkett looked at his granddaughter's sleeping face. As he left, he closed the door quietly behind him.

{Chapter 40}

One Person and One Package at a Time

Dog bites were an expected occurrence in his line of work, but the Rottweiler charging around the corner looked like it could do a lot more than bite. The facts of the situation flashed through his mind. He knew this dog's name was Arnold and that his owner's name was Debbie Holmes. He knew that she ordered books from Amazon regularly and received small parcels from Nuts.com occasionally. He did not know if there was any hope of not being bitten. He pulled a dog biscuit from his pocket and used his happiest sounding tone of voice to say "Good boy, Arnold!" Arnold stopped and sat on his haunches, waiting for Carl to throw the biscuit.

Carl breathed with relief, tossed the biscuit and then commanded Arnold to heel. The massive dog quickly moved in on the right side of the UPS driver and accompanied him to the porch, where Carl pushed the parcel from Amazon through the dog door on the bottom of the front door. Carl asked Arnold to sit again and handed him another biscuit as the canine complied.

Another disaster averted, the delivery driver jumped back into his boxy brown delivery truck, and checked the address of the next delivery. Bettina Chee was getting her monthly parcel from the Puritan Vitamin Company. As he turned on to Llano Street and stopped in front of her house, he thought for a moment about his mother and how much Bettina looked like her, but how the spry and lively Bettina never acted like his perennially depressed mother, who had committed suicide at the age of fifty-four.

As he stepped down from the truck, his mind raced through everything that had happened since he last saw his mother.

Ultimately, everyone who learned of his mother's demise had asked him how and why. 'How' was an overdose of barbiturates and 'why' was just as easy. She grew up in the hopeless atmosphere of the Pine Ridge Reservation. Suicide was common among her peers. It was statistically expected that at least one of her three children would kill themselves, and his sister had obliged the statisticians after a winter of little snow and much wind. Carl knew that the wind could suck the *wakan* right out of one's soul.

When he applied for a job at UPS, he had no real hope of even getting a response from them, so he was surprised when they offered him a route. At first he worked in Sioux Falls, and then he was transferred to Minneapolis, where he met Tammy, a young college student in the Department of Education, who soon became his wife. The UPS culture was demanding. He learned to be accountable. Tammy and Carl started their family after she graduated. They moved to Aztec, New Mexico in 1987.

Then in 1991, he fell into his own vortex of depression. He refused to acknowledge the pain, but it gnawed at his guts until he felt nothing but hollow and aching. The color left his world and the only thing he could sense was grayness. He stuck to the crutch of a strict routine and started self-medicating with gin and tonic. Alcohol helped keep him quiet and isolated. It was a wall to keep Tammy from seeing his true pathetic face. Suddenly, he understood that his mother had responded not selfishly, as he had long thought, but rather in the urgency of excruciating psychic pain. Suicide seemed like the best option for him too.

But the spirit beings had other plans; they botched his attempt and demanded that he explain why he was straying away from his true purpose. He was ashamed and had no answer other than to say "I will do better from now on." He awakened in a pool of vomit, knowing that his destiny was to walk a spiritual path, to be a holy person. He was alive and he was changed.

As he reached the front steps of Bettina's house on Llano Street and strode across the porch, his mind let him return to the present.

Bettina was always at home so it was no surprise that she met him at the front door. She scribbled her name on the electronic tablet and thanked him for the delivery. She pressed a dollar tip into his hand. He thanked her and told her it would be donated to his suicide prevention project. She smiled.

His project funded the purchase of custom made snow globes from Bulgaria. He kept one wrapped and ready in his personal gear bag. He had learned as a *wicasa wakan* to sense people's psychic energy level. He performed a ritual to transfer additional *wakan* into the little globe, so when he found someone who was sinking into depression, suddenly, without warning, they would receive a package from an anonymous friend. When first opened, the globe appeared to contain a small brown bunny in a field of snow, but when shaken, it was a leaping and kicking rabbit frolicking in the snowfall. Thus far, Carl had lowered the suicide rate of San Juan County by twenty percent.

{Chapter 41}

Burrito Queen

Aletta loaded the dishwasher with the last of the lunch plates, then she sorted the silverware by type and loaded it. She flipped the toggle switch and listened to the water spraying inside the machine. John was scraping the hamburger residues from the flat deck before it was allowed to cool down.

"How is it working out for you to have to cook in the afternoons?" Aletta asked him.

"I like coming over here, and this month is okay, but I really can't be doing this during tax season. This place doesn't quite support itself. If I don't keep my tax practice up, we'll be in deep trouble by February," he replied.

"Are you going to advertise for a cook?"

"I've thought about that, but I don't know what to do yet. Things have a way of working out around here in ways I never expected."

Suddenly the radio was broadcasting the loud and obnoxious rantings of the half-drunk hillbilly announcer starting his afternoon show. "Ugh!" sighed Aletta. "Mojo Nixon, the self proclaimed booger-eating moron. I think I'll change the station lest any innocent people come in and are exposed to his profanity."

John laughed. "Hey, he did write a pretty good song about Elvis. *Elvis is Everywhere*. So ol' Mojo has some kind of redeeming qualities, but, yes, please do change the station. Speaking of Elvis, have you seen Duane Hutton lately?"

"The Elvis impersonator? Yes, he usually comes by about three-thirty or so. He seems to have avoided the layoffs. Have you ever got to see his show?" Aletta asked.

"No, but one time he came in while 'In the Ghetto' was playing and suddenly he was lip-synching and dancing on the bar. That was a great show!" the owner smiled.

The waitress put her hand on her hip. "He told me he has a high-collar white jump suit with gold brocade for his shows. I told him he ought to pay the extra money to get one in fire-retardant Nomex material so he could wear it in the oil field. His work clothes just don't do him justice." They both laughed.

"You wanna have a plate of enchiladas with me for lunch?" asked John.

They were sitting at the bar eating flat-layered cheese enchiladas with red chile when the cowbell clanked. A large heavy set woman with a strawberry blonde braid down her back stepped in, trailed by a thin man in a cowboy hat. Smiling, they sat down at the bar counter.

Aletta sat two glasses of water down in front of them and held out a pair of menus. "Would you like to see a menu?"

"Well, actually, we come to see about a job. Carl Klinkett, the UPS driver, said that you all were looking for a cook. My name is Nicky and I have a lot of experience in all kinds of food service. We're from Oklahoma and I used to manage a restaurant there. We come down here and WIllie got a job with the Cabot ranch building some fence, but that doesn't seem like it's going to last the winter. And besides, we are living in our camper trailer and so I really don't have anything to do all day," the woman replied.

John just stood up and shook the woman's hand. "Nicky, you are in the right place at the right time. Now that you have a job, what would you and Willie like for lunch?"

***

That afternoon, Willie pulled their camper trailer off the Cabot Ranch and tucked it in the backlot of the Roadhouse under a juniper while John showed Nicky the essentials of Roadhouse cuisine. If the absence of sweet tea and the paucity of gravy concerned her at the time, she didn't show it. All the important standard Roadhouse recipes were written in magic marker on the back wall of the kitchen, big enough for the cook to see from anywhere in the room. She would take over Guido's slot and be responsible for preparing the sauces the Roadhouse was becoming almost famous for. With her apron on, a spatula in her right hand, and her left hand on her hip, no one doubted she could cook.

***

By Sunday, Aletta was expressing her doubts to her employer. "Nicky doesn't

152

understand anything about New Mexico food. She is making gravy instead of chile sauce. All the Mexican plates are coming out smothered in white gravy. She throws on a few slices of jalapenos and that's it! No green chile except on the green chile cheeseburgers where she is forced to put it on. Way too much cheese melted over everything and french fries on every plate. It is embarrassing to carry out an order for Mexican food since she's been here. You have to talk to her, Mr. Irick. She won't listen to me."

"Calm down, Aletta. Mexican plates are a lot for a person to have to learn that has never eaten them. I really need to make it work because I can't afford to cook here instead of tending to my practice." Then John paused for a few seconds, thinking: "What if we get Mary and Nicky to trade shifts? I think that would work. Nicky could learn to manufacture burritos. Mary has the Mexican food figured out now. I'll call her and see if that would work for her."

"Oh, and Aletta, I almost forgot to tell you this. About those photos on the computer, I don't think Guido ever even plugged it in. I'm pretty sure it was that Australian couple that were here last summer. They were here when I first bought the place. Did you ever meet them?"

"No, it was before my time."

"Well," he said, "they were a little quirky."

{Chapter 42}

La Mujer

Sea level is two feet higher in the Philippines than it is off the western coast of Peru. No one suspected this until quite recently. Sea level was sea level. Period. Then in 1992, the U.S. and French space agencies got together to do some ocean mapping by satellite. Lo and behold, now they were in a pickle. Elevation suddenly got a lot more complicated. Globally rising sea levels added to the confusion. Most countries simply pegged what they considered the average sea level and called it good. It is not the same in all places.

Imagine a large rectangle sitting over the Pacific Ocean. The west side touches Australia, the east side touches Peru. The northern side of the rectangle skims across the ocean at the equator, the base crosses back from Tasmania to Tierra del Fuego, streaking just north of the shores of Antarctica. Turn your rectangle into wind, nice strong winds. Let the wind push the waves it creates. Push the water to Micronesia! Oh, see how it piles up. Sun-warmed ocean water flowing to the Philippines!

Excuse me, but any idiot knows you can't pile up water. Water will simply seek its own level, so along the bottom of the ocean, protected from the driving wind, water flows back toward South America. The water along the bottom of the ocean is cold. This cold water comes welling up along the coast of Peru carrying the deep sea nutrients of sunken organisms; millions of tiny organisms you might not normally be thinking about, such as phytoplankton and diatoms. This upwelling is pushed northward along the coasts of Chile and Peru by the cool dry winds that have returned across the southernmost Pacific, forming the Humboldt Current. Nutrient rich, cold, and only mildly salty, this ocean water creates the most productive ecosystem on the planet. A perfect place to fish.

Much ado has been made of disruptions of these cycles. When the wind currents slow down, the water quits piling up, the cold water stays still at the bottom of the pond, and the surface heats up, then the clouds start building over the mid-Pacific and heading for the driest desert on the planet, which is, by no coincidence, adjacent to the world's greatest fishing hole. They call such an event El Niño. They love to talk about this "boy child" as it is literally translated. El Niño does this, El Niño does that, everything is all about El Niño! What the hell?!

Let's talk about La Niña instead. She didn't even get a name except as an afterthought and she only gets a description of being opposite to the disruptive 'boy child'. Isn't that a perfect metaphor for the kind of gender bias that is running our world? I propose that the readers of this book should collectively petition the government to take a stand on the problem and rename the energized super-cycle of the Pacific circulation system "La Mujer"!! For it is no little girl. It is a fully functioning feminine archetype. The Woman. Henceforth, we will use this improved epithet.

We need a definition of La Mujer. Well, go back to our little rectangle and amp up those winds by several knots. Create a bigger warmer pile of warm water in Micronesia. It starts raining like crazy in Australia. Some of the water gets shunted over to the northern hemisphere, where it starts on the journey to Alaska. It starts raining like cats and dogs in Japan. It starts snowing like hell in Alaska. Canada gets blanketed. If the pressure systems are just right, it gets pushed as far south as the border between Colorado and New Mexico.

Weather Headlines from early November 2011:
- from the BBC: 2,000 People Cut Off by Australian Floods
- from CNN: Bangkok Braces for Flooding by High Tides
- from USA Today: Snow, hurricane-force winds batter Alaska
- from the Denver Post: Wolf Creek Ski Area plans to open this weekend

Can you say "La Mujer"? *La Moo-hair!!*

155

{Chapter 43}

Leather Sniffers

Aletta lifted the small plastic bag full of garbage from the waste bin and shook out a new plastic bag to replace it. The sink and toilet were now spotless. Cleaning the restrooms at the end of the day wasn't a bad job in her opinion because all the supplies were stored under the sink. It was simple.

The next chore, dusting and wiping down the convenience store area was a lot more work because so many things had to be moved to remove any spills, finger-prints, or the special kind of oily dust that comes with deep-fat fryers working all day long. She carried a rag in a bucket of soapy water along with a feather duster to the front of the store and began cleaning.

There was a new product to dust. Two used saddles were on display by the front window. Willy had talked John into buying them on speculation. Actually, they had come with a horse named Ace. The plan was to sell the horse and saddles. John provided the money, Willy would provide the training and find a buyer. They would split the profit.

The response from her customers surprised her. Aletta was unaware of the oil-field men being particularly interested in horses, but hardly any of them walked past the saddles without touching them, feeling the leather, or resting their hands on the saddle horns. There were even some men who got their coffee and stood by the saddle display to chat. It definitely seemed to be an attraction.

The back door squeaked, creaked, and clunked open. She heard the Oklahoma twang of Nicky and Willy coming in to cook their dinner. They stomped their feet at the back door to shake off the snow, then Nicky turned on the light and started getting some pans out.

Willy walked into the front, where Aletta was finishing her chores.

"How is Miss Aletta doing this evenin'?"

"Things are going good, Willy. How is Ace doing?"

"Me and Ace are goin' to the mountains tomorrow. We're goin' to Wolf Creek to do some skijorin," the cowboy said.

"You are taking the horse skiing?" asked the puzzled waitress.

"No, ma'am, '*skee-jor-een*'," he said carefully, and then continued. "It's where a guy on a horse pulls a guy on skis. You try to go real fast. They got to go over ski-jumps, avoid runnin' into things, and then grab the rings. Just like water-skiing but on snow with a horse instead of a boat. You need a fast horse, and Ace is the one to do it. Me and Ace are gonna come home with some prize money. A fella' needs a little green in his pocket, don't you agree, Miss Aletta?"

"What's the purse? How much could you win?" asked the waitress.

"Well, you have to split the purse with the skier. The grand prize is $1000, so I'll have to settle for $500."

"Do you have a skier lined up? Who is on your team?"

"No, I'm goin' to get over there and find the bravest one I can find, because we are gonna be goin' really fast. This is a timed event. I even put special traction shoes on ol' Ace so he don't slip on the ice, and I been trainin' him to start on a dead run. Ace is zero to sixty in three seconds. After the race, we can stick around and people will pay to try a little slower skijorin'. Even if we don't win, we'll come out ahead. And I might find someone that wants to buy Ace once they see him in action. I bet I can get a good price up there. What do you think, Miss Aletta, is it goin' to work?"

"Sounds like it will be fun, Willy." She went to the sink to dump the bucket, and then twisted the rag to squeeze out the water. Nicky came around the stove carrying two plates covered with burgers and fries. She greeted the Aletta as she passed her to sit at the bar-counter. The waitress sighed, "I'm done for the day, but I'll come sit with you for a few minutes before I go."

"That'd be real nice. We done went to town this afternoon," Nicky said as they sat down." I'll tell you, it was crazy down there." She went on to describe the stores where they had stopped and how it wasn't snowing once they got to the bottom of Manzanares Canyon. Aletta pulled out some napkins and silverware and rolled them as they talked about the customers who had stopped in and if there were any prospective buyers for the saddles.

Their plates were clean when Nicky looked Aletta in the eye and said, "I think I need to tell you this because no one else will. Penny don't want to say nothin' about it, but she hates the way you roll silverware. She unrolls any you rolled and re-rolls it ever mornin'. I watch her do it most mornings. I don't know why ..."

Willy excused himself to go start sweeping and mopping. Aletta looked at the roll she held in her hand. She looked at the pile she had just created.

As Nicky got up to carry the empty plates to the sink, Aletta fished around in the back of the pile until she found one that Penny had done. She set hers and Penny's side by side and studied them. She noted no significant differences. She partially unrolled each one, comparing how they were tucked and folded. Penny's were perhaps slightly tighter, but not really different.

Aletta picked up the cell phone and dialed Penny's number. "Penny? ... Would you like me to roll the silverware a different way? ... No, I haven't been drinking; it's just Nicky said you were having to re-roll the silverware I rolled."

Aletta heard the back door squeak and clunk as Nicky left.

"You don't know what I am talking about? Well okay, but if you do want me to do it a different way, I will. You don't have to worry about telling me stuff. I am open to learning new ways of doing things. Okay, well I am glad that you are okay with it. Sorry to call you so late, but I was worried."

"*What the hell was that about?*" Aletta wondered, but Nicky was gone.

Willy had rolled up his sleeves to sweep and mop. She saw that his arms were tattooed almost to the wrist, but it wasn't very pleasing artwork. "*Someone had only been practicing when they did that,*" she thought.

Willy noticed her looking at him and smiled. "This is the institutional way of cleaning floors," he said as he moved the bar stools away from the counter. "First you sweep around the edges, and then you use a bigger broom to do the center of the floors. It saves a lot of time to do it that way."

Suddenly she realized that Willy had spent some time in prison. Where else would you get a crappy tattoo on *both* arms? Where else would you learn to clean floors the institutional way? Where else would you have trained the two-hundred mustangs, that Willy claimed to have trained? Hutchinson Kansas Penitentiary had a wild horse training program. She suspected he probably got there smoking pot because she had noticed the smell on him on several occasions. This didn't seem like the time or place to ask about it, so she said her goodbye, picked up her purse and exited through the squeaking creaking back door.

{Chapter 44}

Navajo City Roadhouse Blog:

Christmas Eve at the Roadhouse

Saturday, December 24, 2011

I got here before daylight and started perking coffee, mixed up some of Stephanie's recipe for fried bread dough, and put the stuff in the bread maker to make regular bread. The cook is in the kitchen grinding up some lamb to make Navajo City Tacos for to-day's special. They are playing a mixture of old country favorites and Christmas songs on the radio. The traffic is light out there on Highway 64. A customer came in at 8:15 and bought a breakfast burrito and a can of V-8 juice. Some folks called to see if we would be open so they could make their breakfast plans. I pulled out all the letters to spell out NAVAJO CITY TACOS on the marquee out by the highway and then just about froze my fingers off putting them on the sign. There's a nice fire in the woodstove, so the pain was only temporary.

I wonder where Rita Mae is today. She might be up in the Canadian northwoods, or she might be wandering around Asia. Things aren't gonna be so quiet once Rita Mae gets back. The parking lot will be full and trucks will be lined up along the road shoulder. The coffee pot won't have time to cook its freshness away. She taught me everything I know about being a waitress, but I've got a long way to go to pick up her charisma. I hope she finds this blog and lets us know when she's coming back.

When John Irick bought this place there was a banner out front advertising some beer company. The sign had a skinny blonde in a cowboy hat and some skimpy outfit serving a beer. John took it down right away. I suppose it was false advertising. None of us waitresses are that foxy. Well, Naomi is kind of a babe, in her own way. She likes to show off, so even when it's zero outside she is showing some flesh. I expect someday to hear that she died of frostbite. Penny and I are never gonna freeze to death. I'm wearing long underwear under my jeans. We are sensible-shoes sort of women.

The cook just came out and told me that the meat grinder died. Hmmm. Brand new, made in China. John bought it at Charter Freight. Junk. He should have known better to buy something from those people.

Well, a couple of people just came in so I better sign off.
Merry Christmas,
Aletta Ramsden

{Chapter 45}

Time to Talk

The old man was asleep on the barstool. It was not unusual for Placido Lucero to fall asleep during his stop at the Roadhouse, but Aletta didn't expect him to show up when there was snow on the ground. *He probably had a lonely Christmas*, she assumed, knowing that he didn't have a family. But the truth was he was just on the last stop of his busy holiday schedule. He had been celebrating Christmas with all of his friends and he was now so stuffed with empanadas, posole, turkey, enchiladas, biscochitos, mashed potatoes, cranberry sauce, tamales, and carne adovada that he could hardly walk. The french fries in front of him were just not too interesting.

The myth of Placido Lucero was that he was super-rich, but actually he was land-poor. Upkeep on his ranch took all of his money and time. At ninety-two years old, he was still running cattle on 3,744 acres. If he sold it, he might be wealthy, but he had no plans to do so. The myth was also that he was lonely, but he was a pleasant-tempered fellow with a strong New Mexican accent and he was never one to shy away from adventure, so he had a lifetime of experiences he could tell if you got him in the mood and asked the right questions. Aletta, like his many other friends, loved it when he stopped to visit and she had time to chat, but after fifteen minutes of conversation the old man would close his eyes and drift off. She thought he might be dreaming about when he was young and strong and could still ride those horses that he liked to talk about.

He might have been dreaming when the cowbell clanked and Pamela Anderson walked in. He jolted awake and watched the two women greet each other.

"I needed to get out of the office for my mental health, so I arranged to take a long lunch to come up here," explained the archaeologist. "Those four walls of my office make me a little claustrophobic some days." Pam turned her eyes to Placido, considering where to sit. He smiled in a friendly way, so she sat down beside him.

"Do you two know each other? Placido Lucero ... Pamela Anderson. Pamela works for the Forest Service, she's an archaeologist. Placido runs cattle on his ranch. It's this piece of land that starts behind the Roadhouse and goes to the San Juan

River, then west down to Turley."

"Oh, yes, I know of the ranch, and I am very pleased to meet its owner. Your ranch must have a lot of archaeological resources on it. People would have been living there, especially the Navajos."

The old man answered with a green-chile accent, "Yes, you can find many potsherds around there. We used to find whole pots when I was a kid, but I haven't seen one of them for a long time. Some archaeologists came one time to survey an old ruin, but I wouldn't let them dig on my ranch. I didn't want the oil companies to be digging around, so I just have one rule for everyone: no digging unless I am watching."

"Are there any caves?" Pamela asked.

The old man thought for a while before he replied. "I think there might be, but they'd be up in the rocks where the cows don't go, so I never bothered to look."

"I'm working on a project on the forest and BLM lands east of your ranch to examine the caves for archaeological materials. We are not removing materials, just inventorying them. If you didn't mind, I would very much like to examine the caves on your ranch, Mr. Lucero."

"I'd like to know what's in them too. If you found a Spanish treasure, would it be mine?" he asked. "I always secretly thought there could be a treasure up there, but I was too lazy or too busy to look. Bring over the papers that say whatever you find is still my property and, yes, then you can look -- without digging. But, now, I better go before my eyes decide to take another nap. They have to help me drive home. Come by my place next week and we'll go drive around and look at things. Unless the snow is too deep—don't come if the snow is too deep."

As he made his way out the door, Pam ordered chicken enchiladas with green chile for lunch and Aletta handed the order over to Mary. "I would have made a cake if you had called me. I've been missing our cake time," said the waitress.

"You've been baking the cakes? I didn't know you made them yourself, Aletta. How nice! Now I really feel special," said the archaeologist.

"Okay, I need some government gossip. It gets pretty thin out here when the forest closes for the winter," Aletta said as she poured herself a cup of coffee. "What's been happening in your world?"

"Aletta, you should know that nothing happens in government offices between the solstice and the New Year. The Christmas party is about it. Everyone brought their families. It was nice. You know who is doing well is Erin Tate's family. Last year at this time, they didn't look very good, but this year they were dressed up. He got his son into a special therapy program. Have you ever met his son?"

"Autistic? ... uh, Kevin?" Aletta dug into her memory bank.

"Yes, well, he is starting to talk. I guess the time he spends in therapy has allowed Denise to actually have a life of her own. She looks a lot better."

"My desk has stayed pretty clean. I went down to the State Historic Preservation Office to dig around in the old files for a couple of days before Christmas."

"What are you working on? Not the freedom construct?" asked the waitress.

"Oh no," replied Pam. "Freedom is not a good topic for December. No, this has to do with my favorite topic."

"Feathers!" smiled Aletta.

"Yes, I was looking to see if there are any Thunderbirds depicted in petroglyphs or pictographs in the Dinetah."

"You are not talking about the car ... some kind of special bird petroglyph?"

"Yes. It's a very widespread symbol. According to legends, the Thunderbird is a powerful spirit in the form of a large bird. Usually people interpret it to be a great Eagle or even a Condor. Thunderbird was used as an allegory for certain forces of nature in the natural order such as wind, thunder, lightning, etc. As the legend goes, lightning flashes from its beak and eyes, and the beating of its wings creates the thunder."

"Isn't that like a universal military symbol of strength? Is it on the dollar bill?" asked the waitress.

The cowbell clanked and Carl Kinkett stepped in carrying several parcels. "Anyone missing some Christmas presents?" The ladies laughed.

He set them on the counter and itemized them as he checked them off the list on his electronic tablet. "Sandy Poole, two packages, Michael Cabot, Devil Spring Ranch, and one for Miss Penny. Okay, scribble your name here, Aletta," he said handing her the tablet. She took the stylus and wrote her name neatly on the line.

"You both know each other?" Aletta asked. Pam nodded.

Carl said, "Pamela Anderson, the parrot lady that works for the Forest Service. I deliver vast quantities of birdseed to her address! Little did I realize that both of you are friends."

Pam said, "And I didn't realize that all the people between here and the forest get their parcels at the Roadhouse. Come join us Carl, we are talking about my favorite topic."

"Birds?" he guessed. "I have a mandated 10 minute break that I would love to spend with the two of you. It's 2:35 now. Tell me about these birds."

"I was just talking about Thunderbird symbolism. It's a little bit different than the symbolism of the eagle in the Anglo culture. In the European mind, eagles tend to be associated with supreme power and authority. The 1792 Congress made it a national emblem because it related to freedom. What about the Lakota? Do you have the Thunderbird?"

"Yes, it's called *Wakịnyạn,* which combines *wakan,* meaning sacred, and *kiya,* meaning winged. There are four types: black, blue, red, and yellow. They are permanently at war with the *Unktehi,* who cause flooding and contaminate water, as well as the *Waziya,* who use snow and ice to cause famine and disease. The *Wakịnyạn* have voices of thunder, but they are the ones who created the grass. If you speak to or dream of the *Wakịnyạn,* you go a little crazy, but you become magical." The UPS driver looked at the archaeologist.

She said, "Well, out here in the west, the Thunderbirds are much less helpful. The Navajo Thunderbird was simply a monster who created thunder when it flapped its wings and disoriented its victims with blinding rain and its shiny beak—nothing noble about this bird. In fact, one of the legends says it was born of some perverse sexual practices that came about when the Navajo men and women went their separate ways."

"The men and women split up?" Aletta asked.

"Yes, the men were on one side of the San Juan River and the women stayed on the other. It was kind of a pissing match to show who needed whom the most. The women ultimately won, but while they were split up, perverse sexual practices created all kinds of monsters. One of the ladies was pleasuring herself with a feather, or maybe a clump of feathers, and nine months later gave birth to the Thunderbird.

"The Thunderbird just did all the things that come natural to birds of prey, but the problem was that the prey was human. So ... it had a nest on top of Shiprock where it fed humans to its chicks after it had dropped them from the sky to render them harmless. The Thunderbird was finally destroyed by Nayenezgani, one of the Monster-slayers.

"Nayenezgani had taken a giant piece of intestine from the last monster he slew and he used it to trick the Thunderbird. He let the Thunderbird capture him, but when it tried to drop him, he dropped the intestine and held on to the bird by its feathers, or maybe he fell but landed safely. Either way, the bird picked up the snack and flew to its nest unknowingly carrying the Monster-Slayer. Nayenezgani fell into the nest of baby Thunderbirds and had to fight for his life to keep from being devoured. He stealthily broke the necks of the baby birds so that the parents would not be alerted. When the parents returned to the nest, he shot them with his lightning powered arrows. Then he turned the bodies of the Thunderbirds and their young into all of the species of birds in the world today."

"Wow!" said the waitress. "I think I like the Lakota walking-yawn better, if I have to come face to face with a Thunderbird. Hey, Carl, do you want a cup of coffee or something?"

"Yes, but I better make a pit-stop first," he said indicating the restroom. Aletta poured a cup and refreshed her and Pam's cups. As Carl returned, he stopped in front of the round-up photo the advocates had presented to the Roadhouse. Studying it, he asked, "Where is this? I don't know all of these men, but there's Shep and his sons, Aaron Shauner, Randall Tapia, Sephra Brooks. Is that Sam Filkins?"

"Yeah, "replied the waitress. "That was taken the afternoon that Aaron was murdered. The wild horse advocates gave it to us to display as kind of a memorial."

"This horse ... I have seen him somewhere recently. He is quite distinctive with that white forelock." said the UPS driver. Both women got up and walked over to stand with Carl and study the photo. The rearing buckskin stallion was in the center of the photo. It was not clear why the horse might be rearing.

"He *is* distinctive," Aletta agreed. "If you saw him, it's because he got out during the murder. He's up there in the wild horse territory running free again."

"I saw him on the Navajo reservation about 2 weeks ago. The horse I saw looked exactly like this one," the UPS driver insisted.

"Get a photo of it next time so we can compare," Aletta suggested.

"I will if I see it again. First, I have to remember where the heck I might have seen it. I've been a few places since then!"

"So Carl, do you have any theories about who might have murdered Aaron? Has your finger on the pulse of this community given you any hints?" asked Pam.

"Well, I saw these other men in the photo; they were staying at the Days Inn. They must have been the contractor's crew. A lot of Shauner's friends sank into a kind of depression since then, but a few people started giving off the energy of a cornered animal. They probably didn't do it, but they might know something about it."

"Like who?" asked the archaeologist.

"I don't want to accuse anyone, but maybe when I have time, we can review the case," said Carl.

"You know that they are treating this as a terrorism case? That is what I learned from the advocates. It's the FBI and no habeas corpus. They have pulled out all the stops on the investigation," said Aletta. "They will probably give the perpetrator the death penalty."

She continued, "Which reminds me, Pam, you didn't give me the BLM gossip. How is Randall Tapia?"

"They put him on leave," replied the archaeologist.

"His wife suspended delivery of mail and parcels for a month, while they go to Mexico on vacation," said the UPS driver. He looked at his wristwatch, "Hey, my time is up. Gotta go! I'll catch that cup of coffee next time."

The cowbell clanked goodbye.

{Chapter 46}

Whatcha Gonna Do with a Cowboy?

Willy picked up a pile of blue jeans waiting in his chair to be washed and threw it on the sink countertop. "This place is too damn small, Nicky. It wasn't bad in the summer when my chair could be outside under the awning, but crammed in here like this ... a man needs room to move, don'cha think so?"

She turned the page of the Western Horseman magazine she was reading and looked up at him. "At least you got a chair. I'm stuck on the bed, which gets damn old, damn quick at my age."

"Well, Nicky, on the bed is just where I like to keep you!" he teased her. They both smiled. He kicked a dog food dish and his cowboy boots out of the way to pull the space heater closer to his seat. "You warm enough?"

"Oh, God, yes! I'm hot back here. I might have to take off some clothes ... at least my down jacket," she teased back. "No, really, I think the dogs keep it warm back here. I'm fine."

"Well, look at that, Nicky, that fellow on the front cover of your magazine looks just like me," said the cowboy.

She closed the front cover to look at it, keeping her page marked with her fingers. "Kind of, yes, but that man has a bigger nose. Most people wouldn't notice, but I would never mistake him for you."

"Well, it sure don't hurt to have a heart-warmin' picture of *me* on the front cover of the biggest horse magazine in the country. It's gonna be in the back of people's minds that they seen me somewhere and I was real nice. This is good luck, Nicky, don'cha think so?"

"Hey," she replied. "There is a good article on King and Poco Bueno in here. It says those horses were around in the 40's and 50's and they produced the most important bloodlines in the quarter horse industry. They bought King for $800 and

169

had to borrow the money to do it," she said.

"Doc O'Lena, Dry Doc, Doc Bar," said Willy. "All those horses come out of the Poco Lena line, didn't they? Hey, I had to borrow money a lot'a times to buy horses, but they never turned out like that. I wonder if they paid the man back the eight-hundred dollars?"

Nicky started turning pages. "There is another article on skijorin'. Oh, where did I see that ... here, page 30. It says that no skijorer is of sound mind. You need to remember that next time you go. They invented it in Finland and used reindeer. It was almost an Olympic sport. Let me read you this paragraph:

"Really, no skijorer is of sound mind. Skiers can hit 60 miles an hour slaloming behind a sprinting Quarter Horse. One misstep or lost ski edge, and they could go down hard. You'd think that would cause skijorers to practice, but one skier in Telluride, Colorado, when asked about how he prepared, said: 'I had a Bloody Mary.'"

Willy was excited. "The one I found didn't settle for Bloody Marys. He was drinkin' Speedballs ... that's a mix of Red Bull and vodka. He was fearless aw'right. You shoulda been there, Nicky. I was right about Ace. I got a good price plus the purse and I paid John back every nickel he loaned me to buy him. That was a good day!"

"There was also a letter to the editor about the article on mustangs in the October issue," she said. "The man had a Navajo Nation mustang he was sure proud of ... maybe that will help you get your mustangs adopted. How's that goin' anyway?" the woman asked.

"Not too good. I got people problems. Jim Brown is a pain in the ass. You know what I mean, Nicky?"

"What's he doing?" she asked.

"He won't leave my horses alone. He's messin' 'em up."

Nicky got really quiet thinking. Jim Brown owned the stable where Willy had taken the mustangs. Jim had taken a few as well. The Bureau of Land Management had a program with an outfit called the Mustang Heritage Foundation that paid people to train wild horses and get them adopted. Most of the horses gathered in the fall round-up were going to Mustang Camp, that place down Largo Canyon, but Willy and Jim had filled out the forms to become trainers. They could each take 4 horses at a time and get paid $750 per horse when they got them adopted. It was some nice temporary income if it worked.

Jim was a big landowner, owned some of the most valuable undeveloped property in the San Juan Basin. At 83 years old, he was still going strong. His eyesight was never good, but it didn't slow him down. He owned a prestigious boarding stable, but he had a soft spot in his heart for mustangs. He had much more economic potential than the Mustang Foundation in Nicky's opinion.

"Ain't he letting you keep them horses for free?" she asked.

"Not exactly, I have to keep his horses trimmed ever' month in trade for the pen he lets me use. I have to buy the hay, but his guys feed the horses twice a day and muck the pens. That don't sound like a bad deal, does it?"

"That's a good deal," she said. "What is he doing to mess 'em up?"

"He goes in and jest starts throwin' ropes on 'em. They get all worked up and they learn to run away from having a rope on 'em. That's kind of how the old timers would train ... jest git the horse used to it ... whatever horses needed to git used to. That stuff's been outdated for years. Now days, you give the horse a right answer for him to find and help him find it. There ain't no right answer to having a rope throwed on you. No horse is going to like that, now are they, Nicky?

"I tried asking him to leave them alone, and when that didn't work, I tried to teach him a little bit about modern ways of horse training, but that man ain't willin' to listen. He can't see across the corral to even know what the horse is doing," Willy looked depressed.

"Willy, those people have money. We gotta get along with them for our own good," she counseled.

"Wait, Nicky, I didn't tell you ever'thing yet. I was at the feed store and ran into Matt Parker, that school teacher from Fruitland, and the first thing he tells me is that Jim has been lettin' him and some other guys come train the mustangs with him. Jim is givin' lessons on how to be a cowboy with my mustangs!"

"Hell, that's not right," she said looking over the top of the magazine, "but I don't think the man got wealthy being especially considerate. That ain't how you get wealthy. Look, Willy, it's probably more important to get along with a wealthy person than train a couple of mustangs. It will pay off better. I don't think you should move your horses unless you find another facility with a rich owner. The blind ol' codger is just too good of a target."

"Well, I don't go too long without another good idea, Nicky. Maybe there is an opportunity to teach guys how to be cowboys ... Maybe that's where the money is? Do you think that might work?"

She responded by holding up her January edition of the Western Horseman. "That's what it's all about, darlin'."

{Chapter 47}

Leavin' On A Jet Plane

Carl Klinkett turned the key in the ignition and shut the UPS van off. He unfastened his seatbelt and sat back deeper in his seat. The plane hadn't arrived so he had time to consider whether he wanted to make any New Year's resolutions.

The highlight of 2011 had definitely been the family camping trip on horseback into the Weminuche Wilderness. Yes, they must make it an annual event. A goal for his work would be to actually take the lunch break the company mandated. This was turning out to be much harder than he anticipated, but the company was cracking down and writing up drivers who didn't have it in their logbooks, so he would force himself to take lunch. A goal for his health ... drink more water; he knew his kidneys would thank him. A spiritual goal ... now that was going to take some deep thinking. Perhaps he could find a mentor to help him see what he was missing? Open new realms to him ... but then he thought that if it was meant to be, the teacher would just appear—making that a goal for the year was counterproductive. Perhaps he should learn to play the flute and see where that took him? Not in the house; it would drive the family nuts. Maybe he should put more effort into talking to the animals ... that was going to be hard with his work schedule. Maybe the best he could do in that department was to get a parrot? Maybe company policy would allow him to have a parrot in the truck with him? When the weather allowed it ... no his truck was either too cold or too hot.

The plane he was waiting for was flying from Salt Lake City. Like the van that he was driving today, it belonged to the special elite branch of UPS, Urgent Services. Like all UPS drivers, Carl dressed up for Urgent Services deliveries. His uniform was spotless. His creases sharp. He had even shaved before he left the house this morning. Would they notice as he delivered the package? Well, they would certainly notice if he was sloppy. This New Year's Day delivery was costing Schlumberger a fortune, but he suspected that it was some item critical to drilling a gas well, so going without it was also costing them a fortune. He knew that standard drill rig rentals were more than $10,000 a day; the oil company couldn't let the rig stand idle more than absolutely necessary.

When UPS had asked for someone to volunteer for special duty on New Year's morning, Carl was the only driver that had no plans for the previous evening. Carl was possibly the only one who wouldn't have a hangover. He wondered if the men he would be taking this to were going to have hangovers.

The noise of the approaching aircraft, alerted him that it was about time to go to work. He pulled up his logbook and noted that he had taken one of his ten minute mandated breaks.

A car pulled into the parking lot. The driver got out quickly. Carl noticed that he didn't take time to lock the door. Another pick-up he assumed. He followed the man toward the terminal. The man was dressed in camouflage fatigues. "This looks like a very depressed hunter," thought Carl, but then he couldn't remember if it was hunting season or not.

The man, hearing the footsteps behind him, turned and Carl instantly recognized that it was the Calvinist preacher, David Donisthorpe.

"Good morning Pastor Donisthorpe. New Year's Day and a Sunday to boot, what could be better?"

The pastor forced himself to smile. "You obviously know me, but I don't remember your name. Are you in my congregation?"

"No, sir, I am not. I belong to a different faith. I'm Carl, the UPS driver."

"Oh, yes, *sniff*, the UPS driver. I see that now. Picking up packages on New Year's day, I didn't know your company did that."

"The Urgent Services Department delivers anytime and anywhere ... but it's expensive!" he laughed, but the other man did not respond. Carl slowed to turn into the Express Package service door.

"Well, I am going to Tahiti on vacation. I need to get away. *Sniff*. See, here are my tickets," the pastor said waving a ticket envelope. "Now, if you will excuse me," the pastor darted into the terminal building through the main entrance.

In reading the paperwork pertaining to the Urgent Delivery parcel, Carl saw that it contained a part for a Revolution Core RSS, whatever that was, and had been shipped from Provo, Utah last night at 7 P.M.. He estimated it would be delivered by 9 A.M. if he drove at the speed limit. Walking back across the parking lot he noticed that Pastor Donisthorpe was staring at him through the plate glass windows from the lobby of the terminal.

"That fellow needs a kicking rabbit delivery," he said to himself.

As he swung himself into the seat of his truck, he realized suddenly that the pastor was probably lying to him. He had no baggage. He wasn't dressed for Tahiti, it was Sunday morning, and there wouldn't be another plane for hours.

He glanced back in the mirror. The pastor was coming out the front door of the terminal, but Carl knew he didn't have time to find out what was really going on.

{Chapter 48}

The Baptism

Everything was in place. The gear was at the river. The car was parked with a note that said "*Gone to Tahiti.*"

He resented the nosy redskin and his happy talk, but at least the idiot had provided an opportunity to show the ticket off. Donisthorpe knew it would be a while before they would find his car. Then, he thought, they will find the note, and if they check deeper they will see the charge on the credit card for the ticket to Tahiti. He savored the idea that he was about to make a squeaky-clean getaway.

He turned west at the end of the road and walked on the little trail between the chainlink fence of the runway and the edge of the mesa. Although he had a good view of the town below, he felt like he was walking in a tunnel. He looked only at the trail immediately in front of him. He wished it were darker.

The little trail took him down the barren badland slope and past the back of some houses. His camo should keep him from being noticed. People will still be sleeping, he hoped. A dog barked and he hurried to get through the housing area.

He had to cross Highway 64 at the confluence of the La Plata and the San Juan Rivers. He waited in the shadows of some trees until he was sure no cars would be coming. He would have preferred to use the Animas River because of its association with the soul but that would have put him in the middle of Farmington. This was infinitely better. He followed the river bank around a lonely bend where the San Juan presses up against a rocky hill. The highway climbs the hill and leaves the river behind. A tawny sandstone cliff and a gray clay slope squeeze the river bank to the width of a foot trail.

His gear was stashed under a willow bush. He filled his pants and coat pockets with lead weights. He dragged two chains and a shotgun into the center of the river. The water was icy cold and waist-deep but he didn't notice. He used zip-ties to attach one of the chains to his clothing. The other chain he wrapped around his neck.

He sniffed one last time.

"Acts two, thirty-eight. I have repented of my sins and have accepted Jesus Christ as my personal Lord and Savior and believe by faith that I am about to be born again. I now desire to be obedient to the command of the Lord to be water baptized."

The shotgun blast echoed on the gray slopes.

The only witness was a coyote with a white forehead.

{Chapter 49}

Dream Catcher

"I dreamed that I was driving down Highway 64 to deliver a parcel; there were golden leaves falling from the trees. I could see the river, it was beautiful ... clear aqua-colored water running over giant boulders. I saw a man in water-colored camouflage dive into the river, but when he came back up to the surface, he was an otter. I wasn't driving. I was sitting in a cottonwood tree watching the otters play. The otter-man swam to the other bank where more otters were laying in the sun. Another otter ran forward and leaped on the otter-man. They rolled in a ball, but they weren't biting so I thought they were playing, kind of wrestling, and swimming in the river. I knew they were old friends and that one was the ghost of Aaron Shauner.

"My granddaughter found me and asked me to tell her a story. I pointed to the otters and said they are getting ready to be reborn. I could see Shiprock in the distance and a Thunderbird was going back to its nest. It was time to eat lunch, so my granddaughter and I walked back to our house."

{Chapter 50}

Conspiracy for Freedom

Aletta carried a bag of ice in from the ice chest in front of the building. Four Corners Ice Company kept the freezer stocked and the Roadhouse sold ice by the bag as well as using it for drinks. Ice made with local tap water would ruin a drink and it was probably too salty to freeze anyway. She broke up the imported ice by hitting it with a mallet, then climbed on a bar stool behind the drink dispenser to fill the ice compartment.

John Irick was on the afternoon shift again this week. Mary had been driving under the influence on New Year's Eve and had to get a breath-alcohol ignition interlock system installed on her car before she could drive it. John didn't seem bothered. Aletta could never decide if he liked having to work here or if he was just a very accommodating human.

Either way, he sat at the bar next to Carl, who was eating his mandated lunch.

Okay," said Carl, "the way you say dog is *shunka*."

"*Shunka*. Sit *shunka*. Good *shunka*," said John.

"Horse is *shunka wakan*. *Wakan* means sacred," said the Indian.

"A sacred dog? A horse is a sacred dog?"

"Exactly. Now try this: *pidama*. It means 'thank you,'" explained Carl.

"Pee-doma?" tried John.

"Not quite. *Pidama*, rhymes with 'the llama.'"

"*Kola* means friend and *Hau* is Hello. So *Hau Kola*, but you would only say that to another man."

John tried to show off by replying, "*Hau kola. Pidama.*" Both men laughed and let the topic drop.

Aletta pulled up a barstool to the back side of the bar. She began, "Carl, I wanted to ask your opinion on something that Pam and I have been discussing." He looked at her expectantly, so she continued. "Is Russell Means dying of cancer or not? They are saying on the radio he will be speaking at Fort Lewis College the first week of March."

"You and Pam were talking about Russell Means?" The UPS driver looked confused.

"Well, no ... we were talking about freedom in general, but I was wondering how it applied to the American Indian Movement," she said.

"Excuse me, but who is Russell Means?" asked John.

Carl replied, "A Lakota movie actor and Indian rights activist from the 1960's to the present."

"A friend of yours?" asked Aletta.

"Sorry to disappoint you, but no. I've seen him around, but I wouldn't say I know him."

John complained, "I don't know who he is."

Aletta had been brushing up on the subject so she started offering John clues.

"In 1983 he was on the libertarian ticket with Larry Flynt ..." John shook his head in reply.

"In 1987 Ron Paul beat him for the nomination as the Libertarian party Presidential candidate ..." Again John shook his head.

"Tried to get on the ballot for governor of New Mexico in 2001. Wait, that wasn't an election year ... I know ... you'll get this one," the waitress said. "Andy Warhol painted 18 individual portraits of Russell Means in his 1976 *American Indian Series*."

"Oh *that* guy," John smiled.

Carl added, "Russell has been important in getting people to notice the problems of indigenous peoples. He's very good at radical theater and has always gotten a lot of media attention. Aletta, you are right that he is always talking about freedom. He also tried to set up his own country, the Republic of Lakota. I might go listen to him if he is going to be in the area."

"I've been trying to figure out how what they did relates to freedom," said the

180

waitress. "They took over Alcatraz ... why?"

Carl pressed his lips together as he composed an answer. He began carefully, "The treaties of 1868 had given Indians rights to surplus federal lands, so when they closed the penitentiary on Alcatraz in the early 1960's, the activists wanted to claim it. For several years, the Coast Guard was able to keep them away, but then in 1969, a large group of college students occupied it for something like 19 months. The government said it was impossible to give them the island. The publicity of the treaty issues forced President Nixon to address return of appropriated lands and self-rule."

"That seems to me to be about broken promises more than freedom itself. Okay, later on they took over the Bureau of Indian Affairs office in Washington DC ... why?" asked the waitress.

"There was a termination policy in place with the BIA that ended tribal rights as sovereign nations, terminated healthcare and education programs, and cut other basic services provided by the federal government. This was widely seen as another way that the government was breaking their treaties, so the activists marched across the country on the 'Trail of Broken Treaties'. When they got to the BIA office there was some kind of misunderstanding that made the activists feel dishonored, so they took over the building for a couple of weeks. Barricaded themselves in, destroyed a lot of records. They had a list of 20 demands for the government. Most of them boiled down to 'Honor the Treaties'.

"In the end, President Nixon gave them a suitcase with $66,000 and freedom to leave the building. Once again, they made a little bit of political progress and this ended the termination policy. Sovereignty was restored to tribes that had been terminated."

"Sounds like a fight over provision of resources," the waitress summarized. "Okay, one last question. They occupied Wounded Knee ... why?"

The Lakota UPS driver responded, "That was about an internal conflict to the Ogallala Sioux. The US was backing a junta type government that the traditionalists wanted to impeach. When peaceful solutions failed, the protesters decided to occupy Wounded Knee. Some people got killed, but the junta stayed in power."

The waitress said, "Pam told me that scientists were measuring freedom by the number of choices available to people and by the probability that people would make a choice. Can we apply that definition to the freedom sought by the American Indian Movement? Were they increasing the number of choices available? Or were they making it more likely that people would make a choice?"

Carl thought for a moment, and then replied, "I don't know the answer to that, but I do know a quotation on the subject. This is what Nez Perce Chief Joseph had to say:

"Let me be a free man, free to travel, free to stop, free to work, free to trade where I choose, free to choose my own teachers, free to follow the religion of my fathers, free to talk, think and act for myself – and I will obey every law or submit to the penalty."

"*Pidama* for sharing that, *Kola*" said John.

"*Pidama* for being interested. Hey, lunch time is over! I better run."

Navajo City Roadhouse Blog:

Ski Navajo City

Saturday, January 07, 2011

Things have been very, very quiet except for the tourists that get lost between Durango, Colorado and Farmington, New Mexico. They always come in the door, obviously in a hurry, and then ask if we *happen* to know how to get to the Farmington airport. I tell them that they sure went a long way out of their way to get so lost and that it's still another hour to Farmington. At least they are heading in the right direction when they leave. It happens more often than one might expect.

Someone came in and told us that Navajo City was incorporated back in the 1970's. That's kind of funny because as far as we know, no one actually lives here except for Milton, Penny, Willy and Nicky. One of them could be elected mayor by any of the others that aren't convicted felons and then the mayor could appoint another one of them to be the dog catcher. They could check about getting federal funding for any other municipal jobs.

Actually, this is pretty important in that you have to have a municipal election to have beer and wine sales. If Penny and Milton are registered to vote, they could decide if we are going to sell alcohol or not. I'm sure there will be a lot of campaigning on the issue. Penny drinks and she would probably make better tips, so she will vote for it. Milton could probably be influenced by a bribe. I doubt that the others would bother to try to get registered and they don't drink either.

Personally, I am not too keen to sell and serve alcohol. I'll probably cut the customers off after one bottle of beer so I don't have to deal with the drunks or clean the bathrooms after them. Cutting them off is going to hurt my tips. Sigh .... Well, I also think we should stop selling cigarettes and chewing tobacco, but no one will listen to me, so I just give the customer the surgeon general's warning and tell them to try to quit as I take their $4.49.

In the Have-More-Fun Department—we set up a mini-ski slope on the east side of the parking lot. John had some old inner tubes to ride and even ol' Milton thinks it's fun. It's definitely a good excuse to come back in and drink hot chocolate. We put a sign up in the front: *Ski Navajo City*. That is really going to confuse the poor lost tourists.

So, I should have done my laundry and gotten things ready to go in tomorrow morning, but, no, instead here I am dinking around on the internet. Shame on me! Gotta go!

Yours truly,
Aletta Ramsden

{Chapter 52

Blood of the Mustangs

As Aletta let two gallons of hot water flow into the repurposed pickle bucket, she tried to imagine how many hamburgers it took to use five gallons of pickles. *Say they sold fifty hamburgers a day with three pickles on each one ... except in the oil-field there were quite a few anti-vegetable types that ordered meat-only. Maybe the vegetable haters were ten percent of the customers, so you could only count forty-five of the burgers as having pickles. How many pickles are in a bucket?* She searched the label. *Three thousand pickles in a five gallon bucket ... that's a thousand hamburgers. Why do we have more than one used pickle bucket?*

She poured a cup of vinegar into the water and was suddenly enveloped in the smell of pickles. It made her nose tingle. She ripped the packaging off the new window washing tool. It had a nice black squeegee backed by a big fluffy scrubber. The telescoping handle was innovative. She dropped the tool into the bucket of water and picked up a yellow rubber glove and a small pile of newspapers to scrub and dry the windows. Her mother had taught her to always clean windows with newspapers. *Was it there something in the ink that made them shiny?* She didn't remember.

Aletta started in the northeast corner, four plate-glass windows away from where Nicky sat by the wood stove reading a novel titled *Lover Unleashed*. Willy was in town shoeing a horse and buying dog food. Having Nicky there made Aletta feel like she was in some fancy coffee house where people sat and read books between sips of espresso.

"What's that book about?" she asked.

"Hmmm. It's a passionate love story about a female vampire and a human doctor," the off-duty cook replied without looking up. "Sounds like that is drippin' on the floor. Is it?"

Aletta looked down and sure enough the water was flowing out of the fuzzy scrubber and down the telescoping handle to her rubber glove. A pool of water was forming at her feet. "Dang!" she said, dropping the tool back in the water. As she

185

walked into the kitchen to get the mop and some rags, she noticed the words of the song on the radio.

"Oh a real man's gonna do what a man's gotta do
Whatever it takes to say, 'Gee, but I'm cool'
Heck, I've got nothin' to lose so I'm gonna try
I'll walk up, give her a smile, and look her straight in the eye
I'll pretend what I have to say isn't lie
That's right I'm going to lie
Somedays I have to lie"

Humans have a love/hate relationship with lies, she thought. *What was a novel anyway but a pack of lies?* As an author, she realized she would have to have an ethic to guide her in how much lying she would allow herself to do. Maybe some standard like a minumum of 50% true would be ethical. She was willing to exclude herself from the fantasy genre.

The water mess was cleaned up and another window half done when the cowbell clanked and Rex Roundy walked in. Nicky looked up and put her book down as she greeted Rex with a big "Howdy, amigo!" The chubby man shuffled over to sit with Nicky as Aletta dried her hands and pulled her order pad from her apron.

"Coffee and a cheeseburger, Cupcake," ordered Rex, before he turned back to look at Nicky.

Aletta was grateful that Nicky had the attention of the man that normally teased and tormented her. Perhaps Nicky could provide her with a model of how to deal with this type of customer. She turned the order in to Mary and then returned to her window washing project to eavesdrop.

Rex and Nicky were in mid-conversation.

"This was all new for me because my mother raised me to be a lady. I mean, my parents were well-to-do and well-known in Tulsa. My mother had a string of racehorses. That's how I got interested in horses. Willy was shoeing horses on our ranch. That's how we met.

"Anyway, I was shocked when I saw how she dresses. Her mother knows, but hell, between Naomi and her slut-for-a-mother, they've slept with half the men in the county."

Aletta frowned thinking about Naomi's being engaged to that oil-field guy. Her mom is a lesbian who doesn't even like men. Then again, it's a very under-populated county; maybe half the men isn't very many. She decided that they have to be talking about a different Naomi.

Rex replied, "Well, next time I come in and she is here, I will have to ask her about that and if I can make an appointment." He laughed loudly.

"Oh, My God!" thought Aletta with shock. *"Why did Nicky just sic him on that poor girl?"*

Mary rang the food service bell to call Aletta to pick up the meal. Aletta stopped by the sink to rinse and dry her hands as she walked into the kitchen. She carried the plate and a roll of silverware out to Rex. She set it down as Rex and Nicky continued their conversation without acknowledging her.

Rex was saying, " ... really, I only work there to have something to do. I don't really need the money. Even when I was recovering from cancer, I just felt I should have a job. They gave me 6 weeks to live when they first told me, but that was 9 years ago. I think it's because I get up and go to work every day."

"What the hell is he talking about?" thought the waitress, *"He's had to come in here to ask to buy cigarettes on credit until payday almost every month!"*

Nicky grabbed the fork out of his hand as Rex unrolled it, "Let me look at that!" she demanded. "It might not be clean ... no, it's okay. You know, Rex, they would have all kind of health code violations in this place if it wasn't for me."

Aletta's mouth dropped open. *How could that woman say that?*

Nicky took over the conversation as Rex filled his mouth with cheeseburger. "I know what you mean about workin', Rex. That's one of the things I hated most about when we was up on the Cabot Ranch. I didn't have no work to do. I spent four weeks just sittin' in the camper readin' novels. But that is not the only thing I hated about that place. Did you know that Shep Cabot paid for that ranch with the blood of the mustangs? He bought that place before the mustangs were protected and he used to just round them up and sell them to kill-buyers to send to the slaughter house. He paid for the whole place with mustangs. No wonder he hates the government for wrecking his little operation. The other thing about this is, I watched them come and go all that time and I think it's pretty suspicious how they are always moving cattle around with no brand inspections. They drive on them backroads to keep people from knowing what they are up to. We had to get out of there because those people were so creepy."

Rex replied, "Well, that ol' Shep is telling lies then, he says you two got run off for suspicious activity involving his tractor." He laughed so hard that Aletta thought he sounded like a donkey braying.

Nicky interrupted glaring, "That's what I mean about that asshole!"

"You wanna know something that's been puzzling me, Nicky? I came in here midday on the day Aaron Shauner got murdered. He was standing out front talking on the telephone, and ol' Cupcake here was crying her eyes out. I always wondered if the murder might of been a crime of passion. What do you think; could she have pulled the trigger?" He turned and grinned at Aletta.

Nicky's eyes flashed a mischievous look, and then she said, "Cupcake wouldn't harm a flea. She even rescues lost ants."

Aletta indignantly picked up her bucket and walked out the door where she started on the exterior glass surfaces. She could hear the hum of the gas field compressors and a few snow birds. She knew better than to let herself get emotional over other people's bullshit. These two really seemed intent on outdoing each other in that department. The word 'psychopathic' popped into her mind.

She watched for Rex to prepare to leave, and then she walked around the building to the front door to return to her post at the cash register to collect for the meal. When he asked for a pack of cigarettes, she looked at him hard and said, "Sorry, we ran out." He seemed to know he had pushed her too far, so he turned and left without another word.

Aletta walked over to the table to pick up the dishes without speaking a word to Nicky. Equally silent, Nicky picked up her novel and exited through the side door.

{Chapter 53}

Missing

Pam opened the kitchen drawer looking for the scissors. She dug through a pile of spatulas and mixing spoons. Finding nothing sharp in that drawer, she pushed the drawer shut and paced through the house trying to think of another place to look. Every Sunday she used them to cut the newspaper into squares to go in the bottom of the bird cages, but she knew that, sometime in the last week, she had used them for something else. If she could remember what else she had used them for, she knew she would find them.

She tried to imagine herself going through the week doing things. Could she have taken them to work? She checked her purse. Nothing on the bedstand or in the bathroom drawers, not in the refrigerator, not in the car. Hmmm.

She finally resigned herself to buying another pair and put a cup of coffee in the microwave to reheat. With a warm cup of coffee, she sat down in the recliner next to the coffee table. Out of the corner of her eye, she saw it ... the basket of yarn she had pulled out to knit some mittens was tucked up against the recliner. The scissors were in the bottom of the basket.

Mystery solved, she set about cutting up the Sunday paper. She pulled the tray from the bottom of each cage, scrubbed it, and lined it with newsprint. The pair of green Quaker Parrots tried to entice her to play with them by bobbing their heads up and down. She fed them each a banana slice, but the male dropped his on the clean newsprint. It landed next to this article:

FARMINGTON | Police are looking for a man who was supposed to be leaving on vacation to Tahiti but did not board the plane and has been missing since then.

David J. Donisthorpe, 42, was last seen at the Farmington Municipal Airport on New Year's Day. He has served as the minister of the Covenant of the Evangelical Church since 2005 and is well known in the area.

Officers are searching the area and checking with neighbors.

Donisthorpe is described as a white male with brown hair and brown eyes. He is about 6 feet tall and weighs 160 pounds and may be wearing a camouflage jacket, blue T-shirt and camouflage pants. His family and friends were unaware of his vacation plans, according to police.

Anyone with information on Donisthorpe's whereabouts is asked to call police at 291-2515.

Navajo City Roadhouse Blog:

Waste not

Thursday, January 12, 2012

The snow plow guy just ordered a burger to go and then went to sand HWY 537 while it's cooking. Hope it doesn't get too cold while he is gone. Fortunately, HWY 537 is the shortest highway in New Mexico.

The owner is in the bathroom texturing the drywall on the restroom upgrade project. He tore out the old urinal and our world smells better now. A little while ago he was out front in his skidsteer scraping the snow off the driveway when a guy came in and ordered six cheeseburgers to go. I would have tried to cook them if there weren't so many, but it raised my anxiety enough that I went out and flagged John down from his snow removal project. It's embarrassing when you have to get the cook out of the skidsteer to cook. However, our customers don't seem surprised.

Some folks down the road have chickens, so we save all the scraps for their flock. It's really too much for them to digest—we end up with a five gallon bucket every few days. Mostly it's stuff that gets old in the refrigerator and we have to toss it out. We have really cut back on the number of tomato slices in the bucket because now that they've gone up to four dollars a pound, we ask our customers if they want tomatoes. The chicken owners came in a while ago and picked up the bucket, but they forgot to leave a clean one. Scraping the food off the plates is such a habit that it's kind of disconcerting to just put it in the trash. The last customer left four French fries which now grace the dustbin. We would like to get some piglets as they would do a better job of converting scraps into something useful to us. Maybe John will build a pigpen out back. Sure enough, I will name the pig Wilbur, and he will not find a spider to save him from his fate.

We also flatten our cardboard for recycling. It piles up until John puts it in his truck and drives it to Farmington. Last week the waste management guys from the Apache tribe stopped in and said they had a recycling trailer that no one ever uses. They might be able to let us keep it down here. They have to ask the tribe.

One thing about this snow ... I haven't had to do any mud wrestling today.

Yrs truly,
Aletta Ramsden

{Chapter 55}

Laugh About It

Aletta stood polishing the water spots off the drinking glasses as she stacked them on the shelf. John was reading the classified ads in Sunday's paper. The radio was playing a Hank III song. The last line caught her attention. *Did he really say he's a candidate for suicide because he never laughs that much?*

She sighed. "You know, John, I kind of miss Guido," the waitress started. John looked up over the paper. She continued, "He was funny and always had a joke about everything. He made me laugh."

"So," John replied, "are you telling me that Mary is not funny?" He tilted his head back and let out a belly laugh. She laughed, too, because Mary was the antithesis of funny, always concerned with her house payments, her kids, or her immature husband.

"Yeah, I miss Guido too," John went on, "I liked when he changed the Loretta Lynn song *Don't Come Home a-drinkin' (with lovin' on your mind)* to *Don't come home a-lovin' (with drinkin' on your mind)*. I really got a kick out of that."

"I think about him," the waitress said, "when a song gets stuck in my head. He told me the cure for it is to sing '*Henry VIII* from Herman's Hermits, and you know what …. it works!"

John sang out a chorus.

John stopped and asked, "Won't that get stuck in your head? That would be really annoying."

The waitress replied, "No your brain seems to just throw it in the dustbin after it's done its job."

The cowbell hanging from the door clanked; John and Aletta turned to look as Pam Anderson stepped in. "Surprise!" she said.

"Hey, stranger!" smiled the waitress. John stood up to shake Pam's hand as Aletta got her a cup of coffee and a spoon.

"If you'll excuse me, I think I will step in back and bake a cake," said John as he dropped the archaeologist's hand. She took off her jacket, laid it on the bar stool and sat down on it.

It took them twenty-five minutes of non-stop gossip to run through all the items of interest. Pam reported that the birds were doing well, desk was still clean, the contract with Placido Lucero was coming together but it had still been too snowy to get out and agree on boundaries, Jessica had told her that Randall Tapia was back at work and looking more like a hippy than he used to, but no, he probably doesn't have a prescription for medical marijuana ... or maybe he does! Aletta reported that Bones had gotten a sore paw on the day she took the dogs sledding, that the bathroom remodeling was going well, that the tile under-flooring was complete, and that she was thinking about switching over from writing to make people cry to writing to make people laugh.

John walked in and sat down at the counter next to Pamela saying, "I hope you like Devil's Food because that was the only mix I had."

"Did you really make me a cake? That is so nice! So, John, you will like this ... do you know why if it weren't for archaeology, Navajo City wouldn't exist?" to which John and Aletta responded with doubtful looks.

"Well," Pam said, "the Navajos got the water rights because there was archaeological evidence that they had been farming along this river since the 1500's when they migrated into the area. They had been pushed out of the best farming land by the settlement of the Anglos and Hispanics, but the evidence that they farmed along the river was undeniable. The land that they were given, some fifteen million acres, has virtually no farmland on it, so there was a justification to provide them a way to have a traditional way of life by providing irrigation water."

John said, "The idea to build a dam had been floating around since the turn of the century. I know that it was promoted by Jay Turley, a surveyor and author of all of New Mexico's water laws. Those Indian water rights must have been the final impetus. It cost a fortune to condemn all the property that was inundated; the whole town of Rosa had to be abandoned. I heard it was the fifth largest earthen dam ever built.

194

"The dam was completed in 1962," John continued, "It was an opportunity for developers to sell any private land in the area for small developments like Navajo City. So, Pam, you are right we wouldn't be here if those archaeologists hadn't found farming along the river."

"Do you know anything about the salvage archaeology project they did before building the dam?" asked Pam. John and Aletta shook their heads "no".

"There were a number of archaeological projects, but the one that is most important to me is the analysis of the rock art. They photographed and sketched all the rock panels of art they could find. There are three layers of rock art in this area. The oldest is the Pueblo-related peoples, then there is a layer of Navajo art, and finally a layer from the early Anglos and Hispanics, primarily sheepherders in the eighteen and nineteen hundreds.

Aletta broke into the conversation, "Where I take my dogs sometimes, there are some triangular shaped people. They look like alien creatures. What layer is that?"

Pam laughed, "Those figures are termed '*broad-shouldered anthropomorphs*'. Anthropomorph means 'human shaped'. Those are from the Pueblo-related people, who lived in pithouses in this area. The Anglo-Hispanic ones are most likely to be someone's name written out along with the date of their effort. Many of them are January and February dates because that is the season that they would bring the sheep down from the high country and spend the winter in these protected canyons. The layer I am most interested in is the Navajo layer."

"Because the Navajos are still a living culture, we know most of their rock art has religious or supernatural meaning. It would have been done ceremonially, not casually to pass the time. And certain sites are where the stories originate. The birthplace of the Monster-Slayers was inundated with the dam building; before that, Navajo Medicine Men would have visited the site to renew their connection to the story and its principles."

The back door creaked, squeaked, and clunked open and the voices of Nicky and Willy Ledoux in the kitchen interrupted the conversation. John got up from his seat and said, "The LeDouxs must be hungry. That cake is probably cool enough for the icing."

Pam and Aletta chatted about where Aletta had seen the anthropomorphs while John and the LeDouxs were cooking. Aletta asked the best way to document the petroglyphs and Pam described how she photographs them and then sketches them. Recording their locations was the more critical and harder step unless one owned a GPS unit.

John dinged the waitress call bell and Aletta went back to pick up the cake slices. Chocolate fudge frosting on a Devil's Food cake ... yummy.

Willy and Nicky filed out of the kitchen with their own meals and sat down at the counter bar, just around the corner from Pam.

"Hey, ain't you the Forest Service lady?" asked Nicky.

Pam nodded, her mouth full of cake.

"I'm Nicky and this is my husband, Willy LeDoux." After which, Willy tipped his cowboy hat. "I heard you was doing some research on Placido Lucero's ranch."

Pam took a sip of coffee to wash the cake crumbs down, and then she smiled. "Yes, I am going to be looking at rock art on his ranch."

"Have you been to his house? Does he really live alone?" asked Nicky.

"Yes, he has a nice place just outside of the town of Turley," Pam replied.

Willy introjected, "The man has a horse he ain't ridden in a coon's age. I'm gonna ride it for him, just to make sure it's still safe for an old man. He might want to ride out and check on his cows, don'cha think so, Miss Aletta?"

Miss Aletta, always wanting to encourage positive thinking, replied, "Oh, certainly."

"Hey, I got a joke for you Miss Aletta. Where do cowboys cook their meals?" asked Willy. The waitress shrugged before Willy blurted out, "On the range!" John and the LeDouxs laughed out loud. Pam and Aletta smiled.

"I got another one. The eastern lady who was all ready to take a horseback ride said to the cowboy, "Can you get me a nice gentle pony?'" Willy said, batting his eyes and using a falsetto voice.

Using a deeper voice, Willy continued, "'Shore,' said the cowboy. 'What kind of a saddle do you want, English or western?'

"'What's the difference?' asked the lady.

"'The western saddle has a horn on it,' said the cowboy.

"'Well, If the traffic is so thick here in the mountains that I need a horn on my saddle, I don't believe I want to ride.'"

Everyone else laughed. Pam only smiled but got up from her chair and started putting her coat on.

"One more before you go, Miss Pamela. You will like this one," said the real cowboy. "Back in the Old West, three Texas cowboys ... no, I should say *New Mexican* cowboys was about to be hung for cattle rustlin'. The lynch mob brought the three men to a tree right at the edge of the San Juan River. The idea was that when each man had died, they'd cut the rope and he'd drop into the river and drift out of sight.

"They put the first cowboy in the noose, but he was so sweaty and greasy he slipped out, fell in the river and swam to freedom.

"They tied the noose around the second cowboy's head. He, too, oozed out of the rope, dropped into the river and got away.

"As they dragged the third New Mexican to the scaffold, he resisted, 'Please! Would ya'll tighten that noose a little bit? I can't swim!'"

John and the LeDouxs were laughing as Aletta escorted Pam to the door. The two women gave each other a hug without saying a word. The cowbell clanked and Pam was gone.

Navajo City Roadhouse Blog:

Got mud?

Thursday, January 19, 2012

All the snow has melted in the lower elevations and it's been raining for a few days. For January it's pretty wet. Our customers come in with mud up to their knees, if not up to their hats. They've been putting chains on trucks in the mud. They linger over cups of steaming coffee or hot chocolate, reluctant to go back into the bog. I've swept five times this afternoon. I could start a garden with the floor sweepings.

Yesterday, I didn't get a chance to write in the blog because Naomi got to be the waitress while I crawled around on my knees in the women's bathroom. We are putting new tile down, so I spent the day mortaring the new tiles in. I was sore this morning and I sure missed yesterday's tips, but the most surprising thing was how many new friends I made in the women's room. Folks of either gender would come in to see what was happening and they would stay for 20 or 30 minutes talking to me while I kept squishing the tiles into place.

One of my new friends claims to be the "Big Liberal Democrat" of the area. This is noteworthy in oil field country. He told me that he had never met a woman in a bathroom before. I didn't tell him about my political persuasion; he might have an idea, but whatever he thinks, I am sure I am more extreme. His wife works on invasive weeds for an oil company. They had the fish tacos and ate almost every bite. Some of my visitors had tile experience and steered me away from a problem I was about to create. Folks have been stopping at Navajo City just to come in and check out the bathroom. It's kind of the biggest construction project in this part of the county after the new highway bridge. I bet John could put a donation box and it would pay for the new fixtures. Well, it's the *only* public bathroom for 30 miles in either direction. I bet it was famous for being stinky when it was a bar. Milton, our elderly maintenance man, put in new vents, so it should be an improved olfactory experience, besides a good place to meet people.

We are probably the most important bathroom for the entire Jicarilla Apache Nation. Everyone from Dulce needs a pit stop by the time they get to Navajo City. We have learned to greet them with "*Dáazho*", which is hello in Jicarilla. We are planning to advertise on the Dulce radio station, KCIE, with something like "You've been stopping here for years. Don't you think it's time to try the food?"

It's six P.M. now and no one has stopped in for the last hour. All the mud is swept up and it's drizzling outside. Glen Campbell is singing about being a lineman for the county. The cook is reading a newspaper back in the kitchen. I could go in and stick up a few ceiling tiles, maybe someone would come in to talk.

Yours truly, Aletta

{Chapter 57}

Hungry as a Horse

The sun was just peeking over the distant snow-capped San Juan Mountains as Aletta pulled off US 550 onto the road leading to the wild horse holding facility. She had bumped into Jessica at the Giant Fuel station in Bloomfield getting an early-morning cup of coffee and, since Aletta wasn't busy, Jessica had invited her to come help feed the mustangs. The whole local wild horse program had fallen into Jessica's lap after Shauner's demise and Tapia's breakdown. Jessica said it was rare to get any help with the morning feeding, so Aletta was glad she had the time to assist.

After Jessica had rolled the chain-link gate open, Aletta pulled her Jeep through and parked in the little parking area where the snow had been pushed away and the ground was now dry. She could see Jessica forking grassy hay from a giant rectangular bale into a large push cart. The horses stood behind the fat gray bars of their heavy-duty pens watching the process. Their breathing looked like fog as it was exhaled from their nostrils. Frost covered their backs, but they looked reasonably warm in their thick winter coats. A few of the horses snorted at Aletta as she walked from her Jeep.

"Take the cart into the first pen and dump it into the feed trough. They might fight with each other but they won't come near you," Jessica said.

Aletta pushed the cart to the gate and looked inside at the four hefty horses. Their eyes were wide and they stood with their necks stretched high. They moved in a swarm, keeping in constant contact with each other, each one trying to hide behind the others. They seemed to take turns bobbing their heads up and down while looking at her. She tried to decide if that was a warning signal as she contemplated opening the gate. They did not look malicious, so she prodded herself to just open the gate and go in.

The ground was a barely frozen field of muck and hoofprints that impeded the cart's forward motion. Aletta quickly realized she could pull it backward much easier than pushing it forward. She didn't really want to get between the cart and the horses, but there was no choice. The low metal oval trough sat in the middle of

200

the pen and she felt more exposed with each step toward the trough. Reaching it, she turned the cart around and tilted it to dump the hay. The horses came forward toward her eagerly, so she hurried to get to the other side of the cart, but then she realized they wouldn't come all the way as long as she was there. As she pulled the cart away, they moved in and began eating.

Jessica had already pulled the other cart to feed the horses in the second pen, so the women returned to the haystack together. On Aletta's second venture into a pen, the horses stood apart rather than swarming, but she soon realized that despite all the rumors about the malevolence of mustangs, they were only frightened horses, needing food to survive. Feeding them wasn't nearly as dangerous as she had imagined.

Jessica asked her to walk through the alley and check that each water trough was at least half full of liquid water. Any ice was an indication that the heating element wasn't working, and any trough with low water would have to be filled, but that was easier in the late afternoon. If they were half full, they could wait, while an emptier tank required pulling a hose out. It wasn't merely good luck that each of the tanks was ice-free and none required filling as Jessica was a very capable facility manager. Meanwhile, Jessica had pulled the tarps back over the hay. Their work was done, so they jumped up to sit on top of the tarped bale while they watched the horses.

"How many horses are still here?" asked Aletta.

"Twenty-one," replied Jessica. "All the foals and a couple of older horses were adopted out before Christmas. We've had five adopted this month and there are sixteen out with trainers in the Mustang Heritage program. We had one die of colic—oh my God—that was a horrid experience! But, I feel good that we have less than half of what we started with."

"Have you named them?" asked Aletta.

Jessica laughed. "No way! We refer to them by number. We use the last two digits of their neck tags."

"Well, I really like that little twenty-two horse in the first pen," said the waitress.

"He's a real cutie, isn't he? See that horse thirty-seven, the black, next to him. They are inseparable friends. They spend all day playing with each other," said Jessica.

"Do you think they are sad to be here?" asked Aletta.

"Sometimes I think they might be depressed a little by the size of the pens and the fact that they have to live on a muck pile, but they spend a lot of time interacting with each other. The geldings play a lot, the mares not so much. They don't seem more depressed than any domestic horse. I do worry about them though. Just look at this place, up here on this exposed windy mesa. No shelter at all and nothing even to block the wind. It's been pretty brutal at times, but these horses are tough. I give them extra feed on cold nights, but I can't help but feeling that they would be better off in the wild where they could find some natural shelter."

"Would you like me to come help you again? I don't work until afternoons except on Sunday. I could come four days a week if you don't mind my dogs coming too."

"We could try it. Do you want to come tomorrow?" Jessica asked.

"Yeah. I'd love it. You have to go from here to your office, yes?"

Jessica replied, "I better head on over there. Hey, Randall is doing great. I really think that trip to Mexico helped him lighten up a little." The women slid down from their perch.

"Tell Randall 'hello' for me. I am looking forward to spring when the range opens up again and the government lunch crowd is back at Navajo City. Well, I'll see you tomorrow!" Aletta headed toward her Jeep thankful to be provided with an opportunity to be around the mustangs.

***

That afternoon, Pablo Aguilar, also known as "the snowplow guy", hoisted his broad butt onto a barstool at the counter of Navajo City. His snowplow run was Highway 64 from Highway 84 west to the Rio Arriba County line and the length of Highway 537 from 64 to the Navajo Dam. Aletta liked getting him to talk even though his dark eyes and swarthy skin made her think of the word "bandito." He was rebuilding an old Harley Davidson in his garage and had tried to clear the place out by getting John to buy his hydroponic grow-light setup. Aletta made it a point to never ask what he had been growing, but had recommended that either the liberal Democrat's wife, Jane, or the lady down at Mustang Camp might have an interest as they were both gardeners.

After ordering a double-meat Green Chile Cheeseburger, Pablo took a long slow sip from the straw in his iced-tea. "I was sure happy to see the snow has melted down here. I'm going to throw a little sand on it on the way back. Except for some icy spots it's clear below milepost 110. Beyond that, *hieee, no bueno! Mucha nieve!* (no good!, A lot of snow!) The poor *pendejos* that have Highway 17 can't even start to catch up.

"I don't know what they're gonna do about them *caballos* on the highway. Those horses are getting pushed out of the forest by the snow. Somebody is going to hit one for sure and then there will be trouble. My boss called the Livestock Board, but they say they have no jurisdiction on either Indian horses or mustangs, so I don't know what will happen; but anyone that is driving that way should sure be careful. Hitting a horse is more likely to kill someone than hitting a cow or a deer. The only other animal that bad is an elk. Horses and elk are just the right size to be hoisted up onto the hood and slam into the windshield. It kills everybody. *No bueno.*"

***

The next morning, Aletta brought up the issue with Jessica, who sighed and said that she knew about the horses, but they were US Forest Service mustangs. She said that Tapia had tried to push them back into the forest, but the cattle-guards were full of snow and since the horses could walk right over them, they kept coming back. People were feeding them along the highway.

"Couldn't the Forest Service feed them away from the highway?" Aletta asked.

"That would pretty much be violating the idea of keeping them wild," the young woman replied. "The American public wants them to be wild, not just like animals in a feedlot. If some of them starve or get killed on the highway that is just the way of nature."

***

By that afternoon, it seemed to Aletta, that mustangs on the highway had become a hot topic at the Roadhouse. The oil-field workers were both nervous about possibly encountering them, especially at night, and heart-broken to see the horses in such desperate straits.

Willy sat down at the counter and told her he had never seen horses in such bad condition. "I can't understand why the Forest Service would let a horse starve like that; can you, Miss Aletta? It makes a fellow ashamed to be human to let an animal get that way. Somebody oughta' do sumpthin.'"

Aletta agreed. An idea occured to her, so when Duane Hutton, the Elvis impersonator, stopped in, she cornered him. "Duane, I need you to do me a favor. You drive up on that La Baca Canyon road every day ... Could you drop a three-string bale of alfalfa off along that road? It might pull some of those horses off the highway. I'll have a bale or two stacked up here ready for you every day. It won't feed them all, but it might save a few human and horse lives." There was no way that the Elvis impersonator could refuse.

She placed a donation jar by the cash register with a sign, "Keep the Mustangs off the Highway. Off-road feeding project. Donate cash or hay." It was full of money before closing time. The plan was going to work.

Navajo City Roadhouse Blog

I might forget your name, but I'll remember if you don't eat red meat.

Thursday, January 26, 2012

The boss decided to try to instill a new lunch habit out here in the oilfield. He wanted to make it easier for them to plan on eating here every day than it was to pack a lunch, so we now have "lunch cards". For twenty bucks the customers can buy a card good for five meals. They can't use them for more than one person and the card expires after 15 days. We knew the men would probably be chowing down on the Roadkill, which is our double meat and everything else on it specialty burger, which retails for $7.65. With meals only running $4 with a card, it's a super deal. But then the morning cook and the owner had a traveling steak salesman show up. He was a good seller and we ended up with a box of steaks in the freezer. For $9.99, you can have a nice steak for lunch, or for $7.99 you can have the same steak after 3 P.M.. But with the lunch card, you get the steak for only $4—heck, that's what we paid the traveling steak salesman! The breakfast cook was freaking out over the margin. She wanted us to quit selling cards.

Well, the owner has a cooler head. He has an idea that the best advertising we can have is to have a full parking lot at lunch time. This week, when the regulars showed up with their lunch cards, the parking lot filled up. There were even trucks parked in the back and across the highway. It wasn't just regulars with their cards, it was a big segment of the oil field population. The owner says to consider the difference between the cost of the meal and the $4 meal card to advertising. It's pretty effective advertising if you ask me and we don't have to do it forever.

Considering that we don't even have a proper sign out front, we are doing pretty well. The advertising plan for Navajo City Roadhouse is a little weak. You have to either know this place is a restaurant because you've been coming here all your life or you have to figure it out by our Breakfast Burrito flashing sign. There is a proper sign in the works though, and when it arrives and gets hung up over the doorway, I'll try to get a photo for this blog.

Benito and Rose came in yesterday. I remembered them from before Christmas when Benito had told me that his favorite place to shop was Chelsea's Pub. I'm really bad at remembering customer's names, but what I am good at is remembering their initials. So I guessed his name was Bernie and her's was Rachel. They feigned indignation, but then they admitted they didn't remember my name at all. Later, another customer came in and as we got to talking, he said his wife drives a semi-dump truck, and I asked if her name starts with a D. Sure enough. One customer, who we really wanted to know by name, was unfortunately called Mr. Mud by the cook, since the guy sells engineered well-drilling mud. Now we can't recall his real name. This memory thing is something I've got to work on.

Still, I can't feel too bad. Last week an Apache EMT came in, and I commented that I hadn't seen him in a while. He looked confused because he claimed that he never met me. I insisted he looked very familiar. I thought he had come in with a very good looking woman who I assumed was his wife. Hmmm. Then I mentioned some of the details that the man and woman had told me. Hmmm ... it was his dad and mom!!!

Yours,
Aletta

{Chapter 59}

Theories

Aletta was dusting the windowsills after the lunch rush. She noticed that although there were no dead flies this time of year, there was still dust. The windows themselves were still clean. She thought about Rita Mae. *Is she in Thailand on a beach or is she bundled up somewhere in the Canadian Northwood's?* Aletta sighed and looked out the window at the landscape across the highway. The juniper trees looked happy with the moisture. The snow was still deep, wet, and crusty in the shade of the trees and bushes. Elsewhere the reddish mud was dark with melted snow—mud just waiting for a boot on which to dry and be carried into the cafe, crushed into dust and kicked into the air, only to land on the windowsill and be dusted off on a quiet afternoon.

She heard the vehicles coming before she saw them, but suddenly Carl's big brown UPS truck lumbered in from the westbound lane and a shiny new red truck crossed the highway from the eastbound lane to pull into the other driveway. The red truck parked next to the UPS truck and Pamela Anderson got out of it. She and Carl walked up to the cafe door together.

Aletta tossed her feather duster onto its shelf and had the front door open before they got to it. She gave each one a big hug feeling the specialness of having her friends drop in. Carl laughed when she hugged him, "I heard the Roadhouse has friendly staff, but this is ridiculous!"

"What are you two doing out here? Let me get the coffee! Lunch?" beamed the happy waitress. They took their coats off and sat down as Aletta got coffee, silverware rolls, and menus.

"Carl and I have been having a little problem after-hours," said Pam with a coy look. Aletta raised her eyebrows as Pam continued. "We both do our grocery shopping at the Safeway in Aztec where we bump into each other … usually in the produce section. Have you ever tried to have a serious conversation in the produce section? It's just about impossible. We decided to meet out here with you instead, because you have a good perspective too. We have been trying to discuss the murder."

208

Carl said, "I only have my lunch hour, so ... hmmm .... I'd like a French dip and a side salad."

"Ranch with that?" asked the waitress, to which Carl nodded.

"Same for me," said Pam. "I have some comp time from that conference I went to, and I wanted to put some miles on my new truck."

"I noticed the new wheels! Wow! It really looks heavy duty!" Aletta said as she left the room to turn in the order.

"Did you get the Off-road Package and four-wheel-drive? Toyotas are definitely top of the line," said Carl.

Pam smiled in reply, and then pulled a small notebook from her purse as Aletta returned. She opened it. "I prepared a list of all the ideas I could come up with. I thought we would go through them one by one. But first, let's see if we can add any more."

She read from the list.

Suspects:

1. Horse activist
2. Sephra
3. Sam
4. Random Hunter out of season
5. Tim, wife having an affair with Shauner
6. Angela, the girlfriend
7. Oil-field guy with a vendetta
8. Someone gunning for Erin Tate
9. Danielle Tapia
10. Cabot boys with Shep covering for them

"Does this list have to have only plausible suspects?" asked Aletta. "I have heard so many ideas on this topic that I basically had to refuse to talk about it after the first day."

"I think we should list them all," said Pam, "because we don't really know."

209

"Okay, add these: skinwalker, aliens, and nun with a gun," said the waitress.

Pam added to the list:

11. Skinwalker

12. Aliens

13. Nun with a gun

Carl said, "I think you have all the obvious ones I would have added. Let's make a list of the evidence we know about. Start a new list, Pam. Shotgun ... out of vehicle ... late afternoon ... two- track road ... Cabots called 911. What else?

"Tracks," said Pam. "No vehicle tracks. Tracks of barefoot human, coyote, and the horses."

"What about the dead deer?" asked Aletta.

"Right!" said Pam, adding it to the list.

"Which of the people on the list had a plausible reason to kill him?" asked Carl.

Both of the woman looked at him with surprise. Aletta said, "Almost everyone had a reason if you count wanting to liberate those horses and including mistaken identities. Let's see, who *wouldn't* have a reason ... the Cabots, and probably the aliens, maybe the nun."

Mary, back in the kitchen, rang the waitress call bell that signaled the meals were ready. Aletta ducked into the kitchen to grab them and Mary followed her out.

Before he bit into his sandwich, Carl asked her, "Mary, did you know Aaron Shauner very well?"

"Yeah ... he was one of the guys that we partied with," she replied in her pinched nasally voice. "He liked to drink malt liquor and shoot billiards. He was an all right guy. He'd put sunglasses on his dog and would wear this crazy hat that looked like a big lizard. My ol' man and him would sometimes work on cars together. They had a mutual friend with a party barge at the lake so we spent a lot of time together last summer."

"Do you know of anyone who would want to kill him?" asked Aletta.

"Besides his girlfriend? No. He never did really fucked-up things. He was pretty cool like that," replied Mary. "He drove her crazy because she thought he was an underachiever. He had a good job; I don't know what she wanted him to do. Well, probably sober up a little—that might have been what she wanted.

"Hey, I better get back to my bacon prep. Nice talking to you all though," Mary said as she departed for the kitchen.

"The bigger question is who would have known that he would be on that road," said Carl.

"The Cabots are the only ones we know about. It is possible that Sephra or Sam might have known or overheard," said Pam. "Tapia told me that the Cabots had told Shauner about that road when they visited the roundup that day."

"You know, I just remembered something. The night that it happened, this Native American guy, I think he was Navajo, came in and ate dinner. Just before he left he said something like they caught seven horses fewer than they thought they caught. He *must* have been talking about the horses that got away. He *must* have seen them! Could he be the killer?

"What time was that?" Pam asked.

"He left just as I was ready to close ... about eight," replied Aletta.

"What did he look like?" asked Carl.

"Handsome, about 50, his hair was dark except for a bright gray or white streak over his eye. He was wearing it in wrapped braids. He was wearing some nice jewelry and even wearing moccasins, kind of dressed up," recalled the waitress.

"Would you recognize him from a photo?" Carl asked.

"Maybe," replied Aletta looking puzzled.

"Tomorrow, I'll bring a photo for you to look at; for now, let's go through the others. I will tell you why I don't think it was him when we get to him."

Pam added a new item to the list of suspects:

14. Navajo customer

Then she said, "Okay, let's start going through each one. Horse activists ... Beth

Hudson is probably the most likely suspect in that group. Perry Bennett—you know, that BLM law enforcement officer—told Jessica, my cousin, that Beth Hudson had gotten really upset when she saw the Cabots looking at the horses that were going to be euthanized. Apparently she left the roundup early cussing like a sailor," said the archaeologist.

"She doesn't live in this area. I don't know her," said Carl.

"She lives in Durango," said Aletta. "She's one of those grumpy ladies that find a problem with everything. It seems hard for her to compromise her ideals with reality, but she's too smart to kill someone to get her way. How would she have known the road?"

"If she knew the Cabot ranch and had a map, she might have guessed," said Pam. "No one seems to have known about the Cabot's contractual arrangements for horse disposal. Tapia would have been able just to call them and request horse disposal services if the total fee was less than $2500 and they could accept a credit card."

Aletta laughed, "I can just see their yellow pages ad for euthanasia services in the phone book! As if this area had a phone book."

"There's no phone book for out here?" asked Pam.

Carl laughed, "Pam, there are lots of places in the Four Corners that don't have phone books. They don't have landlines. Cell phones were the first phones for many people in remote areas."

"Well, you know they had that meeting with the Wild Horse Advocates Council here," the waitress said. "Many of the attendees had not been at the roundup. None of them seemed very suspicious. They all seemed worried about their ability to be advocates. Are there any of them you want to discuss … Lynne Wagner? … Sally Horne? … "

"What if it was an outside Animal Liberation person?" asked Carl.

Both women looked at him with their lips tight. Pam spoke up, "Carl, they wouldn't know the road so they couldn't have set up to stalk him."

"Oh, yeah … what about Sephra and Sam?" asked Carl. "Why are we absolutely sure they could not have done it?"

Aletta replied, "No one told Sephra they were euthanizing those horses before Sam told her that night. She went over to dinner at Sam's to look for older photos of that rearing horse in the photograph, Phantom."

"They did?" asked Carl excitedly. "Do you know if they had photos?"

"Yes, they found some photos from a long time ago as I recall," said the confused waitress. "But the thing is, that shotgun that Sephra had didn't even work. The Feds tested it. You cannot imagine how crushing it was for Sephra's spirit for her to be under investigation. Thank God they cleared her quickly; she couldn't handle it."

"Sam would have known what was happening," said Pam, "and if anyone knew about the road, it would be Sam. He is the most likely suspect in my opinion, except he has Sephra as an alibi. Okay ... we have to dismiss my most likely suspect, but ... well, next we have the random hunter hypothesis. This is a favorite at the government agencies."

"Why would that be a favorite? What would be the motive?" asked Aletta.

"Maybe the dead deer was the reason. Maybe someone got caught looking like they were hunting out of season?" suggested Carl. "They have a gun in their hand and they are in self-preservation mode. They panic and shoot the source of their anxiety."

"How did they get Shauner out of the vehicle?" asked Aletta.

"Maybe he got out to question them," suggested Pam. "They could have been on foot hunting in that area, or they could have even been on horseback ... hmmm. That could explain no tracks other than horses, especially tracks from where the gun was fired. Hunters are rarely barefooted though."

"If I imagine a barefooted hunter," Carl said, "He would have a bow and arrow, not a shotgun. But I can see why this is the favorite hypothesis so far."

"I forget who told me about Tim's wife having an affair with Shauner," said the waitress. "No, wait, I remember; it was Tim himself. Everyone tells me everything out here."

"Well, that wasn't Shauner. That was Joe Simpson, if his truck parked in front of their house means anything," said the UPS driver, "But Tim wouldn't have known that."

"Tim might have had a reason and been in the area, but he wouldn't have known about the road," said Pam.

"Penny told me that Tim was here when everyone found out about the murder, and he called Shauner's mother to confirm it. Penny says Tim was all broke up about it. He couldn't have already known that Shauner was dead unless he is a very good actor," said Aletta.

"Angela Aragon, Shauner's girlfriend, was at work," said Carl.

"Where does she work?" asked Pam.

"The Big Smiles dentist office," replied Carl. "I had delivered a parcel there that afternoon."

"I kind of like the oil-field vendetta hypothesis," said Aletta. "A lot of guys griped about the way Shauner was driving the back roads. They called him 'The Duke of Hazzard'. Guys lose their job in the oil patch for getting in an accident, even if it's not their fault."

"Did he get in any wrecks?" asked Carl.

"Not that I heard about," replied Aletta.

"No," said Pam. "That idea has the problem of no other vehicle tracks and it would have had to be opportunistic rather than planned. There are no oil wells on that road, so no one would have a reason to be there."

"A road without an oil well?" asked Aletta facetiously. "I didn't know *that* existed." She laughed and the others smiled.

"This number eight .... someone gunning for Erin Tate? The Forest Service wild horse guy?" asked Carl looking at Pam.

"Well, it was really weird at the time, but Erin Tate just about went into a mental breakdown during the week after the murder. He's an ex-Marine and I think it reactivated his PTSD. Talk about paranoia! He moved his desk so he could see out the window. He started parking in a different place, and then he traded his personal car for another used car of a different color. I had a private conversation with him about it and he told me that the murderer was probably after him but just confused about the name. He said that there are a lot of people who would want to see him dead, but he wouldn't go into details."

"I don't see how that would work," said Aletta. "Someone laying in wait for the first Aaron or Erin that shows up? I hope he realized how impossible it would be. Why would someone want to kill him?"

"Don't know …. hey, we are running out of time. Let's get Danielle off the list and we will have finished," said Pam.

"Not so fast, lady," said Carl. "We actually have a lot left to go. But as far as Danielle goes, remind me why she is on the list."

"Oh, right, the Navajo customer," replied Pam. "Danielle is on the list only because Randall got his shotgun tested, and she is the only one who would have had access to it. I kind of thought the fact that he checked the gun shows he thought she might have a reason."

Carl regretfully nodded his head. "Yep, she is manipulative and sneaky. I feel sorry for Randall being married to her, but he seems to love her. Personally, I won't deliver packages to her door. I just beep the horn and let her come out of her lair. Her energy scares me." He hunched his shoulders and shivered a moment.

"Enough creepiness, can we meet again tomorrow, ladies?" he continued. Seeing that they were nodding yes, he added. "I have some research assignments for tomorrow. I will bring a photo of the Navajo it might be. Aletta, would you talk to Sephra and get the details on the photos of Phantom? Pam, if you could brush up on what is known about Skinwalkers, I think we will have a very interesting discussion.

"Six dollars will cover my lunch? Okay, ladies, see you tomorrow!"

Pam pulled out two bills from her purse, picked up Carl's money and handed it to Aletta.

Aletta smiled at her friend. "Pam, thanks so much for thinking to include me in this conversation. You two really made my day!"

"Yes, well, get ready to do it again tomorrow!" said the archaeologist as she opened the door to leave.

{Chapter 60}

Theories Two

"Let's get the Cabot boys off the table," said Carl when they met the next day.

Pam and Aletta laughed out loud at the absurd thought of the two surly men sitting on a table.

Carl continued, "They knew he'd be there, they have lots of weapons and they are just ornery enough to kill someone for the fun of it, but Shauner's death was an economic loss for the family. Michael's truck got repossessed and is sitting on a used car lot in Aztec."

"They would not have let the horses go," agreed Aletta. "I'm surprised they didn't figure out how to strip the truck and trailer and just dispose of the body when they realized the horses were gone."

Pam objected, "Shep would have no part in that! He's a decent fellow."

"Yeah, he's the only one with brains in that family. The boys are truly skunks," said the waitress.

"Does anyone know if they tested Cabot's shotguns?" Pam asked. When Aletta and Carl looked at her blankly, she continued. "Okay, say the boys did something really stupid like killing Shauner just for the hell of it ... Shep finds out and arranges to protect them. I like this theory, personally."

"It *is* more plausible than most," Aletta conceded. "More plausible than '*aliens*' or '*nun with a gun*' ... do we even have to talk about those?"

"No point in talking about them if we have nothing to say," said Pam. "Aletta, what did you find out about Phantom?"

Aletta referred to her notes on the back of a used restaurant order ticket. "Sephra told me that Phantom was full grown in 2002, so he is more than 10 years old. There was a mare and foal with him in 2008. Sam named the mare Daisy and the foal Clipper. Daisy was bay with tall stockings on her hinds, Clipper was black with similar tall stockings. Clipper was one of the studs that was returned to the wild after

216

the roundup.

"Where is this information going to take us, Carl?" she asked.

"Okay, team, showtime …" said Carl pulling a photo out of a manila envelope. He laid it on the counter in front of Aletta. It seemed to be a black and white photo taken at night. In the center of the photo a man was caught in mid-stride. He had no shirt on and his chest was muscled but not hairy. He wore a belt with several animal hide parts hanging from it. A horse's tail, a deer tail, a beaver tail, and a racoon tail were clearly visible. His braids hung loose and dark, but the hair above his left eyebrow glowed with a silver streak.

Aletta gasped, "Yes, it's him!"

"Wow," Pam said. "He looks like he is dressed to play a part in a movie, but I have a feeling he is not an actor."

"No, he's the real deal," replied Carl. "In the 1990's I was asked to sit on an investigative panel that was tasked to determine whether Navajo witchcraft was creating social problems. There had been many strange deaths at the time, so they gathered together a group to study the local practices of witchcraft and if it was spreading to the Anglo population. It turned out that the problems were related to crystal meth being introduced to the area instead of witchcraft.

"The man in the photograph, Kenneth Joe Denetsosie has, arguably, the deepest knowledge of Navajo religion and mystical practices of anyone alive. He absolutely refused to be interviewed; he basically disappeared every time we tried to talk to him. In the end, we determined that his interests were more likely to be actually beneficial to the community.

"Phantom, or his identical twin, is currently running free on the Denetsosie allotment near Pueblo Pintado with an older bay mare with white hind legs. The mare was adopted from the roundup by Kenneth Denetsosie according to the BLM. She has a fairly fresh brand. Here is a photo on my cell phone."

The women each turned to stare at Carl, then at the screen on the cell phone. Aletta got up and took down the photo of the roundup to compare against the tiny digital image.

"I am pretty sure that Phantom is Kenny Joe, skinwalking as a horse. I am almost certain of it." stated Carl.

"Are you saying Kenny Joe can change himself into a horse?" asked Aletta. "That's creepy!"

"He can probably also change himself into a beaver, a deer, or a raccoon judging by the tails hanging from his belt," said Carl. "Pam, how about you give the archaeologist's report on skinwalkers?"

"Hey, guys, I am feeling a little uncomfortable here. As a scientist, I have to be quite skeptical of paranormal claims. We are way over the edge here," said the archaeologist. "I have some facts for you. I like facts."

"First, the legendary transfiguration can go either way: animals can turn into humans or humans can turn into animals.

"Some cultures have shape-shifting animals. The Japanese have the Kitsune. They start out as foxes, but when they get to be 100 years old, they grow extra tails, (up to nine of them), and then they have the magical power to shape-shift into various humans, or possess people by entering their bodies. The Kitsune are tricksters and often take the form of human females to seduce men. They are showing up currently as typical creatures in Japanese animation.

"In Scotland and Iceland, they have Selkies. These are seals who take off their coats to become people, usually women. Apparently they make faithful and devoted wives, because young men would steal their coats and force the Selkies to marry them. However, if the wife found her coat, she could not resist returning to the sea even if she had a happy life. Some North American tribes hold that bears can do the same; they take off their coats to become human. I did not, however, find any information about their desirability as mates for humans.

"When it is a human turning into an animal, it's called *therianthropy*. Many cultures have this type of legend and some of the ancient artwork of the caves of France is thought to represent the idea of shape-shifting. One of the most well known legends is the Mesoamerican Nagual, who can be good or evil depending on personality. The Nagual typically becomes a jaguar or puma. I have a colleague who aroused the suspicions of the modern Yucatec Mayans because she did not conform to her expected gender role and because she was collecting animal bones. It is quite serious to be accused of shape-shifting even in today's world.

I've got a lot to say specifically about Navajo shape-shifting, but first I would like to talk about modern day therianthropy. There is an American subculture, actually somewhere between a cult and a lifestyle, of people living as anthropomorphic animal characters. They call themselves the '*Furrys*'. This group is primarily an online phenomenon, but they also wear animal costumes and meet at Furry conventions. There are several of these annually and are well attended, raising money for animal-related charities. Okay, enough about them.

"Skinwalkers are just regular Navajos by day, but transform into animals at night," continued Pam. "They are said by some to gain their immense powers by inflicting pain and suffering on others. The harm caused by skinwalkers includes curses put on people and scaring people with trickster pranks. When they perpetuate greater crimes, it is almost always motivated by revenge and acquisition of power.

"They are more likely to be killed than to kill, as there are many informal reports of someone shooting an animal at night and the next day the neighbor is dead of a gunshot wound. They can also be killed by discovery. Just having pronounced the name of Kenneth Joe Denetsosie would be enough to kill him according to legend. Three days after someone identifies them by name, they die."

Carl interrupted to say, "If that was true, he would have died in the 1990's."

Pam nodded and went on, "The most common animals associated with skinwalkers are coyotes and wolves. Wearing the pelt of any predatory animal is strictly taboo among the Navajos. Sheepskin and buckskin are the only pelts allowed and then only for ceremonial wear.

"No one has seen the ritual performed for the initiation of the shaman to become a skinwalker and some people claim that they have to murder a relative or have sex with a corpse. This matter is of some controversy. It is also said that if you step on a bear track, you could automatically be turned into a skinwalker.

"You know, I could not accept the reality of a literal shape-shifter, but I could see that the role in the community might be valid. Let's just say there could be a strong connection between Kenny Joe and Phantom that we do not understand at this time and may account for some of the phenomena associated with this murder. I am open to the idea of a figurative skinwalker," concluded Pam.

Yes," said the waitress, "but he wouldn't have had a weapon if he was the horse. He couldn't just open the trailer, jump out, grab a gun and kill Aaron."

"What about this idea?" said Pam. "Phantom and him are connected somehow. Kenny Joe jumps on the back of the trailer as it's moving and gets the door opened. He's barefoot. Aaron stops to see what is happening and Kenny Joe shoots him, then rides away on Phantom? It's a crazy idea, but it accounts for everything."

Carl smiled, "Very clever, but the big question is what do we do with your crazy idea?"

"Hmmm," Aletta said crossing her arms on the counter and resting her head where she could stare at the photo of the skinwalker. " .... you know, I remember thinking he smelled like horses. Yes, he definitely smelled like horses."

They all stared at the evidence and chewed on their now cold french fries.

Finally Carl spoke up, "You can't really blame a guy for rescuing his horse. I vote that we don't take this to the police. He's adopted the mare and has gotten Phantom off the range. I always felt guilty for spying on him in the '90s, I think we should just leave him alone."

Aletta noted, "The FBI is never going to have him on their suspect list. Nothing is going to bring Aaron back from the dead. I agree with Carl."

Pam said, "I would prefer not to mention the whole crazy shape-shifting again, so I will happily leave things as they are."

"Hey, I don't know when we will do this again," said Carl, "but next time let's pick out an easier crime to solve."

{Chapter 61}

Navajo City Roadhouse Blog:

Quiet Time at The Roadhouse

Saturday, February 04, 2011

Six-thirty P.M. is a quiet time here at the roadhouse. There are a couple of guys sitting by the woodstove eating mushroom Swiss burgers. I am expecting my two regular coffee customers to wander in momentarily (the only guys that buy coffee in the afternoon). I've been scrubbing the woodwork around the doorways but it still looks grungy. The cook is taking a little siesta so he can be ready for the clean-up.

The big gossip here this afternoon is the Jeep roll-over just across the county line. The thing was crushed, but miraculously, no one got hurt. The State Police have been there about an hour and a half, waiting for the tow truck. I found out recently that the State Police don't call the closest wrecker but rather, they have a strict rotation on a list. In other words, they call someone across the county and the person with the wreck could have a much larger tow bill than necessary. What a racket!

We had a baby in here this afternoon. You know I was glad that I scrubbed that highchair the other day! It was a clean little baby and I would have been so embarrassed to put it into a grubby highchair.

Last night I was getting ready to leave and darned if my battery wasn't dead. Had to push-start my Jeep. It's a lonely feeling out here when you think you might be stranded.

Gotta go ... time to clean up.

Yours truly,
Aletta Ramsden

{Chapter 62}

Candlemas Concerns

Aletta stood next to a table, hip cocked, supporting her weight on her left foot while she absentmindedly prodded the table leg with her right boot. She held the cell phone to her left ear, while in her right hand she held a damp white rag. Her ear was starting to ache from having the phone pressed against it.

"yeah … yeah … right … I didn't know that … I don't know what to do … we're feeding them everyday quite a ways from the road … yeah … I don't know how to move them off the highway … I thought they would too … I hate hearing they look so bad … okay, Jane, I will call you if I think of anything we can do … bye."

Aletta sighed and finished wiping down the table. The Off-Road Feeding Project had successfully prevented more horses from migrating to the highway, but it had not pulled any of the starving horses off the roadway. People in the community didn't realize that feeding them on the road was going to cause them to be killed, so the humans continued to provide just enough food to keep the horses from leaving. She rinsed the rag in the sink and hung it to dry before returning to her normal resting position by the cash register.

The cowbell clanked and three Sisters from the Virgin of the Canyons Monastery stepped in. To Aletta, they looked so formal in their black habits; their heads and necks swaddled in pure white under their black hoods. Each had a wide collar and a crucifix hanging from the rosary around her neck. They looked worried and scurried up to the cash register in a cluster.

"Miss Aletta, we've come to talk to you about Candlemas," said the tallest of the three. She had a strong downward curving nose and thick cheeks. She wore wire-rimmed glasses and her skin was a ghostly white.

"Oh, another holiday to announce in the blog?" Aletta asked.

"No, Candlemas is two days past. The prediction is dire. We need your help," said the Sister.

223

"February second ... wasn't that Groundhog Day? It was a pretty nice day, wasn't it?" asked the waitress. Suddenly she scowled, "What's Candlemas?"

"The Feast of the Presentation of the Lord," the Sister replied. "Forty days after Jesus was born, he was presented to the temple. It is one of the Four Joys of the Rosary."

"Okay," Aletta said tentatively as she realized that what she was hearing was pretty much a foreign language. "What is this dire prediction?"

"Six more weeks of winter. You know the ancient poem:

If Candlemas Day be fair and bright,
Winter will have another flight:
But if it be dark with clouds and rain,
Winter is gone and will not come again.

"It was sunny indeed," continued the Sister. "The Lord's wisdom is infinite, but sometimes he is providing us with the opportunity to act from our higher selves. We think this is one of those times."

Aletta tried to make light of the situation, "Maybe you could get a second opinion from the groundhog network." She laughed.

The nuns looked irritated. The tall Sister said, "Miss Aletta, our quest for humility requires that we be slow to mirth as we have been admonished that only the fool lifts up his voice in laughter. However, we rejoice that you are happy. We must however, in this instance, remain focused on the plight of the animals which are starving even within sight of our holy church."

"I'm supplying just under a ton a week in the Off-Road Feeding Project. I don't know what else I can possibly do."

The shortest sister exclaimed, "The animals are starving. We are feeding Valentino, our elk, and some of the animals at the monastery but we have no budget to do so."

Aletta suddenly imagined rivers of donations flowing to the Vatican while animals died on monastery doorsteps. She felt herself grow distrustful.

224

The tall sister spoke again, "Unfortunately, one of the Sisters has been feeding the animals from our own pantry, which is strictly prohibited. She has been excommunicated and beaten for it, but if she tries to justify her actions, she will be expelled. The real problem, Miss Aletta, is that everyone knows she is right. As compassionate humans, we cannot watch the animals suffer but the only thing we know to do is pray." The Sisters all stared at the floor.

Aletta felt her eyes fill with liquid. She couldn't imagine someone being beaten for feeding starving animals. "Maybe I could share some of my hay funds with you to help alleviate the conflict. I need some help from you all too. You can help me get the horses off the highway."

***

And so it came to pass that on the 6th of February, a procession led by Benedictine nuns—their long black habits in sharp contrast against the snow-—followed some malnourished mustangs down Highway 64 to the gates of the Virgin of the Canyons Monastery, through which they passed, followed by a large number of Catholic riders and horse-loving pilgrims. As the horses were eating their portions of hay, the taller of the Sisters recited a modified version of the prayer of St. Francis of Assisi:

"Blessed are you, Lord God, maker of all living creatures. You called forth fish in the sea, birds in the air, and animals on the land. You inspired St. Francis to call all of them his brothers and sisters. We ask you to bless these horses. By the power of your love, enable them to live according to your plan. May we always praise you for all your beauty in creation. Blessed are you, Lord our God, in all your creatures! Amen."

{Chapter 63}

Good Buddy, Sad Story

Dear Rita,

We went down to John's last night to get a new wood stove to replace the old one here at the City. We are trying to not use the gas heater at all up here since the price of propane got so bad. When we were loading our gear into the truck to head to John's place, Keith Spencer came walking around the corner, totally drunk and looking for some shelter from his life.

You will remember him, he is the dad of the girl that spent a day with you learning to be a waitress, and then you and I went to his parent's place in La Jara for the 4th of July party. Anyway, Keith lost his job at Conoco-Phillips in the mess of his life. I don't expect to see him around the oil patch in the near future.

So we took him down to John's place with us after work. Milton was there adding an electrical outlet. We pulled the wood stove out of the guest room and replaced it with a smaller but more efficient stove. You are going to like this new one better. It has a glass window.

Keith built a big fire in the little stove and slept on the couch with Chica and Milton's dog, Julie. John says that this morning Keith was sober enough to want to go back home and try to salvage his life ... all his kids are now living with their various moms. He might pull it off, but crushing debt and a very materialistic ambitious wife are not easy to live with in a tough economy. When an alcoholic is looking for an excuse to drink, it doesn't take much, does it?

John dropped him off in Blanco at 6:30 this morning and I saw Keith on the side of the road on my way to the mustang holding facility.

There are signs this winter may be winding down. Blanco and Na-vajo City appear to be on different planets right now. There is no snow down at Blanco and even the mud has dried up. My garden has emerged from the snow and my heart wants to dig into it. These days really whet my appetite for spring; it's time to peruse the seed catalogs.

Yours,
Aletta

P.S. I called Keith a couple of times today, but he's not returning his calls. I fear that doesn't bode well for his sobriety.

{Chapter 64}

Mustang Fever

Aletta sat in her Jeep waiting for the left-turn arrow to allow her to proceed. Bones and Koby sat in the back seat watching other vehicles in case one of them should contain a dog. In the old days, the sight of another dog would have set them barking, but now they understood that another dog meant that dog biscuits were available for not barking. It had taken Bones a lot longer to understand he would get a biscuit if he kept his mouth closed, but Aletta didn't mind honoring the commitment of maintaining a biscuit stash if it meant having the dogs under control.

Traffic started moving and she swung her little Jeep onto southbound Highway 550. The dogs had done very well in being introduced to and interacting with the mustangs. Bones had considered barking on the first morning, but the mustangs had just ignored him. Now the whole pleasant routine for the dogs was to check the horses then patrol the perimeter of the facility for the smells of any wild creatures that had managed to get through the chain-link fence.

Mucking the horse manure had been added to the daily tasks once the ground had thawed. Someone had scraped all the winter's muck with the tractor and since then, she and Jessica kept the pens clean by forking it up and hauling it to the muck heap. Aletta considered mucking to be a Zen meditation; it gave her mind time to work things out for itself. The horses quickly got used to the two women moving quietly around the perimeters of the pens and it wasn't long before the horses paid little attention to them at all. Hay was more interesting to the equine mind.

On this particular late February morning, she pulled into the parking area and realized that almost all of the horses were gone. Two pens near the haystack had two horses in each. It suddenly seemed so empty and lonely. Jessica was rolling a wheelbarrow from the barn.

"Hey, Jessica! What happened to the rest of the horses?"

"Mustang Camp took ten yesterday," replied Jessica. "They've been picking them up once a month. We'll try to get these last four adopted from here. Adoptions usually pick up in March; people start thinking about having a horse to ride by summer."

"I guess you don't really need my help with just four horses," said Aletta. "Can I stay and help this morning?"

"Of course!" Jessica replied. "I hope you realize how much I have appreciated having your help, Aletta. You are an excellent volunteer in addition to being a wonderful friend. I am going to miss you."

"Will you be getting any more horses this year?" asked Aletta.

"We won't have another gather for at least five years."

"I don't know if I can live without a mustang that long," sighed Aletta.

"You might have to adopt one. Do you have a space for a horse?"

"I have 10 acres I live on. It's just sagebrush and wormwood, but it is fenced," Aletta replied.

"Well, that cute little Number 22 could be yours for only one-hundred and twenty five dollars. He's at Mustang Camp and should be ready for adoption in two months."

"I'll think about it," Aletta said as she laid her manure fork in the wheelbarrow. She pushed the wheelbarrow into one of the now empty pens and started cleaning up what the animals had left behind. It won't be long before the Off-Road Feeding Project will be over, she thought. "This is going to leave a hole in my life."

Before she and the dogs left the facility for the last time, she had Jessica write down the phone number for Mustang Camp. Maybe Sephra would like to take a trip out there with her?

***

Doc Barlow and her dog, Roy, met the two visitors at the gate. Aletta had called to make an appointment and inquired if she and Sephra could bring their dogs, so the three women carefully supervised the canine introductions to prevent any dog-fights. Bones and Roy sniffed noses, sniffed butts, scratched the ground and turned back to their owners. Koby kept close to Aletta and ignored the males. Sephra elect-

229

ed to keep Duke inside the Jeep since he wasn't mustang savvy and she didn't want him to get muddy.

Aletta knew Doc from the horse trainer's infrequent stops at the Roadhouse, but she had never been to Mustang Camp. "This place is amazing! Was it really an old school?" she asked.

"It was the Largo Canyon School, which closed in the eighties. We remodeled it to look like an Indian pueblo in 2003. If you need to stop by the restroom, it's just inside those double doors on the left. If not, we might as well head back to the pens."

Sephra excused herself and Aletta and Doc stood waiting in the sunlight of the canyon landscape. Horses were milling around the yard. Two bays approached the women; Aletta noticed that they had government brands on their necks. Doc reached over and started scratching the withers of the one closest to her. The horse started wiggling its lips, stretching them farther away from the teeth, lifting and curling them with ecstasy of the scratching.

"So you are thinking of adopting? How much horse experience do you have?" Doc asked.

Aletta described her prior limited experience with horses and how she was an avid dog trainer and used mostly positive reinforcement. Doc assured her she would be successful with whatever horse she chose because all of them had been started with positive reinforcement. They would only vary in the time it would take to teach them what they need to know for their new jobs. Sephra rejoined them and they strolled to the pens.

"When I was volunteering at the BLM place, I liked one they called twenty-two," said Aletta.

"We named him Kiowa. He's in the last stall," said Doc. "He's one of the newbies. Until we can get them to follow us around, they live in stalls."

They walked past the other stalls where the mustangs stood relaxing in the sunshine. Kiowa was licking a brick-red salt block and looked up as the women approached. He walked to the fence and watched them.

"Will he let me get close?" asked Aletta, who had only seen the horse in his previous wild state.

"Kiowa ... oh, yeah," Doc said. "I have some hay here in my shoulder bag, put it on your shoulder and go into the pen. Move really slow and be careful not to grab toward him. He should let you pet his face and his neck, especially on the left side. Just pet him and feed him so you get associated with good things in his mind." She held the gate open for Aletta to enter the pen.

She held out a handful of the chopped hay. Kiowa approached, with his head high and his eyes wide.

"Do you think he remembers me and has already associated me with something bad?" asked Aletta.

"Be patient," Doc replied. "He's interested."

The horse started bobbing his head up and down with his nose stretched towards Aletta's offering of hay. Then he took a step toward her and took the hay from her hand. He did not step away, so she offered him another handful.

"His lips are so soft!" Aletta marveled.

"Uh, oh! You're falling in love!" cautioned Sephra.

"Might already be too late to change that," noted Doc. "He is a good level-headed horse. He'll make a wonderful trail horse. Now, put your hand up and ask him to *target face*, he should touch your hand with his face. It is much less frightening to be touched if it is their choice."

Aletta held up her hand and gently commanded him to *target face*, and he stepped forward to bump his face on her fingers. She broke out in a giant smile.

"Now feed him for his efforts. If you know clicker training from your dogs, instead of a click, we use a verbal bridge '*dee*'."

It was familiar language to Aletta and more so to Sephra, so the next time she offered the target to the horse, when he touched her hand, she said '*dee*' and then fed the horse. Doc looked pleased to be talking to an adopter who understood something about modern animal training. Soon Aletta was petting his neck and scritching his withers. Kiowa was enjoying the attention, when Aletta thought about the time of day. "Oh! We better go. I am going to be late."

"Okay," Doc said holding the gate open for Aletta. "Let me grab an adoption form for you to take with you. Let me know if you want me to hold him for you."

Doc detoured off the path back to the vehicle to go into what appeared to be a dining room with large plate glass windows. She returned with the form before the girls got through the gate. "Here you go," she said handing the form to Aletta.

"If either of you two ladies would ever like to come out and get some practice training mustangs, I surely wouldn't mind," offered Doc. "I can see you have some skill and experience."

The two young women looked at each other and laughed. Sephra said, "We inspire each other!"

They called the dogs, who jumped into the Jeep through the tailgate on cue. Aletta and Sephra found their own seats, and headed north, back to civilization. Sephra turned in her seat to face forward as she finished giving Duke a friendly greeting. "So are you going to do it?"

"I shouldn't have come out here. Maybe my subconscious mind thought the horse's wildness would sober me up and I could quit fantasizing about owning a mustang. *But that horse*! How could I *not* fall in love? How can I possibly afford him?"

"I thought you said he was only $125 dollars?" Sephra said.

"The purchase price of the animal isn't the issue. It's the hay, the tack, vet care, the pen and the shelter. That's the part I have to afford," replied the pragmatic waitress.

"Okay, the price of hay ..." started Sephra.

"Two-hundred and fifty dollars a ton comes out to seventeen dollars a week plus shipping. I could do that," Aletta interjected. "I have to have a saddle and stuff ... that's at least $500 for anything decent.

"I would have to build a pen for him," she continued. "I don't know what it would cost, but I think an estimate for $1000 to build a pen with a three-sided shelter and roof is probably close."

"Sounds like you need $1675 to adopt Kiowa. I can make a donation to help him get a good home," offered Sephra.

Aletta turned to give her friend a grateful smile, then turned back to watch the road. They drove along in silence for several minutes.

"The other thing is how much commitment I would be making. I couldn't really take the horse anywhere without a truck and trailer, so it would limit my time to the trails around my house and on the BLM land around me."

Sephra countered, "It could be worse! At least you have public land around you. You wouldn't have to be stuck on the sides of roads."

"Yeah, but Sephra, it's just the loss of freedom that scares me ... and besides horses are social animals, would it be fair to make him live with a pack of half-Airedales to keep him company when I am away?"

"I see what you mean," said Sephra who always found it easy to see things from an animal's point of view.

They drove for at least five miles before either of the girls felt inspired to continue. Aletta finally broke the silence by saying, "They won't be catching mustangs again for several years. It might be my last chance for a local mustang. I will never find a more perfect one than Kiowa."

"Doesn't Mustang Camp also get BLM horses from Utah?" asked Sephra.

"That's what Doc said," replied Aletta glumly. Sephra knew her friend desperately wanted the young gelding.

They had turned on the pavement before they felt the need to continue the conversation. "I am not going to fill out the application form until I have a pen and shelter built and the money for a saddle saved. Or maybe I can find a cheap used one. Anyway I am going to wait. If I need a mustang fix, I'll go back out there and learn to train. I'll find someone around my neighborhood who has horses and will let me ride them so I know if that is going to satisfy me."

"Sounds like a good plan, girlfriend. Hey, did you call Penny and tell her you were running late?"

"Oh, crap!" said the waitress.

{Chapter 65}

Time to Mosey On

John Irick's father had called his son's accounting degree a *'license to steal'* and John never forgot it. In fact, it became one of those pivotal factors that shape the whole of one's destiny. Not only would John not steal, he rebelled against his father by barely charging for his time and even working for free. He could not force himself to do things for mere self-interest and as a result his clients were an odd lot of struggling businesses and dubious endeavors. John understood failure enough not to fear it.

The current *'basket case'*, as he called them, was a struggling lime farm in south Texas. They badly needed an infusion of cash to stay afloat, so they had come to him, through oil-field connections, to help them sort out their financial affairs and seek additional investors. He agreed to work on a percentage of the money raised. It had taken quite a bit of work to get the records into conformance with accounting standards, but with that in hand, he had set to the task of building an investment package. The company manager, however, was not an easy person to pin down and every time the investment package appeared to be complete, the manager would have a completely different concept to work from. Everything would have to be revised.

John had already invested a couple of months on this project, and he was starting to doubt that the protean manager could possibly appear to be credible to investors. He realized that he was going to have to spend a few weeks at the lime farm to keep the manager in bounds. Once the project was funded, it would be out of his hands and, right now, he needed the money.

He was thinking about the lime farm as he pulled off Highway 64 into the Roadhouse parking lot. Even before he pulled around back, he could see that Willy was hitching his camper trailer to his truck. The snow had been dug away from the front of the trailer tires. It was almost ready to roll.

John parked and got out of his truck holding a newspaper and his briefcase. "Hey, Willy, what's going on?"

"Hey, Mr. Irick, how are you doin' today, sir? It shore is a nice day today, ain't it? Me and Nicky figured we'd mosey on down to Bloomfield, maybe rent a house or somethin'," Willy said. "It's too cold up here on the mountain. We found us a place where we can put up some corrals. It's been nice bein' here, but it's time to mosey on, don'cha think?"

John's inner accountant instantly told him that getting them unplugged from his electric pole would save fifteen-dollars a day plus the cost of their food. "Yeah," he answered, "that sounds like a good idea. Even one thousand feet lower is going to be warmer." He turned and went to the building. The back door was unlocked and Nicky was making pancakes. Aletta had not yet arrived.

"John, I put pancake flour on the shopping list because I used the last of it," said Nicky. "I guess you seen Willy getting ready to drag up and move to town."

"You're going with him, aren't you?" John asked with confusion.

"Oh, yeah," the cook replied, "but I gotta talk to you about it. I know you need me, so I am not gonna just leave, but I want to either cut back the number of days or change to the afternoon shift. It's really hard to get Willy up early in the morning and he is gonna have to drive me."

"Give me until this afternoon to explore the possibilities, Nicky, and then I'll call you and let you know what I can do. I do need you, you are right about that." With that said, John ducked through the hallway to the woodstove where he kindled a blaze.

As he watched the flames grow, he heard the back door and the sound of Aletta tersely greeting Nicky. He wasn't sure why, but the two women did not like each other.

Nicky called out the back door for Willy to come eat, then they brought their plates of pancakes in by the woodstove. John got up and started preparing to make breakfast burritos. Aletta began turning on lights, unlocking the front door, and preparing for customers. She kept herself busy until Nicky and Willy had finished, dropped their plates in the sink, and departed, then she came back into the kitchen where John was working.

"So, are the LeDoux's moving?" she asked with a smile.

"Yep," he sighed, "they are going down to Bloomfield to be warmer. Can't say as I blame them."

"Yes, it's much warmer at that elevation," said Aletta happily.

"How about Nicky being the afternoon cook?" he asked.

Aletta looked suddenly horrified. "That would not be a good thing. I would really hate that because she is such a backstabber."

"What do you mean by that, Aletta?"

"Well, she gets in these moods where she tells mean lies about people. She hurts people for no apparent gain. I've seen her do it many times. Think about it, have you ever heard her say one nice thing about anyone?"

"I see your point," he said. Then he sighed. "I'll cover another day and get her to come out four days a week, still the morning shift."

***

It was mid-afternoon before John called Nicky. "Okay, you take four mornings. What morning do you want me to pick up?"

"Well," she replied, "I am gonna need some money to cover my gas too, so I think about fifteen dollars a day for travel, and I can do it."

John's inner accountant started to cry, but the only thing he said was "What day do you want me to take?"

"You take Monday. I'll do Tuesday through Friday," she said.

"It's a deal," he said feeling thoroughly used. "Talk to you later."

His inner accountant told him to shake it off and not be disillusioned with the whole human race. *People*, he told himself, *don't really do much that isn't in their own self-interest*

{Chapter 66}

Navajo City Roadhouse Blog:

Barely Breaking Even.

Saturday, February 25, 2012

No one can complain about the weather. We've been in our shirt-sleeves all week. The main roads have dried out, but we don't have too many "main-road-customers" so they've all been going to work when the ground is going to be frozen a while. They might be wishing for a breakfast burrito when they go to work at 3 A.M., but at that time of day, there are no breakfast burritos on this side of the county. Then by lunch time, they are about to starve to death, so our parking lot has been packed. No doubt they like our food when the front parking lot is just a sea of muddy trucks.

We've decided, come better weather, that the waitresses here are going to challenge the waitresses at the Sportsman to mud-wrestle. The Sportsman is the bar/restaurant down in the town of Navajo Dam, twelve miles away. Those girls won't have a chance against the three of us. The plan is to publicly challenge them in the newspaper so even if we don't get to wrestle, we'll get some advertising. I just hope I don't have to wear a bikini.

They haven't finished the women's bathroom yet. John, the owner, came over yesterday to move the drain pipe after he couldn't find a toilet to fit in that small of a space. He had to dig a tunnel under the building. He called the operation arthroscopic plumbing. I was glad I wasn't here to have to see or smell it. While he was down there he found out the reason that floor is so spongy is because it's made out of old particle board, so when he screwed the concrete board onto the particle board, well, he might as well have screwed it to a marshmallow. The net result is that he had to tear up my nice tilework and put in longer screws. One step forward, two steps back.

This week was the first week this place has broken even with its overhead. We were jammin' during the week, but today, it's slower than I've ever seen it. We've actually been grateful for every muddy track through the front door. Total tips for the day: $5.36—Pitiful isn't it?

Yours truly,
Aletta Ramsden

{Chapter 67}

It Starts with Ghrelin

Normally when the stomach is empty, a neurochemical called ghrelin is secreted. The secretion of ghrelin continues until the stomach is stretched. Ghrelin travels through the bloodstream to the brain, where it activates brain cells in the deepest part of the primitive brain to increase the sense of hunger and prepare the body for food intake. Ghrelin provides an animal with motivation to seek out food by sniffing, foraging, and hoarding.

Fat is the most efficient way to store energy. Survival is dependent on having the energy resource to fuel life's many necessities. The first priority is providing fuel to immediate metabolic processes especially within the brain. The second priority is to expand the modest glycogen energy reserves in muscle and the liver and additionally to replace any body proteins, such as tissues, that have been broken down. The excess calories, after these needs are met, are stored as triglycerides in adipose tissue, commonly known as fat.

Starvation is the simple inability to obtain the energy needed to sustain life. It can occur when the environment does not provide sufficient energy or the animal cannot utilize the available energy. The liver gives up its stored glycogen in the first few hours. The body then utilizes the fats stored in various areas. This process can take months in robust animals. The last fat deposit to be used will be the marrow of the bones, which will become transparent and gelatinous in a starved animal.

When the body has used all of its fat reserves, it will turn to the protein comprising the cytoplasm of the cells. The animal will eventually reach a point where the cells of the body are unable to perform the functions necessary for life. Death results from lack of sufficient blood glucose to provide the energy needs of the brain. The animal has usually lost no more than 30% of its original weight.

Although horses have only one stomach like humans, they share the necessity of robust gut microbial flora with ruminant animals. Inadequate food intake results in a rapid decline of the bacteria and protozoa present in a healthy animal. The horse obtains most of its energy from by-products of this microbial colony rather than from the food itself. The ability to digest fibrous material declines as the microbes are lost.

Starvation occurs most often in the winter and early spring months in cold climates. Adult animals normally store fat in the fall to use as winter limits foraging. Juvenile, yearling, and old animals are most susceptible to starvation because they have smaller fat reserves, higher nutritional demands, greater heat loss, and lower position in the social hierarchy. It is normal for 60 to 70% of the deaths to be animals less than one year of age. Starvation affects the unborn animals indirectly. The fetus will continue to take nutrition for its development from the mother, using her energy reserves until the mother absorbs or aborts the fetus. If born, the offspring may be stunted, too small to nurse or the mother may reject and abandon her offspring.

The duration and severity of the winter is critical to the animal's chances for survival, as it determines the length of time the animal must depend on its body fat reserves. Deep snow and cold temperatures, especially during the latter part of the winter can result in very high numbers of deaths, whereas protection from wind and low temperature will decrease the metabolic demand for energy.

Wild horses suffering from starvation are lethargic, unsteady, listless, and unafraid of humans. Their heads hang low; ears and tails are motionless; and their eyes are dull and expressionless. They often lie recumbent waiting for their fate to change. Their dull and shaggy hair coat fails to shed. Their skeleton is visible with a backbone rising from a vacuous frame, hips jutting out. Their sunken eyes sit in a disproportionately large skull. They die without a struggle.

It takes weeks of slow refeeding to bring the horse back from the precipice of death. Weeks of careful limited feeding to re-establish the metabolism of a positive energy balance. In nature, this would come about as a slow sprouting of spring's first green. Microbial colonies of the gut must flourish before the horse's world comes back to normal. Sudden access to normal levels of food kills the horse quickly.

Yes, but is starvation painful?

We cannot inquire if equine starvation actually physically hurts, but we can look to some human models where the victims are able to report on the experience. Choosing to starve is not uncommon in the human species. Two examples come to mind: anorexics and hunger-striking prisoners.

We normally think of anorexics as choosing to live in a semi-permanent state of near starvation. This psychological disorder has the highest morbidity of all psychological disorders. We now know that there is a genetic predisposition to anorexia involving decreased ghrelin activity and addiction to the neurochemicals produced by starvation. This disease is best addressed by understanding it as a disorder rather than a lifestyle choice. There is no report of pain associated with the starvation of anorexics.

Hunger strikes are often the only means of protest available to the incarcerated. By continuing to drink water, prisoners can often survive more than 100 days without food. Euphoria is a common sensation during the first stages of starvation. Later, with the onset of depression, comes the loss of interest in water, which complicates the problem of survival. Abdominal pain is observed in some but not all hunger strikers. There is not enough pain to constitute an effective deterrent to self-starvation.

The horses died quietly.

{Chapter 68}

Pickin' Up The Slack

Milepost 89 flew by the window, but neither Willy nor Nicky paid any attention. The discussion was heated.

"I know you don't like to bring me up here, but it's good money, Willy. My wages come to forty-eight dollars, plus the travel allowance that comes out to sixty-three dollars. If I take that job at Little Anita's, I'll only be getting waitress wages plus tips. That's two-dollars and forty cents an hour."

"Yeah, but Nicky, you'll be waitressin' and meetin' people." He put both hands on the steering wheel and looked at her. "That's the only way to get ahead, meetin' people and findin' deals, don'cha think so?"

"Well," she countered, "I've been meetin' all the vee-eye-pees in the patch out here. I know where the money is."

"Yeah, but your oil patch contacts have yielded no economic benefits to my way of thinkin'. The only one that looked to go anywhere was that ol' man, Placido and nuthin' came of that."

"I ain't given up on that yet," she said defensively as he pulled into the parking lot.

Willy pulled to a stop in front of the back entrance. Nicky sighed, looked at the door and looked back at him. "Willy, I hope you have a wonderful day. No matter if we argue, you're still my favorite cowboy." She leaned over and kissed him on the cheek.

He smiled and said, "Go get 'em, Miss Nicky. Your little cowboy will be here to pick you up at twelve-thirty."

The back door was already unlocked and as she walked in she could hear two men talking out by the coffee machine. She instantly recognized John's deep voice, but not the other more nasally voice. She hung up her coat, stopped at the sink to wash her hands, and walked to the front.

"Oh, Nicky! I'd like you to meet the new cook-in-training. This is Bill Clifford. Bill, this is Nicky LeDoux. I brought Bill in today to learn the Roadhouse menu. He's going to be a part-time cook to pick up the slack."

"Glad to meet you, Nicky," said Bill. "I've heard that you're one of the best cooks in the county."

"That's nice to hear," replied Nicky. "I try."

"If you boys will excuse me, I will get things going in the kitchen," she said ducking back down the hall.

"Since I'm here to learn, I better just stick with the teacher," Bill raised his cup in salute to John, and then followed Nicky into the kitchen.

She started going about her daily routine without bothering to explain anything to Bill, but Bill kept up a running commentary on the process, touching the equipment as it was used as if to commit the process to tactile memory. When she had the burrito making materials prepped and assembled in the hot table, she started rolling burritos and wrapping them in the aluminized paper wrappers. The last step was to secure the paper end with a sticky label marked with the type of burrito inside. She turned to warm another three tortillas on the stove and Bill moved up to the table and started rolling a burrito.

Nicky frowned, but started heating more tortillas, letting the man take over rolling. He seemed to catch on immediately or perhaps he had experience. She didn't know and she didn't care enough to ask.

The back door squeaked and clunked as Penny made her way through. She looked momentarily surprised to see someone new rolling burritos, but said, "Good morning," with a happy smile.

"You must be Penny," Bill said turning to look at her with a smile. "One of the legendary waitresses of Navajo City. I'm Bill Clifford, cook-in-training."

"Glad to meet you, Bill," she responded. "Is this your first job cooking?"

"Heck no! I've worked at a lot of Mexican food places. Most recently I was assistant manager at a pizza place up in Telluride. I also recently was a cook's assistant at the county detention center. I have a lot of experience. Can I fix you something special for breakfast later? You're going to love my '*migas*'."

"That sounds nice," Penny responded feeling most flattered by the consideration. "I'll go unlock the front door."

She stopped by the sink to wash her hands and then rounded the doorway, finding John studying yesterday's cash register report. "How's it goin', Boss?"

He lifted his chin in salute and replied, "Things are finally picking up, Penny. I think we are starting to see the end of winter."

"Yeah, it's been super busy. Hey, thanks for making a fire and putting on the coffee."

He grinned as she turned on the '*open*' sign, then as she was coming back from opening the door he said, "After you hang up those keys and get yourself a cup of coffee, come sit with me by the fire. I have something I want to talk to you about."

As she hung up the keys, as was her habit, she turned on the radio. Waylon Jennings was singing about always having been crazy. She filled her cup and made her way to the far side of the restaurant where John was sitting facing the fire. He pulled up a chair for her to sit next to him.

"Penny, Bill is my sister's son. He's been in a lot of trouble and I just picked him up from being released from the county jail. Please don't mention it to Nicky, she doesn't need to know, but since he'll be here with you, just call me if he is anything but on his best behavior. Can you do that for me?"

Penny nodded, "No problem."

"Now what service supplies do we need to put on this week's shopping list?" John asked.

Before Penny could reply, Bill came out carrying a tray of wrapped burritos. "Where do these go?" Penny got up to show him the metal and glass heated case. She liked this pleasant fellow, even if he had a "history" ("*Who didn't?*" she thought), and immediately forgot about the service supply request.

Bill returned to the kitchen with the empty tray and rearranged the location of the cheese relative to the salt shaker before he started rolling the next batch. Nicky rushed over, "What are you doing? The cheese goes over here. I want the cheese here," she said as she rearranged the cheese container.

"Nicky, it's not convenient over there. Look, everything else is lined up in order, but having the cheese over there makes it so you have to go back to the start of the line. When I'm rolling burritos, I'll put the cheese over here."—he thumped it down—"When you roll burritos, you can put it wherever you like. I'm rolling right now ... no, I'm on a roll. Get back, woman," he laughed, "I have burritos to wrap," he said, waving her away with his fingers.

John walked in with his briefcase slung over his shoulder. "Okay. Looks like you two are doing a great job. Nicky, I will call you later to get the grocery list ... could you be sure and get a list from Penny? Bill, I will see you Saturday at seven A.M."

As soon as he was out the door, Bill and Nicky looked at each other fiercely. Then quite suddenly Nicky's face softened and she said, "It's nice to work with someone with experience. Bill, I was the manager at an Applebee's in Oklahoma City for 15 years. My husband and I moved out here to work on some ranches, but this has been a hard winter. We just moved into town. Here, let me show you how to do the English muffin sandwiches."

For the next hour, Nicky was quite charming to the new cook, who waited for a lull in customer traffic to throw together a feast of migas (fried corn chips, with eggs and jalapenos) for the three of them. Nicky commented that it seemed like it needed some gravy on it and both Bill and Penny howled with laughter.

Nicky was standing in front of the hot deck with her hand on one hip and her spatula in the other hand, frying a deck full of burgers. Bill had just finished filling the tomato slice bin and was wiping the food slicer, when Nicky said, "There is something you should know about working here, Bill. Sometimes, John gets in trouble with his gambling debts and can't pay us. He's a compulsive gambler, you know, but he is such a nice guy no one wants to quit on him. He owes me quite a bit of money from over the winter. I think he owes me ... well, somewhere around six hundred dollars. I'd have to look to be sure. And when he's on a binge like that, he has a pretty nasty temper, but only when he's on a binge. We have to try to keep him from just spending all the money on the horses, but, you know, it's hard."

"You lying bitch!" Bill said as he stomped out of the kitchen.

When the hamburgers were pre-cooked and everything was prepped for lunch, she washed the cooking dishes, dried her hands and helped herself to a fountain drink with a straw. She was pleased that Bill had left with so little effort on her part. She sat down next to Penny, who was reading the newspaper. Penny didn't look up. Nicky said, "I didn't mind seein' that guy go," and then she sipped some of her drink.

Penny still didn't look up, but she responded, "Bill didn't leave. He's out at the woodpile chopping firewood." Nicky turned and looked out the corner window. She saw him swinging a heavy axe with a yellow handle. Penny continued, "Nicky, there is something you don't know, but you should ... Bill is John's nephew." The round hunk of firewood exploded under the axe.

Nicky put her hand over her mouth and sat thinking. Then she took her drink and poured it down the sink. She gathered her belongings and sat in the chair waiting for Mary to come in and relieve her, then for Willy to come pick her up.

After she had pulled herself up into the cab of Willy's truck, she turned to him and said, "Willy, you were right about these folks, I thought about it all day and you were right. There is nothing to gain here. I guess I'll be taking that job at Little Anita's."

{Chapter 69}

Mesa and Canyon

Salvador Canyon was as good as any place to start looking for treasure, thought Pamela as she turned off the pavement onto a tiny dirt road. Mr. Lucero had given her a key that would open any of the gates on his ranch in exchange for the rights to any Spanish treasure found. She had convinced him to settle for the *Spanish* treasure and to leave any Indian artifacts in place. It was a perfect solution. She climbed out of her truck to unlock the gate, then she drove through and stopped again to lock the gate behind her.

In a Tony Hillerman book, she told herself, locking the gate might prevent all kinds of dangers to lone female archaeologists. It gave her a sense of security to know the only possible other visitor to Salvador Canyon would be an oil-field operator checking on the three gas wells that had been installed along the roadway. Surveying private land had definite advantages if you didn't want to be disturbed by other people.

She stopped at the first oil pad. The well had been recently reworked and the entire site was dry. She parked on the north side and looked out at the escarpment. It wasn't far away. She wondered if she should even bother taking her daypack, but then decided that her camera and water bottle would be too much for her hands. She rummaged through a file folder lying on the passenger seat trying to decide which map to take. The BLM map was entirely the wrong scale for what she was about to do, but it had the 100+ miles of winding escarpment marked in pink highlighter so she could figure out what roads to use to access each area. The 7.5 minute quadrangle maps were only marginally better, and she had each one keyed to the big map. She decided to leave the BLM map in the folder and just take one quad, which she slipped into her pack. She got out, hung her binoculars around her neck, and shouldered her daypack.

She locked the door and set out hiking toward the rocky cliffs. Immediately she realized that she was walking down an old pipeline right-of-way, now overgrown with Russian thistle and goat heads. Winter had erased all traces of the delicate goat head plants but left a dense carpet of the seeds bearing long pointed spines. She felt them being crushed under her boots.

Suddenly, the disturbed ground was replaced by the sandy bottom of an intermittent stream. No vegetation grew in the wide sandy bottom. In the middle of it, water from the long winter continued to drain down a braided stream. As she approached the stream, the sand started feeling like she was walking on jelly and she realized there might be quicksand. The sand was higher and drier looking on the far side of the stream, so she took two big quick strides and then leaped across the water. She climbed out of the sandy bottom and continued up the old right-of way, which now was covered in shadscale and four-winged saltbrush; both plants that can grow in heavy alkaline clay. She was very thankful that the clay was dry as it made the walking easy.

Coming around a low juniper tree, she saw that it was time to leave the right-of-way and head directly for the escarpment. She climbed a clay slope to where the sandstone boulders began. She stopped to study her map and compare it to the landscape before her. The rocky slope in front of her represented a two-hundred foot gain in elevation. The little cliffs up on the slope were only 20 feet high. She climbed to the base of the cliff to start looking for rock art. The prickly pear cacti were growing in dense patches, so it was unfortunate that when she tripped over a small boulder, she fell hands first into one of the spiny plants. She pulled a pocket knife out and pinched the tiny spines between the knife edge and her thumb in order to pull them out.

She started following the cliff towards the south-east but the slope grew more gradual until there was no cliff at all, merely a talus slope, which she crossed easily. The slope beyond it split into two levels; she decided to stay below the lower escarpment. She rounded the contour of the land and found herself in a little sheltered drainage. A rock face darkened with a deep brown patina caught her attention. She drew her binoculars to her eyes and saw it. Definitely a bird, probably a raven. She knew that if it was a thunderbird, it would have a square god's mask instead of round head. She hurried to the base of the rock art panel and pulled out her map, logbook, and camera to record the site.

It took her about 20 minutes to photograph and sketch the petroglyph, look around for other artifacts, and record the information. To continue following the same level in the escarpment, she had to cross a dry arroyo. It amused her to remember how when she first came to the southwest, she had called them "gullies". She steadied herself on some rocks as she climbed into the narrow trench and then used an exposed root to pull herself out. The escarpment was rapidly gaining height as the mesa above rose in elevation. It seemed to her that there might be three levels of cliffs above her now. She looked up the canyon and estimated the final height of the escarpment would be around 1,000 ft., but that was at least three-quarters of a mile away.

A small flat area in front of her caught her attention. It was ringed with wolfberry bushes which are often found on archaeological sites. She hurried across the slope to it, noticing the slope was covered with low mounds. As she passed into the open center, she realized the mounds were old prairie dog holes; the soft ground collapsed and she was suddenly standing knee-deep in a burrow. She tried to pull herself out, but the edge of the hole continued to grow with her every step. At last, she started to feel solid ground and hoped the prairie dogs would forgive her. She scouted around the edges of the flat area for artifacts and found a small pot sherd. She photographed and recorded it before she continued.

The rock at the bottom level was getting too grainy and fractured for rock art but the escarpment above her looked very promising. The juniper trees were inviting and looked like the natural place for a human to gravitate to, so she started looking for a way to access the second level. A narrow slot in the rock with a series of steps seemed to be the answer to her prayers, so she tucked the binoculars out of harm's way and used both hands to scale the slot. As she reached the top, she felt the sandstone crumbling beneath her feet and the rock steps went tumbling down the slot. She would have to find a different place to climb down.

The little bench had quite a bit of exposed sandstone along its edges. The rear portion was sandy, as if the wind had been building a dune. Near the trees, she found a large rock, covered in lichen, which had some archaic stone working tools—really just harder rocks—and flakes of chert at its base. She suspected some ancient person had sat on the rock and fashioned arrowheads and other stone implements. It took her 30 minutes to record the site. She felt like she had made a very good start on her project.

Looking around for another way down, she realized there were no other options. She returned to the slot and looked down it intently hoping to see some possibility. The rocky jumble at the bottom made risking sliding off the edge too dangerous. She wasn't sure what to do.

She pulled out her cellphone to call for help, but it could not pick up a signal. She stared at the oil-field road below her and realized it could be a couple of days before someone came along. If she started a signal fire there was little chance of anyone noticing it. She retraced the back edge of the bench to see if she might escape by going higher, but the cliff behind rose at least 30 feet.

A couple of piñyon trees were growing below the bench, their tops only a few feet higher than the cliff. It was risky, but it seemed to be her only chance. She secured her binoculars inside her daypack, sat on the edge between the tree and the rock, and then slid off on her rump. She grabbed a main stem of one of the trees, but it broke with her weight and she crashed onto a lower limb. Her hands were sticky with pitch, but she managed to find a way to the ground. Her coat was torn and her face was scratched and bleeding, but nothing was broken.

Heading directly downslope, Pam crossed the dry riverbed. Her descent was fueled by anxiety so she walked in long strides, although she was limping to avoid weight on her right leg. She followed the road back to where her truck was parked.

Pam threw her backpack in the back, but the prospect of soiling her new truck with pine pitch made her take off her coat and examine the rest of her clothing before she got in. Settling into the driver's seat, she took the steering wheel in her hands, took a deep breath, and started sobbing. Fear and tension locking her shoulders started to release as she cried. She felt overwhelmed by the realization that her archaeological project was too large and too complex. It might be different if she was still young and strong. She felt humbled by the landscape.

"It's not fair to have to get old," she said out loud and then she heard herself whine and realized how absurd that type of thinking was. She sat up and stopped crying. She reached over and pulled out the BLM map. Muttering, "older *but* wiser," she started the engine, turned around, and headed north out of Salvador Canyon.

***

Forty-two minutes later, she was parked on Escavada Mesa, sitting on a rock overlooking Salvador canyon. Eating an apple and alternately staring through her binoculars and checking against the topographic map, she put little pencil marks on the map where ever it looked like she would like to look. She wasn't going to find any sherds this way, but she could cover a lot more ground. One hundred plus miles of escarpment would take a long time even at this rate. When it came time to climb to all these locations, Pam promised herself that she would not try it alone.

{Chapter 70}

Rita Comes to the City

Behind the wheel of her rental car, Rita was focused on two things: staying under the speed limit and trying to decide how much cooks were like surgeons. Retired from surgical nursing, she knew surgeons, but she was only guessing about cooks. She reasoned that their jobs basically worked the same way, the surgeon got the order, performed the operation as rapidly as possible, and other people wheeled the results out the door, making room for the next patient. Suddenly a vision of a masked and gloved surgeon having a rack full of open orders, a big kitchen stove, and a line of patients on gurneys made her giggle. "Well," she concluded, "they are both famous for their temperamental personalities." With that thought her foot grew a bit heavier on the gas pedal and the New Mexican landscape flew by.

Eighty miles ago, between Albuquerque and Bernalillo, she had been pulled over and received a warning about her speed, so when she noticed the police car sitting in the parking lot at the Continental Divide, she let her foot off the gas with a gasp. It wasn't that she had any reason to speed through the 250 miles between the airport and Navajo City; it was just that it felt good. The speed limit on Highway 550 was seventy miles per hour, but she was convinced this little rental car would prefer eighty. She adjusted her foot position so that she could barely touch the gas pedal.

Actually, the whole trip had been just a blur since the day John called and asked for her help. The staffing at the cafe was problematic under any circumstance because there was no population nearby with people looking for jobs. He had found a new cook to replace the one who had just left, but he was uncertain if the new man would last very long and John had to go to Texas for some consulting work. Something in his voice gave her the feeling he was overwhelmed. She had immediately arranged for someone to housesit, then cleaned the leftovers out of her refrigerator, stocked up with food for the house-sitter, and bought a ticket to New Mexico.

One-hundred and thirty-five miles later, she pulled into the driveway of John's home and parked. John saw her through the living room window and rushed outside to greet her and carry her luggage into the guest room. He had some soup simmering on the stove and heated a pan to warm the tortillas. Rita Mae lifted the lid on the soup pan and the smell of warm chicken soup with green chile filled the room. "Oh, God, John, how did you know I was craving your Green Chile Chicken Soup? That is one thing that I just can't get in Nova Scotia. I am so happy you called me to come. It's been a long winter up north!"

"It's been a long winter here as well. Wolf Creek Pass just got eighteen more inches of snow."

"Have you been skiing this winter?" she asked.

Nonplussed and a bit defensive, he replied, "No, but I have been to the hot springs in Pagosa a couple of times."

"I'm jealous! I love those hot springs!" she said. "Now what is this about going to Texas? When do you leave?"

"I fly out of Durango on the seventh, that's Wednesday, and I'll be back on Tuesday the thirteenth. Mary's back to cooking the morning shift and the new cook, Bill, is covering the afternoons. I haven't made arrangements for a cook over the weekend because I was hoping you could do it. It's still pretty muddy in the oil patch, so business should be slow."

"John, that seems a short-sighted solution. We need to train Aletta to cook so you always have her as a back-up. I thought about it on the way up here. Aletta can get trained during the week, then she and I can cover the weekend. Oh, and since I got here two days before you leave and you mentioned it, I think I might take my little rental car up to Pagosa Springs tomorrow. That just sounds like heaven."

***

Rita Mae showed up at Navajo City on Wednesday at nine in the morning. They had sold almost forty burritos and the cash register reported receipts of $213. It was looking to be a good day for food sales. Penny was finishing rolling the silverware into paper napkins and Mary was defrosting the freezer. Rita Mae filled a bucket with hot soapy water and started scrubbing the drink dispensers and other front area food service equipment. When she got to the Slurpee machine, she cleaned part of it before she asked Penny about Slurpee sales. Then when Penny said it was a summertime thing, Rita Mae declared it unsanitary and had the cook and waitress help her drag it into the storage room.

Things were looking good by the time Bill and Aletta showed up. Bill arrived at 11:30, walked in the back door, and immediately started checking preparations for lunch. He was slicing onions on the slicing machine when Rita Mae walked into the kitchen and he didn't see her at first. She was wiping off the ticket order rack when he turned around to replace the onion bin in the cold table. He almost dropped the onions thinking it was Nicky for a moment, but when she turned around and smiled, his composure returned and he grinned.

"Another cook?" he asked.

"No, I'm Rita Mae. I'm filling in for John this week. I come to help him out once in awhile," she said.

"Oh, yeah," Bill said, "I've heard about you. You were Merriam's friend and you helped John get the restaurant started."

"Are you part of the family?" she asked.

"The black sheep part," he joked. "No, really my mother is John's older sister. She lives up in Bayfield."

"I probably met your mother at Merriam's funeral, but that was so long ago, I've forgotten," said Rita Mae. "Well, I am going to excuse myself, so you can get back to getting ready, but I am glad you are here, Bill."

"Hey, Rita, save your appetite ... after the rush, I'll cook something special for you and Aletta. You're gonna love it."

"I'll look forward to that, Bill," she said as she walked back toward the dining area.

Aletta straggled in at 11:55 lugging her laptop. When she saw Rita Mae, she squealed with joy and ran to hug her. The cowbell on the front door broke up the happy reunion as the cafe started filling with hungry oil-field workers. Rita Mae's extra hands and attention added enough quality customer service that the tips were better than usual, though Rita declined to take a cut. Her oil field friends were happy to see the smiling waitress from Nova Scotia was back.

By 1:40, things were starting to quiet down. The guys from Dawn Trucking had bought the guys from Conoco-Philips lunch. The guys from British Petroleum had bought the guys from Halliburton lunch. The guys from El Paso Natural Gas had bought each other lunch. Aletta had bought Milton lunch. Jane and Don had sat with Placido Lucero to talk about the current price of cattle. A few men were left lingering over their meal, but Aletta was already refilling the ketchup bottles.

There weren't any customers waiting so Aletta and Rita Mae were surprised when Bill rang the waitress call bell. "Lunch for the staff," Bill announced when Rita walked into the kitchen, "Philly Fajitas." There were three plates covered in tortillas, beans, shredded Philly steaks, cheese, onions, and lime wedges.

"Does Aletta eat meat? I thought she doesn't eat red meat ..." said Rita Mae.

"Oh, that's right. Let me make her one with fish," he pulled her plate back and grabbed a fish steak from the freezer. Within three minutes, it had cooked and the three of them sat down at a clean table.

"Well, Aletta, John and I were talking about needing a back-up cook, and we decided to ask you if you would like to train for it?" began Rita Mae as she watched the waitress for a reaction.

Aletta's eyes widened, but she was chewing on a bite of fish and couldn't reply immediately.

Bill said, "That's a great idea. I can train her."

"I don't know if I have the temperament to be a cook," she said swallowing the fish. "I don't know if I can hold up under the pressure. I manage when it is one hamburger at a time, but beyond that is frightening."

"Well, let's just try it. It won't hurt for you to learn it and since I will be here until next Tuesday, you'll have an opportunity to do something out of the ordinary," said the older woman. "We'll start on it after we finish eating." She purposefully ignored the look of doubt on Aletta's face.

"So tell me about Nova Scotia," said Bill. "What do you do in those long dark winters?"

***

Aletta spent the afternoon learning the protocols for cooking and cleaning the kitchen. Keeping the food items in their designated place seemed to be key to the cook being able to work efficiently. Cleanliness was tied to the bucket of bleach water sitting on the corner of the big work table. It wasn't possible to wipe things down too often. Food-holding temperatures had to be monitored and there was a thermometer to help her learn to gauge temperature by feel. By the end of the day, her brain was tired of learning. She had cooked a few burgers, made french fries, boiled potatoes and baked a sheet of bacon for tomorrow. The kitchen sparkled.

Bill had given her a guided tour, and then supervised by assigning her tasks, but otherwise he had stayed out of the way and spent his time flirting with Rita Mae. By the end of their day, the two of them were singing along with the radio as Rita Mae mopped and Bill swept.

By Thursday evening, they were dancing, and on Friday, he asked if she would like to go fishing with him over the weekend. Of course, she had to stay with Aletta and run the restaurant, but she took a rain-check on the offer. Bill's mother came to pick him up on Friday evening and he gave Rita Mae a hug before he left.

Business was slow over the weekend and Rita Mae steered customers to menu items that would not be difficult for Aletta. She claimed to be *out* of enchiladas, when John Aragon tried to order them. Aletta looked tired at the end of each day.

"Cooking's lonely," said Aletta. "I miss my customers." Rita Mae momentarily wondered if surgeons were also lonely but then she remembered they had assistants and nurses. Cooking immediately won the contest for the hardest job in her mind. Her respect for the profession grew.

On Monday morning, Bill walked into the cafe right after Rita Mae sat down with a cup of tea. She expected a warm smile but he was frowning and looking in any direction but directly at her. "Hey, Bill, what's going on? Did something happen over the weekend?"

"Can Aletta cover for me today? There's something I have to do." He still did not meet her eyes.

"I can call her and see. What's going on?" she asked.

"I have to be in court at 1:30," he replied with a defiant glare.

Rita Mae called Aletta and fortunately, she was available. The neophyte cook was more than a little worried about coping with a lunch rush, so Rita Mae made arrangements for Mary to stay and assist. "It would be good experience for the girl," she told the breakfast cook.

With arrangements made, she approached Bill, who was sitting by the fire and reading some official looking documents. He looked up scowling until he saw her, and then his face softened. "I'm sorry, Rita, but I was in this crazy mix-up where I was mistaken for someone who was shoplifting at Walmart. I was minding my own business when they just came and arrested me. It should be cleared up after today. I had forgotten all about it until I got to my mother's and she reminded me."

"How are you planning to get there?" Rita Mae asked, instinctively prepping for the next event as all good surgical nurses do.

"Well, that's what I wanted to talk to you about. Do you think you could let me use your car?" Bill asked.

"No!" she responded immediately.

"I wouldn't be gone for more than a few hours," he pleaded.

"No," she said, walking away.

"My mother will pick me up then," he said without acknowledging her emotional distress.

She didn't look back.

Aletta managed to make it through the lunch rush with flying colors. The customers seemed happy and tips were good. Rita Mae insisted that Aletta take her share of the tips anyway. At the end of the day, Rita Mae invited Aletta to stop by John's on the way home. Rita had bought a bottle of wine hoping to share it with Bill, and even though that wouldn't happen, she still would like some company. Besides, Aletta's graduation from the Navajo City School of Cooking was something to be celebrated.

{Chapter 71}

The Youngest Mustang

Martha Ramirez hadn't really intended to pick out a pregnant mare, but the mare looked at her so sweetly and hopefully, that a pregnant mare is exactly what she adopted. Martha rationalized as she filled out the application and wrote the check for $125 that she would be getting two horses for the price of one. Then the man told her that when the foal was born, it would be hers and not fall under the terms of the adoption. How fun to have her own little one to play with!

The people that had gentled the mare had named her Maria, but Martha immediately started calling her simply Mom. As soon as Mom arrived, Martha put her on a special diet to make sure that the young one had everything it needed, but it turned out that Mom was a little picky. She ate every scrap of hay that Martha put in front of her, but she wouldn't touch the carrots or the grain at first. The carrots would be sitting in the bottom of the feeder untouched. The grain, Martha eventually realized, was being eaten by the chickens. The mare had a protein supplement block and a mineralized salt block in the corner of her shelter. The salt block now was sculpted by the many hours Mom had spent licking it.

Two weeks ago Martha had noted that Mom's udder was filling up. The bag itself had swollen up first, and then the teats had become turgid at the beginning of the week. Two days ago there were thick waxy drops hanging from the end of the teats. The mare's vulva was sagging under her tail. Martha recognized that the foal could be coming any time, so she called her daughter to bring her twelve-year-old granddaughter, Annie, to stay for a few days. It was time for the girl to learn about birth.

Martha checked the mare every three hours throughout the night, but each time Mom was standing quietly next to the feed trough. At dawn, the mare had moved to the far side of the two acre paddock. Milk was dripping from the teats, so Martha woke Annie to come watch.

It was cold, so the two humans tucked themselves up against the east facing wall of the shelter. The sun would warm them when it came over the horizon. The mare was lying down, looking back over her belly. She didn't seem to care about the humans. She raised her tail several times, then she got up, circled, and lay back down and looked at her belly again. Her left front leg was stretched and arched so that the bottom of the hoof was almost flat on the ground. The young mare grunted softly.

"Does it hurt her?" asked Annie in a whisper.

"A little," answered Martha.

The mare then put her neck on the earth and used it to try to roll her body. A gush of water was expelled from the vulva. She lifted her head and turned to sniff her belly again. "Her water has broken, *hita*. It won't be long now," said the grandmother.

The mare lifted her head high and slipped her front legs out in front of her, arched and curved, ready to push her body up, but the mare didn't rise. Instead she looked around at her surroundings as if the world had become very confusing. She kept her ears back as she focused on the feelings inside of her. She kept the length of her tail bone tense and curved so the hairs of her tail were well away from her body.

She jumped up suddenly and the bluish-white birth sack was protruding from her dark vulva. The mare seemed to relax between the contractions. The sack sunk back into the orifice and the mare started sniffing the ground. After pushing some dead leaves around with her lip, she raised her head high and curled her upper lip back to where her front teeth were exposed. With this odd expression she stood shaking her muzzle ever so slightly.

"*Abuela*, why is she making that funny face?" asked Annie.

Martha laughed quietly, "I don't know. Maybe she is happy?"

The mare put her lips back to the earth and rustled through the leaves. She bent her legs several times as if to lay down, but each time stood back up. Then she looked at the humans, and lay back on the ground.

A tiny white hoof was then visible inside the deflated sack. Martha breathed a sigh of relief that it was in the proper orientation for birth. The mare put her neck back to the earth and lay with her belly exposed to the humans. With each contraction, her body would stiffen, her upper legs sticking awkwardly high and her neck arching towards her withers. A second hoof and the tiny legs appeared in the growing mass of birth sack.

The mare righted herself to rest on her sternum and put her legs in front of her again as if to stand. She pushed her head and neck forward, then rolled back over and lay on her side straining. Her tail quivered and her breathing became labored as each contraction passed.

A small nose became visible jutting out between the mother's tail and the tiny legs, but then slipped back inside. The mare rose, turned a circle and folded her front legs to lay back down. She threw herself on her side again and strained to push the foal out, when nothing moved, she turned back up on her sternum for a minute until another contraction forced her back to her side to strain. She rolled part way over, the legs on her right side flailing in the air, and the baby's nose came out farther. Finding no relief from the pain, the mare stood up again, circled and lay back down.

The contractions became relentless. The mare strained with every muscle in her body and the foal came slipping out in a gush. Its head started bobbing immediately which broke the sack from its nose and allowed it to breathe. Its front legs bent at the knees and it sat up on its sternum to have its first look at the world. Mother rested with her head and neck on the ground. She was exhausted and had no desire to move.

The little foal managed to get her front feet on the ground, the shaggy rubbery coating on them made it appear as though they couldn't be used for walking. The foal scooted its body away from the mother, freeing its hind legs from the birth canal.

"It looks like the baby is wrapped in a blanket," said the young girl.

"That will fall off in a few minutes," replied her grandmother. "Now is the time for them to rest and let the blood drain out of the cord that connects them. This is when we must be the most still."

They watched as the active little baby scooted itself down the length of the mother's legs. The mother was still lying with her head on the earth, so it looked as if the baby might suspect that it had landed on an uninhabited planet.

Finally the mother rolled back up on her sternum and looked at the baby. She reached her neck to sniff the foal, looking somewhat surprised by the new arrival. The baby pulled itself closer to the mother's nose and they finally were close enough to sniff each other.

Fifteen minutes flew by while Martha and Annie watched every move of the foal with great delight. Then the mother rose to her feet and turned to sniff her baby. The umbilical cord broke in the movement but the bulky afterbirth still hung from the mother's vulva. The baby pulled her legs under her and started trying to stand. It looked impossible to the humans, but after a few false starts, the baby was on its feet next to Mom. It leaned and swayed as it learned to keep its balance; then it took a wobbly step forward, only to fall backward and land on its rump. It rose again and started nosing Mom's leg.

"It has to find the mother's nipples, Annie," said the grandmother. "It has to do so many things for itself."

Within a minute, the little foal had found the nipple, experimented with its mouth, and emerged from under Mom with milk dripping from its lips. The afterbirth slipped out of the mare and fell to the ground silently. As the foal turned around, Martha could see it was a little girl, a filly.

"What should we name her, Annie?" asked the grandmother.

"Pebbles. I want to name her Pebbles," replied the girl.

{Chapter 72}

Fears Summer

Eaglets have hatched from the eggs laid in February. They are making their first sounds; sounds which blow away all the bad that settled over the land during the winter. The breath of the Eaglets rustles the head feathers of the Thunderbird. The Thunderbird awakes and rekindles the thunder, preparing it for summer. The Mother Earth stretches out after awakening, and this wakes all hibernating beings. New growth begins from here.   Navajo Legend

Its Navajo name *Shi Yinaldizidi*, means 'fears summer', for it germinates in the fall, continues to quietly develop over the winter, explodes in growth as the days turn warm using every molecule of available moisture to spread its fibrous root system and send its grassy leaves upward. By May, its seed heads are developed, and by June it is only a dried grass falling to the ground.

It is a stealthy competitor in the cold deserts of the Colorado plateau. It leaves no moisture for spring germination of other species. Their seedlings die. *Shi Yinaldizidi*, or cheatgrass, as the ranchers know it, thus creates new unoccupied habitat for itself and marches onward. It was introduced to the American west in the 1890's and now occupies 100 million acres.

It becomes unpalatable before the seed heads develop. The dead grasses provide no nutritional value to grazing animals after May. This increases the grazing pressure on the other species of grass and contributes to overgrazing and erosion. Its spread is far more damaging to the productivity of the ecosystem, than is simple overgrazing. It has a greater impact on grazing than all the American mustangs combined.

Yet it still finds some redemption. Honoring the contrary nature of *Shi Yinaldizidi*, medicine men make a tea of it to wash their faces before donning their ceremonial masks. For the grazing animals, it is the first forb to offer them sustenance, and for that they are grateful.

{Chapter 73}

The Exuberance of Spring

The New Mexico State Police pride themselves on keeping the state's highways safe, but by the end of March, Highway 64 was clearly out of control. The typically empty stretch between Dulce and Bloomfield was packed with oil patch workers, water trucks, fracking convoys, well engineers, geologists, mud operators and all manner of roustabouts. The highway was dry and should have been safe, but every day the area's citizenry were calling the police about oil field trucks speeding, passing on curves, passing on the right on straight-aways and running them off the road.

Officer Fred Anderson took the new stack of complaints and returned to his desk to see if there was anything substantive in the lot. A license plate number wasn't enough. The New Mexico State Police official policy was that it takes several witnesses to complain about the same driver before they'd pull over that person or send them a ticket. Furthermore, the witnesses must also be willing to sign a complaint and testify in court. The residents of western Rio Arriba County were never going to do that.

Giving tickets in the oil field was especially problematic. Competition for good jobs was keen and it wasn't unknown for someone to call in a false complaint against a competitor. The safety programs at almost all of the major oil field companies mandated that an employee receiving a ticket be summarily dismissed from the company, so men falsely accused were likely to act irrationally. It was the kind of thing that might put a man on a downward spiral from which he might never recover.

The only solution was going to be to start patrolling the area more regularly. The mere presence of the patrol car would probably be enough to curb the reckless behavior. Fred sighed as he looked at his calendar. The prospect of lunch at Navajo City was the only redeeming compensation for this assignment.

It was eleven o'clock when the shiny black patrol car crested Manzanares Pass. So far he had found no sign of trouble despite the heavy traffic. As he crossed the county line at milepost 86, a rig-moving convoy of ten semis and two escort trucks waited to pull onto the paved road. Aware that they had limited visibility from eastbound traffic, he pulled over, executed a quick k-turn, and went back to station himself west of the rig-move. He turned on his flashing lights and got out to direct highway drivers to pull over. The convoy, led and followed by the escort vehicles, lumbered onto the pavement heading east. He knew the men appreciated his assistance even if they didn't get a chance to say so.

Back on the road, Navajo City soon came into sight. He noted that there were six white oil-field trucks in the parking lot and then wondered what the special of the day was. They didn't have a special every day, but when they did, it was marked on the little whiteboard behind the counter. He remembered back to when the place was a biker bar, but he never got to eat there back them. He would have had to go undercover. Not that the patrons would mind his presence, but his supervisors would certainly have gotten a phone call about one of their officers spending time at a bar.

He had time to patrol all the way to the Forest Service land boundary before lunch. A water truck was pulled over with its hood up at milepost 98, but it was off the road far enough to not constitute a hazard so he drove on. A pair of semis hauling liquid nitrogen was parked at the General American road turn-off and he considered for a moment checking the driver's hazmat certifications, but then didn't bother. A couple of monastery nuns in a Volvo waved at him as they drove to town; he waved back.

He turned around at the east end of the bridge over the La Jara wash. The bridge was new. He had heard that the pilings on which it rested had been driven into the sand eighty-seven feet deep and never hit solid ground. He tried to imagine what it would look like if all the sand was removed …. perhaps a miniature Grand Canyon?

He sighed … milepost 120 and he hadn't found any moving violations. Damn that quota system! Maybe something would turn up on the way back to lunch at "the city", so he pointed the patrol car west and let it roll. He was feeling the exuberance of spring and a big powerful engine when he came in behind a line of trucks going exactly at the legal speed limit. He slowed down, becoming part of the procession and hoping he might catch someone recklessly passing. Twenty miles later, he pulled out of the line and into the packed parking lot at Navajo City. It was a sea of white trucks. He parked illegally close to the mailbox because it was the only parking spot left.

He called into headquarters to check out for lunch, locked the cruiser, and walked across the parking lot. It sounded like a noisy group shouting and talking over the blaring radio, but when he opened the door and stepped inside, all eyes were on him and only the radio was left making noise. That moment could have persisted for an eternity as it registered in his conscious mind. Then Penny shuffled out of the kitchen and started laying plates in front of hungry men. The soundscape returned to normal. Fred found a seat at the counter, where Aletta handed him a menu and a roll of silverware.

"Hey, Fred, glad to see you! I hope you are arresting speeders today. What can I get you to drink and do you want the special?" Aletta asked.

He thought it wasn't fair for her to already know he would order the special, but he did, and a cup of coffee to go with it.

He had a few minutes before his food came to talk to the other customers sitting at the bar. Carl was eating his mandatory lunch. Jane had come in for a quick cheeseburger. Art was eating fish tacos. They were the only customers present who were not employed in the oil field, so they spoke to each other in hushed voices.

"I hope you guys can do something about this road," said Carl. "It's getting so stressful that I've been going alternate routes lately."

"Oh my god, I know what you mean!" said Jane. "I just about got run off the road twice yesterday. They've all gone crazy."

"You're not going to be able to do anything about it," said Art. "They have an organized communication system. They've got a code for police patrol and they just warn each other when you're coming. There is no way you're gonna catch them."

The idea of a lawless stretch of highway did not sit well with Fred, so when he finished eating and paid the bill, he headed down to a stretch of highway where he could tuck himself away to almost be invisible, and he got out his radar gun. Within half an hour one-hundred trucks had passed him and none had been speeding.

He drove back to the office slowly. He needed a donut right about now, but he didn't let himself succumb to temptation. He parked in the motor pool and gazed across the array of black cruisers. Suddenly it dawned on him.

***

The first day of official spring set a record on US Highway 64. Forty-six tickets were handed out in less than three hours by a lone police officer driving an unmarked white pick-up truck. Our hero, Fred, had made the world a safer place. A few fellows were looking for new employment.

267

Navajo City Roadhouse Blog:

Thanks to the Self-Service Customers

Saturday, March 31, 2012

Last night I had locked up and was sweeping the floor, anxious to get home, when Scooter drove into the parking lot. At the end of the day I usually have a few left over burgers in the hot case that I take pleasure in giving away, so I was happy to unlock the door and let Scooter in. He bought a soda and took a free (left-over) bacon cheeseburger for his ride home.

I finished sweeping, put some new paper in the bathrooms, and counted down the cash in the register, leaving $150 to start the morning. John finished cleaning the grill and sweeping the kitchen. I had ridden to work with John, so we jumped in his truck to do a few errands in town before he dropped me off at my place. I went into the hardware store to get some glue to fix the women's toilet and John went to the grocery store to pick up tortillas and cheese. It looked like we would get to our homes well before dark, with a good days work under our belts.

Then the cell phone rang.

It was Fidel Candelaria. The door of the Roadhouse was wide open. He had called the State Police and was remaining there. We turned a sharp U-turn and headed back up the hill to Navajo City. I realized that I hadn't re-locked the door behind Scooter. For some reason we didn't worry too much even though last month's inventory build-up and the register were at stake. We were prepared for whatever we found.

Two police officers and Fidel were sitting at the counter chatting when I bounded in the front door. There was a little pile of money on the counter near the cash register. A note on a napkin around a couple of dollars read "2 packs of dentyne". The $150 was still in the register and the self-service customers had left $11 to pay for their purchases. It had been at least 2 hours between when we left and when the place was secured by Fidel. It kind of restored my faith in the world.

Thank you, unknown customers!
Yours truly,
Aletta Ramsden

{Chapter 75}

Winterkill

Sam reached over to turn off the radio. Bruce Springsteen had never been one of his favorites and this new song, "Atlantic City" really bugged him. *Everything dies,* yes, but *someday comes back.* "What kind of reincarnation crap is that?" he shouted at the radio. "Life doesn't go anywhere; it just ceases to function. Grow up and get real, Bruce."

He reached to roll down the window and let some of the morning air clean the bitter feelings from his mind, but his left arm refused to lift the crank handle, so he had to hold the steering wheel with his left, and reach across his body with his right. "Damn this getting old crap," had become his mantra lately.

As somewhat of a consolation to himself, in the wee hours of the morning when he couldn't sleep anyway, he had packed a lunch and his spotting scope, climbed into his truck, and left Santa Fe. That was four hours ago, now he was bumping down Rosa Road, heading into the Wild Horse Territory.

That asshole had betrayed him in the end. The plan had been to consistently remove fifty to seventy horses a year until they reached an appropriate number of animals, but the goddamned government had withdrawn the money needed to be consistent and had let the herd numbers get out of control. The power and glory of helicopters trumped any pitiful conception of a gentle gather. His years of hard work to provide a model of what wild horse gathering should look like was shit-canned.

"Fuck those horse-killing assholes," he said out loud, remembering the photos of the 1992 helicopter gather that had killed three horses. It had created so many outcries in the community that the Forest Service had been forced to let him try bait trapping. Twenty years of developing the humane trapping methods should mean something to someone. Paying him a small consulting fee to pick out which horses would be left on the range was more of an affront than a compliment. "A sort of fucking consolation prize," he said under his breath.

The sky had barely become totally blue. The clean morning sunlight was making the tips of the gray-green sagebrush glow. There they were! Three of the chosen ones. Two bays and a sorrel. They stood in vigilance, watching the truck pass. He knew if he stopped they would run and it would break his heart to see these pathetically thin animals use their energy so needlessly, so he drove on.

The Catholics had driven the highway horses from their land as soon as any cheatgrass was visible. The horses that had been down at Aletta's feeding project were in fair shape from what Duane Hutton had to say, but it was the horses farther back who had toughed it out that he worried about most. What about Phantom? Did the old fellow make it?

He came over a rise into one of the Range Manager's brush-removal areas. The cheatgrass was thick and green but the gray shapes littering the pasture shocked him. It seemed like a whole herd of deer had simply lain down and died. He stopped his truck and got out to walk through them. The fur coming loose from their pelts fluttered in the stiff April breeze. The scavengers had only fed on a small fraction of them. He picked up a leg bone and cracked it over a rock to confirm it was starvation and not some kind of epidemic. The marrow was a pinkish-red jelly.

Some darker fur caught his attention. Horses! Some number of small horses, probably foals and yearlings, were scattered among the dead deer. A disarticulated jawbone confirmed his guess about them being young. The front hooves were squared at the toe from the animal's efforts to paw to find food. The cheatgrass under the snow would have been meager rations for this many animals.

He took some photos and solemnly returned to his truck. His thoughts returned to Phantom and his son Clipper—had they survived? He headed toward the last place he had seen them, the roundup site. Four ravens sitting in an oak thicket only hopped on their branches as he approached. He realized that they probably were feeding on dead animals, so he pulled his truck over and got out to check. Six carcasses in various states of disarticulation were scattered among the litter. The coyotes had been spending time in the thicket, eating what was left of the starved animals, but Sam recognized the hide of the pinto that had been spared euthanasia by the murder incident. It was possible that these skeletons were all horses who had escaped on that fateful day ... but they didn't escape fate itself. It was clearly their time to go.

He got back in his truck and continued on toward the roundup site. He recalled that the Santa Fe New Mexican had run a story about the issues last year at this time. He should have seen the betrayal was already planned; the helicopter gather had already been scheduled. "Sam has done a great job for us, but I would say we have not been able to gather *enough* horses," read the interview. He knew they would never admit any responsibility for the population growth. Those years they hadn't gathered any horses would not be mentioned, it was easier to blame the catching method.

The road he was following started to deteriorate into potholes and sand bars where melt water had overrun the road. The first pothole caught him off guard and he bounced so hard that he hit his lap against the bottom of the steering wheel. The second one trapped him until he got out and locked the hubs in four-wheel drive. Suddenly he was reminded of all the times he had driven these same roads in spring, making plans for the year's catch and reviewing the consequences of the prior year's technique. Then he remembered dead horses in his own traps. He hadn't known you can't simply feed a starving horse; one spring, six had died miserable deaths as a result of his ignorance. He recalled a mare that turned and bolted from the trailer, crashing into the fence and breaking her neck. He recalled pulling his rifle from his truck and putting her out of her misery. He thought of the two foals killed by mountain lions while they were in his trap. He had listened to the screaming of the horses and the cats from the safety of his trailer, feeling paralyzed by not knowing how to respond. He thought back farther in time and remembered stallions fighting to the death, stallions intentionally put into the same pen, and suddenly all his bitterness dissolved in an ocean of guilt. The whole career choice suddenly seemed fueled by guilt. Had everything been merely to find a way to redeem himself with the benevolent horse beings? It seemed true. A humane trapping system was to be his gift to them. Tears fell down his cheeks and he wiped them with the sleeve of his shirt so he could continue driving.

By the time he got to the little turn-off for the road where Shauner was killed, the main road was flowing with melt water. He doubted it was worth the risk of getting stuck, so he turned onto the little two-track. It wouldn't hurt to have a look around at the crime scene and the hillside road was dry. The road hadn't been used all winter so there were no ruts or tracks. When he found the scattered bones of the dead deer, he knew he must be in the approximate location. He got out and walked around. A lost pen from the Office of the Medical Investigator near the cattle guard told him he was in the right place. He tried to imagine where the trailer had been, and then he found a line of fine ground organic matter that would have been horse poop last fall. It marked for him where the trailer would have been. The damage to the truck was on the left rear quarter panel, so he tried to guess where that would have been. Searching the ground he found a few bits of what were probably skull particles. He sat down on the road trying to sense the event. He closed his eyes and opened his mind to access his intuition. A vision of a man on horseback popped into his mind. He opened his eyes to visualize him in the landscape, and intuition told him that both the man and the horse had been hidden in the aspen trees.

He struggled up from the ground and crossed the greening meadow. At the edge of the aspens, he looked back at the location of the victim. He could feel fear in the air. Suddenly there was tension in his own body and he tried to just be open to the fear and listen to what it had to say. He tilted his head back from side to side, flexing his shoulders and stretching his neck, then he rotated his head, stretching his neck in both directions. As his head came back to its resting position, his eye caught something out of place. A white piece of paper sticking out of a woodpecker hole.

The little hole was higher than he could reach, so he found a small boulder and dragged it into position. He stepped up onto the rock and managed to snatch the paper from the hole. It was in good shape for having spent the winter in a hole. He unfolded it. It was a gas receipt from the Navajo City Roadhouse Cafe dated 10/28/2012, the day of the murder. The credit card used to pay for it was in the name of Aletta Ramsden. He immediately knew that there was no way that the little afternoon waitress would kill anything, much less a government employee, so he started trying to imagine ways it might have got there, but came up with nothing plausible.

He started walking back to his truck and realized how tired he was. He felt unbalanced and immediately chastised himself for not drinking enough water. When he got back into the truck, he drank some water then found his cell phone and called Tapia. "Randall, this is Sam Elkins. I found something up here at the murder site that I need to show you ..... Can you meet me at Navajo City? .... okay four o'clock, see you there."

Plenty of time, so he closed his eyes. It occurred to him that if he was looking for redemption, it had been granted. He had done the time and paid for the crime. Life had simply released him from having to gather horses. He was free. Perhaps now was a good time to start a discussion with Tapia about the government buying the patent on his secret mustang bait.

{Chapter 76}

It Makes No Sense

As Sam turned the key to the "off" position, his left hand reached up to his shirt pocket to make sure the receipt was still there, and not just something he imagined. Its smooth firmness was assuring to his touch. He was excited to think that it could blow the case wide open and that he would get the credit for solving the biggest crime in the history of the Wild Horse and Burro program.

Randall was sitting in his truck, next to Sam's parking place, talking on his cell phone when Sam pulled up. He extricated himself from the conversation and climbed out of the truck. Sam was leaning on the tailgate of his own truck by the time Randall got to him.

"What's the scoop, Mr. Sam?" Randall asked.

"I found something at the crime scene. I am not sure what it means." Sam pulled the receipt from the shirt pocket and handed it to Randall. Randall scanned his eyes over it, looked up at Sam with surprise, and then studied it in detail. "Cardholder, Aletta Ramsden ... so she gassed up her Jeep in mid-afternoon ... well, we do know that the last phone call he ever made was to her at the Roadhouse phone. She *was* the last person to ever talk to him as far as we know."

Sam said, "So ... she could have known the route he was taking."

"It's possible," said Randall frowning. "This is going to have some problems as evidence. It is just your word as to where you found it. How did it stay in such good shape except for this edge?"

"It was kind of pulled into a woodpecker hole. Maybe it smelled like food," Sam replied.

"Hmmm ... how else could it have gotten there?" asked Randall.

"I have no idea," replied Sam, "and I've been racking my brain for about three hours on the question. What do you say to the idea we go sit down with Aletta and ask her some questions?"

"Yeah, a piece of pie and some questions sound like a very good plan."

Aletta was sitting across the counter from a small silver-haired man who was talking. " ... this makes the animal abuser feel powerful and that's something they usually lack in their lives. Other abusers simply enjoy having dominance over an animal. There are also abusers who feel entitled to do whatever they want, resulting in things such as cockfighting or fighting dogs." Aletta and the customer turned to look at the new arrivals.

Aletta motioned to Sam and Randall to come sit with them at the counter. "We are having the most interesting conversation about the psychology of animal abuse." She grabbed two menus and two rolls of silverware and set them down on the counter. "Ice tea?"

They both nodded and sat down." Hello, gentlemen," the silver-haired man smiled, "my name is George Simon."

"Sam Elkins. Pleased to meet you," said Sam as he reached sidewards to shake George's hand. As the men dropped hands, Randall stood up, saying, "Randall Tapia here." He stepped behind Sam to reach around and shake hands with George.

"What kind of pie do you have today, Aletta," asked Randall as she set the two large ice teas on the counter.

"Blueberry, do you want it heated and with ice cream?" asked the waitress.

"Make mine heated with ice cream," said Sam.

"No ice cream for me," said Randall. As the waitress took the order back to the kitchen, Randall turned to George and asked, "What brings you to Navajo City, George?"

"I'm heading to a speaking engagement in Taos," replied George. "I was in Phoenix and came up through Flagstaff. I live in Arkansas."

"What kind of talk are you giving in Taos?" asked Sam.

"Well, I'm a Cognitive-Behavioral Therapist and I specialize in both the treatment of manipulative people and helping the people that were manipulated to understand the relationship," replied George.

"Hey, I went to Cognitive-Behavioral Therapy for depression and it really helped me," said Randall. "One of my staff was murdered last fall and I spent six weeks in CBT after I totally broke down."

"What kind of therapy are you talking about?" asked Sam. "Mental?"

"Yes," replied George. "We work collaboratively with the patient to identify unhelpful thinking and behaviors, and then we help them learn healthier skills and habits."

Randall smiled, "I had to learn to quit trying to please everyone. I am still struggling with it, but it gets easier every day."

"Sounds very practical," said Sam as Aletta placed a plate of pie and ice cream in front of him. Within moments Randall was chewing his first bite as well.

"We have our fair share of manipulative people around here," said Aletta. "I don't know why, but I swear that I am a magnet for them," said Aletta.

"Let's talk about that for a moment," said George. "Manipulative people need people like Randall here that are going to try to please them. Those tendencies to please others or put aside your own personal needs for the good of the social structure are given the label *neurotic* in psychological terms. In its extreme form, neurotic behavior is driven by shame and guilt and people totally lose track of their own self worth. Manipulative people seem to be able to sense a likely, that is neurotic, victim. It is also apparent that neurotic people may choose to interact with manipulative people as a way to organize their life. Falling in love with a manipulative person is easy for a neurotic person."

The waitress gasped, "Do you mean I really could be a magnet for manipulative people because I am neurotic?"

George laughed, "Don't worry, Aletta, almost all really nice people are on the neurotic end of the spectrum. Look at me, look at Randall. We had unhealthy levels of trying to please people, but we've learned better habits. You just need to learn some better habits."

"People can always make me end up feeling like it's my fault," she said.

"That's a typical tactic that only works if the victim is sensitive or conscientious.

Often they will prey upon the vulnerability of the victim before they make their power-play, so that the victim is afraid that the event is their own fault. The other thing manipulative people do is called *impression management*. They are very aware of how to maintain plausible deniability. They go out of their way to maintain a mirage of innocence."

"What are they usually trying to achieve?" asked Randall.

"Power, dominance, attention, gratification, excitement ... the list goes on. They are not all the same. And that brings up another point: one of the biggest mistakes a neurotic can make is to think that everyone is like them. Unfortunately there is nothing pro-social about the motivations of a manipulator and they didn't get that way through unfortunate circumstances, so don't make the mistake of feeling sorry for them. Trust your intuition; it knows how to smell a rat."

"Wow! That is what I try to do all the time ... trust my intuition. Then sometimes I find out that I've been suckered in again," said Aletta. "I wish I was going to your talk in Taos, I need to learn how to take some control of my world."

"Well, I've written a book, called *In Sheep's Clothing*. You can find it on Amazon. Hey, I better go on down the road; here's my lunch money ... keep the change." George stood up. "It was nice meeting you fellows." He turned and walked out the door.

Aletta turned to face the two men, who now were watching her with wide eyes. "I just love it when interesting people show up at the Roadhouse. I love to learn things about people. That conversation was the most exciting thing that's happened all week—well, until you showed up. What are you two doing out here today anyway? I haven't seen either of you in a long, long time."

"Well, we were out checking out the crime scene now that the snow has melted and decided to come in and see what you know about the events," said Sam.

"I've heard every possible rumor about it and I've talked to a lot of people about it. I kind of think it had to have been a random hunter on foot," the waitress said.

"How did you first hear about it?" asked Randall.

Aletta's eyes registered annoyance. "Randall! You called me up and told me not to blog about it! Then it seemed like you totally forgot about me."

"I did? Oh ... yeah, things in my life were kind of falling apart about then. Sorry," apologized Randall.

"Well, I still haven't blogged about it and some people have said that was suspicious in itself, since I am known to gossip about everything, but I gave you my word."

"I appreciate that, Aletta. I really do," replied Randall.

"You're welcome, Randall. We neurotics have to stick together," she said, happy to hear some appreciation.

"I don't want to be left out of the neurotic club," said Sam. "My guilt and shame is enough to qualify me as well."

"I think you are a junior member," teased Aletta.

"Oh, no, no," Sam teased back, "I get senior membership or I'll quit."

"Are you trying to manipulate us?" queried Randall. They all laughed, and the men rose out of their chairs to dig money from their pockets and toss it on the table with a *keep-the-change* smile.

"Thanks, guys! Come back soon. It was so nice to see you," said the waitress as she started to clear the dishes.

As he got to the tailgate of his truck, Randall turned to Sam. "When we went in there, I was thinking that maybe she was at least an accomplice, but ... well, in my opinion, Aletta didn't have anything to do with it. Would you agree?"

"I was really hoping to score a homerun on this, Randall, but you're right. She's innocent. What should we do with the receipt?" said Sam.

"I'll take it down to the FBI office. They will probably interview her and they might want to talk to you again. It doesn't prove anything, but it is more evidence than they currently have. We just have to trust for truth to prevail," said Randall.

"Sometimes that doesn't happen, Randall." said Sam, biting his lip.

"I know," said Randall, offering his hand to shake. Sam took it, but then Randall reached out with the other hand, and pulled Sam into a manly hug. "It's been hard, but it's gonna get better," then the men turned and climbed into their trucks.

"I'm too old to believe it's gonna get better," muttered Sam to himself as he started the engine.

{Chapter 77}

The Missing Tractor

Pam watched the old man climb into the passenger side of the truck. It struck her that she didn't know if there had ever been a Mrs. Placido Lucero. His pleasant manners and easy going temperament would have been very desirable qualities in a mate. Then again, he could have been a consummate bachelor, never presumptuous enough to take a wife. Or perhaps, maybe his age had tamed a once wilder and more ruthless Placido? It was hard to imagine the man in the passenger seat was ever ruthless, and she didn't want to risk stirring up any grief on what promised to be a very fun adventure. Placido had offered to show her some rock art panels in Gobernador Wash that had been left by his own ancestors in the 1880's.

They followed the San Juan River from Blanco to the Sportsman Bar and then turned south into the bottom of Gobernador Canyon. There was a publically accessible road across this corner of the ranch, so they didn't have any locked gates until they turned off the gravel road into the little side canyon where the main corrals for the ranch sat. Placido insisted on getting out himself to unlock the gate.

The small side canyon had an exceptional stand of cottonwoods, thick and stately, many wrapped with the bare vines of foxgrape. The foxgrape and the trees wouldn't leaf out for several weeks, but at this time of year the trees, which were either male or female, were busy with their sex lives. Their little catkin-like flowers had burst from the twigs and branches. The male trees (defined by who produced pollen) were hung with red pendulous inflorescences, while the female trees (who would eventually bear the wooly seeds) had much more modest whitish green flowers. This little canyon would be an oasis in the summer, but in late July Pam suspected that it might look like a snowstorm as the trees shed the cotton-wrapped seeds.

"This little canyon has a lot of water under it; that's why the trees like it. We built the corrals up here because of the water. I never liked hauling water," said the old man as they bumped over the rutted road.

"It's beautiful. It reminds me of home in eastern Ohio," said Pam.

"Yes, but it gives my cows the pink-eye when the cotton is falling. I had to build another corral for midsummer and so I get stuck with hauling water anyway," said the old rancher. "This corral is best for winter because the wind is never too bad. We always kept the saddle horses here in the winter."

Pam pulled up to the corral and shut off the engine. Suddenly she became aware that Placido was breathing faster and seemed to be staring past the corral. He grabbed the door handle, flung open the door and barely using his cane, walked around the edge of the corral. Pam got out of the truck and followed.

"Somebody took my tractor! It was right here. See these tracks!"

Pam saw deep tracks from tires with giant treads. She and the old man followed them to where they abruptly disappeared.

"They put it on a trailer. Nobody just borrowed it. The thieves took it. No one knew it was here but maybe two or three people and only one of them had a key. I knew I shouldn't give him a key. He gave it back, but I bet he made a copy. I knew better than to trust him, but he was going to do me a favor and put a few rides on my saddlehorse. I didn't listen to my heart. This is my fault."

"Should we call the sheriff?" Pam asked.

"The phone won't work in this canyon. Instead let's go up to the Roadhouse and see if we can find him," said the old man.

As they drove, Pam had the sensation that the key in her pocket grew very heavy. Her whole project seemed in jeopardy. She couldn't blame Placido if he decided to further limit people's access to his property. How would he know if he could trust her? Could she have done anything to prevent this? She didn't know, but somehow she felt guilty of trespassing against him. She wasn't really looking for the Spanish treasure that he wanted her to find. Was that cheating on their deal? Maybe he *shouldn't* trust her? Maybe she shouldn't trust herself? Maybe she was wrong to be doing this at all?

Aletta looked up from rolling silverware and broke out in a big grin when they walked in. A couple of men in fire-retardant uniforms who were eating a late lunch and chatting with each other about natural gas production, looked up momentarily and went back to their conversation. She put the beverages she expected Pam and Placido would order on the counter even before they had seated themselves.

"Lunch? I didn't make a cake, Pam; I didn't know you were coming," said the waitress.

"Neither did we. We're actually looking for Willy LeDoux," said Pam.

Placido picked up a napkin and said, "I'd like french fries with green chile and cheese melted on top." He casually sipped his iced tea and squinted at the other customers to see if he knew them.

"Well, Willy and Nicky moved about five weeks ago. They might be living in Aztec or Farmington. Pam, would you like anything to eat?" said the waitress.

"Okay ... a philly steak sandwich with curly fries," said the archaeologist.

Aletta disappeared through the doorway to the kitchen and gave the order to John, who was standing in front of the stove with a wide spatula. "Coming right up," he said with a smile.

She ducked back into the front room saying, "I heard that Nicky was working at Little Anita's and that Willy was shoeing horses in Colorado. Why are you looking for them?"

Placido turned to look at Aletta through both lenses of his bottle-thick glasses. "Aletta, do you think Willy is the kind of person who might steal a tractor?"

Aletta gulped and struggled to reply. She had never been asked to incriminate someone. "Placido, to tell you the absolute truth, I never knew those people to be thieves, but I do know that they are liars. So could they have stolen your tractor? Perhaps they could have. You should call the sheriff."

The order was ready and John dinged the waitress call bell. Aletta asked him if he could come out and talk to Placido about Willy, so he wiped his hands on a white bleachy rag and followed her back to the dining area. Placido looked at John and asked him the same question he had asked Aletta.

"He could have," replied John. "As I recall he was in some kind of trouble with the Cabots about a tractor before he came here."

"Oh, that's right, I had forgotten that," said the waitress. "You should call the sheriff."

"I don't think I will," replied Placido. "I don't trust the sheriff and besides that tractor is in Colorado by now. It won't bring it back."

"But, Placido, letting them get away with it means they will try and steal more," objected the waitress.

Placido smiled mischievously, "But not from me." Then he started eating his french fries.

Pam reached into her pocket and pulled out her Lucero Ranch gate key. "Placido, if you are uncomfortable about people having gate keys, here is mine if you want it back."

Placido looked at her with both eyes and twisted his upper lip. "Are you crazy? Of course I don't want your key. You're going to find the Spanish treasure. Don't be silly. I knew those people were no good from the start. Everyone always thinks they can put one over on Placido Lucero. First they nose around my house, then they see what else they can rip off.

"I got an idea, Pam. Maybe next week you could take me to Little Anita's so I can see if that Nicky will look me in the eyes." He opened his eyes wide behind the thick glasses and looked around at everyone making them laugh with him.

Navajo City Roadhouse Blog:

Springtime in the Oil-Patch

April 1, 2012

It's spring and business is cranking up as the oil field unfreezes and dries out. The drill rigs come back, the U.S. Forest roads open up, and the highway gets busy. Tourists and fishermen wander in and realize they have found something special.

Waitressing is all about being ready. It's easy when the silverware is rolled, the menus are spotless, the condiments are on hand, the tables are clean, the lemons are sliced, the glassware has the water spots polished off, and the coffee is fresh and hot. It's hell when these things are not ready.

Come see if I am ready for you,
Yours truly,
Aletta

{Chapter 79}

Interrogation Transcript

Stribling: All right, Aletta ... I appreciate you coming in. I'm Greg Stribling and I am with the FBI.

Ramsden: Yes, I met you at the Navajo City Roadhouse where I work. You were there for the Wild Horse Advocate Coalition. I'm the waitress.

Stribling: Uh, yeah. Now I recognize you. We are going to do a pretty thorough interview today.

Ramsden: Yes, I'm excited to get interviewed. I was wondering if anyone would ever get around to asking me what I know about it.

Stribling: So what we're going to do is go over a number of things.

Ramsden: I'm ready when you are.

Stribling: Would you like some coffee before we get started?

Ramsden: Oh, yes. You just made a pot! Let me get it, you drink your coffee black as I recall. Is that right? You didn't have any of the pie that night, but I should have thought to bring some. The morning cook has been baking blueberry pie that is just to die for.

Stribling: Uh ... Thank you. I have a simple rule when I talk to people, I treat everyone with dignity and respect.

Ramsden: I kind of have a rule like that too. I get better tips if I do.

Stribling: I'll ask that you do the same with me. We're going to start off by going through what your rights are—just like everybody else.

Ramsden: Oh, this is exciting. I'm trying to write a novel and this experience is going to be so valuable. Go ahead and act like I am really a suspect so I get the full effect.

Stribling: Uh ... basically in the United States you are guaranteed certain rights under the U.S. Constitution. Now Aletta, just to avoid any confusion, because people do get confused when they are called in to talk to the police, you are obviously not under arrest and are free to go at any time. The door is not locked.

Ramsden: I made arrangements for Brenda to cover my shift in case I am not back early enough, so time shouldn't be an issue.

Stribling: Aletta, if there is anything in our interview that makes you think that you want a lawyer, let me know. We can delay the interview to give you time to talk to a lawyer.

Ramsden: We should be good on that, Greg. I don't have much use for lawyers.

Stribling: I would like you to tell me where you were on the afternoon of the 28th of October.

Ramsden: I was at work waitressing. I had been there since early morning because we had to get a lot of food ready to go out to the wild horse roundup. We catered it, but you probably already knew that. I was there until a little after eight. I had a customer come in just before I closed up so I was delayed from closing on time. I was also waiting on someone, and I think it was probably Aaron Shauner who had called and ordered something to go, but ... uh ... he never picked it up. Hey! You probably have his phone records; was that call from Aaron?

Stribling: We'll talk about that when it's my turn; right now, I'd like you to continue your story.

Ramsden: Well, my last customer of the day was a Navajo and I almost fell asleep listening to the radio because I was so tired by then.

Stribling: Why were you tired?

Ramsden: Man, you've never been a waitress, have you? I was there for fourteen hours.

Stribling: Did you leave during that time?

Ramsden: I walked outside at some point in the afternoon and put fuel in my Jeep. There were some customers I didn't like, so I just needed some fresh air for a few minutes.

Stribling: Besides yourself, who else was working that day?

Ramsden: In the morning, Mary and Penny, and in the afternoon, Guido was working.

Stribling: Would that be Mary Decker and Penny Martin?

Ramsden: Yes, that's them. Penny is the waitress and Mary is the cook.

Stribling: Would you know Guido's last name?

Ramsden: No, I never did know that. I do know that he was an anarchist but he didn't ever do any harm. In fact, he supplied the murder investigators with free coffee and donuts to take to the crime scene.

Stribling: What is your normal work schedule and how was that day different?

Ramsden: Well, I normally come in just before noon on the weekdays and stay until eight, except in the middle of the winter we close at six. Then I work the full day on the weekends. My days off are usually Monday and Tuesday, but I think at that point I also had Wednesday off. That day I came in at six in the morning. I have to admit I was really excited about the roundup and wished that I could be out there with my good friend Sephra ... Sephra Brooks.

Stribling: How did you learn that Aaron Shauner had been killed?

Ramsden: Randall Tapia asked me to call him and he told me.

Stribling: Why did Tapia ask you to call him?

Ramsden: He wanted to ask me to not blog about it. I have a blog that everyone out there reads. But Randall asked me not to, so I didn't. Then he went off and had a mental breakdown and forgot all about it. I didn't blog about it, sir. I want you to know that.

Stribling: Yes, I am familiar with your blog. I was wondering why you didn't mention the murder.

Ramsden: Just ask Randall, he'll tell you. Of course, once Penny found out, I think she called me or something, then *everyone in the world* found out. It was out of control when I got to work.

Stribling: When did this take place—Randall calling you and Penny finding out?

Ramsden: It was the next day. Randall had stopped by the Roadhouse on his way home from the investigation. He gave Milton a card and asked him to have me call. Penny called and told me, so I called Randall right away.

Stribling: How did you know Aaron Shauner?

Ramsden: Well, Aaron was a regular customer. He'd pick up a burrito on the way to work when he was in the field. I didn't see him as often as the girls in the morning saw him. Sometimes he would stop on his way back to town. He'd usually get an order of french fries to go.

Stribling: Did you know him outside of work?

Ramsden: I was at a party at Navajo Lake one time where he showed up. He was pretty inebriated, but I didn't talk to him. Drunks make me nervous.

Stribling: You didn't have any romantic involvement with him?

Ramsden: Well, he was always trying to hit on the waitresses, but nobody took him too seriously. I definitely wouldn't have been interested in a guy like that.

Stribling: Would you like to help me scratch your name off the potential subjects list?

Ramsden: Well, I am kind of enjoying this, but let's get me off the list so we can talk about the real suspects. What do you need?

Stribling: I'd like to photograph the bottoms of your feet and get a print of your feet.

Ramsden: Oh, yeah! I forgot about the footprints, of course you'd be collecting footprints. Nicky, one of the cooks that doesn't work at the Roadhouse anymore, said the fact that I like to go barefooted in the summer was enough to implicate me. I told her that unfortunately for her theory, everyone is capable of going barefoot at a moment's notice.

Stribling: Okay, I am going to have you go into Mrs. Williams's office where she will fingerprint and footprint you. Then we will meet back here in fifteen minutes. If you need the restroom, it is the third door on the right.

Ramsden: Thanks, Greg.

Stribling: Now that you've had some time to think things over, is there anything else you want to add to your summary of the events?

Ramsden: No, but you said we would talk about the phone call ... was I really the last person to ever talk to Aaron Shauner?

Stribling: He placed a call to the Navajo City Roadhouse at about 4:23 p.m. What did you talk about?

Ramsden: He placed an order for a Roadhouse Roadkill with curly fries and said he would pick it up about eight. That was it. Wow, that gives a new significance to the photo of Aaron we have hanging at the cafe. His final words were an order for a Roadkill.

Stribling: What *is* a Roadkill?

Ramsden: Well, it's a double meat cheeseburger, with a ham sandwich on top. The idea is for the cook to make a burger that actually towers over the plate. You should come up and try one, but bring a friend because they are big enough for two people.

Stribling: Is there anything else we should talk about?

Ramsden: Well, yes. I made this list of customers that were in from three o'clock onwards. I think you can scratch them off your list. They couldn't have got there. Here, take it. Then, after considering a lot of possibilities, I've come to the conclusion that it had to be a random out-of-season hunter. Someone with a gun who happened to be near that dead deer when Aaron drove up.

Stribling: Let me change the subject for a moment, Aletta. You said you put fuel in your Jeep. How did you pay for it?

Ramsden: I used my debit card so it shows up on my bank statement.

Stribling: What did you do with the receipt?

Ramsden: The charge shows up on the bank statement. That's good enough for taxes according to what John Irick told me, so I just throw the receipt away unless I have the option to not have it print at all.

Stribling: Do you remember what you did with the receipt that day?

Ramsden: Not really, but typically I would just toss it in the garbage can that sits next to the gas pump. Why?

Stribling: Did you visit the crime-scene at any time over the winter?

Ramsden: No, I am not sure what road it's on other than it's between the roundup site and the Cabot Ranch.

Stribling: Do you have any idea why we would have found a receipt for fuel purchased at the Roadhouse at 2:15 on the 28th of October at the crimescene?

Ramsden: Really? New evidence? Who was the cardholder?

Stribling: You.

Ramsden: Me! Wow! *You're kidding*! When did you find this receipt? The day that it happened?

Stribling: Last week.

Ramsden: Oh, now I get it. That's why Sam and Randall paid a visit. They had found a receipt with my name on it. Hmmm ... who could have fetched it out of the garbage, kept it for all that time, then put it at the crime scene? Anyone could have gone up there! There are people that don't like me. I wonder if one of them did it. Can you get fingerprints off it?

Stribling: Aletta, I think we have enough information for now. Unless you have something to add at this time, we'll terminate this interview. Thanks for coming in today.

Ramsden: Thanks, Greg. Come try the Roadkill someday. Oh, and can I have a transcript of this interview? I want it for my diary.

{Chapter 80}

The Friday Club Reconvenes

George Jones was belting out "Ramblin' Fever" on the radio while Aletta polished the tops of the salt shakers. His *"ears being tired of the same ol' songs"* caught her attention. She certainly did get tired of this station sometimes, but still she didn't change it. Customers liked it and that was enough. She could listen to something else at home, but she never did, preferring to just listen to the wind chimes in the yard and the sounds of birds in her garden.

As the clock hand ticked onto the hour, Pam's red Toyota pulled into the parking lot. Pam's first day back on the forest survey was something to celebrate, so Aletta had an angel food cake with whipped cream ready and waiting. Little did she know that Carl would momentarily pull his big brown truck into the parking lot, so she was quite happy to see Pam and Carl coming through the door of the cafe together.

Pam was talking, "I'm doing field work on the forest on Fridays, but working on the Lucero Ranch on the weekend. The Lucero Ranch project really has me excited because no one has ever done any archaeology there before. I am finding a lot of interesting things.

"Hey, Aletta! It's the Friday Club—ready for another year! I hope you don't mind that I invited Carl to join us," said Pam.

"Are we solving any murders this time?" laughed Aletta. "Carl, have you been skipping your mandatory lunches?"

"No, but I have been reducing my calorie intake. It was nice to have you fatten me up over winter, but now I'm packing veggies and jogging at lunch. My doctor wasn't too happy with my cholesterol level."

"Thank god, Carl!" Aletta teased, "I thought you had started eating at Little Anita's. But you definitely look healthy. Good to see you!

"Pam, did you end up taking Placido down to Little Anita's?" asked Aletta.

"Well, we did go in there, but Nicky wasn't working that day, so it didn't happen. He was going to see if another friend would take him again," said Pam.

"What are you guys talking about?" asked Carl.

Oh ... someone stole Placido Lucero's tractor that he normally keeps by his winter corral. He thought it might be Willy LeDoux, so he wanted to see if Nicky would look him in the eye."

"Oh, the tractor that used to be at Placido's house when he had a garden? I know where that tractor is. I saw it up in Arboles, Colorado," said Carl.

"He said it would be in Colorado!" said Pam. "Could you go by and talk to him?"

"Cake!" announced Aletta, pulling the stunning white dessert from the top of the microwave where she had stashed it. "Carl, would you like some or should I go get you a carrot to gnaw on?"

He looked pained, and then agreed to have just a very narrow slice. "Hey, I had a strange dream last night," he said. "I dreamed that I was in the high country of the San Juan Mountains riding Phantom along the edge of some snow-packed fields. The wind was howling and Phantom's mane was blowing all around me. I didn't know what to do, so I just had to trust that Phantom knew the way."

"Was it a scary dream or a good dream?" asked Aletta as she passed around the slices.

"I was anxious at first, but then I knew I could trust him," said Carl. "A good dream!"

"Do you keep a dream journal?" she asked as she passed around cups of coffee and sat down. When he shook his head with his mouth full of cake, she continued. "I try to keep a journal, but I will be the first to admit that it's very hard to make yourself wake up and write in the middle of the night. Oh, speaking of writing, guess what I got?" Pam and Carl looked blank. "I got a transcript of my FBI interrogation."

"What!" blurted Pam. "You were interrogated?"

"Yes! And there is new evidence. Sam, or maybe Tapia, found a receipt at the crime scene that was from when I bought gas for my Jeep that day." Pam and Carl looked astounded. "Yes, someone put a receipt that I had thrown away at the crime scene. I kind of remember some kind of creepy guy with a horse trailer being at the gas pump, but not enough to really say anything about it. He was creepy though, I remember that."

"Oh my god; were you scared to get interrogated?" asked Pam.

"No, I was really interested in the process; that's why I asked for a copy of the transcript. George Stribling was really quite nice compared to how threatening he was when he talked to the Wild Horse Advocates. He even made a pot of coffee. It was nice to get out of here for a change. Brenda, the new waitress, covered for me."

Aletta's voice brightened as she continued, "You know I had the most amazing customer last week. He was a cognitive-behavioral psychologist and he was telling me about the kind of people that abuse animals and the kind of people that thrive on manipulating other people. He made me realize how manipulators are very aware of other people's vulnerabilities to be exploited. They use our desire to be nice against us and cause us to doubt ourselves. We have to learn to recognize and counter their intent. I'm really interested in this, so I ordered his books from Amazon. I am so sick of exploitative people." She popped a bite of cake in her mouth and chewed happily.

Pam took a sip of coffee, and then turned to the waitress. "Aletta, there is something I wanted to talk to you about. This seems like a good time. I wanted to ask you if you could work for me as an assistant one day a week on either Saturdays or Sundays."

"Pam, I would *love* to, but I work here on the weekends. Then again ... Brenda would love to have another day, I am sure, but what if I couldn't get the day back after the project was done? I might really regret it."

"Aletta, I can pay you ten-dollars an hour for a ten hour day. A hundred bucks is more than you are making here," said the archaeologist.

"Aletta, I think you should do it," said Carl. "It's a totally unique opportunity.

This place will still be here when you get back, and, really, Aletta, you don't want to spend the rest of your life here."

"Well, actually, what I really want to do is figure out how to go to college. It seems kind of silly, but I've been thinking that I might like to have a degree in psychology."

"What is silly about that?" asked Carl. "An education will help you escape from the limitations of being a service worker. I have a couple of other interests that keep me sane, but you can't know how many times I've wished I had gone to school rather than gotten a job delivering parcels!"

"What would you have studied, Carl?" asked Pam.

"Sociology maybe … if I couldn't get into medical school. Or maybe I would be a vet. I don't really know," the UPS driver replied.

"Let me think about it overnight, Pam. I can't go this weekend anyway. I'll talk to John tomorrow and let you know." Aletta looked ambivalent, then her eyes met Pam's and she smiled. "It makes me feel so good that you asked me. I've gotta figure out how to do it."

A car pulled up in the parking lot and a young family with two young children got out. The cowbell clanked as they came in. Aletta smiled at them, "Sit anywhere you like," she said as she grabbed menus and silverware. She placed them on the table in front of the two adults. "What would you like to drink?"

The young girl, who Aletta estimated was four years old, said, "Daddy, I want a menu too." The dad looked at Aletta pointedly and Aletta retreated back to the menu holder to get another menu.

Pam and Carl stood up. "Aletta, we'll see you later. Call me tomorrow," said Pam as she went out the door.

"Take the job!" said Carl just before the cowbell clanked behind him.

Aletta was still waiting for the drink order as the couple silently studied their menus. The little girl put a roll of silverware inside the folded menu and tried to flatten it. The little boy was taking sugar packets out of the holder in the middle of the table and stacking them in a pile. The adults were totally absorbed in their menus, so

Aletta walked away to clear off the cake plates from the bar counter. Before she got there, the man cleared his throat and Aletta turned around. "Are you ready to order, sir? Can I get you something to drink?"

"We'll just have water to drink," he replied.

She went behind the counter and picked up two large and two small glasses and filled them with ice, then dispensed drinking water into them. She returned to the table and set them down. The little boy immediately bumped his, but Aletta caught it before it could fall.

"The kids will have spaghetti," began the man.

"I'm sorry, sir, we don't have spaghetti," replied the waitress.

"Do you have any kind of pasta?" the woman asked in a challenging tone.

"No, I'm sorry, but we don't. Did you notice that we have a child's menu? The most popular thing for kids is usually a toasted cheese sandwich," suggested Aletta as sweetly as she could.

"I don't like toast, Daddy," said the little girl. "I want that cake," she said pointing to the angel food cake on the counter. The family turned their heads to look at the cake.

"How much is a piece of cake?" asked the father.

Aletta hadn't considered the economics of selling angel food cake until that moment, so she pulled a number out of thin air. "Two dollars."

"We'll have three pieces of cake and an extra plate," said the man.

"Great. I'll have that right up," said Aletta, turning to go.

As she cut the cake slices and put them on the plates, she thought to herself: *there aren't even enough literate people around here to get the five commitments we need to get the bookmobile to stop. I'm taking that job and I'm going to college. I really don't want to be here forever.*

When the family was done, the boy's water spilled and mopped up, and the little girl crying, it came as no surprise that they didn't leave a tip, but Aletta felt grateful that they had helped clarify the situation.

Navajo City Roadhouse Blog:

Gossiping about the Cooks: The Cody Special Disaster

April 12, 2012

There is really not time to update this blog, but hey, there is TOO much gossip not to.

We have a new cook named Mike. Unlike the last few, he is clean and sober. I turn in the order and his response is, "Great! Have it right out!" Wow!! I love him. My faith in cooks as human beings has been restored.

Cooks are usually the root of most gossip. Let's start with the last one, Bill. Nice guy when he was sober, but he liked to keep the kitchen in total chaos, all the foods stacked up amidst scattered hash-browns and cheese particles. He wouldn't wash his dishes; he'd just stack them on top of everything else. His claim to any level of cleanliness was his strict maintenance of his bleach water bucket. The food he turned out was good, except for his predilection for making the eggs crispy. One thing our customers don't like is an "over-easy" egg with crispy edges. You put it on the table and the customers look at you with eyes that match their hard eggs, which totally stressed me out. I just started telling afternoon customers they could not order eggs no matter what. Since we have our new cook, this is not a problem.

Bill had a drinking problem. If you looked in the refrigerator next to the burgers in the middle of the day, you might find a beer or a coffee cup full of red wine. John tried to ignore the situation because Bill is his nephew, but everyone else saw the disaster coming.

About two weeks ago, the now ex-cook came to work at noon totally drunk. The kitchen rapidly became a shambles. It was looking grim. I tried minding my own business, but when every order was messed up, I sure wanted to find a reason to leave. I called John to come help and he arrived within fifteen minutes. He took over the front and asked me to help Bill in the kitchen. This set the stage for more drama than Navajo City sees on a regular basis.

Cody is one of our regular customers. He likes chicken strips and white gravy. But he likes them with green chile and cheese on his French fries. He orders this meal every day. We call it the Cody Special. Well, there are a few women in the oil field, about three of whom are vivacious, intelligent women. Needless to say, they *never* have to eat lunch by themselves. Sue is one of these ladies. Sue and Cody don't work together, but they know each other and Sue knew of the existence of the Cody Special. On that fateful day, she made the mistake of ordering the Cody Special *with no green chile*. John wrote it down like that. I would have written "chik strip". Big mistake.

I was back with the inebriated nephew trying to patch up the orders and get things out. No one was talking about the fundamental problem of Bill being totally drunk; John was avoiding the problem by staying in front. We were all just trying to work around it. I had never cooked a Cody Special, so I asked Bill, who said green chile and cheese on fried chicken fillet. When John came to pick up the order he pointed out the "No Green Chile" on the ticket. We took it back, but I was confused about what was wrong with it, so Bill said he would do it.

There were nine guys sitting with Sue at that table (Did I say she never gets to eat alone?) and maybe a dozen other customers at other tables. A bunch of orders were in preparation and the bell rang again for the Cody Special. It still had the green chile on it. The Boss turned the plate back to the cooks since it was still covered with green chile.

The cook started cussing and told the Boss he could come back and cook himself. The Boss said, "Okay, that would be fine." The cook said he was quitting. Fine. Fine with me especially! But it didn't work out so smoothly. The cook stormed out the back door, but in just a few seconds came in another door into the dining area with the customers, making an ugly scene. I grabbed him, and then the Boss and I dragged him out the back door. It would have been so much better if the drunk cook would have just minded his own business, but he was determined to cause a scene, so he kicked in a couple of doors and threatened to do some serious damage to whatever he could. We called the police, but, this far from civilization, you can't really expect them to help you in a crisis.

Some customers stood up and tried to help. Most of them would have run from a real fight because of their jobs, but they at least were a bit threatening. One of the customers, Travis, was in a fightin' mood though, and took the cook's challenge to step outside and go a round. They never had an opportunity to get it done, because I stepped up and, with one blow, decked Bill. Yes! I took him down and some customers helped drag him into the walk-in cooler we don't use. I parked my Jeep up against the door and we all breathed a sigh of relief.

The first state cop arrived about twenty minutes later, but he called for reinforcements and the other one showed up a bit later. We were still busy serving food and the owner was getting the kitchen cleaned up, so we had to give our statements between customers. I watched them try to get the cook out of the cooler. Cuffed and stuffed, he still was mad enough to break the window in the cop car. Alkies bleed easy and he was a bloody mess, so they took him to the hospital for stitches before they threw him in the drunk tank. The boss did not press charges, but the ex-cook was charged with destruction of state property for damage to the cop car.

John and I decided that next time we are going to charge the customers for the floor show. People started teasing me by ordering *a knuckle sandwich*, but it didn't hurt my tips. The Boss posted a notice:

OFFICIAL NOTICE
The Cody Special cannot be ordered without Green Chile.

Hey, I gotta get off of this keyboard and get some napkins rolled. We'll have to save the rest of the gossip for later.

Yours truly,
Aletta Ramsden

{Chapter 82}

One Customer

Aletta self-consciously pulled her green backpack from the bed of Pam's truck. "Will we be coming back for lunch?" she asked Pam.

"Let's take it in case we would rather rest than have to walk back here," replied the archaeologist. "I have a few things for you to carry for me. You can take the GPS, and the altimeter, oh ... and here is the video camera. We probably won't use it, but we should have it just in case."

Aletta tucked the things into a clean compartment of her pack, noticing that Pam's backpack looked much fuller than hers. "How much water should I take?"

"At least a half-gallon. Okay, your main job is to carry that aluminum extending ladder. It weighs less than fifty pounds. The whole point of this ladder is safety. I can help carry it when we are trying to cover ground. I think we are ready to go. Pick up that end, I'll lead the way," she said picking up one end of the ladder.

The ladder felt awkward. Aletta felt as if she was being jerked forward at every step. Pam stopped and looked back at her. "Try getting on the same side of the ladder as me," suggested the archaeologist. Aletta adjusted her position and picked up the ladder again. Suddenly they were walking in synchrony and it was easy.

"That is better," said Aletta. "What are we doing with this ladder?"

"We are going to be climbing some of these sandstone benches on the slope in front of us. It's going to be a pain to carry it up the steep slope, but it might be the only way to get up some of the cliffs. I've glassed this hill and there are three things I want to check."

"Glassed? Looked at it with binoculars?" guessed Aletta. "How can you find artifacts with binoculars unless they are really big?"

"Well, I am not too interested at this point in artifacts like sherds, debitage, et-cetera. There is just too much of it, and we don't have the time. Oh, to be sure, we'll mark any particularly rich areas on the map, but what I am interested in is caves and rock art. We are going to have to lift to get this ladder over the sagebrush. Watch that rock!"

The women walked up the canyon in silence. Aletta heard the wind whistling through the junipers higher on the slope. She heard the distant mechanical sound of a gas compressor with its big engine pushing gas out of a low density well into an already partially compressed pipeline. Their feet crunched on the rocky slope. She could hear the water sloshing inside of its containers inside her backpack. She delighted in her new auditory landscape. She wasn't going to miss George Jones even a little.

Pam stopped. "Let's rest here while I check the map," she said, laying down her end of the ladder and pulling a map from a rear pocket of her survey vest. She pulled a compass from a front pocket and quickly oriented herself to true north, and then she studied the map.

Aletta set down her end of the ladder and wondered if there was something she should do besides enjoy the incredible rocky landscape. It made her slightly nervous not having anything to clean for a change. She got a drink of water from the bottle in her backpack and Pam did the same; then they picked up their respective ends of the ladder and turned to go at a steeper angle up the slope.

"See that dark flat rock surface straight ahead?" asked Pam. "I think it has an art panel on it. Almost all the rock art is on south facing surfaces and the artists always picked out the darker surfaces. They probably did most of the art work in the winter, but it wasn't really art as in decoration. It was probably always tied to ceremony. Winter is still the time modern day Navajos and other tribes tell traditional stories. Hey, watch out for that cactus!"

Aletta lifted her leg higher to keep her boot from hitting the little prickly pear stems, then she stumbled over a rock, and fell forward dropping the ladder. She picked herself up and looked at the scrapes on her hands where she had used them to stop her fall onto the rocks. "I think I will bring gloves next time."

They arrived at the cliff face, and as Pam had predicted, there was a rock art panel. A corn stalk with both tassels and fat ears of corn was the largest and most central figure. A human figure was smaller on the lower left part of the panel. Some turkey-like birds seemed to be strolling around the corn. The tracks of a cloven-hooved creature were carved as if the animal had run up the panel.

They set the ladder down flat on the ground and Pam set her backpack between its rungs. She opened it and pulled out a field book and a sketch book. She pulled out a laser measuring tool. "Pull out that GPS unit you're packing and we'll get the location," she said to Aletta.

Aletta opened her backpack and, not knowing what each carrying case contained, pulled the two small objects out. "Which of these is the GPS?" she asked holding them both out.

"Oh, you have the altimeter too! My old habits die hard," said Pam. "We used those forever, but the GPS gives the elevation more accurately. You can store that square leather one at the bottom of your pack as we won't need it. The one in the cloth case is the GPS. Unzip it, take it out, and turn on the power button, then let it sit on a rock for a few minutes to acquire a signal."

Aletta put it on the rock, and then opened the altimeter case to look at it before she stowed it away. It was a circular dial marked off in units of 250. It looked quite old-fashioned and possibly antique. "How does the altimeter work, Pam? It looks like it was made before the age of electronics."

Pam was busy writing in her field journal. She had an extra pencil in her teeth. She looked at Aletta, took the pencil out of her mouth, and said, "It's quite old. It works on barometric pressure. You have to calibrate it every day." Then she replaced the pencil and went back to her journal.

Aletta put the altimeter back in its case and tucked it into the bottom of her backpack. She pulled out her bag of raisins and ate a few. Pam reached over to pick up the GPS from the rock and recorded its readout into her field book and handed it back to Aletta saying, "We are done with it. You can put it away."

Pam pulled out her camera and started taking photos, taking notes in her field book after each one. Aletta watched with interest but was acutely aware she was doing nothing helpful. Staying out of the way seemed like the best thing she could do. But how could Pam possibly afford to pay her ten-dollars an hour for doing nothing? Aletta was worried.

Pam put away her camera and picked up the laser measuring device. "We are going to need to measure the size of the panel. Aletta, you take my field book. We have to get right up to the panel for this," she said, motioning for Aletta to follow her. Stopping at the right side of the panel, she indicated a shoulder-high location on the panel. "We'll measure from here. You are going to hold the field book up at the edge of the panel, like this. I'll get on the other side and take the measurement."

Aletta had no idea what was happening until she saw that Pam was trying to aim a little red laser dot on the field book. Aletta tried to hold the field book steadier and finally the dot appeared. Pam pressed the button and the device took a measurement, which was duly recorded in the field book.

"It's going to take me about fifteen minutes to sketch this, so you are free to look around and explore the site a little," said Pam.

Aletta picked up the topographic map and studied it for a few minutes. She located all the features she could see in the landscape and studied how they looked when drawn by contour intervals. She read the legend and realized that the ladder, fully extended, was about one interval. She looked at the cliffs across the canyon and imagined putting the ladder up to them. How many of these cliffs could be climbed in that way?

She left her backpack sitting and started walking parallel to the cliff face. A huge pile of giant boulders had slid from above at sometime in the distant past and created a way to climb up to the next bench. She climbed up the pile and sat on a rock where she could watch Pam. *It was like having one customer*, she thought. *I just have to keep her coffee cup filled.* She got up and wandered along the back of the bench. On some crusty dirt, a white object caught her eye. She bent to look and realized it was a perfect little arrowhead. She picked it up and looked around for other artifacts, but there was nothing visible. She climbed back down the rock pile to where the archaeologist was finishing up.

"Look what I found," Aletta said holding it out to Pam.

Pam gasped and looked horrified. "You should not have picked it up, Aletta. It's out of its provenience now. We can't be picking things up. Take photos of things, but don't pick them up. I don't want to have to curate them forever."

304

Aletta felt stung by the unexpected disapproval. "What should I do with it?" she asked. Pam held out her hand to ask for it, and then laid it on a flat rock to photograph it. She handed it back to Aletta and told her to return to where she found it with the GPS and get the location information, then leave it right where she found it.

When Aletta got back Pam was recording the artifact and photograph in her field book. Pam took the GPS and recorded the coordinates and elevation, then handed the unit back to Aletta for storage. Aletta zipped the GPS into its cloth cover and opened her backpack, then dropped the unit inside. She pulled out the bottle and took another drink of water. *Maybe being a field assistant was too boring?* she brooded while Pam was packing her gear.

Pam picked up the front end of the ladder and Aletta put on her backpack and lifted her end. They started traversing the slope. It was steep and rolling between small arroyos and little hillocks. "This next one is why we brought the ladder," said Pam. "Let's stop here and check the map."

Aletta set down her end of the ladder and came up beside Pam where she could see the map over the archaeologist's shoulder. "Where are we?" asked Aletta. "I'd like to learn how to read the map well enough to navigate."

"We are here," Pam said pointing at a little wave in the contour lines, "and we are going to the x over here."

"Pam, I really don't want to annoy you, but I really want to learn everything. I think if you explain all the steps you are doing, I'll get to be a lot more useful. Teach me *everything*, would you?"

Pam broke out in a giant smile, "Aletta, I didn't want to annoy you by telling you about everything. I was worried you weren't that interested. I would love to explain everything, but you also have to ask questions because I don't know what you don't know."

"Start by telling me about everything that would not happen in a small roadside cafe. That's what I know about, everything else is new."

***

305

By the end of the day, Aletta had learned to record the information to the field journal in her neatest handwriting as Pam dictated it to her. Pam was very pleased that the increased efficiency allowed them to get to five sites instead of the three planned ones. Aletta was satisfied, too.

{Chapter 83}

Mustang Mission

Brenda was cleaning out the cabinets under the waitress station, while John sat by the cash register reading the paper. She kept interrupting him to ask if she could dispose of various items that obviously had not been touched in years. He was glad to see someone finally tackle that project, which even Rita Mae had ignored. Naomi had the looks, Aletta had the brains, and he suspected Brenda had the diligence. He knew she was going to be a great replacement for Aletta.

Aletta wouldn't really be gone until August, but he already missed her. She was such a great listener—always ready to engage with him in a conversation about the latest book he had read or some esoteric period of history he had learned about on the history channel. Intellectual women were few and far between in this landscape. Brenda would probably listen, but there was no chance for a real discussion.

He missed Merriam. When she had died, they had simply cremated her and sent her ashes back to him. Sometimes, on the really lonely nights, he would get the urn down from the mantle of the fireplace and sit it on the coffee table to discuss history or politics in his characteristic monologue style. He always imagined what she would say in the conversation. Sometimes he admitted that she would just be rolling her eyes.

He got up to get another cup of coffee. Then he picked up the freshly baked pan of brownies to see if it had cooled enough to cut and put in the display case. Cool enough, he cut it into a dozen squares and put eleven of them into the case. He bit into the last one, and then set it on a napkin while he sipped his coffee.

He recognized the truck pulling in off the highway. The snub-nosed farm truck belonged to Mustang Camp down in Largo Canyon. It was pulling the dilapidated blue stock trailer in which they hauled horses. Doc Barlow was driving. *Now there was an intellectual woman*, he thought as she came through the door.

"Hey, John! What's for lunch?" she asked.

He smiled and said, "I'll bet you'd like a chicken salad." He called back to Bren-

307

da, who was still rummaging through a cabinet, "Brenda, I've got this covered, you can continue what you are doing."

Doc responded with "Yeah, perfect, and a cup of hot tea. Do you have a mug to put it in? Those little brown coffee cups are too small."

He found the mug collection, picked out the big one with the crowing rooster design, and dropped a fresh tea bag into it. He then filled it with piping hot water. He set it and the cream pitcher in front of his customer. "When you get that fixed up, bring it back to the kitchen and come talk to me while I make your salad."

He had already dropped two fillets into the deep fryer before she came down the hallway, stepping over Brenda's project, around the stove, and into the kitchen. "I've never been back in the kitchen before," she said. "That is quite a stove."

He asked her, "How is your training project going? Did you get all those horses adopted?"

"We did, John. The volunteers and I delivered the last one three days ago. I'm actually on my way right now to get more horses," she said. "I have to go to Delta, Utah to get this batch. I have interns coming next week so I need new horses for them to train. I figured out that I could solve some financial problems created by having too many horses if I get paying students, but that means I have to keep getting horses. It's a vicious cycle," she laughed.

"So, do you have any good news for the American taxpayer? Do you think this mustang crisis can be solved?" asked the accountant/cook.

"Well, the Forest Service is looking at saving you some money by euthanizing horses," she said.

"You're kidding," he said, as he chopped the lettuce.

"Not really, the range manager told me he was getting a permit to use a weapon and that the Forest Service policy was they could be humanely destroyed after forty-five days whether they are healthy or not. I don't know what prompted this because we've pretty much kept their horses adopted since 2009. I suspect it has something to do with the existing policy making it hard to justify the expense of training and adoption."

"What's it costing me for you to train and give away American mustangs?" the accountant asked, motioning her to follow him and her chicken salad back out to the front of the restaurant.

"Between eight-hundred and a thousand dollars," she replied. "John, you'll understand the core philosophy to our program. You start with a horse that's not worth anything, that you can't even give away. Then you start training it. Its value starts going up. At some point it becomes valuable enough that people think it is worth the adoption fee. People start seeing them, not as a range pest, but instead as a good deal. They can all get adopted."

He got her a roll of silverware as she sat down and then started talking about the modern-day range wars as she ate. She tried to respond a time or two, but John was both informed and passionate about the subject (the Sagebrush Rebellion) so she just ate and listened. She had eaten the last bite before he stopped himself. "Sorry, I got carried away. So are you going to Delta from here?"

"Yes, I'll head up to Moab and spend the night with some friends there, then I'll get to Delta. I'll pick out the horses on Monday and they'll get their brand inspections; then Tuesday, I'll beeline it back to Rio Arriba County."

"That's a long drive! Do you think that after all of that, you'd want to go dancing in Durango with me next Saturday?"

"I've got a better idea. Why don't you come down to Mustang Camp, and I'll cook you some of my famous lamb chops and we'll dance to the radio," she offered as she got up and took out her wallet.

"Oh, yes, that does sound like a better idea. Hey, lunch is on me. Have a safe trip. I'll see you soon."

{Chapter 84}

Gratuitous Sex Scene

He screamed at her from across the meadow, then curving his neck and loins, he jogged toward her with a springing step. She did not look up, but continued to graze among the dandelions.

He stopped to sniff a still-moist pile of feces, carefully examining each lump with his widened nostrils. The aroma of her feces aroused him. He shifted his weight onto his back legs, lifted his nose high in the air, and curled back his lips, creating a toothy grin that horsemen call *flehmen*.

He took two measured steps forward and lifted his tail. Then he strained to defecate onto her feces. The mass fell and he whipped around to sniff the pile again. She was still placidly grazing. He screamed again, but this time more to the universe than toward her.

She spread her hind legs apart and raised her tail to expose her dark vulva. Still grazing, she flexed the lips of her vulva to expose the delicate pink tissues within. She squirted a few drops of urine. Then she turned to coyly look at him.

He tightened the curve of his neck and loins and walked toward her with his knees raising high at each step. She raised her head to face him but her posture remained relaxed. Their nostrils met. While in nose to nose contact, she shifted her body to put her tail closer to him. His nose felt the side of her face, then traced the bottom of her mane to her shoulder. She curled her neck sideways to watch his movement. Twisting his head, he used his nose to give her a playful push on her belly just behind her front leg. She stood strong and pushed back indicating her willingness to quench his desire.

He stepped back and pushed his nose under her flank. She watched him lovingly but did not move. His penis grew longer, pushing itself from its sheath. At first the penis dangled limply, but quickly it became tumescent and turgid, extending itself for more than half the length of his abdomen. He flexed it and it bounced against his belly.

She raised her tail, and he moved to sniff her vulva. After a moment of aromatic ecstasy, he raised his muzzle in another flehmen display with his penis held high for all to see. He lowered his head onto her back and then put weight on his chin, trying to prepare her for the coming mount. She responded by stiffening her back legs and raising her tail. He moved to align his chest with her tail, then he lifted his front end, rearing on his hind legs, his penis reaching for her vulva, and put his hooves on her back.

Braced against his weight, she widened her stance to assist the penis find its mark. Then she stood staring forward with a mixture of concern and impatience on her face.

Abandoning himself to desire, he thrust his penis into her vulva. He curved his back to touch her withers with his nose. He bit her neck to help stabilize his body as his loins thrust deeply. Suddenly the tip of his penis flared deep inside of her and the semen was expelled into her uterus.

All movement stopped. His body went limp, his head dropped to her shoulder, and he hung on her back with dangling front legs. After a moment, he regained some composure and backed up to slide off her back. The tip of his penis was still flared, but it quickly lost its tumescence and slipped back into its sheath. She turned to look at him, who would be the father of her next year's foal.

{Chapter 85}

Eighty-Sixed

Aletta studied the calendar on the wall. There were exactly one-hundred days until school started. The application had been easy and she was accepted immediately. The process at San Juan College seemed extremely student-friendly and the campus was only a twenty minute drive from her house. It was perfect except for one thing—it didn't offer the program she really wanted. Fort Lewis College, an hour away in Durango, had a strong psychology program, but tougher entrance requirements. Aletta had settled on a plan to attend San Juan for a year to get all of her prerequisite classes out of the way, and then try to get a scholarship to Fort Lewis. She felt slightly self-conscious about the boldness of her plan, but she believed it was doable.

One of the most notable things that had happened today had been spotting the first fly of the year. In Aletta's experience, the first one was never annoying because it was easy to swat. She was writing *fly swatters* on the shopping list, when the cowbell clanked and a tall thin man with a white cowboy hat walked in and approached the counter.

"Good afternoon," he said, politely taking off his hat.

"Good afternoon, what can I do for you?" she asked.

"I'm trying to find out where Sue Kepler lives," he said.

"Oh, Sue, yeah, her place is out off the General American Road, but I don't think she is living there since her husband died. She's moved her camper trailer down to Sandy Poole's place. That's about highway milepost ninety-three on the right. Sandy lives in the middle of the houses there," explained the ever-helpful waitress.

"Thank you, ma'am," replied the cowboy before he turned to leave.

Aletta paused for a moment to consider how much losing a mate seemed to change women. Some women picked up and moved on while others seemed to implode on themselves. Sue Kepler seemed to be self-medicating with a mix of alcohol and marijuana. It didn't seem like that could turn out well. Since there was nothing she could do to change it, Aletta turned her attention to the afternoon cleaning chores.

***

It was nearing the end of the lunch hour on the following day when Aletta noticed that Sandy Poole was in the checkout line. Sandy had never been a Roadhouse customer other than to pick up a giant styrofoam cup of ice-tea now and then, but Aletta was too busy to think about that now. She was ringing up the meals on the cash register as fast as she could to get the men back to work. The tip jar was looking good.

When Sandy got to the front of the line, Aletta greeted her with "Hey! How's married life treating Naomi?"

"How dare you tell anyone where I live," said Sandy with a hateful look. "They repossessed Sue's truck last night, thanks to you."

"I didn't know he was a repo man," Aletta said. "It seems that if they repossessed her truck it was more because she didn't make the payments, not because I told someone where she was living."

Sandy raised her voice to a snarl. "You have no right to tell anyone anything about me. Do I make myself clear?" She bristled with body language that threatened intent to do physical harm.

Alarm bells went off in Aletta's head, but they weren't sounding for physical safety. It was a Freedom of Speech alarm bell. *Do I have the right to tell anyone the truth?*

"Sandy, if you or Sue had asked me to not tell, I would not have told him, but I can't be guessing about what is to be kept secret and what is not. Threatening me is not a good way to handle this, so, sorry, but I am eighty-sixing you. You are not allowed to come in here again until you talk to John. So get out and don't come back."

Sandy looked around her and realized the men standing in line behind her were not looking particularly friendly. She had picked a bad time to do anything more than threaten. Now there were so many witnesses to her threat that she really couldn't do anything to the weasley waitress. She stalked out the door with a huff.

Aletta, with a self-conscious smile, took the ticket from the next customer in line and started ringing it up. "Sorry about that, sometimes this place gets crazy," she said, carefully avoiding eye-contact with the kindly, smiling man.

Aletta wondered what had happened to the meek little bookworm she used to be.

Navajo City Roadhouse Blog:

Rita Mae Objects

Monday, May 14, 2012

Rita Mae says in a letter that what I wrote about the previous cook in this blog is kind of unfair and that I shouldn't have decked him. She says that she is certain that his eggs had gotten less crispy before the Cody Special Disaster happened. That may be true, but the customers have been saying nice things about the new cook's eggs, and tips have improved. The bottom line—money in the tip jar—is a pretty clear measure to me that we are better off without him.

She thinks he is just misunderstood. I will admit that if I thought about it, I might think of some nice things to say about him. He was doing some bad stuff at that point, but he is actually not a bad person. I can understand why she likes him when he is sober, but I am not sure that happens too often.

To be perfectly honest, it should be disclosed that Rita Mae was kind of infatuated with the fellow anyway. Yes, those two had a little thing going on at first. You remember when I told you that Rita got a breast reduction operation? Well, she still has plenty for that cook to cry into about losing his job, having a bad liver, and getting seven stitches in his nose. Lucky for her, she is back in Nova Scotia and safe from getting involved. She can be as forgiving to him as she wants, but it's not necessary for me to do the same.

Can a nice person be too forgiving? Is there such a thing as too much compassion? I kind of think so. I think it enables bad behavior. Holding a person responsible for their actions is the only way we can promote personal integrity, in my sometimes humble opinion.

Yours truly,
Aletta

{Chapter 87}

Over the Edge

Aletta peered into her backpack wondering; *was it foolish to have cheaped-out and put the snakebite kit back on the store shelves*? Snakes could certainly be out there; just because she hadn't seen one *yet* didn't mean a thing. She had, however, let the cashier ring up a small first aid kit, a head-lamp flashlight (Pam's suggestion), some extra batteries, and a pair of deerskin gloves. It would have been more economical to get some canvas gardening gloves, but she couldn't resist the supple buckskin. The cacti and the rocks left no doubt in Aletta's mind that field work was more hazardous than waitressing. Either job, she knew, could be hazardous if a person does not take precautions. *Today, I will make an extra effort to be safety conscious*, she told herself. She shouldered her pack and walked down the driveway toward the gate.

Pam pulled up to Aletta's driveway while Aletta was still saying goodbye to Bones and Koby. Aletta had originally hoped to be able to take them to the field someday, but Pam had told her that today would be a particularly bad day to have them in the field. As Aletta opened the passenger door, she noticed that several coils of braided rope were lying next to the ladder in the truck bed, but she forgot to ask about it as she got in and Pam started asking about the week's Roadhouse gossip.

In a chatty mood Pam drove up Gobernador Canyon and took a right turn about a mile beyond Placido's corral. The road climbed up a steep hill; suddenly they were on top of the mesa. To the southeast, Aletta could catch an occasional glimpse of the back side of Navajo City between the juniper trees. Pam turned on several secondary roads, and then came to a place where the barren and flat slickrock formation edged a majestic deep canyon. Pam pulled up on the slickrock and drove along the canyon edge for a quarter of a mile. "This is it!" she said happily.

Aletta looked out the window of the truck for some idea of where the rock art might be. Suddenly she realized that the closest likely cliff face was between her and the bottom of that canyon. "Pam is the site on the canyon wall below us?" she asked with trepidation.

"Oh, yes."

"Is there a trail?"

"No."

Suddenly Aletta wondered if she was really afraid of heights. She'd never really been in a tall building, but she remembered the fear of going off the high diving board when she was just a kid. Aletta decided to test herself and see, so she walked toward the edge intending to look over the side. At five feet from the edge, she started feeling her anxiety rise. Pam walked past her and peered into the canyon and got down on her hands and knees at the very edge. She had the laser measurement tool in her hands. Aletta watched anxiously as the archaeologist scooted around so her body was at a forty-five degree angle from the edge so she could get one shoulder over the edge to point the laser tool.

"Aletta, would you hold onto my feet, so I don't accidently fall off?" asked the archaeologist. Aletta bent down and put her hands on Pam's ankles. Pam scooted so more of her body was beyond the edge of the rock and suddenly both arms were free to work the laser tool. She clicked the data-capture button, held the meter up to her eyes, and then put her hand above it to make a shadow over the read-out. "Twenty-seven feet," she said with satisfaction and then she twisted her body to get her arms back on the rock and then pushed herself back to safety.

Aletta let Pam's feet go as soon as the archaeologist was back on solid ground. Then the waitress decided to crawl on her hands and knees to look over the edge. The drop off was only three-hundred feet, but to Aletta it was equivalent to the Grand Canyon. At the base of the cliff was a steep gray clay slope with scattered boulders. It was a very long drop to the bottom. That box of Band-Aids in her backpack wasn't going to do much if she fell off that!

Pam said, "Do you see that little ledge right below us? That's where the cave is."

Aletta looked down to see a ledge about six feet wide sticking out from the wall below her. "How are we going to get there? Rappel?"

"Well, we would have to find someone to teach us how to rappel if it had been much lower on the cliff, but we can reach it with the ladder," said Pam as she started walking back to the vehicle. Aletta followed and watched as the archaeologist took a coil of the neon-orange rope from the truck. She then quickly lay down on the ground and shimmied under the truck. "I am tying off to the frame of the truck. Nothing is going to move that. Get some rocks and block the wheels so no matter what, it could not possibly roll."

Aletta found a few heavy rocks the size of a loaf of bread and tucked them in front and back of the rear tires. She stood next to Pam until the archaeologist crawled out from under the truck, then she gave her a hand to help her from the ground. Back on her feet, Pam tested the knot with several jerks on the line. "It's not often that I get to practice my knot tying skills, but I am sure glad I have them," said Pam. "Do you know your knots?"

"Maybe you could teach me some," suggested Aletta.

"When we have time. Right now, take the rope to the edge of the cliff and mark where it hangs over the edge. That is where we will tie the ladder." said Pam.

When Aletta got back, holding the rope to mark the edge, Pam had already taken the ladder out of the truck and had it fully extended although flat on the ground. She took the rope from Aletta and tied it between the top and second rung. "Just for safety, let's put the other rope on too," Pam said. "Would you hand it to me out of the truck?"

Aletta handed her the other rope, which Pam tied to the opposite rail between the same rungs. "We'll attach it to the truck after we get it in place," she said carrying the ladder to the edge. She started pushing it over the edge but when it got half way over the edge it started to teeter. "I was afraid of that," she said. "It's going to be too hard to handle." She pulled it back onto the slickrock. "You take the fixed rope— the one tied to the truck—and hold on to it. I will run the other end of the rope through the ladder between the fourth and fifth rung, then I will be able to control its descent. I don't have to tie it on." She pushed it over the edge again and when it tipped, she sat down on the ground with her legs spread out in front of her, feeding out the ladder rope a little at a time. The ladder slowly tipped up in a fully vertical position and the women let it slide to the ledge. Pam pulled her rope end free. They both got down on their hands and knees to look at how the ladder was sitting on the rock. It looked centered on the ledge with a good three feet between it and the next drop off. Pam took the loose end of the second rope and went back to the vehicle to tie it off.

Aletta looked at the ladder and thought about the actuarial probability of falling from a ladder. *What if I suddenly just let go, or what if I missed a step? Wasn't I going to be careful today?*

"Get your gear, Aletta," said the archaeologist, setting the GPS out for Aletta to pack. Aletta reached for it and then turned it on, setting it on the tailgate of the truck bed while she prepared herself. "Better go pee before we start down because it would be a problem on that ledge." Both women took a bit of toilet paper and went to bushes at the opposite ends of the truck. Aletta got back before Pam and got her cell phone out. She texted a message to Sephra. *Come look for us if you do not hear from me by dark.* In a second message she sent the longitude and latitude from the GPS. In a third message she wrote *In a canyon between Navajo City and the river.*

As Pam walked back up and shouldered her backpack, Aletta asked her, "Pam, do you think this is safe?"

Pam pressed her lips together before she spoke. "Well, personally, I don't know, but I do know that I can't choose to not do this. It is too important to me, so I am definitely going. If you are nervous about it, you are free to stay up here and just mind the camp. I will appreciate knowing you are up here."

Aletta looked to the edge and then back to her friend. "I want to see what's down there, not as bad as you do, but it would be too hard to stay up here and just try to guess."

{Chapter 88}

The Cave

Pam shouldered her backpack and walked confidently to the one rung jutting up over the top of the canyon edge. She tested the tie off ropes with a tug, then got down on her hands and knees and crawled backwards over the edge while hanging on to a rope in one hand and the ladder in the other. "Aletta, come steady this ladder, would you?" the intrepid archaeologist asked.

Aletta crawled to the ladder and held it firmly by the top rung. The archaeologist found a foothold on the third rung, and then pulled herself to be centered between the rails. "That was the scary part," said Pam as she started climbing down. She reached the ledge and didn't let herself be overwhelmed by the desire to immediately go in the cave. Instead, she stepped between the ladder and the cave and held the ladder to steady it for Aletta's descent.

Aletta turned around and crawled backwards over the edge. She held on to the rope until it wasn't awkward to grab the ladder. Her foot fished around for a rung. Pam guided her, "It's about two inches lower; slide down a bit and you'll feel it." The thought of putting even an inch more of her body over the edge terrified Aletta, but she did it anyway and when she felt her boot touch, she was finally able to breathe again. The landing was narrow, but with the ladder to hold, it was by no means terrifying.

The two women turned toward the cave entrance, half of which was closed by a crudely built stone wall. Inside, the sunlight penetrated only a few feet and the contrast with the sunny ledge made the interior seem inky black. Pam set her backpack at the base of the stone wall, rummaged through it, and got out her headlamp. Aletta followed by example. "What we will do is go in and see what we find, then come back and record. If nothing else, this stone wall is a site feature."

As they walked into the cave, the women both flipped on their headlamps illuminating whatever direction they faced. Pam's light focused on a black and white ceramic pot sitting in a small niche on the cave wall. Aletta's light turned toward the corner where the wall met the cave and focused momentarily on a dusty hump that looked like a leather moccasin. The light followed the dusty contour to a heap of what looked to be dusty fur, and then fixed on the bony iridescence of a human skull. "*Pam!*"

Pam's light swung onto the skull. "Oh, cool!" Their eyes were quickly growing accustomed to the dim light and they could now see that the heap was a long dead human who had literally died with moccasins on. "Look how the person was wearing a rabbit skin cloak. It must have been cold weather when he or she died."

In the corner between the wall and the cave there sat a somewhat crumpled half-round shape with a pair of small animal horns jutting outward. From one of the horns dangled a strand of beads of blue, white, and orange. Everything was covered with dust making the most visible parts the vertical surfaces. "That looks like a ceremonial head-piece. Look at the pronghorn antlers. Oh, look at that--it looks like a rawhide rope coiled up there by the feet." The dried frayed ends jutted upward out of the dust, but the half of the coiled rope that was nearest the body was completely covered by dust.

"Can you tell if it's male or female?" asked Aletta.

"I would guess that it is male," said the archaeologist. "But we will have to look at the bones to tell for sure."

"Are you going to collect it?" asked the waitress.

"I'm not going to decide that right now. It's pretty safe right where it is. I don't see any wool, metal, or technology that suggests contact with Europeans. It could have been here for 300 years or more. The question is what would its tribe want to have happen with it. I'm not prepared to ask anyone that right now. It's on private land so it's also up to Placido."

"Do you think it's Navajo?" asked Aletta.

"That black and white pot looks more like Pueblo ceramics. Perhaps Chacoan. It could also be a Pueblo pot in a Navajo site. We might think about collecting some DNA from the body if any suitable tissues are left. But I would only do that if it was important to know."

"Don't the Navajos believe that ghosts haunt places where someone dies?" Aletta asked.

"Yes, if this was a Navajo body who did not die of old age, then there certainly would be a *chindi* to watch out for. It has all the malevolence of the deceased packaged up waiting to infect someone else. Let's assume this was not a malevolent person, but rather some merely unlucky guy whose rope broke when he was down here and he couldn't get out. That's my initial hunch.

"I want to look at the pot," she said turning to focus her light on it. The women walked across the chamber. "Don't touch it, in case it is just waiting to crumble. We will photograph it before we touch it. Look how that niche is carved for it to fit perfectly inside. Someone spent a long time carving that and building the wall, but I don't really see any evidence people lived here. No sign of fire or smoke. Hmmm. Notice the door opens to the east."

At the back of the chamber a short horizontal tunnel seemed to have been mined out of the sandstone. It was only three feet tall, so the women bent down to peer inside. "See any rock art?" Pam asked.

Aletta got down on her hands and knees and crawled inside. "No, I don't see anything." She crawled back out.

"Well, let's get our gear and start recording," said Pam. "We have a lot of notes to take. The wall is a good starting place."

Aletta wrote while Pam measured, photographed, and dictated the information. Some of the rocks still had evidence of a mud mortar between them. "Don't write this down but, the wall could have been plastered over with mud, which would have made this cave difficult to spot. I saw it because of the rock wall, but if it was smooth and the color of the cliff, I might not have noticed anything unusual," Pam commented.

"Where did the rocks come from?" asked Aletta. "Did they haul them in from somewhere or did they get them from mining out that little tunnel?"

"Good question. Let's see if they look like the same material." She picked up a fragment that was lying on the ledge and took it back to the tunnel. "That seems to match, but the layers of the small rocks that aren't sandstone wouldn't have been here. They must have hauled those in. Let's look at the body, now," directed Pam.

Pam pulled a small, soft hand brush from her bag and proceeded to carefully sweep away the dust from the top of the body. "I want to see what this person was wearing in case we can get more clues about tribal affiliation. If we could look under that cloak without breaking it, I would like to see it." The brushing soon revealed a strip of other materials that would have been clothing.

"Looks like woven material," said Aletta. "Does that mean it was after the Spanish came?"

"No, weaving technology goes back to the Neolithic. Production of woven clothing was a principal household occupation all over the world. The pueblo peoples certainly had weaving. Look at the cloak; it's woven rabbit fur. The really early Navajos did not weave but wore animal skins. They learned to weave in the 1600's from contact with the pueblo tribes. This looks like it might be a plant fiber, possibly something like hemp or yucca."

"It looks like there are some kind of leather leggings above the moccasins. Look at those buttons along the seam. They look like bone," observed Aletta. "Did the ancient Native Americans wear socks?"

Pam laughed. "Yes, they did! They used juniper fibers to insulate their feet. Leather moccasins are not often found with the early pueblo people. They were more likely to be wearing sandals, but in the winter sometimes they wore inside-out hides with the fur on them."

"Look at that," she said moving dust away from the edge of the body. "A hand." She turned to her backpack and retrieved a smaller softer brush. With a few deft strokes she revealed the mummified remains of what appeared to be a hand clutching a group of long feathers of which only the central shaft remained. "Feathers that big are usually from eagles," she commented.

"Let's clean the headpiece before we record the body," Pam said reaching over the body to brush the dust from the horns, strand of beads, and dome-shaped hat.

"This hat is the most interesting thing. The Rio Grande Pueblos were most likely to include animal skulls and horn into their headdress. This buckskin cap probably has a pronghorn skull inside of it. Look at the little curly strings dangling … oh, darn, one of them broke. "Let's see if we can get the bead string clean, and then that will be good enough. I really don't want to disturb anything we don't have to."

She finished sweeping dust and got out the camera. Aletta prepared herself to record the photos and, by the end, felt certain that they hadn't missed any details. Pam told herself that she would return someday and do a better job. Then her attention turned to the pot.

She photographed it from several angles. It was vase shaped with a split neck creating two spouts. "This shape of pot today is called a wedding vase," Pam said. "That doesn't make sense to me in this context. Let's see if anything is inside of it." She put on some surgical gloves and picked the pot out of the niche. It had tightly fitting wooden stoppers in each side. She set it on the ground and carefully pulled the stopper out of one side. Inside there were many feathers of various sizes, shapes, and colors. "Yes!" she exclaimed. Then she opened the other side—more feathers!

She sat the pot on the floor and rummaged in her backpack for a folded piece of gray cloth, a ruler, and some forceps. She removed each feather from one side of the vase and laid them in a row on the cloth. "I recognize a few of these. They seem to be primary wing feathers."

"How can you tell that?" asked Aletta.

"They are the most important feathers for flying, so they have more robust quills," said Pam."This tiger-ish looking one is probably a ruffled-grouse. This brown, black, and gray feather with the white speck is a killdeer. This white one with the iridescent black tip is a magpie. This gray one with a blue edge is a scrub jay. This greenish blue one looks a lot like a monk parakeet, but they aren't native birds. The totally blue one is probably a mountain bluebird.

"We'll have to compare them against the Feather Atlas. The Fish and Wildlife Service has a database of feather images we can compare them to. I will lay the ruler next to each one for the photo. Record the colors because there is a chance we won't see them as well on our photos."

When they finished with the feathers from the first half of the vase, they returned them to the container and stoppered it before they started on the other side. By now, they had an efficient methodical way to process each feather. Pam challenged herself to make a first guess as to the species of bird: owl, red-tailed hawk, cliff swallow, robin, peregrine falcon, and heron. She looked forward to working out the puzzle of their identities.

"Okay, any other features in this chamber? Well, let's photograph how the walls meet the floor. It looks like it was at least partially sculpted. Then let's get the little tunnel to nowhere." The women continued working to describe each element of the cave. At the tunnel, Pam stuck her head in, and then twisted her neck to look above her. "Aletta, we're not done. There is a shaft here going straight up." The archaeologist rolled onto her back and looked up into the dark vertical tunnel. "It looks like it goes in about twenty feet. I'll climb in there and you can hand me my backpack." She sat up with her head in the shaft, and then stood up inside the mountain.

Aletta watched as her friend's feet disappeared into the vertical tunnel. Bits of dust and rock fell down the shaft, then after a minute Aletta could hear no sounds coming from the tunnel. She pulled Pam's backpack close to the tunnel and waited, listening. Time seemed to crawl by and she sensed herself losing track of how long Pam was gone. *What if something happened to Pam?* Aletta's mind started racing. She decided she could not risk following her, but rather, she should just go get help. She would call 911 from the top of the mesa and tell them there had been a caving accident. Maybe that wasn't the best idea. Okay, she would climb in just a little ways and see if she could help Pam escape. Maybe she just needed a rope. Would Pam have one in her backpack? Was there another rope in the truck? It was going to be hard to get a person with a broken leg or back out of that tunnel. A broken back would probably be impossible. Maybe they would just give her a big shot of morphine and let her die painlessly ...

{Chapter 89}

Pictographs

A light from the shaft suddenly illuminated the horizontal tunnel like some fancy recessed light fixture. "Aletta, you are not going to believe it!" said the breathless archaeologist. "See if you can push my bag up."

Relieved of her fantasy of having to rescue the archaeologist, Aletta lay down on her back and pulled Pam's heavy backpack onto her stomach. She shoved it upward into the shaft. She held it in place with one hand while she rearranged her body to be crouched under it, then she stood up and pushed it upward with her head. She heard Pam say something like "Got it", and then she felt the backpack being pulled upward out of her hands.

The voice in the shaft said, "Aletta, bring your bag too. We'll eat lunch. I am about to starve." Aletta sat back down on the floor of the tunnel and rolled to crawling position. She dragged her much lighter backpack and repeated the bag stuffing process. Then she stood up in the shaft.

The walls of the shaft had small rocky protrusions but nothing to grasp or actually stand on. She called to Pam, "How do you climb this?"

"Use the protrusions, rock climber's call them *holds*, to secure your hands and feet. Brace your back against the smooth side of the shaft, and then see what holds you can reach with your arms and legs to lift your body. Use the highest foothold you can reach to lever yourself to the next foothold with the opposite foot. Just think of yourself as a caterpillar," came the reply. "Do you want your gloves?"

"No, I can do it," replied the waitress who was feeling more like a spider than a caterpillar. At the top of the shaft it was easier to use her arms and legs than to take the hand that Pam offered. She found herself standing on the floor of a pitch-dark chamber.

"Look at this, Aletta!" said Pam turning to face away. Her headlight illuminated a huge painted panel of figures. "I've been dreaming of finding this ever since I was a little girl." Aletta could hear the emotion creeping into Pam's voice. "I can't believe we are actually here. It's like a dream." Tears ran down the archaeologist's cheeks, but they were hidden from Aletta by the darkness.

"This is painted on, so it's a pictograph? Right?" asked Aletta.

"Yes, pictographs can last forever when they are protected from the elements. This is a perfect place for a cave painting."

"There are certainly a lot of different kinds of birds here," observed Aletta. "They seem to be streaming out of that ... it looks like Shiprock. And look at that big bird with the square head. There is a lightning bolt touching his chest. There's an anthromorph with a funny headdress. This reminds me of the legend of the Thunderbird you told us. Is that a Thunderbird with a square head? It's the evolution of all birds, isn't it? Look how they are they dividing to fly in two directions!"

"Amazing isn't it?" Pam replied. "The procession of birds circles the whole cave. Someone spent a lot of time in here working on this—someone who really knew their birds. Let's grab something to eat because we have a lot of work to do here before our batteries run out."

"Pam, I bought some extra batteries, just in case," Aletta said with pride as she rummaged around for some lunch.

***

Many hours later they finished recording the pictographs. They realized that the birds flying counter-clockwise from their creation were the seed, plant, and nectar eaters, while the birds flying clockwise were meat and insect eaters. The birds that would eat either were on the far-side of the chamber where the two streams overlapped. Pam had new respect for the ornithological understanding of the ancient ones as she and Aletta descended through the shaft and crawled out the horizontal tunnel. Outside, the sun was down and dusk was only softly lighting the sky.

"Dang!" swore Aletta, "Sephra is going to be getting worried." She pulled out her cell phone and walked out onto the ledge. She found no signal. She grabbed the ladder and started climbing. "I'm going up to call Sephra." She was up the ladder and back on the slickrock surface before Pam had a chance to reply.

Pam took a deep breath, sighed, and then climbed the ladder slowly, wondering if she would ever be coming back here. She recognized that this was an extremely important sacred site even if no one else in the world knew about it. Her allegiance wasn't with science's need to know, but rather with reverence for the sacred. She couldn't see herself violating the gift she had been given.

{Chapter 90}

Tears from Alice

It was the first of June and definitely summer. Aletta and Mike, the cook, were sitting at the counter, sipping coffee, and talking about nothing in particular. She couldn't talk about the cave as it was confidential, so she got him talking about his life, though in truth she wasn't really paying attention.

Suddenly the cowbell on the door clanked and a young woman came scurrying straight through the cafe and made a bee-line into the bathroom. They heard the doorknob lock and then watched out the window while a man outside took his time getting out of his truck, kicking the tires and fiddling with the hood ornament. Aletta noticed that it was an art-deco charging ram on the hood of a shiny gray Dodge truck and that his clothes were clean and crisp. He stroked the ram like it was a pet as he stared down the highway. The waitress thought that he didn't look happy. He started to head toward the cafe door, but she watched him seem to change his mind mid-stride and duck back to the passenger side of the truck. He pulled out two brightly colored bags, one obviously a suitcase and quickly set them by the door of the cafe. Then he jumped into the front seat and his tires spun gravel as he headed back onto the highway. His truck was completely out of sight in less than twenty seconds.

The suitcase was a pink and black paisley print and had wheels. The smaller one was a daypack in tie-dye rainbow. If Aletta had looked, she would have seen that the suitcase had an airlines tag on it marked Alice Kelly, Clovelly Rd, Bideford EX39 3QU, United Kingdom.

"Bloody 'ell!" the woman erupted as she emerged from the bathroom and came in view of the front window. She sprinted out the front door. The waitress and the cook set down their coffee cups and turned to watch the English woman frantically checking the parking lot, and then stomping back through the front door. She was scantily clad in shorts and a thin sleeveless shirt. Her long blonde hair was tied into a single loose braid down her back. She was wearing newish-looking roughout boots.

"Did anyone see where that bloke went?" she asked forcefully, but the food service workers just lifted their shoulders and shook their heads with a doubtful look. "The guy, did you see where the guy went? He had all my stuff. He robbed me!"

"Did you see the stuff he put by the door?" the cook asked.

She jerked the door back open, sending the cowbell almost spinning. "Oh, thank god! Yes, that's my stuff."

The young woman stepped out, pulled the bags through the door, then looked up at the waitress and the cook and started to bawl. Lysosomes rolled down her cheeks. "He just dumped me off. He said he would take me to town and he just dropped me in the bloody middle of nowhere."

Aletta responded, "Honey, now calm down. It could be a lot worse than getting dropped off here. Bob must have had an emergency."

"You know him?" she sniffed.

"Yeah, he's a regular customer. Nice guy and a loyal company man. I'm sure he had a reason. Where did you hook up with him? Where are you from?"

"I'm from England." Her face distorted into ugliness as she sobbed. "I was walking from the Mustang training place." She blew her runny nose and cried into her hanky.

"Darlin', what were you doing walking from the horse training camp? That's a long way off the pavement."

"They kicked me out," she wailed. "I tried, I really tried, I didn't want things to turn out that way, but the lady started yelling at me. She was just yelling and yelling. She wouldn't stop. She was so nasty I was afraid. I called the police and started walking, but the police didn't come."

"We know *her* too, but that doesn't sound like her normal behavior. Hey, why don't you sit down and have a cup of tea or something?"

"Yes, but I'd just like some water if that's okay."

"Comin' right up," the waitress said as she filled a glass and the woman seated herself at a table in the center of the room.

Water in front of her, the English girl snapped out her iphone and found four bars of service plus a Wi-Fi signal. She settled more comfortably in her seat and visibly relaxed. They thought she was texting until she put the phone to her ear and started to wail.

"Mum, they threw me out. I was doing everything I could to help them but they went absolutely mad and were just yelling and yelling.

"No, I didn't do aannnyything. It was over nothing. The woman was just yelling and yelling. She wouldn't stop. She was so nasty; I was afraid.

"No, really ... I didn't do anything this time. Why don't you believe me? We were feeding the horses and I put some of the buckets in a muddy spot. She went absolutely mad. I told her that I just didn't think about it and didn't do it on purpose. Everyone has a right to make a mistake without people going crazy."

The young woman glanced at her paisley bag then and jumped up from the seat and looked at the waitress. "Oh, my god, there's an ant on my bag! That is so disgusting! Can't you do something about it?" she asked tersely, pointing from a distance, with the phone still to her ear.

The waitress came around the corner of the counter and searched the paisley bag for an ant. By looking at an angle, she finally located a small black ant on a black dot. She brushed it onto a napkin and carried it outside to near what she suspected was its home—but it actually was from Largo Canyon and never found it's way back. The phone conversation continued.

"Mum, I am stuck in this place in the middle of nowhere and there are ants crawling all over. It's disgusting. I'm afraid. I really need some help.

"No, I can't call a taxi. They don't have taxis in this part of America. I tried calling the police, but they didn't come. It's horrible. I don't know what to do," she said with a more tentative sob.

"Well, when will Dad be home? Maybe he will help me if you won't!" she said with more anger than sadness. "I don't know why you can't get past the fact that I threw all the stuff you were hoarding into the dumpster. Did you get rid of the dumpster yet? It's probably crawling with rats and ants by now. You seriously need to see a psychiatrist, Mother.

"Bye, now." She moved the phone to the table and started sending text messages.

The waitress and cook looked at each other and got off of their stools. The cook had some lettuce to chop. The waitress washed the cups they had used and then walked into the kitchen. She stood by the stove until the cook turned around from the prep table. She snorted and out popped a much suppressed laugh. He chuckled and rolled his eyes.

The cowbell on the door clanked and they looked out into the dining room. It was a State Police officer. He looked at the girl sitting at the table and her bags. "Are you Alice Kelly?"

The waitress appeared around the corner as the English girl nodded and started crying. "Thank god, I'm being rescued! It took you so long I didn't think you were coming. I had to rescue my own self! These people here aren't going to help me. There are ants in this place. I wouldn't eat anything here; it's not safe really. Thank god, you found me!"

"Yes, ma'am," the officer replied. "Get your belongings; I'll take you to town."

"How are you, Fred?" the waitress asked, still looking slightly amused.

"You know each other?" the English girl cut in. "What is with this place? Everyone knows everyone. It's crazy. I don't like it. I'll be glad to be gone from here."

"Yes, ma'am, everyone does know everyone. I got to the horse training school and Doc Barlow said you had started walking but had gotten a ride right away with Bob Ferguson. I called him and he told me you were here. I'll take you into Farmington and you can take the shuttle to Albuquerque tomorrow."

"I'd rather take a cab today," Alice said.

"Suit yourself. Hey, Aletta, while I am here, can I get a green chile cheeseburger to go?"

"Comin' right up!"

{Chapter 91}

Dream Catcher II

"I was riding a horse through the sagebrush. A small group of riders were following me; we climbed to the top of a knoll where we could look down on the valley below. To the west I could see a vast army of militant Navajos armed with antique weapons. To the east I could see a vast army of angry oil-field men armed with pipe-wrenches and oversized trucks. They were waiting for me to start the battle with a sound from the silver horn hanging from my saddle.

"In great fear of the ensuing bloodshed, I desperately tried to come up with a way to call the conflict off. I was crying but I knew my attendants would not understand, so I hid my face in my horse's mane.

"I realized the horse was Phantom. He turned his head and started talking to me. 'Carl, why do you think you are a significant factor in the fate of these people? It was they who chose to be here. They have chosen their own fates and if you try to refuse to sound the call to war, they will, nevertheless, hear you give it loud and clear through their own unconscious desire. War is their pleasure.'

"It started snowing and the armies turned into rabbits. Jackrabbits to the west and cottontails to the east. They started running across the field toward each other and my attendants were now coyotes trying to catch them. I knew I would have to walk home and it was a long way."

{Chapter 92}

Keeping a Promise

Pam was frowning as she opened the tailgate of her truck and pulled the metal detector across it. She was preparing for her fifth Sunday of "Spanish treasure hunting". As she reached to hoist the machine from the truck, all the memories of mother's Saturday housekeeping flooded her mind. She was the child assigned to vacuum. She despised the noisy Hoover. It cut her off from any possibility of pleasant interaction with her siblings. Everyone simply left the room to let her work, walling her in a prison of noise. Her mother never understood her tears or her pleas to change jobs with her sister or brothers. Mother thought it was about having to move the furniture, but it never was. This metal detector reminded her of the hateful Hoover, but here she was, having to drag it across the landscape.

Today, her goal was to finish checking Gobernador Canyon after which she could call it quits. On Public Land, this nasty little business would be illegal. Fines, jail time, confiscation of the equipment were promised for those who were artifact hunting with a metal detector on Forest lands. She had helped law enforcement prosecute looters on the Public Land many times. She knew the profile. They were educated, lazy, and became smarmy when they realized they were talking to a real archaeologist.

The conscience is a tricky thing though, because she knew that if she did not at least make a good faith effort to find Placido's Spanish treasure, she would feel guilty about the bird-cult cave for the rest of her life. Now the metal detector was her cross to bear.

She applied her ethics to the situation as best she could. The detector was only to be used on cave floors and along canyon walls—not the bird-cult cave. She picked out the twenty-five miles of canyon most likely to contain a Spanish treasure; when that was finished, she would have done her duty. She also would not dig for anything deeper than eighteen inches. When Gobernador Canyon was done today, her conscience would be clear.

Gobernador Canyon had changed a lot since her visit with Placido on the trac-

335

tor adventure. The cottonwood trees were now in summer's leaf. The shade took some of the emotional sting out of her task until she thought about the fact that she couldn't hear the birds. No, she had to wear the damn headphones so the machine could signal her it had sensed a metal object.

At lunch, she sat down in the shade. Munching a crisp apple, she inventoried her morning's finds. A small metal toy airplane, a plain gold wedding band, a pipe-wrench, six lock washers, two bolts, and one nail. Each of them had been duly recorded as an artifact although none of them were older than fifty-years. She wouldn't feel like an archaeologist if she didn't record the finds. She considered what the artifacts told her about the culture that left them behind. *It's a technological world.* Even the toy was about technology. The gold ring was for a man's hand. Perhaps he had thrown it as far as he could, bouncing it off a canyon wall, when he found his wife had left him for another oil-field worker. Pam would never know its story, but the ring was probably going to be the only find of any value.

What if it was Placido who had thrown it? What if it represented his former wife, if he had one? The thought of dredging up long dead memories for the man gave Pam a twinge of satisfaction for the devil's pact she had made with him to get access to his private land. She would be watching him carefully when she turned over the booty.

She sighed and tossed her apple core under a sagebrush for the chipmunks to find, and then she shouldered the metal machine, adjusted the headset and turned into Placido's corral canyon. There was a quarter-mile between the mouth of the canyon and the corral, she had been here in the late spring to look at the rock art panels. They weren't Native American panels, but rather Spanish inscriptions, names done in perfect calligraphy. "Elfuego Candelaria, Armando Estrada, Joaquin Martinez". How did these people learn to write so beautifully? She didn't imagine the ranchers and sheepherders were highly literate, so their chisel work on the stone never failed to impress her. Placido's grandfather, Attencio Lucero had etched the date next to his name. *Abril, 1885.*

The panel by the corral also had an inscribed scene of ranch life. Two men leaned on shovels watching water flow into an *acequia* (irrigation ditch). Did they once farm this canyon? With the good water, that would have been natural. She hoovered toward the panel, lost in imagining a prosperous Hispanic family diligently working the land.

The headpiece beeped, so she stepped backwards and re-positioned the machine to go over the patch of ground she had just covered—definitely a beep. She turned at a right angle and hoovered over it again. She set the metal detector aside and pulled her folding shovel from her backpack. As she stuck the tip into the ground, she realized that the shovel in the petroglyph was pointing to the exact same spot. Not only that, the other man's shovel was pointing to the spot as well. *What is this about?* she wondered.

The shovel full of dirt didn't seem to contain any metal artifacts, so she picked up the metal detector and re-scanned the hole. The beep was louder this time, but still in the place indicated by the two shovels. She stuck the shovel into the hole and stepped on it, then picked it up and stuck it back in at a right angle to the first slice. She was hoping for the shovel to strike a metal objects but it just slid through the sandy loam. Again, she searched through the shovelful of dirt without success. Re-hoovering indicated the metal object was still there, but now she was at her self-imposed ethical depth limit. She couldn't stop herself at this point, so she stuck the shovel in again and stepped on it. Another shovel of ordinary dirt. The metal detector was insistent something was down there, so she stepped on the shovel again, and halfway in, she felt it strike something large. She pulled a small trowel from her backpack and started clearing the dirt away. The lid of a canning jar was soon exhumed. She reached down to lift it out and realized it was attached to a jar underneath. The little trowel soon released the jar from its interment and Pam pulled it from the hole. A pile of gold coins glinted through the glass. It looked like they were sitting on a handwritten note.

Working feverishly, she photographed and recorded the jar before she dared to pry off the top. Wax had been used to stick the top to the glass. This, she knew, dated the jar from pre-1900 when the screw top mason jar had been invented. She pulled her Leatherman tool from her pocket and slipped the blade between the lid and the glass. Spanish doubloons! Twelve of them marked as eight escudos each with mint dates of 1885. She rolled them out and shook the note from the bottom of the jar.

Para mis hijos en el próximo siglo. Attencio Lucero, 1886

"For my sons in the coming century"—that would include Placido's father. Pam immediately wondered why it wasn't it dug up at the turn of the century. Perhaps, Placido knew. She sighed and opened up her field book to record the site. The hunt was over; no more hoovering. She had found Placido's Spanish treasure.

***

It turned out that Attencio had died unexpectedly in 1897 and that Placido was the last living member of that lineage. Placido's mother had told him there was a buried treasure, but he had never been able to figure out where to look. The pieces of eight were worth sixteen U.S. dollars in 1885, but in 2012 they would bring just under $6,000 each.

{Chapter 93}

Clipped from the Paper

FARMINGTON (API) -- The San Juan County Sheriff's Office is investigating after human remains were found in the San Juan River near Farmington. San Juan County Sheriff Bill Shultze said skeletal remains of either a man or woman were found. The identity of the body is still unknown.

The sheriff's office stated several human bones, clothing items, two chains, and a shotgun were identified and processed by a crime scene team about fifteen feet from the edge of the San Juan River.

The remains were collected and will be sent to the New Mexico State Crime Lab in Albuquerque for examination by the medical examiner.

Around 10 a.m. Thursday morning (June 13th), the San Juan County Sheriff's Office said they received a 911 call from two people traveling by canoe from Navajo Lake to Lake Powell who said they had found what they believed to be human remains about 0.5 miles downstream from the confluence of the La Plata River.

Police were dispatched to the scene where deputies and investigators soon confirmed that the remains were human.

A more intensive search is underway as the forensic team continues to process the area.

Investigators are going to be looking through missing person's reports both in this area and in the region. Also, they will research old and recent drowning reports.

The investigation is ongoing, according to the Sheriff's office.

{Chapter 94}

Darla West, Private Eye

Mirror, mirror, on the wall ... who's the *sexiest* of them all? You know it's me. Femme fatale, Private Detective, at your service. But girl in the mirror, tell me this ... how are we going to survive this heat? It's one-hundred and thirteen degrees in the shade out there. Phoenix is such a drag in the summer—summer bummer—and I am sick to death of running from one air conditioned space to the next. It hurts my hairdo. Look at our split ends, girlfriend. You *are* dying!

That stakeout job we did last month paid well, but we really did just about die sitting in the black caddie, didn't we? I've got to take good care of you, my love. I need to put a thermometer in there for safety. An SUV should not get hot, but I guess the color was made for the night, not the day. The Escalade is in the shop again anyway. I am so tired of having to ride the friggin' bus to the grocery store. I'd almost prefer to just go hungry, but I am not going back to that anorexia clinic, so we'll ride the bus. Either that or call out for pizza delivery.

Let's check on employment possibilities for a beautiful woman. Does the FBI need my help this week? Isn't it convenient to have their wanted posters on the Internet? Remember when we had to go down to the post office to look at them? Hey, wasn't that a kick when they asked me to rate their site for quality purposes last week? I was glad to see that the FBI is taking my opinion seriously for a change. It's about time they noticed me. Okay, here we go ... let's look at anything north of this hell hole where my license is recognized. What a scam—having to get a different license just because you are in a different state. Criminals don't care what state they are in! They go where they want; but me? No, I have to get a different license. Life is unfair, isn't it, pretty lady? Okay, here's one ...

SEEKING INFORMATION

Arson Investigation

Coalinga, California

January 8, 2012

During the early morning hours of Sunday, January 8, 2012, unidentified suspects cut through a fence at the Harris Feeding Company near Coalinga, California. Once inside, the suspects positioned numerous improvised incendiary devices, or IIDs, beneath tractor trailer rigs parked on the premises. After the suspects fled the area, timers on the IIDs initiated the detonation of each device. The ensuing fires destroyed 14 rigs with an estimated loss in excess of $2,000,000. While no drivers were sleeping in the rigs that night, several Harris Company employees were on site at the time of the detonation and could have easily been seriously injured or killed.

An anonymous claim of responsibility was subsequently released by the North American Animal Liberation Press Office, posted on several websites, and delivered to various media outlets.

===

What the hell!! No reward offered! Assholes! No one is gonna bother calling if there is no reward! What about this one?

SEEKING INFORMATION

Murder on a Government Reservation

Rio Arriba County, New Mexico

October 28, 2011

Aaron Shauner

Victim

Unknown suspects are being sought in connection with the murder of an employee of the Bureau of Land Management (BLM) in the Farmington area of northwestern New Mexico. At approximately 5:30 P.M. on October 28, 2011, Aaron Shauner, a Range Management Specialist at the BLM, was transporting 7 wild horses from a round-up to a ranch adjacent to the public lands. His co-workers used an alternate route to leave the round-up, while Shauner took a little-used ranch road. When he did not arrive as expected, the ranchers went to look for him, but found him dead. The horses being transported had been set free.

An autopsy determined that Shauner was killed with a shotgun-inflicted wound to the head. A murder weapon was never found, and no suspects have been identified.

REWARD

The FBI is offering a reward up to $100,000 for information leading to the arrest and conviction of individual(s) responsible for the murder of Aaron Shauner.

===

Farmington ... hmmm. Let's Google that. Oh! All the way up there! Right next to Colorado—cool, clear Colorado. Oh, yes! Aaron Shauner you might be a mystery now, but get ready 'cause this girl is gonna solve your little ol' mystery. I'll call the mechanics and see if my caddie is ready to roll.

***

We are gonna be needing that hundred-thousand pretty bad, if the caddie doesn't quit breaking down. Those boys just about cleaned me out. If it weren't for my credit card, we wouldn't even clear the city limits. Hey, girlfriend in the mirror, what do you say we stop in Sedona and go shopping in one of those upscale dress shops? Have magic wand will travel! *Magic wand* ... hmm, I like that better than calling it a QuikPod or what I heard the other day—*selfie-stick*—no, *magic wand* is much better.

***

Gee whiz, that clerk didn't have to get so bent out of shape. What a bimbo! It's not my fault if I have good taste in clothes. I didn't hurt anything and I *did* offer to hang them all back up. What's her problem? I'll never go back there but I will definitely give them a one star rating on Facebook. They shouldn't treat customers like that—I *could* be a customer—they didn't know I didn't have any money. Anyway, I made their clothes look fabulous, if I do say so myself. I've got the proof of that right there on my iPhone. I really should have been a model if I hadn't become a detective—maybe I will be a model when I get tired of being a private eye. I'll post some of the pics to my Facebook page as soon as I get to civilization. Let's see, Flagstaff is not too far. I'll bet they have a Starbucks.

We should pull over, girlfriend. Look at those pine trees. We did pack the cowgirl clothes didn't we? Where's that *magic wand*?

***

I don't know about you, cutie pie, but this landscape is wearing me out. Too many photo-shoots, too little time. That one with the sheep and the clouds is stunning. You look like a big-breasted Native American Goddess. Too bad I didn't pack the broom skirt and velvet blouse. The magic wand is a girl's best friend. Let's call and make an appointment with the FBI for tomorrow, and we better get a reservation on a room for tonight.

"Hello. This is Darla West. I'm a private investigator. Who am I speaking with? ... Miss Williams, I'd like to make an appointment to come in and talk to the lead person on the Aaron Shauner case ... Greg Stribling, yes ... Tomorrow, early-morning if possible ... Fifteen minutes should be enough ... Okay, I will see you and Mr. Stribling tomorrow at eight thirty ... Thank you, Miss Williams ... Oh, wait, I'm coming into town tonight, can you recommend a good hotel? "

***

Eighty-seven dollars and fifty cents per night is too much, I know, but I did it for you. You deserve it, sexy babe in the mirror. You might meet some potential clients in a place like this. Let's hand out business cards at the happy hour at least to anyone who looks like they need the services of a detective. That look of anxious estrangement tells it all—*they need me.*

Look at how the lamp light strikes the bed. If I was right there on the pillow, my profile from the left and the shadows—yes! I have to try it. Where did I put those black lace panties? Damn, the magic wand is still in the Escalade. I know ... I'll throw on my bikini and run out and get it. I can stop by the happy hour and see if anything is happening yet, maybe pick up a glass of wine. Oh, wouldn't that be nice!

***

Damn you little vixen, you've let us sleep right through happy hour! Aren't we a lazy bitch! Okay, just get the underwear off, we don't want to get it dirty. See you in the morning. I love you.

{Chapter 95}

Sexy is as Sexy Does

After I finished sorting out and rating my photos, I let the best upload to Facebook while I ate a breakfast of cantaloupe and bacon in the hotel breakfast room. It was the day to pull out the Lady Detective costume. I naturally resemble Carrie-Anne Moss, so it's easy to make people feel like they are talking to Trinity of *The Matrix* by pulling my hair back and wearing my darkest sunglasses. To keep them unconscious of their association, I've had the outfit, with its perky little Nehru collar, done in indigo blue serge. With the Fourth of July just two days away, I'll wear red heels and a belt. First impressions are everything in this business!

I saw Greg Stribling looking out at me through his window as I walked across the parking lot. He thought I didn't see him, or maybe he thought I wouldn't know it was him, but it was no surprise when his secretary let me in and there he was. He's a cagey animal and I don't trust him. Is he gonna try to cheat on the reward? I'll have to expect him to try. Right off, I noticed he had done nothing to personalize his office and he wore nothing that gave a clue about his interests. I felt myself straining to find a point to build rapport.

"Mr. Stribling, how nice to get to meet you. I'm interested in the Aaron Shauner case."

"Are you a private investigator?" When I replied affirmatively, he cut to the chase. "Let me see your license and your identification."

I pulled them from my red handbag. He flipped them onto the top of a copier and instantly had a copy, which he called Ms. Williams to come fetch. Undoubtedly she ran a check on them. As unpleasant as it was, it gave me the opening I was looking for.

"Your operation is impressive, Mr. Stribling. I've seen a lot of agencies at work, but you really are on top of it. I suspect that this is going to make my job easier."

He didn't take the bait. "Ms. West, undoubtedly, you've read the details in the Information Wanted poster. We have prepared a copy of our investigation file which

344

you may study at the desk in the front office. When you are done, you can ask any questions that come up." Ms. Williams brought back the credential copy and handed it to him. He glanced at it and continued, "Now if you ladies will excuse me, I have a trial to attend."

They had a desk for me in a corner of the front office. I toyed with the idea of a photo of me as an FBI agent, but every time I turned around, Ms. Williams was staring at me, so I just looked through the file. Aaron Shauner didn't deserve to die, I could tell that from his photos. I spent about an hour reading interviews with potential suspects. None of them looked worth a damn. I decided to go visit the scene. Ms. Williams creeped me out anyway.

I bought a turkey sandwich—to be my picnic—and a map of the area and headed out Highway 64. The map showed a paved road into the forest, so I followed it. It dead-ended at a large lake, which seemed like an excellent spot for a picnic since finding the crime scene seemed unlikely. The water seemed a little cold for midsummer, but I put on my bikini for some beach shots. Some men with fishing poles were sitting in a boat, so I flagged them over to help me with some of the photos that needed more distance than my QuikPod, I mean *magic wand*, can do. They were kind of old. After they left, I thought I should interview the one person that might know something ... Randall Tapia. I called his office and got an appointment for three-thirty.

At the appointed hour, I met with Randall Tapia and Jessica Anderson at the BLM. Their shared office was highly personalized. Randall had photos of fish he had caught on a cruise to Mexico, Jessica had cowgirl stuff. I complimented them on the job they are doing with the Wild Horse and Burro Program. I could see their eyes light up, so I tossed them another bit of praise. They started talking. They weren't talking to me; it seemed that they were talking to each other or maybe over each other. They told me all about the wild horse and burro program, how they take the horse advocates seriously, how they got all the horses adopted, and on and on. I finally got an opening to ask about the murder of Aaron Shauner, which set them off again. I was caught between two simultaneous monologues. It was hard for me to get away until exactly four twenty-five, when all the government employees exited the building. They walked me down the hall still jabbering, then simply turned and left me at the exit. I am not sure what I learned from them.

I had one other track I wanted to follow, so I called Michael Cabot and asked if he could meet me that night at the Sportsman's Bar. In the photos on file with the FBI, he looked like he might know something and he had found the body. His brother did not look nearly so interesting. I stopped by the hotel to shower and change into something more casual. It was silky green and fit tight. I was conflicted about the shoes. If they had music, we might be dancing. I wore the silver heels, but I tucked a couple of other options into the Escalade, just in case.

I recognized Michael immediately. He was sitting at the bar with his brother. I walked up, introduced myself and asked Don to excuse himself because I needed to talk to Michael privately. I instantly got a sense of a kindred soul as Michael started to talk. After he told me what he knew, I showed him my magic wand and took a bunch of pictures of us posing. He looks kind of dorky in the photos because he was quite insistent about wearing those sunglasses. They didn't have a dance floor and it turns out he was there with his father who is apparently named after a dog, Shep.

Michael took me back to where his dad and brother were sitting and introduced me to them. Shep spit some tobacco juice into an empty can and said to Michael that I surely reminded him of their mother. I asked him sharply if their mother had been a detective who had rock stars and televangelists for clients. He said with some tenderness in his voice, that she was a porn star who had fallen in love with the American West. She was a good woman is what he said, but then he gave me a scowl that left no doubt in my mind it was time to go. I stopped by the restroom for a quick mirror check before I left the bar. The only thing I had to say to my best friend was, "I don't really lie, I merely reorganize the truth." She winked back.

{Chapter 96}

Wrapping Things Up

I woke at dawn and stared at the ceiling. Something Michael told me was to-tally new information. There were some other people on the ranch that day, Willy LeDoux and his wife, Nicky. I had not seen them mentioned in the FBI files. This, in itself, was a red flag. I knew I needed to track them down. That turned out to be easier than I imagined.

I had chosen the Southwest Casual outfit for the day, complete with a turquoise bracelet and a faun-colored suede skirt. It looked great with the high topped western boots. I had to change my nail polish so it took some time to get ready. I was starving by the time I was ready to go out. As luck would have it, I just happened to eat break-fast at Little Anita's and they just happened to seat me in Nicky LeDoux's section— proof that God loves me! I saw her name tag when she came to get my order.

I ordered coffee and a strawberry waffle. When she came back with the coffee, I introduced myself and asked if she would have time to talk to me about the Aaron Shauner case. She looked around and said things would slow down in about twenty minutes and she would take a break and have coffee with me. When I had finished the waffle, she asked me to pay and to then come sit with her at the employee's table in the back. I knew the quality of the information might ride on the size of the tip that I tagged on the bill, so I added ten-dollars to the ticket before I had them run the card.

I stopped by the mirror at the back of the restaurant to give myself a silent pep talk because instinct told me that the case would hinge on what I was about to learn. I sat down with her and told her about being a detective. I told her that they write books and make movies about my cases—I must remember to use that line again. She realized she could trust me, so she laid out the whole story for me.

Willy had seen Aletta, the waitress from the Roadhouse, drive up there in her white Jeep on the afternoon of the murder. He didn't know it was her at the time, he was repairing fences for the Cabots, but later, when Nicky got a job at the cafe, they realized it was Aletta's Jeep for sure. They didn't want to say anything because the owner of the place liked Aletta and might have fired Nicky.

Nicky didn't know what Aletta's motive was until she talked to Rex Roundy, who said that he saw Aaron and Aletta together that morning and Aletta was crying. She assured me that he works in the oil field and I could ask him if it was true. Then Rex and several other people had said that Aletta had closed early that day. John, the owner, could verify this. When Rex had first told her all of that, she was pretty sure that Aletta was guilty, but she had grown fond of the girl as a co-worker so she didn't turn her in. She also said that everyone around knows that Aletta goes barefoot at home all the time. She recommended that I asked Sephra Brooks to verify this.

When I mentioned that all of this made sense of the receipt, I saw a look of fear cross her face. She apparently doesn't know about the receipt. She regained her composure and gave me a contact number for Rex Roundy. I started to leave intending to wrap up the case. She had a favor to ask me: would I suggest that Mr. Stribling offer Willy a plea bargain on his tractor problem? Apparently Willy was involved in some kind of misunderstanding about whether he could use a tractor on a friend's farm in Colorado.

My best friend in the mirror had a happy smile as I left Little Anita's. I stopped by the FBI office to cross-check the new evidence. The smugness of the waitress in her testimony made my blood boil, but the new facts filled in a lot of the story. I asked Greg to talk to Willy about a plea bargain in return for his testimony against Aletta. Greg said that Willy hasn't gone to trial yet, but he is charged with interstate transportation of stolen goods. I asked Greg if I could take a photo of the two of us standing beside his desk shaking hands. Miss Williams got in the picture too. I promised to email the whole report by mid-afternoon so they could read it before the holiday.

Even though now I could afford it, I decided to clear out of my hotel room. I hung my clothes up in the Escalade, paid the bill, and headed up to Navajo City. I wanted to study the perpetrator. Several men with toothpicks in their teeth were walking out as I arrived. She was sweeping.

I picked out a seat where I could watch her, then ordered coffee and a salad. She forgot to ask me what kind of dressing I wanted, but I didn't want any dressing, so

I just had her bring me some lemon wedges to squeeze over the salad. I opened my laptop and started writing the report. She brought me a refill and asked me if I was a novelist. I did the unthinkable and told her the truth--*no, I'm a detective, but they write novels about my cases.* She wanted to chit-chat about being a detective and I humored her. I showed her my magic wand and we took a photo of me and her in front of a picture of the roundup. You can see Aaron Shauner in the photo. He's standing right by my left boob.

I then realized that there were other possibilities in this backwater joint. I asked her if I could wear her apron and pretend to be a waitress and she could take the photos. I look really cute with an apron and an order pad. Then I told her that I had some work to do and sat down and wrote out the evidence report. In the cover letter, I took the opportunity to remind Greg that I expected to receive the reward money as soon as it can be released. I don't know how he will justify it, but I fully expect the man to try to cheat me. I emailed it off to them in record time.

The mirror in the bathroom of the Roadhouse Cafe is possibly the oldest mirror I have ever talked to. I looked rather faded to myself. What I really need is some cooler weather. Aletta told me that the best Fourth of July celebration is 75 miles north in Silverton, Colorado. They call it the Freedom Celebration. I told her, somewhat apocryphally, that she should enjoy it while she can. She won't have any use for the tip anyway, so I didn't leave one.

{Chapter 97}

Indictment

Farmington (API) A Navajo City, New Mexico, waitress was indicted on murder charges Thursday, July 5th, in the death of a Bureau of Land Management Range Specialist who was shot following a wild horse roundup.

A grand jury indicted Aletta Ramsden, 42, on charges of killing a federal employee and animal enterprise terrorism in the October 28, 2011, shooting which left 28-year-old Aaron Shauner dead and allowed 7 horses to escape.

"Today's indictments will allow the state to move forward in the process of seeking justice for Aaron Shauner and to hold accountable those who are responsible for his death," New Mexico Attorney General Jerry Caldwell said after the grand jury hearing.

{Chapter 98}

Celebrity Waitress Program

John opened the bottle and shook one aspirin out into the palm of his left hand. He screwed the lid back onto the container and picked up the glass of water. Staffing always made his head hurt. He picked up the phone and dialed his girlfriend's number.

"Hey, Doc! Good morning! You got time to talk? ... Did you hear about Aletta? ... There is no way she did it, but it might be a while before they get it sorted out. It's gonna leave me without a waitress this weekend. I was wondering if you would be interested in making a cameo appearance as a small-cafe waitress. It would be fun to work together. I'll be cooking ... Oh, you have an intern? ... Well, yeah, you could bring the intern ... Oh, yeah, that would work ... You'll leave the intern to work on Sunday too ... Wow, that solves the whole problem ... Okay, be here by six-thirty on Saturday ... See you then."

He ended the call and dialed the Roadhouse. Brenda answered with a very polished "Can I help you" greeting, but when he identified himself, she launched into an anxious recitation of why she could not possibly work on Saturday. He forced himself to interrupt her. "Brenda, I just was calling to tell you I have a waitress for Saturday and Sunday. No worries. How busy was lunch?" He could hear her anxiety evaporate. Before hanging up, they chatted for a few minutes about items for the shopping list.

***

The intern turned out to be a young dark-haired Irish woman with a strong, but entirely pleasing accent. Rebecca O'Brien had some experience as a barmaid at a pub in Dublin, so she already knew much of the job although the New Mexican food items were unknown to her. She realized the problem before she even arrived, so after John had given her a tour and orientation of the facility, she grabbed a menu and started studying it. John and Doc retired to the patio to have space for a private conversation.

"This girl is really conscientious," said Doc, "and I know she could use a little pocket money as she is stopping in New York for a few days before going back to Ireland. I'll stay to help through lunch, but then she'll be able to handle it."

John replied, "You have no idea how much I appreciate you both coming over. How many interns do you usually have?"

"I try to have four per month and sometimes I have volunteers as well. Oh, here comes a customer; let's see if Becca and I can handle it," she said heading toward the patio door to join the girl at the register. John sat back and listened to the voices through the screen door.

After a few minutes, John realized that the young male customer must be trying to flirt with the Irish girl. John smiled and suddenly felt light hearted. The idea of a nascent romance on the wind made him feel a connection to the billions of young men who had ever flirted with a pretty young lass on a Saturday in July. Doc tiptoed out the patio door, leaving the two young people to themselves. She sat down beside John, who took her hand in his and stared off to the high Colorado mountains on the north horizon.

***

Word must have gotten out about the pretty Irish lass because the men of the oil patch showed up in record numbers for a Saturday afternoon. They all wanted her personal attention and her experience as a barmaid helped her respond to her sudden popularity with grace. Her tip jar started to overflow before lunch was over. Doc Barlow was visibly tired, but Becca was still going strong when Doc finally went home.

On Sunday morning, John realized it would be another record setting day when a dozen young men showed up for sit-down breakfasts and personal attention from the Irish girl. It was going to cut into his kitchen nap time, but the cash register kept rolling out receipts. He couldn't really complain.

Many of the young men asked Becca about Aletta being in jail. Becca confirmed Aletta's temporary incarceration but assured the men, who she assumed were friends of Aletta's, that the misunderstanding would soon be sorted out and Aletta would be back to work. The men looked disappointed to learn that Becca's presence was only temporary and that she would soon be going back to Ireland.

At four-twenty, John's cell phone rang. It was Rita Mae calling from Nova Scotia to see if he could pick her up from the La Plata County airport the following day. She was coming to help keep things under control and no amount of protesting could convince her that things were okay. He realized that she would want to be present for Aletta as well as for the Roadhouse, so he agreed to pick her up at three-ten the following afternoon.

Becca thanked John profusely before heading back to Mustang Camp. She had definitely enjoyed herself and it had been valuable to take a break from horse training. She told John that another one of the interns was hoping to get to come over next weekend if he needed her. John, who was putting the day's receipts into a bank bag for deposit, couldn't help but think it sounded good to him.

***

Rita Mae was absolutely shocked that John would simply drop a random stranger into his waitress position as if just *anyone* could do it. It was the first time the two of them had come anywhere near quarreling, but the Irish girl had worked out so perfectly, that John couldn't avoid the conclusion that Rita Mae was over-reacting. The next morning he was confronted with the fact that both Penny and Brenda shared Rita Mae's doubts about the concept of temporary employment for foreign women as an oil-field attraction. *Damn, but it had worked!* John loved the idea, which he now called the Celebrity Waitress program.

The ladies' opinions were challenged as the day wore on and many of the young men inquired about the Irish girl. After lunch, the three professionals stood staring out of three different windows, scowls plastered to their normally smiling faces.

Penny spoke first, "Aletta better get out of there and get back to work before things get worse."

Brenda responded with realism. "She could get sent to prison for a very long time, even if she is innocent."

Rita Mae chimed in, "We have to get her out of there."

Penny laughed. "A jail break. Then the criminal waitresses of Navajo City can go on a crime spree! Okay, it's not funny, but the problem is basically there is no one else that wants to drive all the way out here for a quiet little cafe job with no possibility of good tips. The idea of those little hussies from Mustang Camp cutting into my tips is what bugs me."

Brenda and Rita Mae looked at Penny with surprise. Brenda said, "I don't think they will have any effect on weekday tips. I just don't want them not doing their share of the cleaning, or worse, leaving messes that we have to clean during our shifts."

Rita Mae said, "The issue for me is that they don't necessarily have training in basic hygiene and food safety."

The ever-practical Brenda turned away from her window to look at the others. "John could have a short training program for them."

Penny laughed again. "John never trains anyone, he just turns people loose and watches to see if they are going to sink or swim."

Rita Mae turned to the others and smiled. "We could train them *ourselves* without ever having to meet them. Let's make a training video that shows all the things an aspiring waitress needs to know. We can cover all aspects of the job. It will be fun, I think. What do you say ladies? Do we want to try?"

The three waitresses worked hard the rest of the week to produce a training video before the arrival of the young Danish intern. Whether their waitress education program was effective or not, no one could ever say. The young woman may have done just as well without it.

{Chapter 99}

Letter from Mom

July 6, 2012

Dear Aletta,

I'm still trying to get over the shock of finding out you're in jail. You've always been one who has to go her own way, but in my wildest dreams, I never thought you'd be arrested for murder. My heart still speeds up every time I think about it. I swear, if your uncle Fred hadn't of been here, I don't know what might of happened to me. I haven't been feeling all that good here recently in the first place. I couldn't imagine what was going on when that woman called to tell me you were in jail. I never did catch the woman's name. It sounded like Seferer ... Do you know who that is? Anyway, she cried a lot and it was hard to tell what she was saying. Well, Fred and I made a deal. Neither one of us is gonna say a single word about this to anyone else. Not even Fred's wife. Especially not Fred's wife. That woman hasn't shut her mouth since the day she was born.

I guess I should tell you that the reason we're not telling anyone is not because we're ashamed of you. Well, we are a little bit, but not a whole lot more than we have been, knowing that you've been working as a waitress in the back end of the world. Why you ever wanted to go to New Mexico is beyond me. The people who love you are here in the place you grew up in and if Missouri was good enough for your dad, and Fred, and me, then it's darn good and well good enough for you too. Anyway, as I was saying, the reason we don't want anyone else to know about your trouble is that we don't want them snooping and feeling sorry for us. Heavens! I don't even let people know you're living in New Mexico. When they ask me where you are, I just say out west. And I sure don't say you're waiting tables.

I was sort of afraid something like this might happen to you. You've always been too trusting and too willing to go along with someone else's ideas. I don't think you killed anyone, but I'm not surprised for you to be accused of one thing or another. I just felt in my bones that being surrounded by all those people from Mexico was not a good thing for a young woman on her own.

Well, I don't know what else to say. I hope you can keep your chin up, and I also hope that even in New Mexico, they'll have to hire a lawyer to help you.

With love from your mother

{Chapter 100}

The Public Defender

Aletta stood behind the long wooden table wearing an orange jumpsuit provided by Rio Arriba County. On the other side of the aisle stood a man she assumed to be the prosecutor flanked by Greg Stribling. Behind them sat Sheriff Attencio Candelaria and Aaron Shauner's mother, Beatrice. Aletta assumed that her case had been assigned to a public defender, but she had not been informed of who it might be. The judge entered the room and the bailiff announced her arrival. The judge looked at Aletta and asked if she had a lawyer. She replied that she had applied for one and been told she would have one, but she hadn't met him yet. The judge turned to the bailiff, who looked at his watch. Before he could raise his eyes to the judge, the back door of the court burst open and a woman in a blue business-woman's dress, carrying a briefcase, came running to Aletta's table. She threw down her briefcase on the table, nodded to Aletta, and turned to face the judge.

The Honorable Susan Dorsey called the court to order in the matter of the United States of America vs. Aletta Ramsden. She asked Aletta to remain standing while the charges were read.

"COUNT ONE: The Grand Jury of Rio Arriba County by this indictment accuses the defendant, Aletta Ramsden of the crime of killing a federal employee during the performance of his duties in violation of Title 18, United States Code, Section 1114. On or about October 28th, 2011, at or near the Joint Wild Horse Territories of the BLM and Carson National Forest, Aletta Ramsden killed Aaron Shauner, a federal employee hauling horses from a wild horse roundup.

"COUNT TWO: The Grand Jury of Rio Arriba County by this indictment accuses the defendant, Aletta Ramsden of the crime of animal enterprise terrorism in violation of Title 18, United States Code, Section 43. On or about October 28th, 2011, at or near the Joint Wild Horse Territories of the BLM and Carson National Forest, Aletta Ramsden intentionally caused disruption of the wild horse gather by setting free seven wild horses which the BLM spent $10,010 to gather."

The attorney remained standing next to Aletta, who turned to look at her. Suddenly Aletta had the sensation that none of it was real. She watched the attorney breathe, her chest expanding. The attorney's eyes blinked and Aletta noticed how liquid the pupils looked. She turned to watch the judge, who continued speaking, but in slow motion. The judge picked up the gavel and in slow motion hammered it against her desk. The sound slowly traveled across the room. Aletta watched the sound toward her. Then, with a bang the world resumed normal speed and her jailers suddenly surrounded her and escorted her from the courtroom. The attorney followed close behind. Aletta was put into a small room with a desk and two chairs; the attorney stepped inside, closed the door, put her briefcase on the desk, and sat down. She looked up at Aletta and said, "You can sit down."

Aletta slowly lowered herself to the seat as the attorney continued. "They assigned me to your case this morning, barely in time for me to get to court, so I'm just getting oriented. My name is Kerry J. Lincoln. I work for the Public Defender's Office. I'll be representing you as your attorney." She pulled a new yellow legal pad and a pen from her briefcase. "Your name is Aletta Ramsden, right? Why don't you just take a few minutes and tell me how you came to be accused of ... what ... Section 1114, killing a government employee and Section 43, animal enterprise terrorism? What you tell me is confidential and I will be able to defend you best if I know the truth."

"What evidence do they have?" demanded Aletta.

"I don't know, we won't know until the preliminary hearing," replied Kerry.

"As far as I know, they found a fuel receipt with me named as the cardholder at the crime scene five months after the murder. It was a receipt that I threw away into the garbage right after I bought fuel, so I have no idea how it got to the crime scene. I never went to the scene, neither before, during, nor after the murder," Aletta said.

"They must have more than that because the Grand Jury needs more than that to indict you," the attorney said. "What were you doing at the time of the murder?"

"I work as a waitress at Navajo City. I was on the clock until eight."

"Was anyone else there with you?"

"Guido, the cook was there."

"Well, if we can get a statement from him that puts you at work, we can get this cleared up at the preliminary." Kerry looked pleased.

"Guido left the country last winter. I think he's in Chiapas. No one even knows his last name or if Guido was really his name at all," said Aletta dejectedly.

"What about customers, were there any regular customers who can speak to your whereabouts?" asked the lawyer.

"I had a list of them. I gave it to the man at the FBI who interviewed me. I've tried to remember who is on that list, but I just can't think clearly since I was arrested. Can you get it back from him?"

"I can try," said Kerry. "They might not give it to me before the preliminary hearing, but we will have it in discovery if we go to trial. It sounds like you want to plead *not guilty*."

"Absolutely!" affirmed Aletta.

"This is one of the worst things that can ever happen to a person—are you doing okay?" asked Kerry.

"I don't know. I keep having a sense that this isn't really happening, like it's a dream or a hallucination," ventured the waitress.

"That's an effect of psychological trauma. It's not uncommon for people to respond like that. It makes a big difference if you keep yourself from feeling like a victim of circumstance. I know that sounds impossible but finding ways to adapt to the situation needs to be your priority."

"Do you have an extra yellow tablet that I could have?" asked Aletta.

"Let me ask the guards if you are allowed to have a legal pad. You might have special rules being a terrorist suspect. You are my first terrorist suspect so there are things I don't know." Kerry stuck her head out the door and asked the guard, who said he would check to make sure. As she sat down she said, "Seems like pencil or pen could be a problem as well."

"No, they let me have little three inch long pencils in my cell, but I haven't managed to get more than one sheet of paper at a time."

359

The guard knocked on the door and gave them a thumbs up signal through the glass.

"Okay, we're about out of time, Aletta, but I want to go over the guidelines for you to follow to help me represent you. First, and this is extremely important, don't talk to anyone about the case, especially the police or the guards. Keep very careful track of your court dates, don't depend on the jail to inform you—it's not as important to them as it is to you. Dress to impress when you go to court; look your very best. Is there someone who can bring you some good clothes for your preliminary hearing? I'll need their phone number to arrange it. I doubt that they will set bail in this case, so you'll probably be doing everything from jail."

"Miss Lincoln," started Aletta.

"Call me Kerry unless we are in the courtroom," cut in the attorney.

"Kerry, then, can you give me some idea of what the process is. Not knowing what to expect is really hard for me."

"Oh, yes, I always forget to go over this. Today you had the Initial Arraignment where the charges were read to you. The next step is the Preliminary Hearing in which the prosecution presents evidence to a judge to show why you should be tried for this crime. We can also present evidence at that time to show why you should not be accused of this crime. You could be released at this point. If not, you will have a Second Arraignment at which point you will officially enter a plea. You can also make a plea bargain at that time. In a bargain, you would basically plead guilty to a lesser charge, which is what happens in ninety percent of all cases. Then there is a period of discovery where information is exchanged. At this point we can file motions, such as a motion to dismiss. Then finally the case goes to a jury trial."

"So what can I do to get ready for the Preliminary Hearing?" asked Aletta.

"Come up with some evidence to substantiate your alibi. When we go to trial, they will have to prove that you did it, if you show why you could not have possibly been there, you will make it impossible for them to do. I'll meet with you tomorrow afternoon. I'm going to call your boss to see if he knows anything about Guido. I'll check with the detective about the list.

"Okay, here is my card in case you need to call me," Kerry said, handing it to Aletta, as she stood up and shouldered her briefcase. Aletta looked at it

Kerry J. Lincoln

Public Defender

President, Rio Arriba County Association of Fiction Writers

{Chapter 101}

Filling the Legal Pad

Kerry was deeply disappointed as she hung up the phone. John Irick didn't know how to find Guido and worse yet, John said he had gotten a call at about seven that evening informing him that the Roadhouse had closed early. The caller was someone named Rex Roundy. She realized sadly, that Aletta might be a very good liar.

The situation distinctly reminded her of Antoinette, the female antagonist in the second book of her romance/mystery series, *The Cyclone Waits*. Antoinette's seeming strength of character was ripped asunder by the constantly shifting multitude of alternate personalities that drove her to evil. Kerry was quite proud of handling the complexity of Antoinette's personality in a way that kept her simultaneously interesting and yet believable. Antoinette had gotten away with murder, perhaps Aletta would also. *Would I be proud to have helped her? Would I have helped Antoinette? Maybe I did help her. I gave birth to her through the power of my imagination. The real question is would I want to have her destroyed? No, I saved her in the end: I have to save her.*

Kerry sighed, and then she laughed. Synchronicity between her day job and her novels was always such a gift from the universe. It made her feel that life is magical. Sometimes it even gave her those *"woo-woo shivers"* that she knew should be called numinosity. The best part—the very best part—was that Kerry got to play the part of a protagonist in every scene; otherwise, being a public defender would really suck.

Greg Stribling had been cordial on the phone. He said his files were public documents and that she was welcome to come look through them. The problem was the three hour drive from Espanola to Farmington— she just didn't have time. There were too many cases on her desk, and things were already starting to get chaotic.

Aletta was the only client that was not out on bond, so Kerry proceeded through security then directly to the attorney/prisoner conference room to wait for the guards to bring her client. It irritated her to no end that they insisted on referring to her clients as *offenders*. *Alleged offender* or maybe *accused person* would be more respectful. The attorney was thinking about how institutionalized disrespect was in

362

the penal system as they brought the prisoner into the room. Aletta put her yellow pad and a tiny pencil on the table before sitting down. Kerry noticed that Aletta seemed to be in good spirits.

"Looks like you've been busy," the attorney commented.

"Yes, I started writing a book about the death of Aaron Shauner. Kind of fictionalized, since I don't know all the details, but I took what I do know and put it together with the people I know and I think it's turning out pretty good. You know, I've wanted to be a novelist all of my life, this is the first time that I haven't had anything else I had to do. Solitary confinement is really an advantage for a novelist. Can I have another yellow pad? This one is full."

Kerry reached into her briefcase and pulled out another new pad and a small book. "I'd like to read what you've written, if you don't mind. It might help me understand the case."

Aletta responded, "I was hoping you would want to read it. So far it covers the events leading up to the murder. All the people are real people who were there."

Kerry handed Aletta the new yellow pad in exchange for the old one. "Your work will be safer with me than in here. Someone could mess with it as a way to punish you. I also brought you a present," she said handing Aletta the book. "This is a book I wrote on doing yoga in small spaces. I got special permission to give this to my clients during their incarceration. The jail is run by the Sikhs from Akal Security and they support yoga for offenders, oh, I mean prisoners."

"Wow, that's really nice. How did you get it published?" asked the alleged offender.

"Self-publishing. It's easier than you imagine, but Aletta, we have to talk about your case. I called John Irick and he said it wouldn't be possible to find Guido and that he had gotten a call at seven that evening that the Roadhouse was closed."

"Oh, that!" Aletta cried out. "I forgot to turn on the 'open' sign. This one customer who is always trying to start trouble called John about it. The man's name is Rex Roundy. You'll read about him in what I've already written. He tried to make a big deal out of the fact that I was sitting at the counter with tears in my eyes when

Aaron was outside in the parking lot. For christsakes, I was writing about a little baby elephant getting rescued. I would never waste a tear on a 'good ol' boy' like Aaron Shauner, no disrespect for the dead intended, but the man was an alcoholic and a drug user. Everyone that didn't know him assumes he must have been an all right guy and that a woman would automatically be attracted to a man with a government job. The reality, however, was that the guy was an asshole playboy character with a substance abuse problem. Kerry, could we just assume *you* had a romantic interest in him? How would that make you feel? Do you ever get that kind of thing … people assume because you represent someone, you must be secretly in love with them?"

Kerry looked chagrined. "Yeah, that happened to me. I met a man online on a dating website but I never met him in person. About a year later he was arrested for embezzlement and I was assigned the case. That was a mess," she said shaking her head with distaste for the memory.

The attorney side reasserted itself and she picked up her pen. "Aletta, this might be one of those rare cases that actually go to trial. Everyone will be expecting you to make a plea bargain to avoid the possibility of a death sentence. If we don't get the case dropped at the preliminary, we need to have thought out what our preference for a crime you would plead guilty to would be."

"Kerry, I'll plead guilty of forgetting to ask what kind of salad dressing they want. I'll plead guilty to jaywalking if it needs to be an actual crime. I won't plead guilty to *anything* having to do with the death of Aaron Shauner. No, in years to come maybe I'll plead guilty to having written a novel about it. But *I am innocent. I didn't do it. They got the wrong person and they need to keep looking for the right person.*"

Kerry suddenly got the feeling that she might be working on this case for a very, very long time if they kept her all the way through the death penalty appeals. No, she would retire before that. Of course, if they wrote a book together—after the sentence, of course—where Aletta told her version and Kerry described the complexity of Aletta's character, she could possibly retire even sooner. The title "*Round Up Murder*" popped into her mind.

Aletta broke the silence. "I'd like you to call the other woman I work for, Pam

364

Anderson, and tell her I need her to work on finding someone who will remember seeing me that evening. Let me write her number on your pad. She will know what to do."

{Chapter 102}

Good vs. Evil

The reservation was covered with bad roads. Carl had driven most of them, but this one, he considered to be the worst. It was so bad that he normally left the parcels for this address at the Pueblo Pintado post office, but today he was on a special mission. He would have had to invent the necessity for this delivery if an actual package from Amazon hadn't fortuitously been in today's parcels. In his estimation, the package from Amazon was a sign that the mission was going to be successful.

His UPS truck lurched across a rut then plowed through a pile of wind-drifted sand. The road wound up a sloping mesa out of the grass covered valley and into the piñyons of the mesa top. Carl had saved this as his last delivery of the day, so the shadows cast by the piñyons were starting to lengthen toward the east. The contrast between the still bright sun and the sprawling shadows made it difficult to see the ruts. The rabbit brush along the road was waving in the wind.

His destination was an isolated hogan at the very edge of the windy escarpment. Although isolated hogans were common on the reservation, Kenneth Joe Dinetsosie's hogan was truly unique. It was built of stone with the care and workmanship of the Chacoans, who had been master stone masons in this very area seven-hundred years ago. An old Volkswagen bug was parked next to a small open shed in which some bales of hay were stacked. The tracks made it seem like the Volkswagen was the primary means of transport. Perhaps Mr. Dinetsosie was home?

Carl picked up the parcel from Amazon and pulled an envelope from the glove box. He stuck the envelope in his signature tablet and climbed down from the truck. The path circled clockwise around the north side of the hogan which had no windows to the west or south. Kenny Joe was sitting outdoors in a rocking chair which was placed between a large east-facing plate-glass window and the edge of the escarpment several yards away. A yellow mongrel dog was sitting at his feet. The dog stood up and walked to Carl with its tail wagging. Carl bent down to acknowledge the dog with a friendly pat. Then he looked at Kenny and, walking between the hogan and the escarpment, said in his best Navajo, *"Yá'át'ééh, shik'is,"* (Hello, my friend).

Kenny smiled and answered in his best Lakota, "*Háu, kolá,*" then he switched into Navajo. "*Áá' ha'íí baa naniná?*" (What are you doing?)

Carl stretched his resources to muster a reply, "*'Áh nísts'íid*" (Very well, thank you). Then, feeling like he had just learned some new vocabulary, he asked "*Áá' ha'íí baa naniná?*" (What are you doing?)

Kenny laughed and replied in English. "Carl, I asked you *what* you were doing. Me, I'm sitting here, looking out over the landscape and thinking about learning to fly. I assume you are delivering packages to me, or maybe you are on a different mission."

Carl lifted the package from Amazon and held it out toward the Navajo, who furled his eyebrows and said, "Wait ... I thought I had two packages."

Carl felt his heart rate suddenly rise. "No, there was only one on today's shipment. I am sure. Is the other one coming from Amazon too? Most of your parcels come from Amazon that is the only reason I would guess that. I could check the truck, but I am sure there was only one."

Kenny Joe laughed. "Yes, I do spend a lot on books. Would you like to see my library?"

Carl suddenly realized that the hogan must be stuffed with books. "Yes, that would be great."

Kenny Joe stood up and stepped to open the bright yellow eastward facing door. He held the door for Carl to enter saying, "Welcome to my home."

Carl was surprised to find no books at all. Instead, he found himself in a strictly utilitarian room with a little wood cooking stove in the center and a number of rolled sheep pelts tucked against the wall. A tiny table near the woodstove held a few dishes and plates. Overhead, a magnificent ceiling was built out of peeled poles stacked like they were a woven basket, with each progressive layer on top of the last and reaching closer to the center, where a small aperture was left for the stove chimney. Kenny Joe directed him to walk to the left with a gesture and Carl saw that there was a ladder poking up from a hole in the floor. "My library is downstairs," said Kenny Joe. "Use the ladder. You can go first if you want."

Carl descended into a room that was larger than the one above it. It was lit by a huge glass door that opened to a ledge in the escarpment that had not been visible from the ground floor. The glass door was open with a simple screen door letting the breeze in from the east. The walls were lined with books. While Kenny Joe climbed down the ladder, Carl walked around clockwise and looked at titles. Almost all the books had to do with philosophy, religion, magic and mythology. He realized that Kenny Joe was perhaps not a simple skinwalker at all.

"Have you read all of these?"

Kenny Joe laughed and started opening the package from Amazon. He pulled out his latest acquisition, *A Metaphysics for Freedom* by Helen Steward. He dropped it onto the coffee table and sat down on the couch. He indicated a comfortable looking chair and said, "Sit down, Carl, and let's talk about what you really came here about."

Carl sat down and found his voice. "Aletta needs you to testify that you ate dinner at the Roadhouse on the night of the murder. She needs to have an alibi."

Kenny Joe looked sideways at Carl. "You'd like me to tell them more. You'll get them to ask what I know about the murder."

"Well, what *do* you know about the murder?" Carl tersely asked.

"The man who killed Aaron Shauner is dead. He killed himself. I watched him do it, but you know why I can never testify about that," replied the Navajo shapeshifter.

"How do you know things are going to happen?" asked Carl. "How did you know to be there?"

"Little Wind whispers into the folds of my ears. It whispers into your ears as well, but you don't know how to hear it," replied Kenny Joe. "It told me you were coming, but it told me you had two packages, so it's not always right, I suppose."

Carl realized he might never again have the opportunity to talk to a high priest of the Navajo religion again, so he played his best card, "Can I ask you some things about shape-shifting?"

"Shoot."

"Did you have to have intercourse with a cadaver to learn how to change form?" asked the Lakota *wicasa wakan* earnestly.

The Navajo skinwalker responded with a howl of laughter. Carl felt a little embarrassed to have asked. Kenny Joe wiped the tears from his eyes with the sleeve of his flannel shirt. "Carl, do you believe everything you read?"

"No, but I do want to know," Carl persisted.

"No, sex with a cadaver is not required to become a shape-shifter. It's more of something like an accessory ritual to make sure you'll be embarrassed and disempowered the rest of your life. I didn't choose that option. Call me old fashioned, but I like live partners.

"It is nothing at all like that. To become a shape-shifter you have to have animal skins that still have the life of the animal in them. Normally what you do is run down the animal on foot and smother it with sacred corn pollen, but if you are willing to embody an aged animal spirit, you can simply take hide or tail of an animal that dies of old age. I have mostly mammals in my repertoire. Then if you are bold enough to step out of your own skin and you know the magic words, presto chango!"

"Does it only work with mammals?" asked Carl.

"Someday, I will know how to do birds," replied Kenny Joe. "It's one of my long-range goals. I have mastered snakes, but I don't like the whole slithering thing."

"Are some skinwalkers evil and some good?" asked the Lakota UPS driver.

The Navajo philosopher howled with laughter again. This time, Carl thought it sounded like a coyote howling. Carl would have preferred a straightforward answer so, as soon as he could, he said, "Please don't make fun of me. I ask because I am trying to learn."

"I am not laughing at you, Carl," replied the shaman, "I am laughing at one of the world's oldest questions—what is good and what is evil. I think that thirty-six percent of the books in this library are about that very question. But ... let me answer your question. Because they are people, shape-shifters can be good and they can be evil, but the best ones—the ones you want to share your world with—are a little bit of both."

"Don't we have a moral obligation to not be evil?"

Kenny Joe smiled and looked at the ceiling and spoke with a Chinese accent. "Those who say that they would have right without its correlate, wrong, do not apprehend the great principles of the universe, nor the nature of all creation. One might as well talk of the existence of Heaven without that of Earth, or of the negative principle without the positive, which is clearly impossible. Yet people keep on discussing it without end; such people must be either fools or knaves." He dropped the accent and continued, "Zhuang-Zhou said that in three-hundred BC and here we are discussing it two-thousand three-hundred years later ... Actually, I think we have just as much moral obligation to not be *too* good. Our obligation is to be authentic. We can only be authentic if we are neither too evil nor too good."

The Navajo continued, "Actually, evil and good are not the most accurate words we could use. They are ambiguous constructs that are hard to apply. Are we really discussing selfish versus social? Creative versus destructive? Assertive versus passive?"

Carl said, "Right versus wrong has problems too, doesn't it?"

"Same problem ... We Navajos have *hózhó* and *hóchxó*, which are more like good and evil, than, say, something like *yin* and *yang*, but the duality is always there and no one has ever figured out how to have one without the other," replied Kenny Joe. He continued, "Actually I believe that things *do* get out of balance and people suffer—that should be avoided. One way it gets out of balance is when we suppress our natural assertiveness. We don't use it in appropriate ways and it becomes our shadow, either as resentfully repressed negative energy or projected onto someone else. We often find a scapegoat to carry our own "evil" for us and then pretend it has nothing to do with us. It's our own desperation to think of ourselves as "good" that creates the drama of victims and monsters."

"Wow," said the UPS driver, "I'm gonna have to think about that for a while."

"Yeah ..." sighed Kenny Joe. "Hey, you wanna see some shape-shifting? I'm trying to work out how to talk like a human while being an animal."

Carl sat up straighter and his eyes grew bigger, "Oh yes, I would love to see some shape-shifting!"

Suddenly, the Navajo he had been talking to became a large rat sitting on the couch. He jumped between the three cushions on the couch, then raised his paws and started talking, "Carl, how does it feel to talk to a rat?"

Carl laughed and replied, "It sounds like I am talking to an Italian rat."

The rat replied, "Well, I wanted to model this rat after Topo Gigio. People already have a very favorable impression of him. It will make them less fearful if the rat that talks with them reminds them of a friendly character they know." Kenny Joe shifted back to human form.

"I think it works well. It certainly brought out warm fuzzy associations for me," said Carl. "But what I came here for is to ask you to testify. I know you won't respond to a subpoena and no one is ever going to find you that you don't let find you. Will you please show up at court? Have some compassion for the poor woman. She is a good person."

"Oh, dear, Carl! We are back to the "good" thing again. I'm sorry, but I can't buy into this whole courtroom drama thing. I just don't see myself as the white knight who rides up to rescue the damsel in distress. It's no fun to be in a courtroom. I get nothing out of it."

"Kenny Joe, please! I'm asking you to help us."

"I guess that now is when I get to be a little bit evil," said Kenny Joe. "Nope. I don't want to do it. I don't totally trust you. You're holding something back but I don't know why."

Carl stood up and opened his signature tablet. "You are right, there were two packages." Carl handed the white envelope to Kenny Joe.

Kenny Joe carefully snatched it from Carl's hand and held it up alongside his face grinning. Then he pushed his finger between the flap and the bottom to break the seal. He pulled out a photocopy of a page from Pam Anderson's field book where she had been sketching the bird cult panel. It showed ten birds. All the labels had been cut away from the illustration. Kenny Joe stared at it. Carl felt the possibility that the shape-shifter would change his mind.

"Kenny Joe, I'm going to go now. I can find my way out, but I really hope to see you in the courtroom. It's on this Thursday, the nineteenth, at nine o'clock. That's three days from now. It's at the U.S. courthouse in Santa Fe."

Kenny raised his hand in a vague wave and continued to stare at the photocopy.

It was dark outside and walking between the house and the cliff edge in the darkness made Carl tense. He was relieved to round the hogan and see the dark shadow of his truck. Out in the backyard, three horses nickered as he came around, but then spooked into the trees when they realized it was a stranger. He started his engine and backed up to turn around using his running lights. When he looked in the mirror, he saw Kenny Joe hurrying around the building. Carl hesitated in case Kenny Joe was trying to catch him, but then he realized the man was heading to get hay for the horses.

Even though Kenneth Joe Dinetsosie had made no commitments, Carl was convinced the man would be there. The dirt road back to the pavement seemed as if it had magically gotten better. Life was good.

{Chapter 103}

Just the Facts

"Hear Ye, Hear Ye, the District Court of Santa Fe, the most Honorable Judge Denise Glore presiding, is now in session!"

The door behind the bench opened, and a blonde woman robed in black stepped forth and took her seat at the bench. She looked at the papers on her desk, then leveled her withering gaze to make eye contact serially with the defendant, the prosecutor, and then the bailiff. Everyone looked humbled by the woman.

"This is the case of United States versus Aletta Ramsden. Council, make your appearances."

One of the men at the counsel table on the left smiled as he rose to his feet. "Good morning, Your Honor, James Henson for the United States. I am an associate deputy Attorney General. This is my assistant, Bill French," he said indicating the man sitting at his left side.

The diminutive woman in the forest-green business dress at the counsel table with Aletta stood up and said, "Kerry J. Lincoln representing the defendant, Aletta Ramsden, Your Honor. The defendant is present, in custody. May I ask the Court if the handcuffs on my client could be removed?"

"That is a decision for the U.S. Marshall's office to make."

A young man stepped forward and removed the handcuffs from Aletta who smiled at him and whispered, "Thank you."

Judge Glore looked at Aletta, "The Court's appointment of counsel is made under statutory provisions that provides that two counsel—two attorneys—shall be appointed for any person that may be charged with a death penalty offense, and those attorneys are required to have certain skills and certain experience. And I wanted the record to show that the court had erred in appointing only one attorney with little pertinent experience to this case. Since this is a preliminary hearing, and not the actual trial, some leniency in the application of rules is allowable. I would like to ask the defendant if she will waive the requirement for two attorneys for the purpose of expediting this hearing or if we should have a recess until after you have been able to meet with your new attorneys, which could not happen until tomorrow. You will have new attorneys assigned to you either way."

Aletta, stood up, blinking in surprise, and turned to look at Kerry who looked uncomfortable as if she should have known it in the first place. Then Aletta turned and looked at the spectators. Aletta recognized several people she knew including Sephra, Rita Mae, John, Carl, and Pam, who were sitting in the third row behind her.

"Basically, Ms. Ramsden, you can either go back to jail today and start again tomorrow, or you can elect to waive your rights and proceed," said the Judge. "It puts us at a disadvantage on appeal, but, frankly, we have run out of time."

Aletta felt empowered by her friends' presence. "It doesn't seem like it will change the facts, and I have full confidence in Ms. Lincoln, so I am willing to waive having two attorneys appointed for this hearing."

The Judge turned to Mr. Henson, "In light of the accommodation by the defendant, I would like to remind the prosecution that your job is to show there was means, motive, and opportunity. Please keep your evidence relevant to the defendant.

"Ms. Lincoln, are you prepared to go forward at this time," she asked, turning to defense counsel.

Kerry unconsciously clutched her jacket together in front of her sternum. "Your honor, we are ready to proceed."

Rita Mae had a small laptop computer on her lap. She started typing.

Preliminary Trial: 9:05am

Court did not appoint correct number of experienced attorneys but Aletta has waived this in favor of expedient hearing. Judge seemed to appreciate her accommodation.

Then she clicked 'publish'. Aletta might not be able to blog, but Rita Mae had her password.

***

At Navajo City, Penny kept checking the monitor on the computer for a blog update to appear while she was rolling silverware. Shortly after nine, she saw the screen change. She called back to the kitchen, "Mary, the first one is up. It says she didn't get the right attorneys but she is going ahead anyway."

The phone rang and Penny picked it up. "Navajo City Roadhouse, how may I help you? Oh ... Jane ... yes, the hearing is being blogged on Aletta's blog ... Yeah, I think if you check it every hour or so ... Yeah, come by this afternoon ... I'll be staying for it, so I will see you then."

***

Preliminary Trial: 9:10am

First witness was Dr. Anna Parsons, MD with the Office of the Medical Investigator. They are establishing the facts of the crime scene. Aaron Shauner was killed by a shotgun blast to the head at about 4:30 P.M. on 28th October, 2011. She showed some pretty graphic photographs and a diagram of the crime scene, which was on a little-used road near the Cabot Ranch. So far she hasn't revealed anything we didn't know before or anything that would link Aletta to the crime.

***

Brenda showed up early—before ten—which confused Penny who was used to being the only morning waitress. The cowbell was surprisingly busy as people stopped by to check on the status of the trial. Placido hobbled in on his cane, telling the waitresses he wanted to arrive while there was still good parking. Wanda looked around and didn't notice too many other customers and wondered what he was talking about. Milton and his dog arrived. Milton and Placido sat out on the veranda and talked about all the different dogs they had each owned over the years. Placido didn't mind talking loudly. When the next blog posting arrived, Brenda brought out a printed copy to read to them. Milton snatched it out of her hand when she finished reading to read what he hadn't been able to hear.

Preliminary Trial: 9:50am

Dr. Parson's testimony is finally over. It was a lot of tedious details. Some new information for me—there was blood and dents on the rear quarter panel of the truck that showed the shot had been fired from the northeast edge of the meadow. Aaron had been either bent over or ducking when it hit him. Also on the crime scene: the dead deer. It had been dead much longer based on body temperature and the development of flies on the carcass. She can tell how long something has been dead by the stage of hatching of the flies. Yuck!

The defense had no question for this witness. Aletta is holding up well.

***

The two elderly men were quiet for a couple of minutes after Brenda read them the newest update. Then Milton started talking about being in the army during the Korean War and seeing guys get killed. Brenda put her hand on Milton's shoulder in empathy and he looked up to smile at her. Several trucks and cars pulled into the parking lot, giving Brenda an opening to excuse herself and retreat into the cafe. The men started talking about the horrors of war.

The vehicles were a convoy of wild horse advocates. Beth Hudson, Lynne Wagner, Sally Horne, David Quinn, and Andy Milligan came in and found a large table. They ordered drinks and discussed the blogs up to that point. The irony of Aletta, the one person at the WHAC meeting who wasn't an advocate, being the one charged with terrorism was the topic of much discussion. No one believed she did it.

***

Preliminary Trial: 10:15am

The second witness called was Mitchell Loomis of the U.S. Marshall Service. He collected evidence at the crime scene. As we all knew, there were bare footprints found in the back of trailer and on the ground behind the trailer. He made dental stone casts of three of the prints. He also collected fingerprints from the handles of the truck and trailer. He said there were horse tracks coming from the trailer going north along the road as well as more horse tracks in the meadow. He said the deer had left a trail of blood from the forest across the meadow.

Defense asked three questions:

1. Were there other tracks on the scene? Answer: Shauner's, Cabots', and the barefoot tracks.

2. Vehicle tracks in the area? Ans: Checked road north and found no tracks. Did not check road going into Cabot's ranch as they had used it and it terminates at a locked gate.

3. Were any of the horse tracks from shod horses? Ans: Definitely all horses were barefoot.

***

Penny, tiring of reading the blog to each person who asked, printed the post and taped it alongside the previous updates on the wall by the door. There was a great deal of confusion about the difference between a Preliminary Hearing and an actual trial. Andy Milligan's dad was an attorney. Andy explained how it works to the other horse advocates. He said that the defense never knows what evidence the Prosecutor will present until the preliminary hearing. It seemed to all of them to be a violation of the idea that you are innocent until proven guilty. The defense has no way to be prepared for the preliminary trial. The significance of the injustice was lost when Duane Hutton, the Elvis impersonator, arrived in full costume.

{Chapter 104}

Star Witnesses for the Prosecution

Preliminary Trial: 10:35am

The third witness was Randall Tapia, the area range manager for the Bureau of Land Management. His testimony was the support for the severity of the charges against Aletta. The pertinent facts being that Aaron Shauner, a government employee, was hauling wild horses rounded up on a government operation and horses were liberated. Randall shared his calculation of the value of the horses based on the cost of the total roundup divided by the number of horses gathered. I think it's interesting the government could value the horses at $10,010 and intend to euthanize them. I suppose that would have made them even more valuable! Did starving to death make them more valuable? I'm sorry, but the valuation irritates me because it is slightly above the minimum amount required for the terrorist charge. Under $10,000, they could not charge her under that act. Coincidence?

Defense asked these questions:

1. Who made the decision for Aaron to haul the horses? Ans: Randall needed to get home as he and Danielle were supposed to go somewhere, so he assigned it to Shauner.

2. Why didn't he drive his own truck? Ans: Shauner's truck was starting to have steering problems and Tapia didn't want him to take it down the switchback above the Cabot ranch.

3. When was it decided to use that road? Ans: The Cabots came by the roundup and told Shauner the shortest route.

4. Who knew it would be used? Ans: Besides the Cabots, himself,

and Shauner, no one else as far as he knew.

Brenda carried out an order of chile cheese fries to Milton and Placido on the veranda. Shep Cabot and Fidel Candelaria were sitting with them when she got there. She had a new order for drinks and more chile cheese fries as she went back into the cafe. Penny was having a hard time doing anything with the phone constantly ringing, but she managed to carry the coffee pot back to the advocates' table, where they sat watching Duane Hutton eat a cheeseburger. Andy Milligan suggested to Penny that she could change the message on the phone to tell people the blog link address. The new message said, "You have reached Navajo City Roadhouse. For information about Aletta's trial read her blog at www.navajocityroadhouse.blogspot.com. For anything else, leave a message."

Lunch customers had just started filling the parking lot with white oil field trucks when the next blog update arrived.

***

Preliminary Trial: 11:50am

Greg Stribling of the FBI was the fourth witness.

According to phone records, Aletta is last person that Aaron ever called. He called the Roadhouse phone as he left the roundup at which time he could have told Aletta the route. Anyone with half a brain would know it is more likely that he ordered food to go.

The FBI calculated that the time required to travel between the Roadhouse and the crime scene was no less than one hour and fifteen minutes. If the killer drove from the Roadhouse they would have had to leave by 3:15 P.M. and they would not have gotten back before 5:45 P.M. Sunset on October 28 was at 6:18 P.M.

Back in the kitchen, the two cooks realized the morning had seriously depleted their French fry stock. They debated who would make the run to town and who would get left behind to what promised to be total chaos. They decided, instead, to send Milton to town to pick up more French fries. Brenda said a prayer that he would drive safely and not break down on the way. The dining room filled, the patio and all of its benches filled. Penny had never, in all her years, seen such a crowd.

***

Preliminary Trial: Summary So Far

Noon recess. Aletta looked calm as she was led from the court-room. Kerry has been on the phone since then. We brought her a bean burrito when we came back from lunch. She said an impor-tant witness was on her way from Farmington, but so far there has been no evidence implicating Aletta.

At the Roadhouse, so many customers bought lunches for other customers that Penny totally lost track of which tickets were whose and which had been paid. None of the customers left to return to work; everyone was speculating what the evidence against Aletta might be. People were emotional about this. Being emotional called for more iced tea! Brenda was bringing the fourth bag of ice in the door when the next blog appeared.

Preliminary Trial: 1:15pm

The fifth witness called was Rex Roundy. He testified he had seen Aletta and Aaron earlier in the day and Aletta was crying. He stopped at the Roadhouse at about 11:45 A.M. Aaron was walking out the door and Aletta was crying at the counter.

He also noted that the Roadhouse was closed early on the day of the murder. He drove by at 6:50 P.M. and the lights were out. He called the owner to report it at the time.

Defense asked three questions:

1. How do you know it was closed? Ans: Parking lot was empty and open sign wasn't on.

2. What time did you drive by? Ans: It was around seven-thirty.

3. Is the parking lot normally empty at that time? Ans: Occasion-

ally there is a car, but normally it is empty.

4. Was the interior dark, were the lights out? Ans: The lights might have been on, he couldn't really see.

One of the Conoco-Philips men shouted, "I never did like that asshole." Everyone shouted in agreement. Tim Tucker started talking about how Rex got his cousin fired by calling up and complaining about his personal hygiene. "My cousins' a water-hauler not a surgeon, damn it. Rex is always trying to get people in trouble."

Penny and Brenda realized they were in over their heads and settled down to just keeping everyone's drinks refilled and picking up the plates as customers finished.

***

Preliminary Trial: 1:25pm

Willy LeDoux was the sixth witness. He was brought after lunch in by the San Juan County sheriff's department and sat in a chair between two guards. We did not recognize him without his cowboy hat. He was wearing an orange prison uniform and handcuffs. He testified that he saw Aletta driving toward the crime scene in late afternoon. He was repairing fences on the Cabot Ranch. On a map provided by the prosecution, Willy was able to show the court where he said he was when he saw her. He said that he recognized her white Jeep by the "save the mustangs" bumper sticker on it.

Defense asked him a few questions about his credibility:

1. What are you in jail for? How many times have you been arrested? Convicted? Willy said he was charged with interstate transportation of stolen goods this time and that he had been arrested for tractor theft twice before, but he always saved the American taxpayer by accepting the plea bargain.

2. Did the prosecutors offer you any special concessions if you testify today? Ans: They said they might remember him being cooperative when it comes time for sentencing. He is hoping to be

able to plead to simply unauthorized use of a tractor.

Shep Cabot held up his hat and asked the crowd, "What is it with that guy and tractors? He was trying to load mine on his horse trailer when I caught him." Cody called out, "Raise your hand if you believe Willy LeDoux!" The crowd got silent as people looked around, but no one raised a hand. Cody went on, "That makes him a piss poor liar! Shame on the Judge if she believes him." The tables of customers fell back into individual discussions, most of which centered on how the prosecution can arrange too many favorable deals for people awaiting trial. The customers were looking sullen about evidence against Aletta when the next blog post arrived.

***

Preliminary Trial: 1:45pm

Sam Elkins was called to testify as the seventh witness. On March 31, he found a receipt on the crime scene. The cardholder printed on the receipt was *Aletta Ramsden*. It was for fuel purchased on 28 October, 2011 at 11:50 A.M. The receipt was in a woodpecker hole. He was surveying the winterkill of deer and horses when he went to the crime scene and found it.

Defense asked Sam two questions:

1. How many months were between the time when the receipt was found and the day of the crime? Five months and two days. He admitted that there was no way to know when it got there.

2. Does he know how the receipt got there? It was rolled up in the woodpecker hole, so an animal might have pulled it in, or someone rolled it up.

***

Few people in the crowd knew about the receipt. Art Jacquez pulled out a Roadhouse fuel receipt and held it up, shouting, "Hey, there's no *cardholder name* on this receipt!" The crowd angrily turned to Penny for an explanation. "After they passed that new privacy law, we had to take the names off, but it's up to the store to set what prints on the receipt."

Brenda looked suddenly frightened as her husband, the tall long-haired gray-bearded JL Hartman, walked through the door with his 'Liberty or Death" tee-shirt proudly on display. "Hello, honey," she said meekly. "Would you like some lunch?"

"I saw where the god-damned son-of-a-bitch lied about seeing Aletta on the forest. I loaded my truck with enough ammo and weapons to bust her out of that place, but then I realized it was in Santa Fe. That's a long drive." He looked around at the crowd, "Does anyone want to go with me?" "Hell, yeah!" the crowd roared but no one got up. Andy Milligan called out to JL, "Wait and see what happens. It will be easier to bust her out of the Rio Arriba County Jail." Everyone laughed and Brenda, proud of his honorable underlying intentions, gave JL a hug.

The Alternative Plan is Jailbreak

JL was eating a French-dip sandwich with curly fries when the next post appeared. He started screaming, "Damn lesbian bitches!" after Penny read out the first sentence, but Duane Hutton moved to sit next to JL and help him maintain a more positive perspective by having Elvis talk to him. Penny started reading from the beginning again.

***

Preliminary Trial: 2:55pm

The eighth witness was Sandy Poole. She testified that Aaron Shauner was a frequent customer at the Roadhouse. She said he was almost always there when she drove by, she assumed he and Aletta were having an affair.

Defense objected to conjecture. Judge Glore overruled because it is a preliminary trial with less strict rules.

Defense tried asking questions to show Sandy is a prejudiced witness:

1. Is it true that you are not allowed in the Roadhouse? Prosecution objected to this as irrelevant. Judge sustained the objection.

2. Why did Aletta ban you from coming into the Roadhouse? SANDY: "For telling her not to tell people anything about me. I have a right to privacy."

3. Did you threaten Aletta to retaliate against her? Sandy admitted she did threaten her, but claimed she didn't really mean it.

Tim Tucker shouted, "Aletta shouldn't have eighty-sixed her." Penny said, "I would have just given Sandy time to get over it." Brenda said, "Sandy had no right to threaten anyone." Immediately the unity of crowd disintegrated into two camps divided by the alcoholic beverage consumption habits of each person. The drinkers sympathized with Sandy. The non-drinkers maintained no one should walk into a place and make demands. Milton said, "How was Aletta supposed to know it was a secret?" JL, who was a neighbor of Sandy's, called her *a little scum sucking rat*. Tim looked like he might get up and start a fight with JL, then six nuns from the Virgin of the Canyons monastery walked in the door.

"Can we get some French fries?" asked the tallest nun. Five Hispanic men sitting at a nearby table jumped up to offer the sisters their seats. While they were waiting for their fries, the next blog post appeared. Penny climbed up on the step ladder to read it aloud.

***

Preliminary Trial: 3:05pm

Sephra Brooks was the 9th witness. Tears were flowing down her face the whole time she was on the stand. The prosecutor got her to testify that Aletta normally goes barefooted when she is at home. Instead of answering his questions, she got angry and screamed out, "She didn't do it!" The Judge had a bit of an emotional outburst as well and threatened to have Sephra locked up.

The defense asked Sephra several questions about people, herself included, going barefoot. She made it a little bit funny so everyone thought about how often they take their shoes off and it broke the tension. Aletta was wiping tears away when Sephra was dismissed.

***

Outside of the Roadhouse, a reporter from the Farmington Daily Times parked on the shoulder of Highway 64 behind a line of other trucks. He took a photo of the amazingly crowded parking lot before he walked into the cafe. Inside, he caught the eye of Penny and told her the reason for his visit. She shouted out to the crowd, "Listen everyone, they sent this guy from the newspaper to find out why so many people are calling in sick from the Roadhouse! Did you all call in sick?" The crowd roared. The County Health Inspector peeked through the doorway before he stepped in and, seeing no signs of anyone feeling less than good, decided to "not notice" they were way over capacity. He made his way to the other side of the counter where he stood with Mary, the cook. She was nervous; they were running out of French fries again.

***

Preliminary Trial: 3:20pm

The tenth and final witness called by the prosecution was William Bodziak, a footprint expert witness. He gave an interesting presentation on procedures for analyzing footprint evidence. Bare feet prints are interesting to him because they can't be changed. He was rather poetic and mesmerizing, for example he showed a slide with these words: *"Wherever he steps, whatever he touches, whatever he leaves, even unconsciously, will serve as silent witness against him. Not only his fingerprints or his footprints, but his hair, the fibers from his clothing, the glass he breaks, the tool mark he leaves, the paint he scratches, the blood or semen he deposits or collects ... All of these and more, bear mute witness against him."* I think he was quoting someone there. Fascinating witness really, although they showed side by side comparison of Aletta's prints and the ones collected at the crime, the crime scene prints looked bigger. The shape was the same, high arches and wide balls of the feet relative to the width of the heels. The detail that might have shown whorls was lost due to the wetness of the horse manure. He said the shape was common in areas with high percentages of Native Americans, such as Oklahoma. He said the footprint evidence was insufficient to exclude the possibility

386

of it being Aletta's print.

Kerry got up and got him to admit the prints didn't exactly match, but then he had to insist that they didn't exonerate her either.

The prosecution has rested and we are in a short recess until 3:30. There is a handsome Native American man sitting with Carl who I think will be called, but she is calling John Irick first.

***

Brenda, overcome by the day's tension, put her head on JL's shoulder and started sobbing. He patted her back and kissed her on the ear. The lack of French fries was a crisis as far as Penny was concerned. People who noticed the scowl on her face assumed the evidence was going against Aletta. The line for the bathroom started growing and Mary went out to the storage shed to get more paper for the toilets. She was carrying it through the back door when the next blog entry appeared. Penny waited for Mary before she began reading.

***

Preliminary Trial: 3:45pm

Defense called John Irick and asked him about the business flow on the day of the murder. Did the business close early? He said that the last transaction on the cash register was about 8 P.M. and that business was above normal because of the take-out orders for the round-up. He saw no reason to suspect that anything at the restaurant was amiss, except for Rex Roundy had called him to tell him that Aletta had forgotten to turn the 'open' sign on.

The prosecutor got up and started asking questions about Guido including whether or not he was an anarchist. Then he asked if he could tell from the cash register report if Aletta, and not Guido, had entered the transaction. He asked if John could be certain that Aletta was there until eight. John had to admit it was possible that only Guido might have been there.

"Guido is never anywhere when you need him," said Penny, recalling the day when he bailed on her. Don Schrieber called out from the corner, "Defense needs to pull a rabbit out of the hat!" Mary had found a forty-pound bag of popping corn in the shed and she called the waitress to start passing around bags of still hot popcorn. A group of drummers from the Apache Tribe arrived carrying big Native American drums. They set up the drums outside the side door to the patio. The next blog arrived as they settled into a circle around the drums. Penny read to the silent waiting crowd.

**

Preliminary Trial: 3:55pm

Defense called Kenneth Joe Dinetsosie, a Navajo man. He had stopped in for a late dinner. His was the transaction at eight. He said the open sign was not on, so he was afraid to enter at first. He said the cook was already gone, but Aletta was there and cooked him a good meal. He said she seemed to be very tired and had fallen asleep in the chair behind the cash register.

The prosecutor started asking him questions about where he had been and what he was doing, but the man got indignant about the invasion of privacy. He said white people ask too many questions about irrelevant stuff. The judge agreed it was irrelevant.

**

The Apache drummers broke into a lively rhythm which at first drowned out all other possibility of conversation, but after a moment they quieted down to just provide a steady watchful beat. At some tables, people discussed when she could have gotten back to the Roadhouse if she had killed him. At other tables, the discussion centered around why no one remembered coming into the Roadhouse that afternoon. The general consensus was remembering something you do everyday five months later was unlikely but all agreed if Aletta had not been there they would have remembered it for sure.

Just before the next blog entry arrived, Duane and the Apache drummers started trying to work out a way to add an Indian beat to an Elvis song. Boom boom. I'll have a blue Christmas without you. Boom Boom.

***

Preliminary Trial: 4:00pm

We are having a short recess. Apparently there is another witness on their way. OMG! Jessica Anderson just *ran* into the courtroom—Pam's cousin that works for the BLM.

***

This time the Apaches took over rhythm totally and it was up to Duane to sing in time.

Love-me-tender, Hey-O

Love-me-true, Hey-O

Never-let-me-go, No,No

You-have-made-my-life-complete. Hey-O

And-I-love-you-so. Hey-O, girl, Hey-O

Everyone clapped their hands or tapped their feet keeping time. When the next blog appeared, Penny climbed up the step ladder and waved the printout to get the crowd's attention.

Preliminary Trial: 4:05pm

Defense called Jessica Anderson, who had just driven down from Farmington. The first she heard about Aletta's indictment was when Pam told her that she was going to Aletta's trial. Jessica remembered that she had stopped at the Roadhouse on the way back from the roundup to use the bathroom. Aletta was there re-filling salt and pepper shakers. Jessica said she distinctly remembered it because the pepper made her sneeze and she knew from the sneeze she could never be a waitress. The prosecutor looks very upset.

***

Elvis and the Apache drummers repeated *Love Me Tender*, then people started calling out suggestions for other Elvis songs. *Heart Break Hotel* flopped, but they managed half of *You Ain't Nothing but a Hound Dog* before the next blog arrived. Penny started screaming "Yes! Yes!" as she pushed the print button. Everyone silently stared as the chubby waitress breathlessly read from the paper.

***

Preliminary Trial: 4:10pm

The prosecution has withdrawn its case!!! Aletta is FREE!!! Everyone is exhausted, but we are coming home.

***

The crowd jumped up roaring, cheering, screaming, and shouting. People were jumping for joy. The nuns were clapping and turning in circles to smile at everyone. Penny was standing on the ladder screaming, "Yes! Yes! Yes!" Brenda and JL started dancing a jig. The health inspector started sobbing into a bar towel. The Apaches pounded the drums and the horse advocates pounded the table. The reporter's camera flashed as he caught the joyous celebration for the paper.

Penny felt her personal cell phone vibrate in her pocket. She pulled it out and looked at the screen. John Irick was trying to call. She answered, shouting over the din. People started quieting as they noticed the concerned look on Penny's face. Soon everyone was standing quietly trying to hear. She took the phone down from her ear and said, "It's John Irick. He's going to put Aletta on the phone." She pressed the speaker button on the phone and held it up over her head, then Aletta's voice said, "Hey, I love you guys!"

"We love you, too!" the people shouted. Many people were reaching for napkins to dry their eyes.

This was a day that would live forever in the history of Navajo City, thought Penny as she watched the happy customers filing out. Milton had started sweeping.

Brenda was washing down the tables. JL was washing silverware. Penny, herself, had been taking care of any customers trying to pay for their food; although, it had degenerated to an honor system by the end. Now she turned to help with the cleanup. Better get some silverware rolled for the morning, and the hard water spots should be rubbed off the glassware before it's put away. She sighed as she picked up the bar towel.

{Chapter 106}

Farmington Daily Times

Murder and Terrorism Charges Withdrawn

FARMINGTON, N.M. (AP) – Prosecutors dropped all charges against the Navajo City waitress, Aletta Ramsden, after an abbreviated trial in U.S. District Court. The waitress had been accused of killing a government employee and involvement in animal liberation activities relating to the murder of Aaron Shauner on October 28, 2011.

Hundreds of supporters gathered at the Roadhouse Cafe to follow the trial which was being blogged from the courtroom. Emotions ran high during the day-long trial. The crowd was a mixture of oil-field customers, Catholic nuns, animal welfare advocates, Jicarilla Apaches and even an Elvis impersonator.

When the blog announcing the charges being dropped was read to the crowd, there was a collective whoop as the crowd erupted in joy. The whole of Navajo City was a riot of shouts, tears, and drumbeats.

Ms. Ramsden was reached by phone and told her Navajo City supporters "I love you so much!" They responded with a resounding "We love you too!"

Brenda Hartman, one of the waitress that organized the event, said, "I prayed for this day, and at times, I worried about the outcome, but I *never* thought she was guilty."

Ms. Ramsden is planning to return to her weekend job at the Roadhouse and will start a study of psychology at San Juan College this fall.

{Chapter 107}

On a Raven's Feather

The eastern horizon was a whitish band under an indigo sky. The sun wouldn't be above the horizon for another hour, but Mr. Dinetsosie insisted on meeting before dawn. Pam and Aletta sat in the truck, waiting in the Roadhouse parking lot, steaming cups of coffee in hand. A Volkswagen with off-road oversized headlights roared over the hill and raced into the parking lot. A lithe man jumped out and hurried toward them. He wore a buckskin shirt with a beaded yoke. A necklace of claws and talons hung around his neck and several animal skins hung from his belt. As he got closer, they could see that his face was painted. The women were terrified.

When Pam asked Aletta if she would accompany her, she had tried to make sure Aletta didn't feel obligated, even though the whole reason was, in fact, the deal she made with Dinetsosie for showing up at the trial. Instead, Pam explained to Aletta that it was an extremely unique opportunity to interview an informant about the anthropological implications of the bird cult cave as well as gain some assessment of shamanism. She had then admitted to Aletta that she was also afraid to meet the man alone. Neither of them had any prior experience with skinwalkers, so they did not know what to expect and *now* he was at the door.

Aletta seized the opportunity to give her seat to the shaman and get into the bed of the truck, claiming that it was easier than crawling in the jumpseat. Pam felt abandoned to her fate. Kenny Joe smiled at the archaeologist and slid into the passenger seat. She wasn't sure she could get her mouth to talk, but she managed to mumble, "It's not far."

"Carl told me you are an archaeologist. I live near Pueblo Pintado, you know where that is? I've met lots of archaeologists from Chaco over the years. You ever been to Pintado?"

She shook her head no and felt like she just fell in his estimation. He looked out the window into the dark landscape. He turned back to her with another topic she might show more interest in, "Carl said you know that I was there when Aaron got killed. Do you want to know who did it?" he asked, grinning.

A rabbit jumped from the sagebrush and ran to the middle of the road, then abruptly stopped to stare at her headlights. She slammed on the brakes. Aletta slid forward from where she was sitting and slammed into the rear of the cab. Pam got out to make sure Aletta was okay, then she insisted that her friend ride in the front.

Pam looked at the shape-shifter again and found her voice. "Aletta, do you want to know who killed Aaron Shauner?"

"Didn't Carl say the murderer was dead?" asked Aletta.

Kenny Joe eagerly offered, "Yeah, he's dead alright. I watched him commit suicide," but neither of the women felt comfortable enough yet to talk to him directly.

Aletta broke the ice, "Well, one thing to note; it wasn't me. I am still alive and living free. If the killer was alive, I would surely want to know who it was. Have I grown to cherish the mystery? No. Okay, who was it?"

Kenny replied, "I'll give you a hint .... *sniffff.*"

"Oh my god! It *was* that guy. I always wondered if it could have been him," Aletta cried.

Pam, overcome by curiosity, dropped her defenses. "Who are you talking about?"

Aletta replied, "This creepy dude that bought gas at the Roadhouse that day. I was filling my Jeep when he pulled up .... oh my god ... that's how the receipt got there. He picked it out of the trash." Aletta got quiet for a minute. "You saved those horses, didn't you?"

"Not the ones in the truck with me, they died in the winter," he said.

"No, didn't you adopt some of them? I meant those older mares," Aletta said.

"Yes, they live at Pueblo Pintado with me. Their age was a disadvantage for them in the adoption system and frankly, I love them."

The three rode along in the growing light of dawn. Pam broke the silence, "This is where we go off-road," she said turning along the rimrock. Still quiet, she parked on location and the three got out of the truck. Pam and Aletta grabbed the ladder out of the truck. Pam scooted her body under the truck to tie off the ropes, while

Aletta looped the free ends of the two ropes through the highest rung of the ladder. She handed the ends of both ropes to Kenny Joe. Then the women picked up the ends of the ladder and took it to the cliff edge. Aletta came back to Kenny for one of the rope ends, while Pam continued to push the ladder over the cliff.

The waitress and skinwalker controlled the descent of the ladder while the archaeologist made sure it landed in the right place. Then Pam took the rope end from Kenny Joe and tied it securely to the top of the ladder. Aletta tied her own end of the rope and Pam inspected the knots. Pam immediately crawled onto the ladder and started her descent to the cave. "Follow me," she said looking at Kenny Joe. "Grab the headlamps," she said to Aletta.

The agile man climbed down eagerly behind her. Aletta hung the headlamps over her arm and followed. Pam and Kenny Joe were silently looking at the wall and the body, when she caught up to them. A glint of sunlight sparked over the eastern horizon, reminding Aletta it would be another hot day. The shaman asked the women to stand to the side of the ledge to keep their shadows on the side of the cave. He watched intently as the rising sunlight illuminated the cave. It lighted the cave walls and even penetrated the tunnel. "That's it! You two wait here," he said scampering into the tunnel. The women watched him disappear up the shaft. There was nothing for the women to do but watch the shadows, cast by the rising sun, move. After fifteen minutes, the light no longer penetrated the tunnel.

"Do you think he needs a flashlight?" whispered Aletta.

Pam responded in hushed tones, "No, he will probably take the shape of a nocturnal animal if he needs to see. Do you hear him chanting?"

Aletta strained her ears and turned her head. "Yes, he's singing in there."

Pam whispered, "We don't want to make any shadows on the floor of the cave, but if we slip along the wall, we could sit where we could listen."

"Pam, if you don't mind, I'd like to go back to the truck and work on my novel. If you are worried about him, I will stay instead."

"No, it's okay," whispered the archaeologist as she turned to hold the ladder for Aletta.

Pam was glad to be left alone with her thoughts as she lowered herself to sit beside the tunnel. His song was rhythmic and he had a strong tenor voice. It reminded her of Luciano Pavarotti somehow, some kind of yearning quality in the way the chant was sung. She loved Pavarotti. What would Kenny Joe be yearning for? She had really expected a skinwalker to be indifferent to his social environment but this man seemed to be unexpectedly friendly. Suddenly she realized how unfriendly she had probably seemed. Not that one could expect to be chatty with a skinwalker, but the man *had* tried to make conversation. She suddenly felt her body tighten and her eyes slam shut in a pang of regret. She was surprised by the gasping sound that came from her mouth.

I'm not being a good scientist nor am I being a good role model for Aletta! What's wrong with me? I can't let myself just melt down in a pool of emotion or I will miss this opportunity. It's now or never. I need to keep reminding myself.

She listened to the chant drone on. Suddenly it wasn't Pavarotti, but instead Elvis singing "It's now or never." She shook her head and leaned to put an ear to the tunnel—no, it was a Navajo song that she recognized and translated in her mind:

> *I am nayéé' neezghání.*
> *Where I walk is dangerous*
> *Long life being the one that causes fear I walk*
> *Where I walk is dangerous.*

It's the Bear's song, she realized. It's sung to separate the male and female energies of the singer in order to diminish any female compassion in preparation for battle. The purpose of this song, anthropologists speculated was to disassociate the integrity of the personality, set aside social conscience, and allow the singer to become a ruthless warrior. She knew there was a second ceremony required to reintegrate the warrior into the community, but that wasn't the song that he was singing.

"Who or what was going to emerge from the cave?" she wondered. She felt the fear creeping back into her mind, but she didn't have to wait long for an answer.

A dusty moccasin touched the floor of the tunnel, and Kenny Joe dropped down to crawl out. Pam jumped up from her sitting position and wondered for a split second if she should bash his head in with a rock as he emerged from the tunnel. *Now or never?* She had to admit that she couldn't do it. She consoled herself with the thought that dying by the hands of a skinwalker was at least an interesting death.

His eyes were gleaming as he stood up. "Feathers?" he asked. Before she could answer, his head turned to look at the double-spouted vessel and his hand reached up to pull it off the shelf. He pulled out one stopper and shook the feathers out much like a smoker shakes a pack of cigarettes. He ruffled through them, then shook them back in, stoppered it, and opened the other side. This time he selected a large black feather with a white quill.

"The thing is, that guy," pointing to the body, "was an Anasazi coward—*I'm not* ... Give me an hour." Saying this, the shaman, set the vessel on the floor, turned on his heel, sprinted to the edge, and dove head first off the cliff. Pam watched him disappear over the edge in horror.

She was afraid that she might faint if she looked over the edge and saw his carnage, so she climbed the ladder, trying to hold back her tears for safety's sake. She couldn't believe that he just suddenly committed suicide and there no way to stop him. As her head poked over the rim, she started sobbing. Aletta saw her friend was in trouble and rushed to help the archaeologist onto the top.

"He jumped!" sobbed the archaeologist. "I didn't have a chance to stop him."

Aletta leaned out over the edge to look. "Did he turn into a bird?"

That possibility hadn't occurred to the scientist. She wiped her eyes and leaned over the edge. Nothing suggested pain, suffering, or violence in what was visible. "We'll have to go back down to look over the edge where the body would have landed. Let's go together," she said, already with one foot on the ladder.

As soon as Aletta had both feet on the ledge, Pam directed her. "Hold my hand to pull me back in case I faint—I will look first." To Aletta, who had never been particularly squeamish about blood, this seemed like overkill, but she did not want her boss to faint so she held her hand tightly.

"Nothing!" Pam stepped back from the ledge and shook free of Aletta's grasp. She and Aletta both stepped to the edge and studied the slope below them. the sheerness of the cliff face gave way to a steep clay slope, under which there was a jumble of rocks. "I expected him to be on the clay slope."

Suddenly a raven swooped down from above. It landed on the ladder and was carrying a feather in its beak. It hopped down from the ladder and put the feather next to the double-spouted vessel, which Kenny Joe had left open and sitting on the floor. The bird flew back onto the rock wall and, looking at them, emitted a deep gurgling sound, then flew off.

The women looked at each other, then looked at the feather. It was the same black feather with a white quill that Kenny Joe jumped with. Aletta, overcome by her waitress instincts, put the feather back into the vessel, re-stoppered it, and re-placed the vessel into the niche.

"Is this permanent? Does he need a ride back to the Roadhouse? Do we wait?" asked Aletta.

"His last words to me were 'Give me an hour'," Pam said with surprise. "I guess we wait. I shouldn't have freaked out."

"I don't blame you for freaking out, but I had a suspicion that he was hoping to fly. Carl said something about it the other day," said Aletta. She sat down in the shade of the cave to wait. Pam sat down next to her and they chatted about where they would fly if they were birds and what kind of birds would they want to be.

After a while the raven swooped back over their heads and into the tunnel. The creature suddenly, from the limits of what the women could see, had moccasins and human legs, but they disappeared by climbing into the shaft. "Kenny Joe is back," observed Pam casually.

They heard him shouting from up in the shaft, "Hey, did you bring a flashlight? Can you toss me a flashlight?"

Aletta grabbed a headlamp and crawled into the tunnel. She turned it on, then stood up to toss it to the shaman. She crawled back out, and he crawled out close behind her. "Yeah, I left my skins up there and couldn't find them in the dark."

Standing, he reached out his arms, wrapped them around Aletta, and pulled her into a hug. "This is the best day of my life! I have dreamed of this for so many years." Tears suddenly welled up and ran down his cheeks.

She ascertained his intentions were friendly, so she hugged him back. Then Pam, who was now standing, put her hands out and asked, "Group hug?" Kenny Joe responded by pulling her to them.

"The thing is," Kenny Joe began, resting his chin on top of Aletta's head, "Little Wind couldn't tell me about the cave, because Little Wind can't get in there. That shaft shuts him down. He told me instead to put the receipt in the woodpecker hole and see what happens. I'm sorry you had to go to jail."

Aletta extricated herself from the hug to look at him. "Well, it was actually good for me because it made me start writing. I met Kerry, she's a great editor and mentor. It was okay. Thanks for spurring me on."

Pam, realizing it was another *now or never* moments, found her voice to ask, "Did you need that feather to fly?"

Kenny Joe squeezed her tighter in a two-person hug, but still pleasantly, as he replied, "Those are special feathers plucked from birds on the wing, so they still embody the power of flight."

"Like the skins you have still embody the animal spirit?" she murmured.

"Exactly!" He pushed her back to look at her. "Like the spark plugs in my vehicular medicine bag."

"Spark plugs?" the women cried in unison.

"Yeah, you take a spark plug out of a running car, it can be used the same way. That's how I change my vehicles. Of course, you get a hell of an electrical jolt changing spark plugs that way, but, hey, it's just part of the ritual." Seeing that the women desperately wanted to doubt the plausibility of vehicular shape-shifting, he said, "I'm starving. What do you say we head back to the Roadhouse? I hear they've got green chile cheese burgers to die for."

Pam took a deep breath and started talking about what she had been thinking about while he was out flying around. "You know, Placido is ninety-two years old, and I don't know what will happen to this land when he dies ..." Because she had a lot to say, no one else got a word in edgewise until they reached the pavement of Highway 537.

{Chapter 108}

Asdzáán Nádleehé Strikes Again

Aletta carried a tray through the side-door. The tray was covered with large glasses of iced tea, iced tea spoons, a dish of lemon slices, and a glass sugar-dispenser. The veranda was shady and the cooling breeze was preferable to the swamp-cooled air inside. She sat the tray down and distributed the glasses to her friends. Placido poured what the others considered an obscene amount of sugar into his glass and stirred it. Pam and Carl dropped lemon slices onto the ice cubes jutting like icebergs from their teas. Aletta sat down and everyone took a sip or two and relaxed.

The eastbound traffic on Highway 64 drew their gaze to the landscape. The road hugged the side of the wide valley bottom, skirting the rocky escarpments of the mesas, which were forested with scrubby piñon and juniper trees. The color of each layer of roadside hill was more muted and blue with distance. The most muted was a wall of high mesa which framed the skyline.

Carl lifted his glass and waved it toward the distant mountain. "You know, I've never been down that road. UPS doesn't go there, and I never thought to just see where it goes."

Pam's mouth dropped open, snapped shut, and she snorted the air out her nose. "I can't believe that! I've spent most of my career out there. I can't imagine!"

Placido said, "It goes to Dulce, then to Chama. That's as far as I've gone."

"Several years ago," started Aletta, "I tried to get it designated as the 'Sister Road' to Route Sixty-Six, which is called the 'Mother Road'. Highway 64 runs from Whalebone Junction, North Carolina to Teec Nos Pos, which is 87 miles west of us. It turns into Highway 160 when it crosses into Arizona. I never really got any support for the sister-road idea."

"I didn't know you did that. Hey, Carl, do you know about Gobernador Knob?"

"I know Gobernador is down that road," he replied.

"Well … see that hump on the farthest ridge," Pam said pointing to the muted mountain. "That is a sacred site for the Navajos."

"It looks like there are a bunch of cell towers next to it … is that the one?" asked Carl.

Aletta snorted in disgust. "That was such a dumb place to put them. Goes along with the disrespect people have for history around here. The oil-field knows it as "Molly's Nipple" because of the shape. I get so tired of having to tell them how disrespectful that name is."

Carl turned to Pam and asked, "Why is it sacred? Is it one of their sacred mountains?"

"The fifth one," she replied. "It's the very center of their world as demarcated by their four sacred mountains. The deity associated with this mountain is Changing Woman. Her Navajo name is *Asdzáán Nádleehé*. She was the child of First Man and First Woman—gods who emerged from the four previous worlds. These were not people. First Man is an archetypal force associated with creation, birth, and dawn; First Woman is associated with destruction. The Knob is the forked-stick hogan Changing Woman was raised in, or in some versions of the story, she was found in. Either way, the Navajos all say it represents the very heart of the Navajo world."

"What did Changing Woman do?" asked Carl.

"Well, she created humans," said Pam. "She got her name from her changes of dress corresponding with the change of seasons and the cyclic nature of life processes. She is associated with birth, all traditional women's roles, and renewal. Changing Woman also represents the cycle of changes in her age: young in the spring, mature in the late summer, old in winter, and young again the following spring.

"She gets us back in harmony. In the Navajo view, life endlessly flows between hózhó, which is beauty, order, and harmony, and hóchxó, which is ugliness, chaos, disorder. Our job as humans is to keep finding our way back to hózhó. But the process never stops."

Aletta pushed her lips together, thinking hard, and then she turned to her friends. "It's kind of like writing a novel—an endless cycle of conflict and resolution. I'm going to look at that mountain more often."

Carl stirred his iced tea, took a sip and looked at Placido."Placido, why did you want to meet with us today?"

"I hate to be the one that has to tell you this, but I'm getting old," Placido replied. "But I never thought I would bother writing a will because I couldn't see it would matter. But two nights ago I had a dream when I was sitting on the couch trying to read a book. I dreamed there was this Italian mouse and he could talk. He was a pretty smart mouse and what he said made me realize that my whole life has been about my connection with my land. I've been foolish to let the fate of my land be undecided. Nothing good will come of it.

"Some people have told me to give it to the Catholic church. If my sister was still alive, she would want me to give it to them, but the church isn't interested in what that land actually represents. It would be meaningless to the church. They would just sell it and send the money to the archdiocese, or just collect the oil and gas money and let the land be ruined. I don't want it to turn out that way.

"At one time, I had notions that there were still cowboys with the romance of the land, but, if they exist, they are few and far between. I don't know of any cowboys that would do right by it. It's never been about weight gain of a bunch of calves. It's been about listening to the wind in the cottonwood trees and watching the shadows move across the landscape. I even went to that cowboy poetry event in Durango but it turned out most of those guys have office jobs."

Pam shifted uncomfortably in her seat, took a quick sip from her tea, and stared off at the horizon. Carl looked at his fingernails. Aletta stood up, "Placido, we aren't ready to have you die. Don't get in a hurry. Would anyone like more tea?"

"No, I'm not done talking about my plan. Please sit back down, Aletta," said the old man. "So when the talking mouse showed up in my dream, he gave me an idea of setting up a non-profit foundation with the land. It will have three related missions: research bird-safe wind generation, preserve antiquities for future generations, and provide a sanctuary for old mustangs. There are tax advantages to setting up the foundation before I die, so Pam, I would like to ask you to take the position of Director of the foundation and work with the lawyers to get it set up. Carl, you are the most honest man I ever knew, I'd like you to be Executor of my estate and make sure everything ends up where I want it. I want to leave something to Aletta in my will to help her get through school.

"It's not that you are all going to live happily ever after," the old man said. "There's a lot of damn hard work and unforeseeable challenges ahead for each of you, but with this plan in place, I can die satisfied."

***

Personally, dear reader, I think Navajo philosophy has much to teach us about living. The goal of life, for the Navajo, is *Sá̜a naagháí, Bik'e hózhó* (harmony according to the cyclical recurrence of life of which natural death is a part). May you achieve that simple goal.

Epilogue

Herman Melville was wrong, the drama is never done. We only stop telling the story for our own personal convenience.

You can't get a hamburger in Navajo City. The Roadhouse is closed and boarded up. John finally came to terms with the obvious; it was always going to be a cash drain. He's been trying to sell it for several years but he hasn't found anyone who could take it on.

He and Doc Barlow got married and they live at Mustang Camp. He's still doing a little accounting between feeding the mustangs.

Penny got a job as the manager of a convenience store in Aztec.

Rita Mae hasn't been back to Navajo City in years. She turned seventy this year and is still a world traveler. She and Kerry J. helped me write this book.

Old Milton is getting close to ninety, he moved down to the Gulf Coast for better fishing.

Willy LeDoux went to prison in Colorado for a couple of years on some old warrant, then was picked up by the State of Oklahoma for unauthorized use of a farm vehicle. The sentence was thirty-seven years. Nicky is still working at Little Anita's.

Sam Elkins died of a progressively debilitating disease.

The mustang numbers have risen steadily over the past several years. It is soon to be a crisis.

Randall Tapia is nearing retirement. His wife left him and moved to Nevada.

Erin Tate is still suffering the cognitive dissonance of listening to hate-talk radio, sympathizing with the Sagebrush Rebellion, and simultaneously managing USFS rangeland.

Bill Clifford got himself in a ponzi scheme with fake certified checks from Nigeria and went to prison for a few years.

JL Hartman threw some rocks through Sandy Poole's window, then holed up inside his fortified house when the sheriff came. The law enforcement officers waited him out and he went to jail. He was let out on bond and he fled to Kentucky, where he is an active militia member.

Brenda got a divorce.

Sephra moved back to Georgia where she is raising show dogs.

Placido was in a nursing home for about a year before he died.

Pam is splitting her time between the Foundation and teaching archaeology at the Community College.

Carl retired and moved to Montana.

Kenny Joe ... well, you don't even want to know about that.

Uncle Fred died and my mother moved to Florida.

I attended one semester at the local college and then went to the Psychology and Brain Science Department at UC Santa Barbara. I finished my dissertation last semester. (Thanks, Placido!)

Acknowledgements

I could not have written this book without help from my mother, Audrie Clifford, and my good friends, Jerri K. Lincoln and Donna Ramsden. I was additionally helped by Patty Robinson and Patricia Anderson, Thank you for the unflagging encouragement. Thanks to my husband, John, for making sure I had something to eat. He really learned to cook at the Roadhouse.

66333737R00224

Made in the USA
Charleston, SC
16 January 2017